Nicole Kilpatrick

FAE'S ASCENT
Copyright © 2021 by Nicole Kilpatrick

ISBN: 978-1-955784-57-3

Fire & Ice Young Adult Books
An Imprint of Melange Books, LLC
White Bear Lake, MN 55110
www.fireandiceya.com

Names, characters, and incidents depicted in this book are products of the author's imagination or are used fictitiously. Any resemblance to actual events, locales, organizations, or persons, living or dead, is entirely coincidental and beyond the intent of the author or the publisher. No part of this book may be reproduced or transmitted in any form or by any means, electronic or mechanical, including photocopying, recording, or by any information storage and retrieval system, without permission in writing from the publisher except for the use of brief quotations in a book review or scholarly journal.

Published in the United States of America.

Cover Design by Ashley Redbird Designs

To my mom, who taught me how to dream.

I

"What are you staring at?" Finn teased as he gently tucked a stray strand of hair behind Clover's ear.

"I heard you need to keep your eyes on your leprechaun at all times, otherwise he'll escape," Clover said playfully.

Finn leaned in for a kiss. "You've already got me. Not going anywhere."

The kiss was sweet, yet intense, as almost all their kisses had been. Clover still couldn't wrap her head around her life's turn of events. Not so long ago, she was just a regular teenager—an exceptionally lucky teenager—then, on her eighteenth birthday, all of that had changed. Now, she was having an early morning outdoor picnic with an absurdly good-looking leprechaun.

As first light broke, the grass, plants, and trees surrounding them changed colors, from vibrant greens to muted oranges and reds. Fall Valley. It had become their special, magical place. It was where Finn had first told Clover he loved her.

On her eighteenth birthday, Clover had discovered that her exceptional luck had been a gift and a curse, born from an agreement her father had made with an evil leprechaun even before she was born. Alistair McCabe. The mere thought of him sent shivers down Clover's spine.

"What's the matter?" Finn asked.

"It's nothing," Clover lied.

Clover hadn't told a soul, but ever since what happened two weeks ago—ever since Alistair McCabe kidnapped, forcibly married, and attempted to murder her—she'd been feeling a sick, unshakeable foreboding at the pit of her stomach. She may have survived, but the curse remained, and now she felt inextricably linked to him, which was why she knew with certainty that Alistair was coming back to get her. It was just a matter of time.

"I know it's a lot to take in. Honestly, I'm amazed at how well you've held up. It's perfectly normal to freak out right now. About Alistair. Your mom. Your powers. Us. It's okay to be a little scared," Finn said.

It had been pretty tough. Not only had Alistair tried to kill her in an attempt to close the portals between Earth and Faerie forever, she'd also discovered her mom was still alive and had met her for the first time. Her mom who just happened to be a very powerful mermaid.

Everything had seemingly changed in the blink of an eye. Clover's father, who had been absent for pretty much most of her life, was back in her life, too. Her once estranged father, her newly found mermaid mother, and her half-faerie self, made for one happy family. Sort of.

Of all the sudden and drastic developments of late, there was one that Clover was crazy-giddy and thrilled about: Finn. She never would have imagined having a leprechaun for a boyfriend, if she could even call him that.

"What? Quit staring, will you?" Finn joked.

"Finn Ryan. How lucky am I to have you for a boyfriend?"

"I don't think anyone's ever called me that before, Clover O'Leary," said Finn, his devilish grin endearing as hell.

Clover picked up a strawberry from the picnic basket and flung it at him.

"Easy there, tiger," said Finn, smothering a laugh.

"If not my boyfriend, then what are you?"

Finn's expression turned thoughtful. "Does it really matter that much to you? That you can call me your boyfriend?"

Clover felt her cheeks warm, suddenly feeling ridiculously juvenile. Sometimes it was easy to forget that compared to Finn, she had almost zero experience in the love arena. How silly she must have seemed.

Finn reached for Clover's hands and gently pulled her to him, so that she was straddling his lap. The closeness made Clover's breath hitch in her throat, her face turning a noticeable shade rosier. She expected Finn to kiss her then, but instead he nestled his face against the hollow of her neck and inhaled deeply, seemingly devouring the very scent of her.

Finn came up for air and gave Clover a soft peck on the lips, his silver-gray eyes hazy. "What am I going to do with you?" he asked tenderly.

Before Clover could respond, an unfamiliar sound pierced the air. Heart-breaking in its soulful lament, it reverberated like the cries of the earth itself. Clover couldn't help but cover her ears; the loud, mournful wails too much to take. It felt like her heart was being emptied of joy and replenished with grief.

"What is that?" Clover screamed.

Finn was ashen and visibly shaken. "When a banshee cries, it means someone has died. When that many of them cry...." Finn shook his head.

"No," Clover said. "You don't think...?"

"We have to go. Now."

"Bansheeeeeeee," Cordelia screamed as she flew in and out of every room in Anna's house in a frightful panic. Day had just broken, and their houseguests had all been asleep in their beds. When the piercing, desolate cries began, Cordelia knew right away that something horrible had happened. "The women of the faerie mounds are keening! Someone of great significance has perished," she cried.

When Cordelia flew into Clover's bedroom, her heart stopped. "Where is she?" The frantic flapping of her faerie wings took on an increased intensity. At that moment, Clover's father and grandmother walked in, confused and clearly affected by the banshee's ominous cries.

"Where's Clover?" Nick asked in alarm.

While Momma Ruth shielded her ears from the ongoing screams, Anna entered holding a candlestick. "Shhh," she chastised Cordelia. "There's no reason to panic. Clover left early with Finn. They're probably at Fall Valley. She's safe."

"But what does this mean?" Momma Ruth asked, gesturing at their surroundings as piercing wails engulfed them.

"A great death has befallen us," Cordelia replied dramatically.

Anna shot Cordelia a hard look before responding, "Actually, Cordelia is right."

Cordelia flapped her wings in smug concurrence.

"We should go," said Anna, concern plaguing her eyes.

The entire realm had heard the cries of the banshees. Most of the faeries bolted their doors and weathered the great lament in their homes, keeping death away. Those who knew and loved Queen Helena Roche rushed to the court. The significance of the banshees' announcements was not lost on Scobert Rott. It meant that someone important was dead, and the most important person in the realm, and to him especially, was Helena, the Seelie Queen.

At the entrance to the queen's throne room, a group had already gathered. Scobert immediately recognized the concerned faces of Anna, Ruth, and Nick. He wondered where Finn and Clover were and relaxed visibly when he saw them approach hand in hand. When he saw his mother, Mary, Scobert let out an involuntary sigh of relief. If what he feared was indeed true, he would need Mary by his side.

Guarding the door to the queen's private quarters were Archie and Alfred, the two ginormous gnomes who were among the many loyal protectors of the queen. They both held their hands up, holding back the crowd that began to form, their feet firmly planted on the great oaken trapdoor that was the entrance to the queen's throne room.

"Listen," Archie bellowed, "the queen is safe. Nobody has been in and out of here since Scobert left last night." When Archie spotted Scobert in the crowd, he shouted, "Tell them Scobert!"

Scobert wasn't the least bit thrilled that Archie had just briefed a bunch of people of his comings and goings. A clurichaun, he was known for his affinity for drink and fiercely independent nature. Although it was no big secret that he and Helena had a special relationship, he still felt uncomfortable at being called out so openly.

"The banshees cry, and I haven't seen Helena since last night. Open the door Archie, I need to enter," Scobert said, the look on his face brokering no argument.

"The queen is fine," called a small voice from seemingly out of nowhere. Queen Helena emerged from the shadows, dressed in a hooded cloak, an intricately carved walking stick in her hand.

"Jaysus Christ, woman," Scobert cried in relief. He went to her and scooped the petite Helena up in his arms, indifferent to the stares from the crowd. With Scobert's considerable girth and height, she almost disappeared into his cloak as he hugged her tight, her feet dangling in the air. He knew then that Helena had used the magical walking stick to leave her quarters without anyone knowing. The *shillelagh* had once belonged to him, a handheld portal with the ability to transport its bearer anywhere in the world in the blink of an eye. He didn't really care where she had been, all he cared was that she was safe.

Archie and Alfred looked like they'd either just seen a ghost or a brilliantly executed magic trick. The rest of the group was just as happy to see the queen alive.

"You had me worried," Scobert whispered as he gently released Helena from his fierce hug.

Helena blushed slightly. "When I heard the banshees cry, I took it upon myself to investigate."

Scobert couldn't believe what he was hearing. "You took it upon your wha—"

Helena shot him a pointed look. "I am quite capable of taking care of myself."

Scobert bit his tongue. He had little doubt. The woman would be the death of him.

"As I was saying," Helena said, "when I heard the banshees cry, I feared what a lot of you perhaps suspected, that a person of great importance had gone. I took it upon myself to go to the dungeons and check on our VIP prisoner, King Boris of the Unseelie Court. My suspicions were confirmed. The King of the Unseelies lay dead in his cell, while the Sorceress Iekika was nowhere to be found."

After the shocking news, they had assembled in the queen's throne room below ground. Clover sensed the uncertainty and apprehension in the air. It wasn't so much the fact that King Boris was dead that caused the stir, it was the breach in the Seelie Queen's security that posed a bigger problem. A prisoner and king who was under Queen Helena's power and protection had been murdered, his throat slit from ear to ear, his head nearly decapitated.

Finn stood in the corner with some of the queen's soldiers. They whispered about increased security measures, justice, and revenge. Revenge against whom? Clover wondered. Who would want to kill King Boris? The King of the Unseelies had banded with Alistair McCabe and was instrumental in the attack on the Seelie Queen and her army. He had played a part in the attempt to kill Clover and offer her up as sacrifice on Midsummer's Eve. Clover's blood turn to ice. Truth be told, if there was someone who had something to gain from King Boris's death, it would be her.

Could Iekika have killed Boris? Clover wouldn't have been surprised. That woman was another level of creepy. She still recalled the wedding ceremony straight out of a horror movie: Clover in a white dress, her collar soaked with blood, Iekika playing priestess, binding her with magic to Alistair. For the spell to work, they'd needed the blood of a half-Fae bride, and Clover was the perfect pawn to further Alistair's plans. She had to shake the memories away. That she was married to Alistair McCabe made her sick to her stomach.

Clover spotted her grandmother, Momma Ruth, and her dad, Nick, in a tight huddle with Anna and Mary. All of a sudden, all she wanted to do was hug them both. The past month had been surreal, to say the least, and she wasn't sure if she could have withstood any of it without them by her side. She walked over to their group and surprised her grandmother with a hug.

"Clover!" Momma Ruth shrieked. "I'm so glad to see you here. Are you okay?"

"I'm good, Momma," Clover said. She gave Nick a kiss on the cheek. "Hi, Dad."

"Hi sweetie," said Nick as he ruffled Clover's hair a tad.

At that moment, Queen Helena entered the room and took her throne. Liz, Finn's ex-girlfriend and the Queen's courtier, was at her heels as usual. She stood by the queen's throne looking as beautiful and resplendent as ever and Clover felt a gnawing urge to choke her out.

Helena, as was her way, got straight to the point. "We will need to send an emissary to the Unseelie Court. King Boris's remains will be returned to the Unseelies so they may pay their proper respects and grieve. The Unseelies must be assured that we will make every effort to find out who killed him. Who will volunteer to do this task?"

All the soldiers' hands, including Finn's, shot up.

"Kean, you will go to the Unseelies," said Helena.

The choice was expected; Kean Mackey was the queen's favorite. Kean stood a little bit taller, evidently proud for having been selected. He was the poster boy for the perfect soldier—extremely loyal, indisputably deadly, and pretty darned handsome. Not too long ago, Kean had professed his feelings for Clover, and admittedly she had been flattered. But in the end, she chose to be with Finn.

Kean glanced in Clover's direction and offered up a small smile and a tip of his head. Clover waved clumsily, hoping she didn't seem too awkward. Of course, Finn had noticed and raised an eyebrow in inquisition. Busted.

"If I may, Queen Helena," Scobert called from the back of the room. "Kean shouldn't go alone. I volunteer to go with the lad. Besides, he'll need someone to help with the corpse, won't he?"

It was plain to see from Helena's reaction that she did not think this was a good idea. Clover totally got it. She would have hated to have Finn in harm's way too.

The queen pursed her lips. "Fine. You and Mackey will go."

Scobert nodded. "Thank you."

Clover admired Helena's stoic resilience and strength, always a queen first before anything else. At the battle with the Unseelies, King Boris had caught the queen unawares and had almost killed her, but Clover had seen him. Before she knew what was happening, Clover had unleashed her dormant, untapped powers on King Boris. One moment Boris was about to attack the queen, the next moment he was carried off by a giant tidal wave that sprang from the tips of Clover's fingers. The queen had not forgotten that. After the battle, she had promised Clover a favor. Clover demurred, insisting that it was an honor to have helped at all. The queen simply nodded and said, "I never forget a debt."

Queen Helena continued, "While Scobert and Kean liaise with the Unseelies, we shall be on high alert. A faerie was killed in my realm, in my court. We will do everything in our power to safeguard the Seelie Court, and the friends under my protection."

Suddenly, all eyes were on Clover and her family.

"Clover," said Helena, "How are your lessons going?"

Clover wished she could disappear into the stone walls of the queen's throne room. Her lessons hadn't really been going great. Her self-defense trainings with Finn went smoothly enough. Wrestling had never been quite so stimulating. It was the lessons with her mom, Meara, that she worried about. Ever since the day she first used her powers, Meara had been trying to coax her abilities out of her again, but to no avail. Several times, Meara had tried to take her to the Land Beneath the Waves to meet the rest of her kind, but she couldn't get herself to breathe under water. It was useless.

"Uhm. They've been going pretty well."

"Now, more than ever, you need to be able to defend yourself. More importantly, you need to be able to go beneath the waves. The merrow-folk's territory is foreign even to most of our kind. Use this to your advantage. You will be well hidden there."

"I understand, Queen Helena. I've been trying, but I can't hold my breath long enough to enter their realm. Maybe it's just not possible. Maybe I'm too human."

"Try harder. My army will do their best to protect you, but you must do your part."

At that, the queen chose to end their conversation. She continued addressing the rest of her army, but Clover barely heard her. She was mortified. As if she hadn't caused enough trouble for the realm, now she was turning out to be a mediocre faerie, barely able to defend herself. With trouble lurking beneath the shadows, all she'd really been able to do the past two weeks was canoodle with Finn. As she tried to slip away from the gathering unnoticed, her dad caught up before she could make her escape.

"Hey, kiddo. Don't let the queen get to you. Woman's so uptight, if you stuck a lump of coal up her—"

Clover shushed him. "Dad! You'll get us into trouble."

Nick eyed her intently. "What's the matter, sweetie? Is it just the lessons? You'll get better, believe me."

"It's not just that. It's pretty much everything right now. So much has happened, and I feel like I don't know where I fit anymore." Clover exhaled. "Does that even make sense?"

"Of course, it makes sense. None of this is normal, sweetie. It's a huge adjustment for all of us. I went from being a convict to a guest in the Seelie Court. Not to mention, my ex-wife is a mermaid, and my daughter, well, my daughter's the bravest person I know."

Nick's words warmed her heart. "Dad—"

"It's true. You've been amazing. None of this is easy. I mean, imagine how Aquaman must have felt," Nick said earnestly.

"Aquaman, seriously?"

Nick doubled over in laughter, and Clover couldn't help but laugh alongside him. No matter how unreal everything had been, she had her dad back, and that made all the difference.

※

Helena called Finn and Scobert into her private parlor. Of course, Liz was there, which made for quite an uncomfortable scene. Finn hadn't really talked to her much, not since he realized his true feelings for Clover. He and Liz had been together for a very, very long time, but Finn had never really considered her to be his partner. Sure, they had a strong, physical connection, but had it been love? Finn didn't think so. All he knew was that he'd never felt for anyone the way he felt for Clover.

"Finn," Liz greeted him curtly. "Scobert, good to see you." Then to Helena, "My Queen, if all is well here, may I please be excused?"

"Of course. Thank you, Liz. You may go."

Helena raised her eyebrow at Finn after Liz left the room. "I suggest you fix that, soldier."

Scobert thankfully changed the subject. "Clover should be farther along in her training by now. This is serious. Alistair will come back for her."

"Ease up on her, will you? She's going through a lot," Finn countered. "I'll protect her from Alistair if he comes for her."

"Your feelings for her are clouding your judgement. You can't be everywhere at once. Remember that you're still a soldier in the Queen's Army. You're no good to us if your only focus is the girl," Scobert said.

"That's not fair and you know it." Finn bristled at Scobert's comment. How were his feelings for Clover different from Scobert's for Helena?

"We're only thinking of her safety," Helena chimed in. "If she's in the land of the merrows, she'll be safe. We'll be better equipped to fight Alistair if we know she's safe."

Finn raised his voice. "I know this. But—"

"You can't bear to be apart from her, not after all that's happened," Scobert continued.

Finn raked his fingers across his head in frustration.

"She needs to be able to fend for herself, Finn," Scobert said. "She is, after all, Fae."

Helena had the final say. "I will ask Meara to fast-track Clover's training. The sooner she's able to hone her powers and go beneath the waves, the better for us all. It's settled."

※

Liz was in a rage. It was bad enough that Finn chose that horrible half-human girl over her, but he didn't even have the decency to look at her in the queen's parlor. What had she seen in him, anyway? She listed all of Finn's shortcomings. He had left her for Clover. He was a sub-par soldier. That second part wasn't true. Finn was a superior soldier. None in the Queen's Army could ever rival him, not even that snot-nosed wannabe, Kean. Alistair was his only true match, but Finn was way hotter than he could ever hope to be. He was kind, too. At least, he *was,* before he'd decided to break Liz's heart.

"Aargh!" Liz struggled to contain her frustration. She could name dozens of Fae and humans alike who would jump at the chance to be with her. She was, after all, so irresistibly beautiful. Yet, Finn cast her aside and chose to be with an eighteen-year-old mutt. She had every right to be angry, every right to hate him, but despite everything, she couldn't stay mad. She couldn't help herself. Finn was the best thing she'd had in her life, and she still loved him.

She didn't have a choice, really. When the sorceress, Iekika, telepathed a message to her, it had been clear. If she wanted to get rid of Clover, she had to help Iekika and King Boris escape. Down to the dungeons she went, and in the cover of darkness, she unlocked the enchanted restraints keeping Iekika's powers at bay. When she heard the banshees' cries the following morning, she'd thought her prayers had been answered. She hadn't expected Iekika would kill King Boris instead.

2

Alistair stood before the Unseelie Court atop a grassy hill, Iekika next to him, serious and terrifying, her red eyes stark against her warm, mahogany skin. A natural leader, Alistair was in his element. Since Boris had been captured, the Unseelies had put their trust in him. In the end, although they'd lost the battle with the Seelie Court, they'd accepted him as one of their own.

Bonfires were lit across the vast plain as the Unseelies milled about, waiting to hear what Alistair had to say. A distant radio blaring nearby and the copious amounts of booze being passed around gave the gathering the bohemian feel of a drawn-out musical festival. The lands of the Unseelie Court were not quite as picturesque as the Seelie Court's, and its inhabitants less genteel, their morals questionable at best. Being a former member of Queen Helena's court, he found the Unseelies' way of life refreshingly honest.

Boris's soldiers, whom he trained at the behest of King Boris, were front and center. When he'd first met them, they were embarrassingly sub-par, inept drunkards, but he'd managed to mold them into acceptable soldiers. They wouldn't be happy about his news, but Alistair felt he was the best person to deliver it.

He cleared his throat and went straight to the point. "King Boris is dead."

A deafening silence fell over the gathered crowd. As the Unseelies slowly registered the horrible news, grief and anxiety spread like a current across the masses. Women sobbed and hugged their children closer while soldiers bowed their heads in mourning. Boris was well loved among his people, Alistair had to give him that. Soon there were raised voices, questioning, and indignation. The Unseelies wanted answers.

"Settle down," Alistair commanded.

"How did he die?" Vincent, one of Boris's soldiers, called from the crowd.

Alistair readied himself. "King Boris was slain by one of Queen Helena's men." Like casting a line out to sea, all he needed to do was wait.

Uncertainty and mourning quickly morphed into blind rage. Guns were fired into the air as battle cries were heard all around. Bloodlust was one hell of a drug, Alistair thought. He simulated grief and addressed the crowd again. "Ladies and gentlemen, please—"

"Death to the Seelie Queen!"

"Vengeance on the Seelie Army!"

His plan was in full motion. "Now's not the time for talk of revenge. We need to mourn the great king's passing. We'll deal with the Seelie Court later."

"What we need," Vincent proclaimed, "is to elect a new king and go to battle with the Seelie Army."

The Unseelie soldiers roared in agreement, while chants of "Alistair" were heard from the crowd. As the calls grew more rapturous, Alistair smiled to himself in quiet jubilation.

"I hereby submit Alistair McCabe to be the new Unseelie King. All in favor, say aye," shouted Vincent.

"Aye!" the crowd roared. Alistair gave a nod of thanks to Iekika. Desperate times called for desperate measures. The

Unseelie Court needed a proper wartime king, and he was more than ready to step up to the plate.

The best part of Clover's lessons with her mom was that she got to swim. The beach in the faerie realm was the most magnificent she'd ever seen. The white, powder-soft sand was almost luminescent under the sun, while the crystalline water sparkled with every wave that came crashing to shore. Wearing a pair of shorts and a tank top, she braced herself for the day's lessons. Her joy from swimming had been quick to turn into angst and disappointment as she'd failed, again and again, to swim deep enough into the ocean to cross over to the Land Beneath the Waves.

Despite the many failed attempts, Meara seemed hopeful. "Ready to go for a swim?"

Her steadfast confidence in Clover was encouraging, if not perhaps misguided. Meara had a dignified and calm self-assurance about her, as if nothing were difficult and everything came ridiculously easy, which made it even harder for Clover to repeatedly bomb in front of her.

Clover plastered on a smile. "Let's do it."

Together they waded into the ocean and, without further ado, Meara dove in and glided into its depths, her legs transforming into a large fin with every stroke. Clover dove in after her, and instantly her spirits soared. Although she didn't grow fish scales and flippers, she swam expertly nonetheless, more than able to keep up with Meara as she swam farther into the ocean.

For a moment, all else faded away. The saltiness of the water, the deafening sounds of the sea, and the feel of the water against her body occupied Clover's senses. She had always loved to swim, but there was nothing like being out in the ocean with her mother swimming beside her. They swam past the waves, where the water was bluer and calmer. Clover marveled at the sights of fish and coral as they both dove deeper and deeper toward the ocean floor. Then, it happened again as expected—her lungs ached, her breathing shallowed, and panic engulfed her. She had to come up for air. Instinctively, she reversed course and started swimming up to the surface.

Don't let fear stop you. You're my daughter, and as sure as I am a merrow, you can breathe under water. You just need to change your thinking.

Although Clover heard Meara's words in her head, she felt powerless to do anything about it. The instinct for self-preservation was so strong that there was nowhere to go but up. She gasped for air as she breached the surface, her heartbeat pounding in her ears. She slammed her palm against the water in frustration, making her eyes sting from the salt.

Meara's head soon popped out of the water; her long, auburn hair perfectly combed back like she was in a shampoo commercial.

"Perhaps today's not the day," Meara said. "But that doesn't mean we have to head back yet." She tilted her head toward the horizon, the ocean vast and inviting. "Care for another swim? No pressure, this time."

It was an offer she couldn't resist. She enjoyed her time with Meara immensely and couldn't wait to explore with her. She nodded. "I'd love to go for a swim."

"Catch me if you can," Meara called out before she swam to the open sea.

◈◈◈

"Two cubes of sugar, please," said Mary.

Anna dropped two sugar cubes in Mary's tea and sliced three pieces of apple pie.

Momma Ruth enjoyed being a guest at Anna's house. It felt like a fairytale-themed bed and breakfast, with its stone walls, beflowered window arrangements, and quaint furnishings. Finn's mother was the most gracious host and was truly a remarkable woman. She'd also formed a bond with Mary, Scobert's mother.

Although the two ladies looked like they could be Momma Ruth's granddaughters, in reality, they were much older than she could ever fathom. Nonetheless, they had plenty in common, most of all their steadfast and unrelenting devotion to their families.

"With King Boris dead, the Unseelies are even more volatile, and who knows what Alistair may do. That's why Queen Helena is concerned for Clover's safety, now more than ever," Anna explained to Momma Ruth.

The two women were trying to placate Momma Ruth. She didn't appreciate the way Helena put Clover on the spot about her training, and the two ladies were quick to defend their queen. Truth be told, she understood where they were coming from, but she couldn't help it. She was overly protective when it came to her granddaughter, especially since Clover had been through so much.

"Sometimes, I wonder," Momma Ruth said, "maybe we're better off returning to Earth. We could go on the run for a while. It's a big world out there. If we keep moving, Alistair will never find us." She took a sip of her tea and looked expectantly at Anna and Mary.

"No, dear." Mary shook her head. "Don't underestimate our kind. Alistair *will* find her. That's why you, Nick, and Clover are safest here."

Momma Ruth sighed. As much as she loved that Clover, Nick, and Meara had reunited under the strangest of circumstances, sometimes she missed their normal life in New York, which on closer inspection, wasn't that normal at all. All their blessings could be traced back to a leprechaun, the guy who ran the deli across the street was a mermaid, and their cat could talk to faeries.

Another reason she wanted to go back to New York, one she didn't readily admit to, was she was feeling less and less like herself in the faerie realm. Ever since Finn used magic to save her life, she'd been feeling stronger, younger, and more powerful by the day. That wasn't necessarily a bad thing, but its implications frightened her. She glanced at Anna and Mary; ethereal creatures suspended in time. Would this be Clover's fate, she wondered. Would it be hers?

"I suppose you're right," she conceded. "Clover is safer here. Thank you again for all that you've done for us."

"Think nothing of it," Anna said as she reached out and squeezed her hand. "We're family now."

※

Back on the beach, Clover and Meara lounged on a spruced-up beach blanket made of a velvety, magical, fabric that was as thin as a sheet of parchment, but as comfortable as a plush mattress. Laid out on the blanket was an assortment of nuts, cheeses, fresh fruit, and wine. Meara had changed into a crisp, linen dress and was looking out into the ocean, her legs stretched in front of her, a look of absolute calm on her face. Her long, auburn hair was swept against her right shoulder, still wet from the swim. Looking at her, nobody would think that only moments ago she'd swam to shore as her glistening fin reflected the light from the sun and waves. Sometimes, Clover still found it hard to believe that the goddess beside her was her mother.

No wonder her dad was so crazy about her. With an otherworldly grace that was difficult to replicate, Meara was the type of woman who made other women feel glaringly ordinary in comparison. The only thing Clover had in common with her mom was their piercing, dark blue eyes. Other than that, Clover felt they couldn't have been more different.

Nibbling on a piece of cheese, Clover wanted to prolong lunch as much as she could. She knew that after they'd eaten, Meara would try to get her to use her powers again. Over the past few weeks, nothing had worked—visualization, chanting, wishful thinking—nada. As much as she enjoyed spending the day with Meara, her persistent ability to prove over and over again that she was insipidly human had started to chafe at her. Had it all been a fluke? Did she really have it in her to perform magic? To swim beneath the waves? She shook her head in doubt.

Clover heard Meara's voice in her head. *You worry too much. Magic isn't planned or orchestrated. It just is.*

It hadn't been the first time that Meara spoke to her telepathically, but had she been listening to her thoughts, too?

"Sorry," Meara said sheepishly. "Didn't mean to get in your head."

Too late, Clover thought sarcastically.

Meara chuckled despite herself.

"Mom! Stop it, please."

Meara's otherwise composed demeanor changed as she averted her gaze, focusing instead on a seashell nearby.

Guilty for her curtness, Clover tried to make amends. "Sorry for snapping at you."

"It's not that." Meara turned to her. "You called me mom. It was nice."

Not having realized she'd even said it, her cheeks warmed.

Meara reached for her hand. "I didn't mean to make you feel uncomfortable. You can call me anything you want."

The moment Meara touched her, a stream of consciousness entered her mind, markedly different from brief messages delivered telepathically. This time, it was as if she were in her mother's head, feeling as well as hearing her innermost thoughts. *I hope I didn't turn her off. What kind of mother am I when I can't even talk to my own child? She has so much power in her. If she only knew...*

She pulled away and brought her hand to her mouth. "Wow."

Meara grinned from ear to ear. "You read my thoughts. You used your powers."

"Can all faeries do that?" she asked, suddenly mortified. If Finn had been reading her thoughts all along, she'd die.

"Some can," Meara said. "There are different types of magics. Sometimes, the Fae can control minds, like Alistair did when he made you believe he was Finn. Faeries who are related also have strong telepathic connections, but the ability is innate to merrows, born of our need to communicate while in the water."

"I don't want to read people's minds and I don't want it done to me, either." If she was being completely honest, it freaked her out to no end.

Meara nodded encouragingly. "I promise to never breach your mind again, except to communicate. If you choose to not use this power again, that's completely fine. It's really not the point, you see."

"What *is* the point?"

"The point, my child, is that you *can*."

※

With Clover busy with lessons and with nothing pressing to attend to at court, Finn lounged on the deck of his lakeside cabin, a beer in one hand and a large, old, untitled tome in the other. The book was held together with rope, uneven pages sticking out like some disorganized, overstuffed filing cabinet. The book was Anna's–a compilation of the oral histories of their people, passed down from generation to generation. Finn flipped through it, looking for information on Cuchulainn, the greatest known commander of the Red Branch Knights, infamous and eulogized as a demi-god by the Irish since the time of the Roman Empire.

What the folktales never mentioned was that Cuchulainn was a great faerie warrior, believed to one day return from the grave to stand alongside a worthy faerie warrior of his equal. Alistair had always believed himself to be that warrior. Over the course of Finn's apprenticeship and later partnership with Alistair, one name had come up over and over as the epitome of soldierly excellence. Cuchulainn, the fallen warrior who would one day fight alongside Alistair, proving once and for all that his abilities equal that of the greatest faerie warrior in millennia.

It all sounded pretty absurd; all things considered. Finn had seen ghosts, ghouls, banshees, headless horsemen, you name it, but even among the most powerful of the Fae, he'd never seen anyone rise from the dead. The only person known to have done that was Jesus Christ, and Finn wasn't even sure if he actually had. The thing was, Alistair had been a firm believer in Cuchulainn's legend, and with all that'd happened, Finn wondered if Alistair was crazy enough to attempt to bring him back. Or perhaps he was the crazy one.

Finn slammed the book shut in frustration. He was grasping at straws, no doubt about it. In the two weeks since Alistair got away, he'd been looking over his shoulder, anticipating his next attack. He figured if he could somehow predict Alistair's next move, then he'd be at an advantage. The man was, after all, his mentor. He was probably the only one in the whole realm who knew him best, which meant he knew exactly how dangerous he was. The thought of Alistair getting near Clover set him off so much, he hardly knew what to do with himself.

"Finn! Are you out back?"

Hearing her voice still made Finn's heart beat just a wee bit faster, especially since he hadn't expected to see her so soon.

"Hey, you," he called as Clover came running to him, her cheeks flushed and sunburnt. She got on her toes and hugged him tight, the scents of juniper, jasmine, and seawater enveloping him. He rested his hands around her waist, pulled her closer, and kissed her. She felt so incredibly good to him, it was almost impossible to describe.

"I have good news." Clover beamed. "I was able to use one of my powers."

"That's awesome! Which one?"

"I can read minds! I read my mom's accidentally, and I really don't want to do it again, and I asked her not to read mine if she can help it, and I just feel so psyched right now—"

"Slow down, slow down," Finn said.

She inhaled once and exhaled in one long breath, looking up at him eagerly. "I was just so happy to have made some progress, and I couldn't wait to tell you about it."

"Of course, and I'm so proud of you. I always knew you had it in you."

Clover smiled mischievously. "Shall I try to read your mind?"

"At your own risk," Finn teased.

She traced her fingers up his chest and draped her arms around his neck. "I've been looking forward to this all day." She kissed him with an urgency which Finn was more than eager to reciprocate. When she slipped her hand under his shirt, her cool touch created goosebumps against his skin. He held her tighter out of sheer impulse as she kissed his neck and mildly toyed with the top button of his jeans.

"Slow down, slow down," Finn said as he gently pulled away, struggling to catch his breath.

With mouth parted and breathing hitched, she looked at him questioningly. "I thought you wanted to." Then she stepped back and looked away.

Of course, he had wanted to.

"I did," Finn said. "I mean, I do. Believe me, I do, but I don't want you to rush into it. We can take our time."

Clover turned beet red as she looked down at her feet and shrugged. "Sure. Whatever."

How stupid was he? The last thing he'd intended was to hurt her feelings. "Clover, please. Don't get me wrong, I—"

"No. I understand. Listen, I better get back to Anna's. I shouldn't have dropped in unannounced anyway."

"Wait. Don't—" Before he even finished his sentence, Clover had already walked away from him.

Safely ensconced in her bedroom, Clover grabbed her pillow and heartily screamed right into it. Beyond humiliated, she wanted to crawl under the covers and hide. Suddenly, she needed more than ever to speak to Andie, her best friend. When she and Momma Ruth disappeared into the faerie realm months ago, they'd left letters to close friends saying they'd gone on vacation. A letter had gone out to Andie, but Clover knew she never would have bought it. It wasn't like her to just leave like that. Andie would have known that something wasn't right. She felt bad for abandoning her best friend like she did, and she wished there was a way to see her or at least talk to her. She needed her now. Andie had more experience with dating and men. Clover, on the other hand, had very little forays into the love department. She tried to imagine what Andie might have said to her if she were there. "Chill out" was a prime candidate, or "who cares that he told you to slow down while you were laying the seduction on thick?"

A knock on the door interrupted Clover's thoughts.

Momma Ruth poked her head into the room. "Can I come in?"

"Of course, Momma."

Momma Ruth sat beside her on the bed. "I saw you walk in. You looked upset."

Clover rubbed her eyes, as if the act might clear her head. "It's nothing. I'm fine."

"Don't lie to me, young woman."

Clover considered her grandma's order. On the one hand, she really needed someone to talk to. On the other hand, did she really want to have the relationship-slash-sex talk with Momma Ruth at that moment?

"I just get so confused and overwhelmed sometimes."

"Tell me," Momma Ruth said soothingly.

"It's just that everything is new all of a sudden. With dad back in my life and meeting Meara for the first time, discovering my powers, falling in love with Finn—it's just been a lot, you know? It's not just that either. I'm scared." She took Momma Ruth's hand as she tried to hold back her tears. "I'm scared all the time that Alistair will come back, and I won't be ready for him. I'm scared that Finn doesn't feel as strongly for me as I do for him. Mostly, I'm frightened for all the people I love. I don't want any of you to get hurt."

"That certainly does sound daunting, doesn't it? It's not too late to make a run for it."

That was certainly not the response she'd been expecting. "What?"

Momma Ruth wiped a tear off Clover's cheek. "Oh, sweetie. These are all valid worries, but none of them insurmountable. You have all the time in the world to get to know your mom and dad better. Same goes for your powers. Don't feel pressured to learn everything all at once. As with everything that requires honing, it will take some time. As for Alistair, if and when he comes for you, you won't have to fight him all by yourself. You've got a whole village of people who care for you and who'll protect you. Don't you worry about us because we can take care of ourselves."

Her grandmother always knew just the words to make her feel better.

"Thank you, Momma."

"Now, what's this nonsense about Finn and his feelings for you?"

Clover suddenly wished she hadn't mentioned anything, but she was certain Momma Ruth would wheedle it out of her, so she figured she'd just be honest.

"I feel like he's not really that into me."

Momma Ruth cocked an eyebrow. "What makes you say that?"

"I'm not like the other women he's been with."

"And this is a problem, because…?"

"Take Liz, for example. I mean, just look at her. She's so beautiful, sexy, and experienced."

"Oh. I think I see where this is going. Clover, you don't have to go all the way with someone just because you think he expects it, and you feel pressured to. If he truly loves you, he'll slow things down and wait until you're ready. If he doesn't, then he wasn't worth it to begin with."

Clover suddenly felt like a fool. Why had she been in such a rush to take things to the next level with Finn, anyway? She realized that, like everything else, their relationship would require time to run its own course. She didn't have to prove anything to herself or Finn. All she needed to do was trust him and see where that took them.

Clover smiled. "What would I do without you?"

"Just because he's a leprechaun, doesn't mean he gets to get lucky," Momma Ruth said with a wink.

"Momma!" Clover shrieked.

As they both giggled like little girls, it felt like home again. Never mind that they were in the faerie realm, or that she was half-Fae, or that she'd fallen in love with an insanely hot leprechaun. With Momma Ruth by her side, she could take on anything.

3

In Boris's house, before a roaring fire, Alistair reclined on a leather armchair, pondering his next move. He knew Queen Helena would send an emissary to the Unseelie Court. Having served under her for many years, he relied on her just and diplomatic nature to prevail even in times of conflict. In fact, he had counted on it.

To be an ambassador for the queen was no small task, usually reserved for the best and most respected of her court. He, himself, had often served as emissary for the queen. Both an honor and a privilege, there no doubt would have been a throng of volunteers, and if Alistair were a betting man—and he was—he would have wagered that Finn would be one of them. He would have been the perfect option, but Helena would have wanted him close to court. If he were Helena, he would have sent Scobert instead. He would have probably thrown in Kean Mackey for good measure. It took at least two strong men to transport a coffin across territories.

If his assumptions were correct, and he was fairly certain they were, then at least two of Queen Helena's best soldiers were on their way to the Unseelie Court. It would be the perfect opportunity to get the girl. Finn, he could handle. He was, after all, the boy's mentor. He'd taught him everything he knew.

Having no desire to sleep on a dead man's bed, one whose death he was responsible for, Alistair opted to stay in his old room in King Boris's house—his house. The slain king's quarters were as spartan as his and every other room in the residence. King Boris was a simple faerie, utilitarian and devoid of class. Alistair decided to remedy that situation. He enjoyed a little pomp with his power; it was just the way he was.

Securing the Unseelie throne had been simple. The charade worked out perfectly. Iekika proved to be a most valuable asset, a worthy right hand, powerful and loyal. He would have many a use for her yet. Feeling pretty pleased with himself, he poured a drink —absinthe, a gift from King Boris. He recalled the day they toasted in that very room as their plans came to fruition. Neither of them knowing at the time what lay ahead.

Alistair raised his glass. "To the great king." He poured a thimble-full on the stone floor and drank the rest.

Small, yet strong, hands squeezed his shoulders from behind.

"A knock would have been nice," he said as he glanced up at the sculpted features of Iekika.

"I hardly think there are secrets between us now, *my King*," Iekika said as she walked in front of him and sat on his lap. Her mouth was warm against his in the next instant. Clearly, she was demonstrating her usefulness, Alistair thought. He kissed her thoroughly, savoring the taste of their shared victory.

"My love," Alistair said in between kisses, "you do know I will never take a queen."

"Yes," Iekika said. "And you and I both know I'm not your love; neither are you mine. Just shut up and kiss me, King of the Unseelies."

❦

They placed King Boris's body in a casket befitting his station and loaded it into a bronze rickshaw with two poles on either end. Finn fastened the straps that secured the coffin in place and helped load

Scobert and Kean's supplies into a compartment at the backend of the wagon. Returning King Boris's remains to the Unseelies was an important diplomatic mission, and if he was being completely honest, Finn was a little peeved that Queen Helena entrusted the job to Kean and not him.

"Are you sure you don't want me to go with you?" Finn asked Scobert.

"Kean and I will manage just fine. You stay here with Clover and her family," Scobert said.

Kean looked away at the mention of Clover's name. It wasn't lost on Finn that the lad still had feelings for her. He couldn't really blame the guy, but as far as he was concerned, that needed to stop. It was one thing that he was being touted as the queen's new favorite and *the new Finn*, but it was quite another thing to have designs on his girlfriend. Also not lost on Finn was the fact that he just referred to Clover as his girlfriend.

"I have a bad feeling about this," Finn said. "The Unseelies are likely to blame us for his death."

"And perhaps they will, but the Unseelies will not strike until after they've mourned their dead. Those are our rules of war, always have been," Scobert said as he lifted the front pole off the ground, testing the rickshaw's weight and balance. "We'll send word as soon as the deed is done."

Another thing that was making Finn uneasy was the fact that Scobert and Kean would have to travel to the Unseelie territories by foot because portals didn't allow for the transport of dead bodies. It'd take at least two days to get there and back.

Kean fished two compasses out of his pocket. "Commandant Ryan, we'll communicate through these," he said as he gave one compass to Finn and put the other one back in his pocket.

"From Helena's stockpile of magical objects." Scobert laughed. "A relic from the old days. It will serve us well in this situation. If you need to relay a message, point the compass due north. If we need to speak to you, the thing will vibrate."

"Like a cellphone," Finn said.

"Put that way, doesn't sound so magical after all, does it?" Scobert chuckled, then shook Finn's hand. "Check in on Helena, will you?"

Finn nodded. "I will." He turned to Kean and clasped his hand. "You two watch your backs out there."

"Yes, sir," Kean said.

At that, Scobert and Kean lifted the front and back poles of the rickshaw respectively and walked toward the vast plains that led to the Unseelie Court.

※

Nick O'Leary had loved only two women in his life. The first was his mother, and the second was Meara. When Meara was pregnant with Clover, Nick had messed up their lives when he gambled them away to Alistair in Las Vegas. Meara had left him shortly after. Little did he know at the time that Alistair was actually in love with Meara and that years later, to exact his revenge, he'd try to murder Clover and close the portals between Faerie and Earth forever.

It sounded like the plot to a supernatural soap opera, but that was the story of Nick's life, which included jarring plot twists like breaking out of prison and finding out that his wife was actually a merrow—a mermaid in layman's terms. He wasn't complaining, though. He had his daughter back in his life, and he and Meara had agreed to get to know each other again so that they could be better parents to Clover.

Waiting near the big fountain at Market Square, Nick had never been more nervous. It was, by no means, a date, but his nerves were frayed, regardless. He was wearing a pair of khakis and a blue button-down shirt Clover had picked out. He decided he looked presentable enough, all things considered. The years in prison hadn't been kind to him, and yet, Meara hadn't aged a day. While he wondered idly whether it was too late to call the whole thing off, he saw her.

God, she was beautiful. She waved tentatively as she

approached the fountain. She was dressed casually in a white tunic, yet she looked absolutely stunning. Not for the first time in his life, Nick was astonished at how someone like her had fallen in love with someone like him.

"Hi," Meara said.

"Hey," Nick replied, sounding like a goofy teenager to his own ears.

"Let's get something to eat?" Meara offered.

"Absolutely."

He followed her through the plaza and into a narrow alley, feeling a bit stalkerish as he watched her navigate through the crowds with elegance and grace. She stopped in front of a shop with a green awning under a sign that read, "Osteria Luna."

She turned around and motioned to the restaurant. "You still like pasta?"

"I love pasta."

They walked in and got a table by the window. A robust lady wearing a bright red dress and a white apron walked over to their table carrying two carafes of wine.

"Red or white?" she asked unceremoniously.

"Red," Meara and Nick responded at the same time.

When the server saw Meara, her eyes widened like saucers. "Lady Glass! I didn't notice you walk in. Forgive me. Such an honor to have you here today."

"Thank you, Luna," Meara replied. "I'd like you to meet a good friend of mine, Nick O'Leary."

The woman graciously shook Nick's hand and recited the day's specials. Nick ordered a lasagna, while Meara ordered zucchini flowers and linguini. Luna left with their orders and promised the food would be out shortly.

"This is a cool joint," Nick gushed as he surveyed the restaurant. There were cured ham legs, salamis, and prosciuttos hanging from the ceiling. Jars upon jars of vegetable confits lined the shelves on the stone walls, while the smells of hard cheese and the aroma of garlic and olive oil filled the room.

Meara nodded as she took a sip of wine. "Although it's called Osteria Luna, they close shop whenever there's a full moon."

"Why is that?"

"Luna and her staff are lycanthropes, cursed to forever be at the mercy of the full moon. Queen Helena took them in a long time ago, gave them their own lands to roam and a means to make a living. They don't harm anyone in Faerie, and they've actually become really strong allies to the court," Meara whispered. "Plus, Luna makes the best handmade noodles in the realm."

"Lycanthropes? You mean werewolves?"

Meara laughed, the familiar sound tugging at Nick's heart strings. "Don't act so surprised. You are, after all, having lunch with a mermaid."

"Touché," Nick conceded. Looking at her then, he realized there was nowhere in the world he'd rather be.

Before he knew it, lunch was served, and they both dug in while they caught up on each other's lives. They talked mostly about Clover and how she'd grown into a fine woman. Aside from a few awkward topics that led to loaded silences—Meara dating Alistair, the fact that Clover was cursed—the conversation had flowed smoothly. Nick was having a great time and from the looks of it, Meara was, too.

"How's Clover's training coming along?" Nick asked as he sipped the last of the wine.

"There's been progress," Meara said thoughtfully, "but she's still resisting her powers. She'll come in to her own, in her own time."

"You said *powers*. What exactly are these powers?"

Meara swirled her wine and took a sip. "It's safe to assume that she would have inherited most, if not all, of my abilities."

"Such as? If you don't mind my asking…"

"For one, the ability to penetrate minds, which she's already displayed an aptitude for. Then, there's control over the elements, telekinesis, healing, astral projection, time manipulation—"

"Whoa, time out. You think Clover will be able to do all of those things?"

Meara nodded. "I know she will."

<hr />

When Finn was summoned by Queen Helena that evening, he feared something bad had befallen Scobert and Kean. When one of Helena's valets showed up at his door saying the queen urgently needed to see him, he wasted no time in getting himself to court and tried to contain his anxiety as he was ushered into the queen's private quarters.

His heart sank when he saw the look on Helena's face. Pale as a ghost, tight-lipped, and obviously distressed, she held a piece of parchment in her hands.

"My Queen, what is it?"

"Alistair is coming to see me. He wants a parley."

"Reject him. It's your right as queen."

"I can't," Helena said, resigned.

"Of course, you can," Finn countered.

"Alistair is the new Unseelie King!" Helena snapped. "I'm *obligated* by the rules governing our kind to receive him."

Finn had not expected that curveball. His thoughts immediately went to Clover. He needed to go to her.

"Clover is safe," Helena said, as if responding to his thoughts. "The farther she is from here, the better. As per custom, the Unseelie King will be accompanied by one person, and so will I. You will stand with me while I parley with Alistair."

"No—"

"Soldier, I am your queen. You are honor-bound to do as I say."

Finn clenched his jaw while his mind raced. A parley signified a momentary truce, a ceasefire. Nobody had ever been known to violate those laws in his lifetime, but he wouldn't put it past Alistair to be the first to try.

"I don't trust him."

"Neither do I," replied Helena. "But you better trust that he's honorable enough to abide by the rules of parley, because he'll be here any second."

Finn barely noticed Liz enter, but when she announced that Alistair had arrived, his blood turned to ice.

"Send him in," Helena said.

Finn went to stand by his queen, even as every cell in his body told him to go to Clover. A soldier to the core, he held his chin up, prepared for anything.

Alistair walked in looking like a gameshow host, wearing a shiny blue suit and pointy leather loafers. Vincent, who had once attacked Clover, followed closely behind. Wearing a leather vest and a blue mohawk, he looked like a degenerate punk. At that moment, it took all of Finn's self-control not to tackle them both.

Helena motioned to a nearby rectangular table and took her seat at its head. Alistair, following her lead, took the seat opposite her. Vincent sat to the right of Alistair, while Finn positioned himself behind Helena.

"I suppose felicitations are in order, King of the Unseelies," Helena said with a small nod of her head.

"Thank you," Alistair said.

"You must know I've sent emissaries to the Unseelie territories. They carry King Boris's remains and I expect they will be received peaceably by your court."

"Indeed, they shall," Alistair replied with a straight face.

"For the record, I'm not responsible for the Unseelie King's death," Helena avowed.

"I will pass that information on to my people," Alistair said, while a wicked smile formed on his lips. "Whether they'll believe it is yet to be seen."

Finn couldn't keep his mouth shut a second longer. "You killed him, didn't you?"

"Finn!" Helena chastised. "This is not the forum for that."

"It's quite alright, Helena. No. I did not kill Boris. You have my word," Alistair said as his gaze focused on Finn, his voice dripping with malice.

"Let's get to the point, gentlemen," Helena said. "Alistair, what is it that you want?"

"I think it's pretty clear what I want." Alistair sneered.

"Get to the point," Helena commanded.

"Very well. To prevent war, all I want is my wife back."

Finn lunged in the time it took for Alistair to finish his sentence. Vincent and his king were on their feet in the same instant. Standing face to face with Alistair, Finn wanted nothing more than to finish him off. Laws of parley be damned. Alistair's death meant Clover's safety.

"Gentlemen!" Helena roared. "Enough."

Finn's bloodlust momentarily abated as he eased his stance, and Alistair took his seat. He would not shed blood in the queen's quarters, no matter how badly he wanted to. His vengeance, for the moment, would have to wait.

Helena placed a hand on the table. "I've considered your demand, and the answer is no. Are those your only terms?"

"Yes."

"Then the parley was for naught. You, Alistair McCabe, King of the Unseelie Court, remain an enemy and a threat to my people. In honor of King Boris, I propose three days of continued ceasefire to mourn the slain king. After which time, you can do whatever the hell you want, but be assured that my army stands ready to defeat you at every turn."

"As you wish," said Alistair.

※

Laying on the grass in Anna's backyard and looking up at the stars, Clover sought to relax her mind. She tried to find the north star but found it impossible to identify the right one. Every time she thought she found the big dipper, a duplicate constellation would pop up right beside it, as if the stars were replicating themselves as she lay there watching them. She wondered if Andie was looking up at the same strange sky in Manhattan. Fat chance of that happening, she decided. The city itself shined so brightly that its glow overshadowed the stars; people looked up to skyscrapers and never the night's sky.

As her vision filled with multiplying stars, she sat up and gave up the search. Anna's backyard overlooked a forest framed by mountains in the distance. Under the starlit sky, she was able to make out the silhouettes of the tall oak and pine trees and was awed by the peaceful majesty of it all. She wished Finn were there with her. She hadn't spoken to him all day and felt foolish for the way she behaved the last time they were together. She resolved then and there to make things right with him again, and while she was on the topic of resolutions, she promised to try even harder during her trainings with Meara. Feeling fairly satisfied with her new goals, she got up to head for bed. Looking out at the forest one last time, something made her do a double take. She thought she saw eyes in the forest, most probably an animal's. Then, she saw them again, ruby red eyes that glowed in the night. She would have recognized those eyes anywhere.

On impulse, she made a run for it, beelining to Anna's house as fast as she could. When she looked back, she saw Iekika charging toward what looked like a version of her, immobile and rooted to the spot she'd just left. She barely understood what was happening. It was as if she, like the stars, had doubled, and decoy Clover appeared so the real Clover could escape.

She collided with Anna when she entered the house. "It's Iekika."

Anna immediately positioned herself in front of Clover as she looked out over the backyard. By then, Iekika had discovered fake Clover and was on the hunt for the real one. Clover was frozen in place as panic engulfed her.

"Run," Anna whispered.

Watching Iekika enter Anna's home was like something out of a slasher movie. Unhurried and intense, she eyed Anna up and down with her deathly eyes. "Get out of the way, or I will kill you."

"I'd like to see you try," replied Anna with a self-assured haughtiness that blew Clover's mind. Then she whispered to her again. "Run."

Iekika's feet lifted off the ground as she charged at Anna with arms outstretched in front of her. The horrifying image would forever be etched in Clover's brain. Anna held her right hand up like a traffic cop. The smell of electricity and lightning permeated throughout the room as sparks flew from Anna's fingertips, rendering Iekika momentarily petrified. Then, Anna delivered a high kick that landed on the sorceress' chin, drawing blood.

Clover chose that moment to heed Anna's advice. With no idea where she was going, she ran. Out of the house and into the night, she sprinted, her pulse racing as she worried about Anna and her family. Even in her panicked state, she promised herself that she would kill Iekika herself if she harmed any of them.

She didn't realize it at first, but she was headed to the path in the woods that led to the beach, the familiar route from her many lessons with Meara. In the dark, she ran into low-hanging branches and twigs as she plowed through the dense forest. Minutes later, bruised and scratched up, she emerged at a clearing on the beach. She stopped to catch her breath, feeling oddly safer even though the threat remained.

With her heartbeat still pounding in her ears, she heard something that made her insides go cold.

"There you are," said Iekika. "What a little witch you are, making me run after you like that."

She slowly turned and was face to face with the sorceress. "What did you do to Anna?"

"Don't worry about Anna."

Clover's thoughts were on overdrive. Should she run? Fight? No doubt about it, she was in over her head.

Mom, it's me. I need you.

"What do you want?" she asked Iekika.

Iekika wagged a bony finger at her face. "Stop this nonsense. You know perfectly well that I came for you."

"Yeah? So, come and get me."

Even though her legs were spent, and it felt like her heart was about to burst out of her chest, she turned and ran toward the ocean. Iekika was hot on her tracks. When her feet touched water, she continued running, figuring she'd dive in when it got deep enough. To her utter amazement, her feet stayed above water as she glided farther into the ocean. She was levitating.

So was Iekika. Clover was only ever an arm's reach away as she crisscrossed over the water, trying to lose her. Dread coursed through her veins as she realized Iekika would catch her, eventually. As she wondered whether she'd be better off taking her chances in the water, something propelled itself from the depths of the ocean, breaching the surface and shooting up like a torpedo. Clover didn't have to look to know it was her mother.

The sea turned angry, and the skies grew gray, seemingly reflecting Meara's state of mind. From high above, a voice boomed over the sound of crashing waves. "Leave my daughter alone!"

A crackle like thunder reverberated across the sky, then a lightning bolt exploded from Meara's outstretched hands, hitting Iekika on the chest, sending her crashing into the ocean. The sea seemed to swallow her up, then spit her back out as Iekika quickly recovered, rising from the water, her crimson eyes fixed on Meara.

Her expression turned grotesque as Iekika launched herself at Meara. Looking like an enraged angel, her auburn hair blowing in the wind, Meara's lips curled up in a frightening smile. She thrust her right hand forward and squeezed at nothing. In that same instant, Iekika's hands went to her neck as she gagged and gasped for air.

It's time, Clover. Go beneath the waves.

Mom, I—

Now!

Without another thought, Clover dove deep and kept going. Her eyes immediately adjusted to the darkness as she propelled herself to the ocean floor. Gone was the usual tightening around her chest and lungs. She breathed as deeply and as effortlessly as if she were lounging on the beach under an umbrella. It was second nature. A pod of dolphins appeared and swam alongside her, playfully leading her closer to the ocean floor. As she dove deeper, the ocean changed. Luminescent guppies swam around gigantic corals while schools of fish moved in graceful synchronicity. She had never seen a seascape so mesmerizing.

Meara's voice interrupted her thoughts. *Swim to the trench. Quickly.*

Clover swam toward a faint light which shone from a break on the ocean floor. Looking down a narrow crevice with seemingly no end in sight, she hesitated.

You're almost there. Go.

She swam headfirst down the abyss, casting her fear aside. The gap got progressively narrower as she swam farther down. After what felt like forever, she reached the bottom. Against a barnacle-ridden rock wall, an opening seemed to have been carved out, like an entrance to a cave. She stuck her hand in the hole and was amazed to discover that it was dry inside. She swam in and came out dripping wet and on all fours on the other side. The change in atmosphere left her catching her breath, the stone floor sharp and abrasive against her knees.

"You made it. Atta girl." Tony offered his hand to help her up.

She hadn't seen Tony since the battle with the Unseelies, the day she found out that the man whom she'd known all her life and who owned her favorite deli back in New York, was actually Anthony Glass, Meara's brother, her uncle. Standing before her now, he looked markedly different. Firstly, he wasn't wearing his usual blue jeans and white T-shirt. He wore light colored trousers and nothing on top. Secondly, and more notably, he looked *younger.*

She hugged him as tight as she could. "I was hoping to see you again."

Getting her bearings, she realized they were in a small cylindrical space, like the bottom of an old well.

"Listen," Tony said as he motioned to a wooden door etched into the stone wall. "Go ahead and enter. I need to go up and check on your mother. I only waited for you to pass safely first."

The door gave off an odd "Alice in Wonderland" vibe—weathered wood bordered with mismatched stones, a large brass doorknob.

"What's in there?" Clover asked, her heart beating hard against her chest.

"Home."

4

As Clover gathered the courage to walk through the door that led to the Land Beneath the Waves, water gushed from the entry that led back to the trench and Meara emerged from it.

"Mom!" Clover shrieked.

"It's okay," Meara assured, "Iekika has left for now. You're okay."

It was then that Clover noticed a deep gash across Meara's chest, staining her white dress.

"Oh, my god. What happened?"

"It's nothing," Meara said, shrugging it off. "The important thing is that you made it through beneath the waves, not a small task for even the most powerful of faeries. You did it. Your powers are emerging, Clover."

Suddenly, the night's events came rushing back to her—creating a decoy of herself to divert Iekika, levitating, breathing under water, and making it through the trench.

"Oh, no," Clover gasped. "Anna tried to fight Iekika off. We must go back. Momma Ruth and my dad were in the house, too. We need to go now—"

"You're safer down here. I'll go and check on Anna and your family," Tony interrupted.

"He's right," Meara said. "You mustn't go back up. Not yet."

Clover's mind was racing. So much had happened in such a short amount of time.

"Could you let Finn know where I am? And let my dad and grandmother know that I'm not hurt?"

Tony nodded. "Of course. I'll take care of it."

She turned to Meara. "What are we going to do in the meantime?"

Meara smiled as she held her hand out in invitation. "Don't you want to meet the rest of your family?"

The enormity of Meara's question nearly knocked the wind out of her. Was she ready to enter yet another foreign world to meet her long-lost supernatural kin? She decided she'd made it that far down the rabbit hole, no sense changing course now.

She took her mom's proffered hand and followed her home.

※

After Alistair and Vincent left the Seelie Court, Finn assigned a handful of their best soldiers to guard the queen. He would strategize with Queen Helena later, after he made sure that Clover was okay. Never mind that it was late, or she might be in bed, he would see her that night or he would lose his mind. As he made his way to Anna's house, Alistair's words kept replaying in his mind. *All I want is my wife back*. With every step, his fury multiplied. If it was the last thing he ever did, he would kill Alistair before he laid another hand on Clover. He would respect the three days of ceasefire in honor of the slain king, but after then, all bets were off.

In his rage, he almost didn't notice the wide-open front door to Anna's house, but the smells of sulfur and lightning were unmistakable.

"Clover." Her name came out in a whisper as Finn dashed into the house like a madman.

Momma Ruth and Nick were crouched over Anna as she lay on

the ground, motionless. Cordelia hovered over her body, panic and concern etched on her tiny face.

"Finn!" Momma Ruth screamed. "Something's terribly wrong. We heard a commotion and found her like this."

He rushed to his mother's side and found her unresponsive, yet conscious. Even as her body lay stiff as a board, the anger in her eyes mirrored Finn's. He'd seen this type of magic before. Iekika had used it on the Seelie Army during the battle with the Unseelies.

"Anna," Finn whispered as he leaned in closer. "I've got you."

A slow-spreading warmth snaked its way to the palms of his hands like it always did before a healing. He placed both hands above Anna's heart and closed his eyes. His arms turned rigid as Anna's face and upper body regained mobility. His torso and legs cramped up as he absorbed the full force of the magic that left Anna's body and entered his.

She grabbed hold of his arm. "That's enough, son."

Exhausted, Finn let go. "Did Iekika do this?" he asked between labored breaths.

Anna nodded.

Bile rose up his throat as he uttered the question he was afraid to hear the answer to. "Is Clover okay?"

The looks on Nick's and Momma Ruth's faces were answers enough.

"Where is she?" he asked, feeling his heart collapse into itself.

Tony walked in at that moment. "She's with Meara. Clover is safe."

※

Nothing could have prepared Clover for what she saw when she walked through that door. Before she entered, she momentarily held a vision of mermaids lounging on giant seashells while lobsters danced and sang nearby. The reality couldn't have been farther from her cartoonish expectations. An ancient city, vast as the eye could see, dotted with lakes, rivers, and streams that meandered through intertwining stone walkways and passages, seemingly enclosed in a gigantic sheer globe, where the sky was the ocean, and the constellations were the ripple of the waves. The merrows weaved effortlessly between water and land, fins transforming into limbs and vice versa in the blink of an eye. The women were dressed in linen tunics and the men in what looked like white pajama bottoms. Some of them looked their way and nodded knowingly. They'd been expecting her.

Two women approached, one with silver blond hair and sparkling green eyes, and the other, a statuesque brunette, both lovely. Like Meara, they had feminine yet strong physiques—the types that conveyed, *I look good in a dress, but I can kick your ass.*

"Clover," Meara said as she motioned to the blonde, "I'd like you to meet Boann—"

"And I'm Sinann," said the brunette with a smile.

"They're my nieces," Meara said. "Your cousins."

Totally blown away that she had cousins her age—or at least *looked* her age—Clover hugged both of them.

"I'm so happy to meet you both."

If Boann and Sinann were taken aback by her display of affection, they didn't show it. They were both gracious and delightful, hugging her back with equal enthusiasm.

"We've been waiting to meet you for a very long time," Boann said. "Come and let's head to grandfather's house. He's very eager to meet you, too."

She looked to her mom. "Grandfather?"

Meara nodded. "My father."

Her heart was fit to burst. All her life, she'd only had Momma Ruth, with no cousins or relatives from her father's side. Then, as if by some karmic turn of events, she discovered not only her mother and her true nature but also a whole new side to her family. If that wasn't lucky, she didn't know what was.

She followed Meara and her cousins as they traversed the narrow, winding streets. Boann pointed to a fort-like structure in the distance. "That's where we're headed," she said as she led her over subterranean pools and streams that snaked through the city's alleys and side streets. She imagined that even if Venice in Italy somehow magically morphed with Santorini in Greece, it still wouldn't be nearly as breathtaking as the Land Beneath the Waves.

Merrows did somersaults off a nearby cliff, their legs transforming into fins as their bodies glided silently into the water.

Sinann caught her staring. "Some of the pools connect to the human world," she said. "We like to visit every now and then," she added with a playful wink, "and sometimes we bring back souvenirs."

"Oh," Clover replied not-so-eloquently as she pictured beautiful mermaids sitting atop rocks, luring weary sailors out to sea with their enthralling siren calls.

Up close, what she thought was a fort was actually a castle, complete with a drawbridge and a moat, which in that environment appeared purely recreational as merrows splashed around in its shallow waters. She once thought the faerie realm epitomized a carefree and bohemian spirit. The Land Beneath the Waves had the feel and essence of spring break in Miami Beach.

They crossed the drawbridge and walked under the raised portcullis. As castles went, her grandfather's certainly didn't seem well-protected. In the courtyard, there seemed to be some kind of party underway. Merrows sipped wine as they lounged on daybeds and schmoozed around cocktail tables.

"What's going on here?" Clover whispered to Meara.

Meara shrugged. "It's always like this."

A dashingly handsome man with shoulder-length, golden curls approached. Sporting the same breezy linen pants and bare chest look like the others, he stood out because of the beautiful tattoos inked like mosaics on his torso and arms that surprisingly conveyed neither biker boy nor escaped convict. He looked like a living, breathing, masterpiece.

"You must be Clover," he said to her. His eyes, which were the same indigo shade as Meara's, bore such depth and maturity.

Before she could respond, Meara made the introductions. "Clover, this is Manannán mac Lir, your grandfather."

He flashed her a dazzling, yet warm smile. "Everyone calls me Lir."

Her mind strayed to an elective class she once took on Celtic mythology. "Lir? You mean, like the sea god?"

His laugh was deep and spirited. "I'm not sure I'd call myself a god. You, my dear, may call me grandfather. That is, if you'd like to."

"Grandfather." She tried the word out, and felt a warmth spread inside. "Yes. I'd like that very much."

※

Finn gripped the compass in his hand and pointed it north.

"You'll break it holding it that tight," Anna scolded.

He couldn't blame her for her foul mood. All of them were on edge. Iekika's brazen attack held many implications. Chief among them, the fact that the Unseelie King had just broken ceasefire and that a full-on war was inevitable. Even though he had feared it, Finn never expected Alistair was capable of such a blatant act of disrespect. The first thing he needed to do was get in touch with Scobert and warn him. He would then brief Queen Helena, and then he would go see Clover.

"This damn thing is not working." His patience was wearing thin.

Mary had joined them and was helping Cordelia serve tea to everyone. "It will work, Finn. Scobert enchanted that compass himself. If it was good enough a gift for the queen, then I daresay it should be good enough for you."

"Everybody, calm down," Nick chimed in. "We do each other no good by biting each other's heads off."

Although he knew Nick was right, and even though Tony had assured him Clover was safe, the longer he stayed apart from her, the more restless he became. He jumped when the compass shook violently, leapt from his palm, and landed on the floor, vibrating. An image of Scobert projected from the compass, filling a clurichaun-shaped space in Anna's living room.

"What's the matter?" Scobert asked. His voice crackled and his image blurred, like from an old television.

Finn went straight to it. "Alistair has been named Unseelie King. He parleyed with the queen, but it was a ploy. Iekika attempted to snatch Clover and fought both Anna and Meara in the process. Clover is now safe beneath the waves."

"What a damn fool he is," Scobert mused. "Is Helena secure?"

"Yes."

"Kean and I will return shortly via portal. King Boris is getting an unmarked grave in the middle of nowhere. In light of Alistair's actions, all courtesies are off the table. We go to war."

Finn nodded. "Agreed."

Scobert's image flickered, dimmed, then disappeared.

"I told you it would work," Mary said with an air of smugness.

"I never doubted it." Finn took the compass and put it in his pocket. "I'm heading to the court to brief the queen. Who's coming with me?"

"I am," everyone answered in unison.

<hr />

Clover always imagined it would be nice to have big family dinners, like the ones in movies depicting thanksgiving feasts—the father carves the bird, platters of food are passed around as everyone loads their plates. She'd never had that. Not that dinners with Momma Ruth weren't special—because they always were—but there was something about a loud, festive meal that screamed hominess and a sense of belonging. She never imagined her first big family dinner would be with a bunch of mermaids, ten thousand feet beneath the ocean's surface, but she was going to take what she could get.

Lir walked around the long table depositing trays of food, while

Meara refilled everybody's glasses with wine. Boann's husband, Nachtan, and her son, Aengus, had joined them and were both eager to get to know their new kin. They peppered her with questions about her life in New York, what she thought of the faerie realm, and how she felt about being half-Fae.

"They're really dying to know more about your father, but they're too proper to ask," Boann said as she reached over and tore off a piece of bread.

"Oh, hush," Meara said as she poured her cousin more wine. "Another topic, perhaps?"

Sinann laughed and shook her head. "This one's always tight-lipped about the mysterious Nick, who stole her heart away. Auntie, c'mon now. Isn't it about time we talked about him?"

She locked gazes with her mother fleetingly before Meara looked away and glanced at Lir.

"Ladies, that's enough." Her grandfather's tone, although light, didn't leave room for argument.

A brief silence followed while everyone seemed to rack their brains for a new topic. Clover took a crack at it. "Sinann, will your husband be joining us as well?"

Sinann threw back her drink. "No husbands for me, I'm afraid," she said with a naughty twinkle in her eye. "I'm more inclined to the female persuasion, if you will."

"Of course." With her foot in her mouth, her words sounded garbled to her. "I'm sorry for making an assumption."

"Don't be," she whispered conspiratorially at her. "I'm not." Sinann's eyes shifted to the entrance to the dining hall. "Speaking of persuasions, here she comes now."

A petite girl with dark hair and a kind face walked in. Looking about seventeen-years-old, she was wearing the same linen tunic that all the women donned, but she didn't have that same air of confidence and otherness the other ladies had. Instead of gliding into the room, like Clover's mom and cousins would have, this girl sort of scurried in. Looking self-conscious and fidgety, she mumbled her hello's and took the empty seat in between Clover and Sinann.

She bowed her head slightly at Lir. "Your Majesty."

He shook his head and stifled a laugh. "For the umpteenth time, Button, you may call me Lir."

Clover had to consciously keep her expression passive to hide her confusion, but more importantly, her curiosity. Who was this girl and why was she addressing Lir like royalty?

Sinann provided some clarity. "Cousin, this is Button, my special friend." She planted a kiss on the girl's lips.

Clover extended her hand to her. "Pleased to meet you."

"Me, too," she said. Then with a hushed voice and only to her, "Who brought you down here?"

"What?"

"Clover is Meara's daughter," Boann chimed in. "She's half-Fae."

"You two will have a lot in common," Sinann added. "She's also from New York."

Suddenly, things started to make sense. Her fairly natural looking appearance, her aloofness, her deference to Lir. Button was human, presumably brought down to the Land Beneath the Waves as—in Sinann's words—a *souvenir*. Clover wasn't sure how she felt about that.

Seemingly sensing her discomfort, Meara added, "Button has been living with us for many years. This is her home now."

Button nodded as she loaded her plate with food. "I love it here."

"Oh, good," Clover said while she made a mental note to befriend Button and get to the bottom of that situation.

Before another uncomfortable pause could commence, Tony walked in.

"Ilbreac!" Lir called out. "Come join us."

Clover searched his face for answers. Was everyone okay? Tony nodded and went straight to her.

"They're fine. Anna's fine. Nick and Ruth are a bit frazzled but doing well."

"Thank God. Finn?"

"The lad's wrecked with worry," Tony whispered. "He insisted on going with me, but I couldn't take him without Lir's consent first."

Clover chewed on her lower lip. As much as she'd enjoyed being beneath the waves with Meara, she had family up in the faerie realm, too, and they would be worried about her. As if balancing two worlds wasn't hard enough, now she had to add a third one to the mix.

"Yo, princess," Tony said, using a familiar and often used endearment. "Care for a walk?"

"I'd love one."

Meara and Lir looked on as she followed Tony out a side entrance that led to a courtyard.

"Looked like you needed a break," Tony said as he walked toward a vast rose garden with every colored flower imaginable.

"I want to go back up."

"You're safer here," Tony insisted. "Our lands are unreachable, even to other Fae. There's the faerie realm and there's the Land Beneath the Waves, the Otherworld. Although we are one, we are removed from the rest of the Fae. This is how it's always been. Queen Helena herself insisted that we keep you safe here."

"For how long?"

"Be patient, kid. This is all for your own good."

When she didn't respond, Tony changed the subject. "So," he said sheepishly, "how was it meeting the family?"

Clover didn't know where to start, but if there was anyone she wanted to talk to at that moment, it was Tony. She'd known him all her life and there was practically nothing that she didn't share with him. "It was awesome and scary and confusing all at once. I have a *ton* of questions."

"Let's hear 'em."

"Okay. Why did Lir call you by a different name? How come you look at least twenty years younger now? Why did Button address Lir as *your majesty* and what's the story with Button? Did Sinann kidnap her? And—does my mom still have feelings for my dad?"

Tony guffawed. "Pump your brakes, kid. One thing at a time."

Hearing him laugh like that, it was like old times. Before she knew it, she was giggling along with him.

"All right, first question. My real name is Ilbreac mac Lir. It's hard to pronounce and even harder to spell. When I started spending more time on Earth, I chose an alias. Tony Glass. Your mother and I use the name Glass in honor of our mother. Fand Glass. She died many years ago."

"I'm sorry," Clover said. "I didn't realize she was dead."

"She was very powerful, and she loved Lir deeply. Some considered her queen of the Otherworld. I suppose that sort of answers one of your questions. Lir is, in a lot of ways, looked upon as not only king but a god down here, although he would never acknowledge it. My father wears his power well, with grace, and not like a sword to be brandished about."

As she imagined a powerful, regal faerie queen who once ruled the Otherworld with Lir, she felt nostalgic for a history she didn't even know she was a part of until recently. She wanted to digest all she could, as fast as she could, to make up for all she'd missed.

"Hey." Tony interrupted her thoughts. "You okay?"

"Yes. Now, on to my other questions."

"Right. Why do I look younger? Because I used glamour on myself back in New York. I figured I'd be more trustworthy if I looked older. I apologize for the ruse. All those years, it was all to watch over you for your protection. I don't regret a day of it." He stopped to pick a purple rose from a nearby bush and offered it to her.

"Thank you." Clover took the flower and remembered all the little gifts Tony had given her throughout the years, the sea glass bracelet on her wrist, the most recent one.

"Now, as to Sinann and Button, that's none of my business.

There's something you should understand, Clover. Faeries have not always treated humans as equals. I mean, we call you lackeys. It's not uncommon for Fae to forcibly take mortals from their homes and bring them here, as companions, or at times, playthings. I'm not defending it. I'm just telling you the way of things."

"That's horrible." Button was her age. She'd barely even had the chance to live her life before Sinann chose her path for her. "Can she still go back if she wanted to?"

"It's been many years." Tony shrugged. "Again, it's not my business, but I will say that I do believe they love each other dearly."

The barrage of information was enough to keep her mind occupied for years. "If Boann and Sinann are my mother's nieces, then does that make you—their father?"

Tony erupted in his trademark reverberating laugh. "Hell, no. They belong to my other sister, Aoife."

As her family tree grew bigger by the minute, Clover's mind reeled. "How many other brothers and sisters do you have?"

"Just us three." Tony peered at her closely. "Hey. I know this is a lot to take in, but I'll be here for you every step of the way. So will your mother. If it makes any difference, the only time I've ever seen Meara cry was when she left you and your father. I don't know if that answers your last question about her feelings for Nick, but I do know that it was one of the hardest things she's ever had to do."

She wrapped Tony in a tight hug. "I'm so glad you're here. Thank you for everything." Then she steeled herself for what was to come. "What do we do now?"

"I don't know about you, but I could use a drink." Tony offered his arm. "I say we start there, and the rest we'll figure out as we go along."

Locked arms with the man who had been there for her all her life, she walked bravely toward an uncertain future.

Alistair walked along a deserted, provincial street in the middle of nowhere, his expensive loafers scratching against the gravel underfoot. He wasn't sure what peeved him more—the fact that he'd ruined his best pair of shoes or that Iekika bungled the simple task of snatching Clover from under Anna's nose. The subterfuge of a parley would have worked like a charm if only she'd done the job she was supposed to do. How hard was it to nab one teeny human? Clover was the perfect instrument to achieve his goal of closing the portals between Earth and Faerie forever—a half-human sacrifice whose death would pierce the hearts of his enemies. He imagined Meara's would-be anguish and felt his own jaded heart flutter. He would take his small victories wherever he could get them.

A bat flew overhead, which meant he was nearing his destination. To Alistair, there was no habitat more depressing than rural America. Devoid of anything to entertain aside from the occasional county fair, it was the epitome of the type of small life he wanted nothing to do with. For those same reasons, it was also the perfect place to hide people he didn't want found.

At the end of the dark street, the light from a small cabin shone like a little ray of hope in the distance. He gave himself a much-deserved mental pat on the back. He'd done a lot of things in life he wasn't proud of. Not exactly the most honorable or kindest of men, he instead prided himself in being strategic and thorough. Eighteen years ago, when he set his plan in motion by inserting himself into Clover's life, he also considered the possibility of failure. Since half-faerie children weren't easy to come by, a degree of preemptive action became necessary.

He entered the cabin at the end of the lane like he owned it. "Ladies, I'm home."

In the eighteen years since he'd *adopted* them, Therese had certainly warmed up to him, although not entirely of her own accord. When he took them those many nights ago, she'd tried to bite his finger off. He made sure that would never happen again by employing a little mild-altering magic and she'd been an angel ever since.

Still beautiful, if not a bit beaten and bored, she rose from her seat by the hearth and ran to him, wrapping her arms around him.

"I've missed you," she whispered.

"Where's Mirabella?"

The girl walked in through the back door, her long, curly, golden hair held up in a messy knot, the familiar look of disdain and resignation evident on her face. Not as malleable as her mother, the mutt proved a little harder to control over the years.

"To what do we owe the pleasure of your company? she asked, sardonic as all hell.

"I have news. The time has finally come to reunite you with your father." He turned to Therese. "And you, your husband."

Therese nodded. "We'll do as you instruct."

Mirabella just glared at him.

"Remember," he said, glaring right back at her. "Your loyalty lies with me. You will report to me. Failure to comply by either of you means death to the other. Do you understand?"

Mirabella's face reddened and her breath hitched as she reached for Therese's hand. "Yes," she hissed. "I understand."

"Good," Alistair said. "Well then, ladies. I believe Scobert is in for quite the surprise."

5

The knife flew from Finn's hand and landed on the bullseye of a crude wooden target forty feet away. He walked over to retrieve that knife, along with the four others that were sticking out of the red circle like quills on a porcupine. With a grunt, he pulled them out and walked sixteen paces back to his throwing spot: the tread marks on the ground evidence that he'd been at this for a while. Closing in on four days since he last saw Clover, Finn was starting to get angsty. Their last meeting hadn't exactly been perfect, either. She wanted to get closer, and, like a jerk, he told her to *slow down*. He threw the next knife so forcefully that it landed less than five feet away, embedded in the ground like a tent peg. A colorful barrage of expletives escaped his lips.

"At ease, soldier," Scobert joked as he approached with two beers in hand. He offered one to Finn. "Nothing like an early morning beverage to take the sting out."

Finn grabbed the bottle and took a long swig. "I'm going out of my mind."

"She's safe down there. Meara will make sure of it. Besides, we've got a lot on our hands right now. The less distractions, the better."

"She's not a distraction, Scobert."

"You know I didn't mean it that way." Scobert picked up one of the knives, a quick flick of his wrist sent it flying through the air, landing on the target, and vibrating for a second before settling. "We need you now. A good chunk of the army has disbanded over these years of peace. Many of our men are scattered all over the world, growing fat and lazy. You need to corral our soldiers and get them back down here—before Alistair gets to them first."

"Is there nobody else that can play army recruiter besides me? I'm more useful here. I can retrain the men that we do have."

"The men trust you. They will follow you—especially after they've learned what Alistair has done."

Finn knew this to be true. It had to be him. "When do I need to leave?" he asked, resigned.

"In the morning? The sooner, the better."

He nodded. He would have to find a way to at least get a message to Clover before he left. Remembering Scobert's magical compass, he wondered whether there was a way to get one to her.

Taking a swig from his beer, Scobert eyed him curiously. "What's going on with you?" he asked.

He raked his fingers over his head in frustration. "I don't know. There's just so much at stake, you know?"

Scobert picked up a blade and balanced it on the tip on his finger. "I get that." The knife wobbled but he willed it upright. "A few years ago, you could have cared less about stakes. It was just you, your mission, your queen. A few extra-curricular activities here and there. Am I right? Now, you've got the girl to worry about and all of a sudden, you're on shaky ground. Everything's shifted."

Finn sometimes forgot that Scobert and the queen were together and that he was probably going through the exact same frustrations as him. He realized they were, in many ways, in the same boat.

Scobert spun the blade on the tip of his finger. "You just have to find a balance." The knife rotated like a globe flipped too fast. It crashed to the ground when Kean came running up to them, destroying Scobert's concentration.

"For Chrissake's, lad. You call yourself a soldier with footfalls that heavy?" Scobert asked.

"Queen Helena has called for you. She says it's urgent."

※

"How come your legs don't turn into a fin?" Button asked.

They were lounging by one of the many beaches in the Otherworld, their legs almost submerged in the water, sitting on the shore as the tide came in. It was the first time Clover and Button were alone together, and she was eager to get to know her better.

Clover shrugged. "To be honest, I'm actually kind of glad. With all the changes I've had to deal with lately, I really didn't need an extra appendage."

Button laughed like young children did—full of unsuspecting and careless mirth. "You're funny," she said.

"Can I ask you something?"

"You already did." Button covered her mouth and giggled, clearly pleased with her own joke.

"Is Button your real name?"

"No."

Clover waited for her to tell her what it was. Nothing.

"What is it?"

"Adele."

"That's a pretty name," Clover said, and meant it. It was a hell of a lot better than Button. "Why don't they call you Adele?"

She wiggled her nose, then started scratching at it. "Sinann said I was 'cute as a button' once. I suppose it sort of stuck."

"Did you also enter the realm through the portal in Ireland?"

Button shook her head. "Nope. We swam here from the Atlantic."

Clover's eyes grew wide. "All the way?"

Button's answering laugh was just as joyful as the last. "No, silly. There's a secret portal only known to merrows—the Ninth

Wave. Every once in a while, when the sea is at its angriest, a giant wave creates a direct entrance to the Otherworld."

"I thought humans could only enter through the portal at Lough Derg," Clover said, thoughtful.

Button chuckled. "Once you've been here long enough, you'll see that merrows follow their own rules. They're not like other Fae."

"How long have you been here, Adele?"

She tilted her chin up to meet the rays of the morning sun, a peaceful smile on her face. For a moment, Clover thought maybe she hadn't heard her question. Finally, she looked at her. "Depends."

"Depends on what?"

"On what year it is now."

Clover was flabbergasted. How long does it take before a person stops counting the days? Even people with life sentences mark the passing of days with etch marks on walls.

"Do you know what year it was when Sinann took—I mean—when you met Sinann?"

"Of course. The war had just ended. I was queueing for the Parachute Jump in Coney Island. It was my seventh time to get on it. I just love the feeling of falling. Don't you? Anyway, that's where I met Sinann. She was lovely."

The Parachute Jump in Coney Island had been shuttered for as long as Clover could remember. It was a landmark on the boardwalk, sometimes lit up for special occasions like the Fourth of July. One question loomed in Clover's mind—which war was she referring to?

"Button. What *year* was it?"

"1947."

"Wow," Clover whispered as her shoulders slumped forward. The enormity of what had happened to Button hit her. Taken from her world when she was barely an adult, she was forced to live the rest of her years in another realm, suspended in time, a *plaything* for Sinann. The injustice of it all made Clover's blood boil. The life that she could have had, snatched from her decades ago on the Coney Island boardwalk.

"I know what you're thinking," Button turned to her, her expression earnest, "that many years have passed and there's no getting them back, but I do like it here; and I do *love* her."

"Don't you want to go home though?"

Button seemed to ponder her question when a big wave crashed to shore, nearly knocking them both over. Drenched, yet exhilarated, Button combed her hair back with her fingers, clearly enjoying herself. Then she turned somber, as if remembering something. "Home is where you're cared for. I don't think there's anybody left to care for me in Brooklyn."

The simplicity and truth to her reasoning pierced at Clover's heart. She wondered about her own situation. Would she still have a home in New York when she returned? Or would everyone have forgotten her? Was she prepared to be like everybody else in the faerie realm—suspended in time, forever young?

She got distracted by a loud splash as a mermaid's fin breached the surface close to shore. Soon Meara was walking toward them, like some sea goddess, which, in a way, she actually was.

"Hi, Mom! Way to make an entrance," Clover deadpanned.

"It was faster to swim than walk," she explained. "Hi, Button."

Button waved. "Hello, Miss Meara."

"Is everything all right?" Clover asked.

"I have good news. Lir agreed to have Finn visit, if that's still what you want."

Her heart beat loudly against her chest. "Of course."

"You can go back up for a little while. I'm sure your dad and Ruth are eager to see you, but on one condition. You'll need to perform a little magic, but I'll guide you through it. Training starts now."

Button stood to leave. "I better get going then. See you gals later."

Meara held a finger up. "Actually, Button, we may need you. Do you mind staying a little while longer?"

Faeries stared as Scobert walked past. Covering their mouths, they spoke in hushed tones, averting their gaze when he looked their way. He picked up his pace as he made his way to the queen's private quarters.

"What's going on here?" Scobert bellowed at Kean as the soldier struggled to match his stride.

"I have no idea. The queen dispatched me with no explanation."

"Did she seem okay? Is she hurt? In danger?" His pulse quickened as he explored myriad possible complications.

"She seemed—distressed."

"Jaysus, Kean. You didn't think to ask why?"

Kean shrugged. "She's the queen. I can't very well just ask—"

"All right, all right. Just shut up, will you?" Scobert was a mess of nerves by the time they made it to the queen's quarters.

Liz met them by the door. She looked like she'd just seen a ghost. "Before you go in there—"

Scobert pushed past her. "Get out of my way, Liz."

The scene that greeted him when he walked in was, at best, anticlimactic. Helena was seated on a floral couch with an unreadable expression on her face. On the bench in front of her, two women had their backs to him, one with wild, curly blond hair, the other, red, tied up in a ponytail. Judging from Helena's attire and the early hour, he quickly surmised that the guests were unexpected. Whoever they were, it was safe to expect they brought bad tidings.

"What's the matter?" Scobert demanded.

The redhead turned at the sound of his voice.

"Scobert," she said.

He recognized the voice instantly.

He stepped back. "Wait. What's going on here? Helena?" He had lost his wife and child many years ago; they were taken from him and replaced with changelings. He'd spent the better part of the last two decades searching for them. Was this some kind of cruel joke?

"These women were found by the Enchanted Pond, having no memory of how they got there. They were brought to me, and I—I recognized Therese. It is truly her. This woman is no changeling, and she remembers you."

Therese got up and walked to him. "Everything else is hazy, but I recall our life together in Fairyhall—"

"It can't be." He stumbled back and felt Kean grip his elbows, steadying him.

"It's really me," Therese said as she took another step closer.

"What—Where were you all this time?" Scobert asked, touches of incredulity and excitement in his voice.

Therese seemed to think her answer through. "Somebody took us from our home and kept us hidden all these years. I don't recall much. They must have altered our memories—"

"Us?" Scobert interrupted. "You mean the babe is alive? Mirabella lives?"

The woman that was with Therese stood up and faced him. She was tall and wiry, her green eyes steely and unwelcoming. With arms crossed and blond curls falling to her waist, she looked like a fierce Amazonian warrior. Who was this woman? Scobert wondered. The challenging look on her face turned to something resembling anger the longer he stared at her. Then he realized it wasn't anger at all, but hurt. She was hurt because he hadn't recognized her.

"Mirabella?" His inexperienced heart thundered against his chest; if he made one wrong move, he feared it would break into a million tiny pieces.

Therese motioned for the girl to come closer, and she did, one slow step at a time, as if she feared her heart would break, too. When her mother reached for her hand, she took it. They both approached and enveloped him in a fierce hug, their arms intertwined as they formed a tight ring around him. In that moment, his world shifted yet again. He snuck a quick look at Helena's unflinching, stoic, face and saw her pain underneath the façade. *I'm sorry,* he mouthed, then he hugged his wife and child with all he had.

༄

Finn stopped at Market Square to pick up a few supplies for his trip. At a small storefront with a sign that read "Lackey Survival Shoppe," a bell rang overhead as he walked in through the front door. The woman behind the counter offered up a smile, then continued ringing up an item for her customer.

He walked around the little shop, idly checking out the merchandise. A tiny, stoppered bottle purporting to be "Leprechaun's Luck" caught his eye. He rolled his eyes at the obvious counterfeit. In the apothecary section, he found the little green pills he'd been looking for. "Glow Away: One pill a day keeps the glow at bay." Faeries needed to soften their appearance when on Earth and sometimes, it was hard to concentrate on holding the glamour all day. The little pills helped. He picked up a couple of boxes; he didn't know how long he'd be up there.

Next to the pills was a transparent spray bottle that read, "Lackey Repellent: Three sprays ought to do it." He chuckled softly, thinking Clover would have gotten a kick out of that. As he browsed the local lackey dailies, the bell dinged, and a young woman walked in. She stared at him for a good long second before pretending to choose between two varieties of faerie dust: extra sticky or barely there.

She had short, dark hair, an upturned nose, and kind, brown eyes. Despite being very particular with her faerie dust, she looked like a fish out of water, completely out of place in the small space as she kept darting furtive glances at him. What was up with this girl? She seemed to feign interest in a pair of vintage corduroy jeans and slowly sidled closer, inching her way to him as she stepped over boxes of used clothes and sports equipment.

"Hey," she said with a tentative smile.

Was this girl hitting on him? Finn shook his head and laughed inwardly. "Hey," he said as he picked up a newspaper and headed for the checkout counter.

The young lady tugged at his arm. "It's me." She whispered.

"I'm sorry, miss. Do I know you?"

"We need to get out of here," she breathed.

Finn stifled a laugh. "Whoa. I'm flattered, but—"

"Finn!" she hissed. Then her face turned blurry, like a lens out of focus. "Look."

Brown eyes turned blue and dark hair, auburn. In the next moment, he was face to face with Clover, then as quickly as the magic lifted, it came back like a veil, hiding Clover and revealing the stranger.

Grabbing both her hands and pulling her to him, he didn't care who saw; he was going to kiss her right then and there.

"Not here," she said, pushing him away.

"Right," Finn said, gaining a modicum of self-control back. They shouldn't draw attention to themselves. "Let's go. Follow me."

Clover shook her head and motioned to the boxes of pills and the newspaper that lay discarded on the shelf. "Go and make your purchases. I'll wait outside," she whispered before she walked out.

Finn rushed to the cashier, avoided small talk, and paid for his items in a hurry. His every thought was of her—how proud he was of how powerful she'd become; how much he'd missed her; and how he couldn't wait to be alone with her.

Outside, he nodded at Clover-in-disguise and started walking. Even without looking, he knew she was following him a few paces back. Without a plan, he racked his brain for a destination. His house? Safe option, but way too far. Anna's was closer, but everybody would be there and, selfishly, he wanted her for himself —for now. Without another thought, he made a quick right on a quiet street and ducked into an abandoned flower shop.

From the little bit of light coming in through a broken window, he could make out a worktable in the middle of a deserted room and shelves littered with old supplies; the smell of flowers still lingering. The door opened with a creak and Clover—*his Clover*—walked in. Even in the dark, he would have recognized that silhouette anywhere. Her eyes seemed to settle to the darkness, but when she saw him, she closed the distance between them in an instant, jumping and wrapping her legs around his waist. He held her up and buried his face in her hair, inhaling her scent: jasmine and juniper, now mixed with something else. Magic? He kissed her then; deeply and with an intensity that astonished even him. He stumbled back against the worktable and turned around, lifting her, and placing her on the surface. When Clover sighed and pulled him closer, he was pleasantly surprised to discover that her passion matched his own, and in the dimly lit, shadowy, abandoned room, he didn't want the moment to end.

Clover pulled away, her breath rasping and her body trembling. "Wait," she said. "Not here. Not like this."

He rested his forehead against hers, equally out of breath. "You're killing me, but I get it." It took him a moment to catch his breath, then he gave her one soft peck on the lips and sat next to her, both amazed and a little surprised at how tightly she had him wrapped around her little finger.

She held his hand and leaned her head against his shoulder. "Did you like my disguise?" she asked playfully.

"Very cute," Finn replied. "Could you bring her back? I didn't get a good enough look the first time."

Clover punched his arm, hard.

Finn laughed for the first time in days. Being with her again felt so right. Suddenly, he wanted to know everything that happened since they'd been apart: her magic, the Land Beneath the Waves, escaping Iekika. He sat crossed legged on the table and faced her. "Start from the beginning and don't leave anything out."

Clover felt like she could have stayed in that dank, forgotten, flower shop forever. She told Finn about her newfound powers, about Lir and her cousins, about Button, and how Meara taught her to use magic to borrow Button's appearance. Finn briefed her on the whole Alistair-turned-King situation, and for a moment, she thought she might throw up. They talked for what felt like hours, recapping the events of the past few days, and just enjoying their time together amidst all the crazy. When Finn told her he'd been ordered to go to Earth to round up wayward Seelie soldiers, their momentary happy bubble burst wide open.

"I'll go with you," Clover said.

Finn shook his head. "Absolutely not. It's not safe."

"But when will I see you again?" Clover asked, not wanting to sound like a pouty teenager but failing miserably.

"I don't know." Finn bowed his head and ran his fingers through his buzz cut, a habit that pulled at Clover's heart strings. She really didn't mean to stress him out any more than he already was. She decided that if they were going to survive their predicament, she would have to let him be a soldier without having to worry about her every minute.

"Look at me," she said as she raised his chin up to meet her gaze. "I'm sorry. I was being selfish. Do what you have to do for the queen—for the realm. I'll be okay. It turns out I have the makings of a pretty powerful faerie. You and I can do this. Alistair won't know what hit him." The boldness in her tone masked her true emotions. She was frightened to be apart from him.

He took her hand and brought it to his lips. "I love you so much, Clover."

"I love you, too."

Finn exhaled and got off the table. "Where to, now?" he asked.

"I need to see my dad and Momma Ruth. After that, would you care to join me for a swim?"

A giant smile formed on Finn's face. "I'd love nothing more."

Helena had ordered Liz to see to the rooms for Therese and Mirabella; they were her special guests. So special that Scobert was, at that very moment, escorting them to their temporary lodgings, rolling out the red carpet for his long-lost family, returned from only God-knows-where. Pacing in her rooms, Helena's nerves were a jangled mess. She would never deny Scobert his happiness, but something about his family's return was not ringing right to her. Why now? Where had they been all this time and who had taken them? Those questions were just the tip of the iceberg. What worried her more was what could come next. Would they go back to Earth—resume their interrupted lives? No. Helena decided. Scobert would never do that to her. He wouldn't abandon her at the brink of war to play house with his domesticated lackey family. Or would he?

Helena inhaled sharply and almost collapsed on her settee. She wiped a traitorous tear with the back of her hand and tried desperately to regain composure. He must not see her in this state. He must not see her at all. What was she to say to him? *Congratulations?* She saw her magical *shillelagh* leaning against the wall and considered leaving it all behind. She could do it; escape somewhere far, far away and never come back. She would have—with him. In fact, she'd wanted to, and they had discussed it, albeit hypothetically, over a bottle of wine. She could abdicate. Travel. Have a life other than the one she'd been indentured to. *A life with him.*

Liz returned with freshly pressed clothes and hung them in her wardrobe. She noticeably avoided Helena's gaze, eyes planted on the floor, more awkward than a jester at a funeral.

Helena decided to put her out of her misery. "Out with it, Liz."

At first, she pretended not to hear, appeared to reconsider, then let loose. "This can't be happening again!" she half-shrieked, then seemingly realizing the insolence in her tone, added, "My Queen."

"Oh, don't hold back," Helena responded sardonically.

Liz took out a corset and motioned to her to assume the position. "He chose her over you once before, had the gall to ask your permission to marry, then *blamed you* when she disappeared." With each enumeration of Scobert's perceived faults, the corset got progressively tighter around Helena's waist.

"In the name of the gods, Liz. I can't breathe."

Liz loosened her corset an iota. "Sorry. What do these plebeian lackeys have that we don't, anyway?" she scoffed. "I swear to all that's holy, Queen Helena, if he hurts you again—"

"That's enough." Helena said, attempting to hide the quaver in her voice.

Liz exhaled audibly but held her tongue while she helped her into a dress and fastened the buttons lining the back. Helena welcomed the momentary reprieve; she needed to gather her own thoughts.

The image looking back at her from her full-length mirror looked every bit the monarch: composed, regal, formidable. For a woman her size, who also happened to look like a teenage girl, it was a tough feat to accomplish. Liz towered behind her as she took care of the last of the buttons. Helena's heart went out to her. She had loved the same man for an eternity, and from the looks of it, he had cared for her too. Then the rug was pulled from under her feet when Finn chose to be with someone else. Unexpectedly, maid and monarch had much more in common than they were prepared to admit.

"There," Liz said when she finished, "you're perfect." Then, after a pause, "What are you going to do now?"

"What I do best—be a queen."

6

Clover-as-Button was introduced to Anna, Nick, and Momma Ruth as Finn's *new friend*, whom he'd just met at the Lackey Shoppe. Eyebrows were raised and judgmental stares were had from all three as Clover put on the ruse of being Adele, half-merrow gal from the Otherworld. Finn thought it would be fun to test her magic and see how far she could keep it up. She was doing a pretty awesome job. When she first donned the disguise, she'd had to deliberately concentrate on sustaining the magic, imagining it stretch and mold around her. The longer she did it, the less she had to think about it. Like breathing under water, this too became second nature. The newly tapped magic coursing through her veins both excited and frightened her. It made her wonder if she was in danger of forever being lost behind new masks, identities, and discoveries. With every change, every fresh revelation, she worried that one day she'd barely recognize herself.

Lost in thought, she almost missed Finn's segue to the big reveal. "...Adele has something to share with you guys. Isn't that right?"

"That's right." She played along. "Tada!" she yelled as she lifted the invisible veil and revealed her true self.

Momma Ruth shrieked and came barreling toward her,

wrapping her in the tightest of hugs. "How—what—oh my goodness!" She couldn't find the words, but her hug spoke volumes.

Clover tried not to fall apart as she hugged Momma Ruth back. There was so much she wanted to tell her. In a matter of days, it seemed like her world had changed drastically—yet again. Her new powers, her new merrow family. The tectonic shifts had nothing on the recent cumulation of jarring events in her life.

"Oh, Momma. I've missed you so much," she said. Talk about change; it didn't escape Clover's attention that her grandmother looked younger and more vibrant than she'd ever seen her. "You look amazing," she added.

While Momma Ruth brushed her compliment aside, it was apparent that it made her feel uncomfortable. Clover decided to let it go for the moment but reminded herself to carve time for a private conversation with her grandmother before she had to head back beneath the waves. She wanted to make sure she was okay.

Nick lifted Clover in a quick hug, then mussed up her hair like he always did. "Look at you," he whispered. "So brave and powerful. Just like your mother."

Clover tried not to blush, but her face had other ideas. "Oh, stop it, Dad," she said. She was nothing like her mother. It was like comparing Disney on Ice to Swan Lake, if that even made any sense.

Anna watched their little reunion unfold with a smile on her face. Clover made her way to her and took both of her hands in hers. "Thank you so much for what you did with Iekika. And I'm so sorry you got hurt. I should have stayed with you."

"No, *I'm* sorry," she said, her voice cracking. "If I had succeeded in stopping her like I was supposed to, she never would have gotten to you. I should have done better, and believe me, next time—I will."

As she looked into Anna's eyes, something occurred to Clover. She was, for the first time in her life, surrounded by family. In many cases, not the family she was born into, but family, nonetheless.

"Thank you," was all she said, but deep inside, her gratitude was boundless and indescribable. From the moment she crossed over to the faerie realm, she'd experienced nothing but support, acceptance, and encouragement. She owed them so much, and promised herself that she'd pay them back, one way or the other.

"Well, then," Anna said. "You must be hungry. Why don't we all sit down for a nice brunch? You can tell us all about the Otherworld and your new shapeshifting skills."

"I'd love to," Clover said while inwardly her mind raced. Shapeshifting?

Finn sidled next to her and took her hand. "What's the matter?" he whispered. "You look frightened."

"Did I *shapeshift*? I thought that was glamour. All faeries can do that, right?"

Finn shook his head. "That was no illusion, Clover. What you did, that was shapeshifting. Very few faeries can do that."

She drew a sharp breath. Once again, the ground seemed to shake from under her. She leaned on Finn to steady herself, this last startling realization almost knocking her off her feet.

※

At brunch, they caught Clover up on all that had happened since the night of Alistair's faux parley. Apparently, while she was away, Anna had taken it upon herself to teach Ruth and Nick a thing or two about warrior arts and self-defense. According to Anna, Nick displayed a proclivity for the arts and had even proved a worthy sparring partner to Kean on more than one occasion. The mention of Kean Mackey elicited a tight-lipped unease around the table. Everyone knew that Kean had openly declared his feelings for Clover and that he was always well liked by everyone, most notably Nick. The fact that Finn and her dad never really had the chance to warm up to each other didn't help, either. Even Anna seemed to sense the awkwardness when she tripped all over herself in her attempt to explain.

"Kean comes by every now and then to check up on—well, the lad enjoys Nick's company." Anna shot a glance at Finn. "I don't see anything wrong with—the truth is—Oh, to hell with it. The truth is that Kean is a fine lad, one of the best in the army, good to have around in wartime. I'm glad for the time he spends with us." Anna focused her attention on Finn. "You, my son, will just have to get over yourself and not flinch every time you hear the lad's name. There's room enough for good men and respectable soldiers among our lot. Understood?"

Silence rang like a gong.

"Gee, Anna. Why don't you tell me how you really feel?" Finn asked, not missing a beat.

Momma Ruth cackled first, and the rest of them boisterously followed suit, breaking the momentary unease in conversation.

"Seriously, though. I have no problem with Kean Mackey. As long as he understands that—"

Clover playfully pinched Finn's side. "He knows you're my guy. Understood, soldier?" She rolled her eyes. "Somebody, please change the topic."

Nick was up to the task. "I've befriended some werewolves," he said with an enthusiastic glint in his eye.

"Seriously, Dad? Leave it to you to seek out the most dangerous creatures and somehow manage to get chummy with them." Half-mocking, but full-on worried, Clover didn't want her father to get messed up with dubious characters.

"Don't worry," Anna assured. "The lycanthropes are our allies and they're trustworthy."

"Your mom and I had lunch at an Italian place owned by werewolves. I went back there the next day by myself and ended up playing pool with some of the chefs and waiters afterwards. Cool troupe. Good people," Nick said.

Clover tried to imagine her dad in a pool hall with a bunch of werewolves and chuckled. As strange as their new reality was, she was happy to see Nick and Momma Ruth adjusting well to their altered lives. She wondered how long they'd have to stay in the faerie realm before it was safe to return to Earth, or if that day would ever come.

Momma Ruth chimed in. "Beware the full moon, son. It's one thing to dine with them; It's another thing completely if you're what's for dinner."

"Momma!" Nick and Clover both yelled.

A fresh spell of easy laughter made its rounds across the room.

"They like me. They won't eat me. Wait," Nick said, a look of alarm on his face. "Would they?"

"It'll sure take the *fine* out of fine dining," Momma Ruth quipped.

As another wave of laughter wove its way across the table, Clover realized that despite the seriousness of what lay ahead and the banality of their current preoccupation, she'd never been happier. Her sides started to hurt as Momma Ruth pantomimed a werewolf attack on Nick; even the usually restrained Anna couldn't keep her giggles in. With Finn by her side, and her family close at heart, Clover found the ground steady beneath her feet, solid and supportive. Remembering what Button had said about home being a place where you're cared for, she felt assured she was at the exact right place.

※

Ruth packed a bag for her granddaughter. If white tunics were all they had down there, then at least she should be able to wear her own clothes. She packed one of the ratty, worn-out jeans Clover had brought from New York, a couple of clean shirts, and underwear. She found comfort in the mundane activity of folding clothes and stuffing them in a bag. With all the fantastical events of late, this was something that felt familiar: looking after Clover. She stopped short when she realized where Clover was going. She wondered whether she should wrap the bag in plastic to keep it dry.

While she was at it, she stuffed a bar of soap and some other toiletries in the bag. Who knew what kind of plumbing they had under the sea? Better to be prepared than wanting for a toothbrush in the middle of the ocean somewhere. She closed her eyes, took a calming breath, and reminded herself that Clover was more than capable of taking care of herself. She had changed so much. Even after she took off the disguise, Ruth barely recognized her. Not that her physical appearance was much altered—other than that new touch of otherworldly glow—it was more her demeanor and bearing that transformed. While vestiges of her lighthearted, carefree granddaughter remained, there was now a perceptible strength and confidence that wasn't quite there before. Her heart blossomed with pride.

Clover walked in through the open door. "Hey, Momma. What are you doing in here?"

"You caught me," Ruth replied. "I'm packing you a bag."

Clover peeked in the backpack. "I could use some proper soap. They use some kind of perfumed kelp down there that I haven't gotten used to."

Without warning, Ruth turned to Clover and held her in a tight embrace, cradling her head against her bosom as a suppressed sob escaped her throat.

"What's the matter?" Clover asked softly.

She released Clover and sat on the bed, straightening her skirt across her legs a couple of times before finally looking her granddaughter in the eye. "Sweetie, there have been changes happening to my body and my overall heath—"

Clover nodded. "You look younger, more vibrant."

"You've noticed?"

She smiled. "It's kinda hard not to."

"Right," Ruth conceded. She wondered if the changes were more noticeable than she'd originally thought. "It started when Finn healed me and saved my life, but it's gotten gradually worse—better—I'm not sure I know the right word."

"How do you feel?" Clover asked.

"I feel like I haven't felt in years. I have no joint pains, no shortness of breath. I feel like I could run a marathon and climb a mountain afterward. I have never felt stronger or healthier in my entire life. I'm also frightened. This type of thing must have consequences. Right? It's simply not normal."

A cloud of worry seemed to settle over Clover as she chewed on her lower lip. "I'm sure Finn never would have done anything that could hurt you. He healed you and saved your life. These are all just probably after-effects from his magic. But I'll speak to him about this. Okay, Momma? You'll be all right."

With her sitting on the bed, Clover held her in the same way that she'd held her only moments ago, against her bosom in a tight embrace. Ruth allowed herself to be comforted as Clover whispered reassuring words. She wondered when their roles had reversed, then realized it had been that way from the start. She and Clover took care of each other. Always had and always will.

※

Scobert barged into his mother's house and sat down by the fireplace. The embers from the previous night's fire still glowed a calming auburn. Burying his face in his hands, he allowed himself a much-needed moment to find solid ground. The weight of the flask securely tucked in the inner pocket of his jacket was a lifesaver amidst the raging storm. Instinctively, he reached for it and took a long, painful swallow.

Being true to the nature of the clurichaun, Scobert admittedly indulged in drink, and had always been the happier for it. When he lost Therese and the babe those many years ago, he'd turned to rage and violence initially, but when there'd been nobody left to fight, torture, or kill for information on his family's whereabouts, he'd returned to the bottle, only this time, not so much to delight, but to deaden.

For close to two decades, he had gone numb, a degenerate recluse in a deserted pub in the middle of nowhere, wallowing in self-pity, isolated from even himself. Prepared as he was to live the remainder of his life in the shadows, when Finn came to him for help a few months past, he couldn't say no. He'd journeyed with the lad and Clover to the faerie realm. Slowly and painstakingly, his crusted-up, decaying excuse for a heart began to thaw. He had opened the door again to parts of his life he'd long ago turned his back on, his mother included. And Helena.

Scobert never imagined he'd ever love again, but faeries make plans and the gods mock. Helena was the elixir that brought him back from the brink of barely existing—the powerful queen, the curious girl, his truest friend.

Now, his wife and child were back, and his life was a cruel joke. Even his trusted whiskey failed to dull the sharp pain in his chest. He wondered whether his decrepit heart was fit to contain all his conflicting emotions, and he cursed the liquor for not doing a better job at masking them.

Even with his back turned, Scobert knew Mary had entered the room. He heard her approach and stop short, hesitating. He delayed looking at her, prolonging the relative calm before facing his predicament. His mother, always patient, kept her distance but remained in the room, as if she felt his torment and was allowing him space to just be, to sort of float for a while. Scobert took another sip to keep from drowning. He half-laughed, half-wept, letting out a god-awful chortling sound as the reality of his situation slowly dawned on him. The loves of his life were back in his life, but in order for them to be a family again, he would have to give up his heart.

He knew what he had to do, and he knew that when he turned around, Mary would be there, ready to listen.

※

Clover walked hand in hand with Finn through the path in the forest that led to the beach. She recalled the last time she'd traversed that route. A mad sorceress was in hot pursuit, and she was on the verge of a heart attack. What a difference a few days can make. Now she was about to take Finn beneath the waves. For the first time, *she* was the one showing him a place he'd never been and letting him in on a new experience. It had always been the other way around. As they neared the clearing and glimpsed the first view of the ocean, her pulse quickened. Barely able to contain her excitement, she let go of Finn's hand and ran to shore.

"Catch me if you can!" she yelled.

Finn laughed and chased after her, as lighthearted and carefree as Clover had ever seen him. "Gotcha," he said as he caught up and wrapped his arms around her waist, planting a soft kiss on the top of her head. They both stood still for a moment, looking out at the vast, sparkling ocean, the crash of waves at their feet. Savoring the moment for as long as she could, Clover closed her eyes and leaned against Finn's chest, comforted by the rhythmic beating of his heart, wishing the day would never end. Tomorrow, they'd be apart again, and although Clover wasn't quite ready to accept that, she knew the clock was ticking.

She turned to Finn. "Are you ready"?

Finn looked nervous. "Tell me again how this works."

"You're to hold my hand the whole time. We'll swim to a trench on the ocean floor. It's a narrow passage, but it shouldn't be a problem. The entrance to the Otherworld is at the very bottom. Lir knows you're coming."

Finn exhaled in a low whistle. "Never imagined this was how I'd meet Manannán mac Lir. A bit out of my element here."

Clover knitted her brows. "What do you mean?"

Finn rubbed the back of his neck. "He's practically royalty—a god even; I'm a soldier. His granddaughter's my girlfriend; I'm a leprechaun."

The resident butterflies in Clover's belly were throwing a parade over the *girlfriend* comment, but she tried her best not to let it show. "Buck up, soldier," she teased. "It'll be fine."

"Yes, ma'am," Finn conceded, a warm smile forming on his lips.

"Let's go." Clover picked up the bag that she'd dropped during their mock chase. It was enclosed in some kind of heavy-duty plastic wrap. She smiled to herself, appreciating Momma Ruth's gesture.

Finn took off his shirt and handed it to Clover. "Is there room in the bag for this?"

The sight of Finn bare-chested stirred the already harried butterflies into a frenzy. Clover silently reprimanded herself for letting her teenage hormones get the better of her, but seriously, she would have to be dead not to have a reaction. She'd known he was built, but seeing and imagining were two different things, and in this case, reality won hands down.

"Actually," Clover said, "you don't need the shirt. You'll fit right in without it."

Finn raised an eyebrow.

Clover offered her hand to Finn in invitation. He dropped the shirt, took her hand, and followed her into the water.

꘎

Finn considered himself to be a strong swimmer, but Clover was something else. The way she glided through the water was both graceful and effortless. He held her hand as they dove deeper and deeper toward the ocean floor; Clover's magic allowing him to breathe and see without a problem. As Finn took in his surroundings, it became clear why the merrow-folk chose to keep their world hidden. There were just some things that were too precious to share.

Swimming parallel to the seabed, Finn brushed his free hand against the sand beneath them while schools of fish flanked them on either side. A laugh escaped his lips, and a swarm of bubbles enveloped his face; translucent pearls slowly making their way up to the surface. He tugged at Clover's hand and pulled her closer, wanting so badly to kiss her. Clumsily, he leaned in to give her a soft peck. She flashed him the most brilliant smile, wrenching his heart into a pulp. The smooth feel of her skin in the water, the way her body moved in tune with his, and the fact that his life was literally tethered to her touch, made for one of the most sensual experiences in Finn's life. In that moment, leagues upon leagues under the sea, Finn became absolutely certain of one thing. He was one hundred percent, unequivocally done for. This girl was it for him.

Clover led him to the trench, stopping every now and then to point at strange looking fish or breathtaking coral reefs. She squeezed his hand when a monstrous looking creature with razor-sharp teeth approached. Attached to its head was a skinny appendage, a floppy pole with a blinking light at its tip. Clover gently flicked at the rod atop its head and the fish started chomping for the light, like a pesky firefly that would always be just a little out of reach. The gentle creature seemed to enjoy the game, and Clover gave it a little pet before swimming on.

When they finally reached the trench, Clover pointed to herself and then to Finn, making a diving motion with her hand. Finn nodded. They plunged into the narrow crevice hand in hand. Enveloped by jagged ocean rocks on either side, their descent was slow, yet steady. When they couldn't descend any further, Clover led him into a large hole in the trench wall. When they swam through, Finn was amazed to discover that the other side was completely dry. He coughed out water as they landed on a rough stone surface.

Clover smoothed her hand over his back. "Are you okay?"

He grinned. As far as adventures went, this one topped the charts. "I'm fantastic," he said, breathless.

Clover got up and rung water from her tunic. She straightened herself out and stood in front of an old wooden door. "Well, are you coming?"

Finn got up, reached for her hand, and brought it to his lips. "I'll follow you anywhere."

Mirabella plopped down on the grand four-poster bed with the plush feather mattress, feeling like she was in some twisted, unearthly reality show. Her mother—God bless her heart—was looking out the window with the same vacant, flimsy look on her face, the one that said, *I'm not entirely stable and may break at any minute.* It was a true wonder that she'd grown up to have any sense at all, being raised by someone who was never, ever wholly there.

Over the years, there were times she'd thought she'd glimpsed a relic of who her mother used to be, but Alistair had made certain that the true Therese would never be unearthed. So completely punch-drunk with Alistair's magic, her mother was a shell of a human-being, moving and functioning at the behest of her captor, like a sad and empty marionette. Easy as it would have been to blame her mother for their lot in life, she simply couldn't. Therese was the true victim; snatched from her home, forced to obey a heartless fiend, left with no other recourse than to raise her daughter in an isolated cabin in the middle of nowhere, eternally awaiting a visit from the man who stole her will.

Mirabella had considered leaving. She'd longed to be with other teens, to go to school, meet a guy, get a job. Instead, she'd been trapped in that house by the same devil who'd trapped her mother. Only *her will* was her own. Try as he might, Alistair had never been able, and would never be able to control her mind—a tiny comfort since she was a captive through other means. Her mother. Mirabella's obedience meant Therese got to live to see another day. Alistair had been clear: her mother's survival in exchange for her submission. The choice had been made long before the promise of an option.

Even as a small child, Mirabella knew her mother needed her. She had always been strong, and she'd known from the start that she was different. When she was five years old and desperate for somebody to play with, she had willed her stuffed teddy bear to life. A toddler puppet master, she'd tugged at the invisible strings that animated the unmoving and made herself a friend. When her mother had seen her handiwork, she had punished her for the first time in her young life. She still recalled the anger and disgust in Therese's face when she'd called her magic an abomination. Even at that young age, she recognized the irony. What Therese loved about Alistair were the very things she hated in Mirabella. She knew then to hide her magic from Therese because she was ashamed of it and from Alistair because he was threatened by it.

To keep the peace, she had tried to make herself as invisible and as pliable as her stubborn will would let her. She knew that was what Alistair required from them, but she never understood *why* he needed them at all. Why were they holed up in a cabin like prisoners, yet provided food, books, DVDs, and other leisure items on a regular basis? Why had Alistair treated her mother like a concubine and she a bastard, and yet made sure to visit every chance he got, cementing his place in their lives as the only husband and father they'd ever know?

She never understood until a few months ago when her mother revealed that her real father was still alive. It was only then she'd realized they were pawns, weapons honed and nurtured by the illustrious Alistair, to be deployed at his will at the right time. Like pigs bred for slaughter.

As if she'd just realized Mirabella was in the room, Therese suddenly left her spot by the window and sat on the bed with her.

"Alistair will be very pleased with our progress here today," she said, not really looking at Mirabella, but sort of vacuously addressing the wall in front of her.

Mirabella lay still and squeezed her eyes shut, silent teardrops falling across the side of her face and landing on the bed below. Was her mother that far gone that she was oblivious to seeing her own husband for the first time in close to eighteen years? A frantic thought entered her mind. If Alistair's magic controlled Therese's mind, could her own powers be able to release her from those bonds? Alistair would surely find out and he'd kill them both, but might it be worth it if she could have her mother back, even for just a moment?

"Mother," Mirabella whispered in between sobs.

"Yes, dear."

"Do you still love him?"

Therese seemed lost in thought. For a quick second, Mirabella could have sworn she saw her mother's face crumple up in a sorrowful grimace.

Then, with the familiar blank, expressionless countenance she'd grown so accustomed to, Therese turned to her, a question on her lips. "Who?"

7

As instructed, we are safely ensconced in the faerie queen's court. Scobert is pleased to see us, but Queen Helena seems leery. To be honest, I am quite frightened of her. I also fear that seeing her father for the first time has upset Mirabella. I will make sure she stays the course. There has been no sign of the girl, but it is early still. My husband was accompanied by a soldier, not matching your description of Finn Ryan. I didn't get his name but am of the impression that he is well regarded by the queen. We've been invited to dine with the queen and Scobert this evening. Will report back afterwards. Always, T.

Alistair inserted a ribbon to mark the page in the journal where Therese's words had magically appeared. With the other half of the enchanted diary in Therese's hands, their communication would be instantaneous, and he wouldn't have to expend so much energy breaching her mind. He couldn't have picked a better infiltrator. He dipped a quill in black ink.

Find out where the girl is. Find Finn. Remind your daughter of our agreement. Be a convincing wife. Your efforts will be rewarded.

He gently blew on the drying ink and closed the book, leaning back into his chair with a satisfied sigh. It was just too easy. Soon, his army would be battle-ready and the feast of *Lughnasadh* fast approached, opening another window to fulfill his mission. With Iekika by his side and the Unseelie Army at his behest, he could almost taste his long-awaited victory.

A knock sounded on his chamber door, interrupting his daydreams of grandeur. "Enter."

Vincent walked in, looking every bit the degenerate with his blue mohawk and sleeveless denim vest. Sadly, this fool was the lead soldier in his army, but what he lacked in intelligence and acumen, he more than made up for in bloodlust and desire for vengeance. He had attempted—more than once—to seize Clover but had failed miserably each time. During the battle with the Seelie Court, he was attacked and beaten unrecognizable by Clover's father, a mere lackey. Although the cuts on his face had scabbed over and his bruises had started to heal, the irreparable damage to his psyche was nowhere near mended. With enough training, he would make for an invaluable assassin. His insatiable hunger for retribution almost matched Alistair's own.

"Speak," Alistair commanded.

"The soldiers want blood, and they want it now," Vincent said, his nostrils flaring, eyes bulging from their sockets. "King Boris's remains have been found buried on the border between the Unseelie and Seelie Courts, cast away like refuse, left to rot in an unmarked grave. The Seelie Queen deliberately defiled the fallen king, even when you came in peace to parley. The Unseelie Court will not stand for this!"

Alistair nodded solemnly, feigning disgust at how horribly they'd been treated by the queen. "Although I agree that her actions are an affront to the civility I've afforded, I must caution against hasty action. We are not, as yet, prepared to fight. The army will continue their training, under my expert tutelage, of course. If reinforcements should be needed, I will arrange for them. In the meantime, put your trust in me, and when the moment is right, we will obliterate Queen Helena and her Seelie Court."

Vincent let out a snort like a bedeviled bull. "King Boris trusted you, and so shall we, but I will remind you that you wouldn't be king right now if it weren't for me."

Alistair was delighted to discover the thug had balls. "Is that a threat, soldier?"

"Nah." He shook his head. "Not a threat. A truth. The army will stand down—but not for long. The Unseelies need leadership, and if you're not delivering, then who's to blame them if they start looking elsewhere?"

Alistair scoffed at the half-veiled ultimatum. "Don't you worry your banged up little head. I *will* succeed, and if you think for one second that you could somehow replace me, then perhaps the damage to your noggin is permanent, but if you have *any* sense at all, you should know instinctively not to cross me." He stood and looked him in the eye. "Today, I give you a pass. I will forget your insubordinate insinuations, but should it rear its ugly head again, it will get chopped off—along with yours. Do I make myself clear?"

"Yes," Vincent spat, a gelded bull. He turned on his heel and walked out.

Alistair shook his head and poured himself a drink, half-marveling at how the greatest commander in the Seelie Army became the sitter for this sorry bunch. *A means to an end*, he reminded himself. *A means to an end.*

※

Lir welcomed Finn into the Otherworld in requisite merrow fashion—by throwing a cocktail party. With the men in their linen bottoms, tans resplendent under the sun, and the women looking stylish in their crisp, white tunics, the whole affair had the feel of a professional photoshoot. *Ibiza Chic Meets Under the Sea.* Clover could almost see the magazine spread. As she'd predicted, Finn fit right in, and she was pleasantly surprised to see that he and Lir were getting along splendidly. She watched from across the courtyard as her grandfather and her boyfriend gabbed on, looking like a couple of handsome frat boys. When Finn met her gaze, he gave her a playful wink. She raised a glass of champagne in their direction. Surreal had lost any meaning long ago. Her world was now a whole new level of strange, which in many unnerving ways was quite delightful.

Meara sidled next to her, a wine glass containing a rich-looking tawny liquid in her hand. She tipped her glass. "Cheers."

"Cheers," Clover replied and took a sip. "What are you drinking?"

"Mead. A vintage. Almost as old as I am," she said chirpily before she licked her lips.

Clover chuckled and shook her head. Sometimes, she forgot that even though everybody around her looked her age, she was the only true teenager in the bunch. When she tried to imagine everything that they'd lived through—Lir, Meara, Tony, even Finn—it was almost impossible to fathom. To live that long, to survive so much, and still maintain the same zest for life. What could be more amazing than that? She observed Lir, with his gazillion tattoos that told countless stories, god of the sea, gesturing with his hands, an unquenchable twinkle in his eye. What a wondrous life he must have lived.

Meara motioned in their direction. "You really care for him, don't you?"

"Lir?"

Meara simply smiled and shook her head.

"Oh," Clover said, her cheeks warming.

"Just be careful, all right?" Meara cautioned. "I'd hate for you to get hurt."

"Why would I get hurt?" Clover asked, attempting to feign disinterest but coming off totally defensive.

"He's been around for a long time and has never committed to a serious relationship. He's a Seelie soldier; loyal to the queen *first* before anybody else. He's a leprechaun, the most nomadic of the Fae. Rarely will you see one of his kind tied down to one particular place, or person, for that matter. I've known Finn for a while. He was Alistair's right hand for as long as I can remember and they weren't exactly angels, those two."

Clover took in a breath to speak, but Meara interrupted her.

"All I'm saying is mind your heart. That's all."

Clover was pretty sure she'd just received the most disturbing advice ever, and the worst part was, it actually made total sense. In truth, she hardly really knew Finn. Meara, on the other hand, had known him since she'd dated Alistair before she met Nick, which was really what started the whole mess they were in. Alistair had specifically targeted Clover to get back at Meara. He had kept Finn in the dark as to the identity of her mother, pretending Clover was just a regular beneficiary of the *luck trade*, Alistair's brainchild and cash cow. Finn found out too late that it had all been a farce, and that Alistair's intentions had always been malicious. He broke off all involvement with Alistair and had been at Clover's side since. Surely that showed some kind of commitment, Clover assured herself.

Before Clover's worrisome thoughts led to a complete tailspin, Button approached, a napkin laden with appetizers upon her open palm. "Hiya gals," she said, indeed looking as cute as a button.

"Hi Button," Clover replied, happy to take her mind off Meara's dire warnings.

Button offered her stockpile of finger-food to both ladies. "Are the rumors true?" she asked Meara. "Will His Majesty join Queen Helena in battle against the Unseelies?"

"Where did you hear that?" Meara asked.

Button shrugged. "I don't know. Everyone. He plots with the Seelie soldier now."

Meara shook her head, an air of defiance evident on her brow. "Don't believe all you hear. Lir hasn't breached the surface in close to a hundred years. Queen Helena's fight is not his. *My* fight is not his. My father will not battle with the Unseelies."

Button popped a piece of cheese into her mouth, seemingly oblivious to Meara's agitation. At that moment, Finn joined their group, giving Clover's shoulders a gentle squeeze from behind. When he saw Button, recognition dawned on his face.

He gave her a heart-stopping smile. "We haven't met, but I know your face well." He extended his hand. "I'm Finn Ryan."

Button, who was normally the poster-girl for nonchalance, blushed like her cheeks had been pinched and smiled coyly. "I'm Adele," she said, extending her hand.

"Very pleased to meet you," Finn said, every bit the charmer.

Clover rolled her eyes despite herself. "I need some air," she said. "Excuse me." She downed her drink and walked toward the gardens.

"Wait up," Finn called as he followed her through the wrought-iron gates that opened out to the rose bushes.

She kept walking, embarrassed and a little frightened of the way she was feeling. She was afraid that face to face, she wouldn't be able to mask her doubts, so like a child, she stood by the edge of the rose garden, her back to him. "I just need a minute."

"Clover, what's the matter?"

Her shoulders went up. "Nothing," she said, trying her best to sound unaffected but not trusting the tremor in her voice.

Finn inched closer. "I know you. Tell me what's wrong."

She turned around but didn't meet his gaze. "Do you? I mean, do you really know me?"

"I know something's bothering you," Finn said as he brushed a thumb against her cheek. "I know when you crinkle your brow and bite your lip like that, you're trying to hold back tears—and I know I will never forgive myself if I'm the reason."

Clover blew out a gust of pent-up emotions. "It's nothing, really; probably just nerves." Despite Finn's concern, she didn't really feel like telling him what Meara said. Her mother was right. She should be careful. There was a boatload of scarier and more pressing things afoot for her to waste time and energy worrying about a boy. She forced a small smile on her lips and diverted to a different topic. "I wanted to speak to you about Momma Ruth. Ever since you healed her, she's been feeling stronger, younger, and more powerful; she's worried there might be consequences to the magic, that it's somehow too good to be true."

Now it was Finn's turn to furrow his brow. "I've actually been thinking about that."

"And?" Clover asked, a knot forming in the pit of her stomach.

"When Momma Ruth's heart stopped, and you made the wish to save her, a very powerful magic was at play." Finn paused, faltering. "A captive leprechaun's ability to grant wishes knows no bounds. The power comes not so much from the leprechaun, but from the magical bond created from its capture. We are able to fulfill any wish, big or small, but—"

"But what?" Clover demanded, her patience wearing thin. If there were consequences, she had to know. Momma Ruth had to know.

"But the magic can be quite literal," Finn explained. "Do you remember what you wished for that day?"

Clover nodded, reliving the horrible moment when she thought she'd lost her grandmother. "Yes. I wished for you to heal her."

"Yes, but not in those words," Finn said, his face grave.

"I know what I said," Clover argued, suddenly feeling like punching Finn in the face. What was he getting at?

"Your exact words were, 'I wish that Momma Ruth won't die.'"

"Yeah, so? That's the exact same thing," Clover said, getting progressively more pissed by the second.

Finn shook his head. "It's not, though."

She wished for her grandmother not to die, and she didn't. The wish was granted. Clover didn't see what the problem was. She simply wished that Momma Ruth—*won't die*. She brought a hand to her mouth and stepped away from Finn. "No."

"I'm not positive. But there's a possibility."

"A possibility that you've turned my grandmother into an immortal?" A cold wave shot throughout her body as if she'd been doused with a bucket of ice water. "And you didn't think to mention this to me?" The cold turned to heat as fear morphed into anger. "You didn't think my grandmother would have wanted to know that even as everyone around her will one day drop dead, she will live on like a cursed vampire?"

"Immortality isn't a curse," Finn said softly. "Being half-Fae, you'll be around for a very long time, too, and the longer you stay in this realm, the less you age. Don't you want to have your grandmother with you as you go through this new life?"

Of course, she would have loved nothing more, but it still didn't make it right. Momma Ruth didn't choose that fate, neither was she born to it. "That's not the point, and you know it." Clover looked away, pissed at Finn for not being forthright and angry at herself for getting Momma Ruth mixed up in this circus to begin with.

"Look, I'm sorry. I never intended to hurt anyone," Finn explained. "If there's anything that I can do to—"

"Oh, I think you've done enough," Clover snapped.

Finn was about to say something but seemed to think better of it. Instead, he shoved both hands into his pockets, his lips forming a thin line.

Suddenly, Clover felt bone tired. The highs, lows, and the ever-growing tally of recent earth-shattering changes left her feeling on edge, like a tuning fork struck too hard. "Maybe you should go," she said.

The look on Finn's face broke her heart. She immediately wanted to take back what she'd said and wipe the hurt from his face.

"I probably should," he said, his grey eyes unwavering.

Clover crossed her arms. "Tony will see you back to the surface."

Finn nodded, his spine straightening. "So, that's it?"

For a moment, they held each other's gazes, unmoving and at an impasse, perhaps waiting for the other to bend. There was so much that Clover wanted to say. She wanted to tell him that she understood why he did what he did, and that losing Momma Ruth would have broken her heart. She wanted to tell him how scared she was of what was to come, of being apart from him; of possibly having her heart broken at the end of it all. Most of all, she wanted to tell him that even though she was royally pissed at him at that moment, she'd never loved anyone the way she loved him.

Instead, she said, "Yeah. I guess so."

"Take care of yourself," Finn said finally.

Before Clover could form a reply, Finn had turned on his heel and walked away.

※

Helena was still as a statue as she gazed at the glittering lagoon in the middle of her throne room, her back to Scobert. A little harp floated overhead, playing the most enthralling melody. The queen's throne room was the most wondrous in the court, with its high vaulted ceilings, ivy snaking up its walls like live garlands, and its moss-covered walkways. The plants and flowers that adorned the expanse of the room were lit up as if infiltrated by the tiniest of fireflies. On a raised dais on the far side of the room was Helena's throne, an imposing slab of quartz decked with feathery pillows and luxurious silks—a most befitting seat for a woman who was both soft and unyielding. As Scobert observed his queen amidst this magical setting, both pride and loss tugged at his insides. No matter what had happened in the past or what the future may hold, Helena would always be the most significant person in his life.

Helena turned. "How long have you been standing there?"

Scobert fidgeted at his beard, shoved a hand in his pocket, and took it out, suddenly unsure where his hands belonged. "A while."

Silence stretched like a fog, dense and suffocating.

"Helena—" Scobert began.

"Stop," Helena ordered, then pleaded, "I beg you." She held her head down.

It took everything he had not to go to her and take her in his arms, even for one last time. There was so much he'd wanted to say, yet no words would have sufficed.

"You don't have to do this," he said instead.

Helena straightened. "I am the queen, and they are my guests.

This is exactly what I have to do," she said, her voice firmer, colder. She walked past him and made her way to the dining table that had been set up near the lagoon, making a play of checking the table settings. The empty charade squeezed at Scobert's heart; half of him needed to hold her, while the other half wanted to run and hide.

"There is much to say," he said.

As luck would have it, the valet chose that exact moment to escort Therese and Mirabella into the throne room. His wife wore a simple beige dress with her hair down, her expression tentative. An image popped into Scobert's head—he wasn't sure if it was real or imagined—his hand upon a lock of her red hair, twirling the fine strands between his fingers before tucking it behind her ear. The bittersweet image was a shot to the heart. Hardly knowing what to do with himself, he dared a quick glance at Helena. She simply inclined her head.

He went to them, his raging emotions like a rabid dog in a cage. Therese picked up her pace and met him midway. "My Scobert," she whispered as she gently stroked his cheek. She gave him a kiss right then and there, in front of Helena, Mirabella and the valet—and like the bastard that he'd always known he was, he let her. His own longing overcoming any hope of propriety. While he was buoyed by the pleasure of holding his wife again, he was drowning in self-loathing and looked forward to a long and painful supper.

After their sudden, uncomfortable display of affection, Scobert signaled to his daughter to come closer. "I hope you're hungry."

Mirabella approached, something mimicking a smile, but was at its core a scowl on her face. A child after her own father's heart. She nodded awkwardly at Scobert and went to Helena. "Thank you for having us," she said as she shook the queen's hand.

"Of course. My pleasure. Please," Helena said to both Mirabella and Therese, "take a seat. Dinner will be served shortly."

They all took their seats at the marble table, Helena at the head, Scobert and Therese to her right, and Mirabella to her left. After everyone had settled, the valet poured cold water into their goblets and inquired as to whether they'd like anything else to drink.

The queen deferred to Therese. "Would you care for some red wine?"

Therese nodded. "Yes, please. Thank you."

Helena turned to Mirabella. "For you as well?"

Mirabella fiddled with the stem of her empty wineglass, her fingers slender and sure. She cast a self-conscious glance at Scobert, her long eyelashes fanning upwards, then resting on her cheek as she looked down again. What a beautiful creature she was, Scobert marveled. She cleared her throat and fixed her gaze on Helena, the steadiness in her green eyes unnerving. "Actually, I'd like something stronger if you have it. Whiskey?"

Scobert was taking a sip of water, but his mouth had sinister plans. A mini geyser erupted from his pursed lips as he half-choked on his drink, a comedic *pffftt* emanating from his mouth as meddlesome droplets of water made their way down his beard. All eyes were suddenly on him as Therese gently patted his back.

"Are you quite alright, dear?" his wife whispered.

Mirabella was staring at him, and while her face remained completely passive, Scobert could swear he spied a glimmer of amusement light her eyes. He coughed into his fist and righted himself, dabbing at his chin. "Excuse me. Went down the wrong pipe. Actually, make that two whiskeys, please."

The valet nodded and turned to Helena. "My Queen?"

"Red," Helena replied in her usual resolute and regal manner. At the head of the table, yet the smallest one seated around it, her presence was large enough to fill a room. As the valet turned to leave, Helena focused her attention on Mirabella. "I see you and your father share the same taste in drink—that must be the clurichaun in you. When did you develop an affinity for it?" Helena asked innocently.

Mirabella smiled to herself, as if recalling a long-ago memory. "I used to pinch a thimble-full every time there was any to be had; it warmed my belly during cold nights."

"It got chilly where you grew up?" Helena asked in the same casual tone.

Mirabella turned noticeably paler as she shot a frantic look at Therese, then at Scobert. "I grew up in a cabin," she said, her eyes now on Helena. "We were alone for the most part, but I think sometimes somebody brought food and supplies over. I don't recall. I fear that our memories have been tampered with, and try as I might, I can't make myself remember everything. Forgive me."

Helena placed a hand on top of Mirabella's. "Say no more. It was not my intent to upset you."

Scobert knew exactly what Helena's intent had been. His wife and daughter had returned to him armed only with a flimsy tale of selective amnesia and invisible captors who had no logical or apparent motive. He was no fool. He knew how implausible it all seemed, and while he had every intention of giving them the benefit of the doubt, he'd also planned to get to the bottom of things, one way or the other. Helena, as always, was one step ahead of him.

The valet returned with their drinks, serving Helena first, then Mirabella, Therese, and finally Scobert. By the time Scobert had raised his glass to his lips, Mirabella had already taken two large gulps of hers, her hand betraying her composure as it shook ever so slightly when she placed her glass down.

"Perhaps a toast?" Helena suggested.

Scobert raised his glass and scanned the table. If someone had told him a few months ago that one day he'd be back in the faerie realm, right hand to his queen, and reunited with his family, he would have told them to yank somebody's else chain. And yet, there he was. His past had somehow caught up with his present, and despite the way it tore his heart in two, it was a misery he was glad to shoulder. "To our present," he said, his voice throaty with emotion, "a gift not to be wasted."

"To our present," Therese exclaimed, while Helena and Mirabella quietly raised their glasses and drank to the toast.

As the servers laid out an assortment of freshly baked

appetizers, an uneasy silence descended on their table. Scobert downed his drink, willing the minutes to tick faster toward the end of the meal. He picked up a croquette and popped it in his mouth.

Therese took a small sip of wine and cleared her throat. "Queen Helena, our rooms are most comfortable and quite big. We could have easily shared one room, to be honest. Thank you so much for your hospitality."

"Not at all," Helena replied. "I'm very pleased to have you." She reached out and offered a small platter of mini pigeon pies to Therese. "The bigger bedroom was meant for you and Scobert and the room adjacent for Mirabella."

Therese blushed as she picked up a pie and placed it on her plate. "Of course."

Scobert interrupted. "Unless you'd prefer some privacy. I could go back home to Mary's and come back in the morning." The thought of spending the night with his wife in Helena's home was a bit too sacrilegious to consider.

Therese brushed a hand across Scobert's thigh, her eyes darting from Helena to Scobert. "Don't be silly. You're staying with me," she mock-whispered.

Mirabella looked like she'd swallowed a toad. Scobert couldn't blame her; no kid had the stomach to endure their parents being all lovey-dovey. For the life of him, he couldn't make himself look at Helena. Whatever expression he might find on her lovely, stoic face was just too much for his bedraggled conscience to handle. When Liz entered the throne room unannounced, Scobert was grateful for the reprieve and the distraction.

"Forgive me for the interruption, My Queen," Liz said.

"What is it?" Helena asked, the picture of composure.

"Finn is here to see you. I explained the...*situation*, but he wondered whether he could see you briefly before he left for mission in the morning."

Helena got up. "Pardon me," she turned to Therese. "If you will excuse me, I'll be right back. I just need a quick word. I won't be long."

"Why don't you ask your friend to join us?" Therese suggested.

Helena seemed uncomfortable at the prospect. "I suppose we could."

Scobert shrugged and left it up to Helena. It was her dinner party.

Helena sat down and motioned to Liz. "Send him in."

Therese smiled, seemingly eager for more company. Scobert wondered whether she too was drowning in awkwardness.

Finn walked in and approached their table, an incredulous look on his face.

"Queen Helena," he nodded. "Scobert," he ventured tentatively, "is it true?"

Scobert stood up, his heart doing that thing again, where it felt like a balloon fit to burst. "I'd like you to meet my daughter, Mirabella, and my wife, Therese."

Therese extended her hand graciously. "I'm sorry. I don't think I caught your name."

"My name is Finn. Finn Ryan."

8

Watching her mother fawn over Finn Ryan made Mirabella feel sick to her stomach. Throughout the meal, she'd made it her mission to be the guy's new best friend. The woman did not have a discreet bone in her body. It was as if an inner alarm went off when she heard the name *Finn* and all of a sudden, gone was the emotionless zombie who'd raised her. She was now Alistair's creature, solely intent on doing her master's bidding. If they ever found Clover, she was afraid her mother might have a conniption. Gold star for Therese—Alistair's star minion.

Mirabella took another sip of the wonderfully aged whiskey and was overcome with guilt. Faulting Therese for bowing to Alistair was akin to blaming someone for their own head injury or debilitating illness. If Therese had full possession of her own faculties, she would never have acceded to that monster. At least, that was what Mirabella hoped.

Therese was in full-on stalker mode. "Tell us, Finn. Where are you off to tomorrow?"

Finn smiled graciously; a quick glance thrown in the queen's direction was met with a subtle head shake from his monarch. "Just a quick errand run. Nothing that would interest you."

Scobert gave Finn a meaningful look. "Is everything okay with—"

Queen Helena promptly shot him down. "Let's limit the conversation to mutual interests, shall we?"

Scobert seemed to bristle at the subtle reprimand, but quickly recovered, signaling at the valet for another round of drinks. Mirabella sneaked a look at Finn, who was sitting beside her. He had a calm and easy way about him that masked the fact that he was on high alert, the way his gaze continually patrolled the room even as he sipped his drink in apparent leisure. His steel grey eyes, while intense and sharp, were also warm and inviting. His light blond hair was cut close to the scalp, his features chiseled, and his lips, full. Not that she'd seen her fair share, but as far as men went, this guy was pretty much drop-dead gorgeous. He also used to be Alistair's right-hand and from what she'd heard, pretty deadly, too. Growing up with hardly any company, Mirabella completely misplaced her manners and stared.

Probably assaulted by the weight of her ogling, Finn slowly turned in her direction. "So," he said, a warm smile on his face, "have you been given a full tour of the realm? How are you liking it here so far?"

Mirabella quickly gathered her composure. "Actually, we've only been in court. I'd love to see more of the realm."

"I'd take you," Finn said, "but I'm leaving in the morning."

"Don't worry about it," Scobert chimed in. "I'll take you and your mother out tomorrow. We could go for a picnic. Have a couple of drinks. Maybe I'll teach you to throw knives—who knows. How's that sound?"

If she was being completely honest, that sounded particularly awesome, but she had to remind herself she wasn't there to have fun. They were on a mission—and their very lives depended on it. "Thank you Scobert. That sounds great," she said while she searched Therese's face for approval.

Her mother snapped back to her role and turned to Scobert. "Yes, dear. We would absolutely love that."

"It's settled then." Scobert's grin stretched from ear to ear.

The queen laid her dessert spoon down across her plate, and Scobert and Finn shortly followed suit. If that signaled the meal was over, Mirabella figured she'd have another sip of her whiskey. She didn't know when she'd get another chance.

"Find a free moment to see me tomorrow," the queen said to Scobert, "for a quick word."

"Absolutely. I'll see you first thing," Scobert assured Helena.

Mirabella wondered idly at the nature of Scobert's and Helena's relationship. While there was obvious deference on Scobert's part, there was also a certain familiarity. One thing she gathered for certain was that while soft-spoken and affable, Queen Helena was not somebody to be underestimated. The woman screamed power and commanded respect. Her very presence gave Mirabella the shivers.

Mirabella was never one to turn away from what frightened her. "Queen Helena," she began, "thank you so much for your hospitality. It is sincerely appreciated."

"It was my pleasure," Helena said as she pushed her chair away from the table and stood. "Unfortunately, the hour is late, and the morning promises a full day of tasks that require my attention. A pleasant evening to you all."

As they said their goodbyes, the queen nodded once at Finn before leaving the room.

What happened next was no surprise. Finn bid them farewell and promised they'd see more of him on his return. He promptly followed Queen Helena out of the room. Mirabella exhaled a breath she hadn't realized she was holding. She realized then that she was on a suicide mission. Whether Alistair or Queen Helena would deliver the fatal blow was yet to be seen.

※

It had been nearly eighteen years since Scobert had shared a bed with his wife. Alone in the room with her that night, he felt like a pimply-faced nervous teenager, hardly knowing what to do or say. He sat on the edge of the bed and waited like a man on death row. Therese was in the bath for what seemed like an eternity. In the past, being with Therese had always been easy. From the moment they met until the day she'd disappeared; their relationship had been effortless. He never had to pretend or try to be anything other than his true self, and Therese loved him for it. Now, things were different, and understandably so. The attraction, at least on his part, was stronger than ever, but he felt like he hardly knew this new Therese. It occurred to Scobert that she may have been thinking the exact same thing about him. He'd admittedly changed over the years. Maybe not physically—he looked the same as the day they met—but emotionally. Surviving what he had and coming out alive on the other side; it changed a man. Largely, he had Helena to thank for his redemption.

He got up, unsheathed the knife that hung by his belt, placed it on the table, and paced the room. He muttered a curse. Thoughts of Helena were not helping his predicament. He was doing nothing wrong, yet raw and unadulterated guilt was eating at his insides. Just as he considered calling the whole thing off, Therese stepped out, her hair wet, skin flushed, a leather journal clutched in her hand. An unbidden smile formed on Scobert's lips. Though she'd aged subtly over the years, she was still as beautiful as ever. Self-consciously, he wondered whether she'd written about him in her journal and if it was good or bad. Again, feelings of adolescent insecurity resurfaced, making him feel like a total fool. He raised his right hand in a silent greeting, then rubbed at his jaw and silently vowed he'd have to be much smoother than that.

"Are you tired?" he asked.

Therese flashed him a familiar smile, bringing back a barrage of memories. "Not really," she said.

Scobert took a couple of tentative steps closer. When she was within reach, he dared to tuck a stray lock of her red hair behind her ear, twirling the fine strands in his fingers before he did. "I've been wanting to do that," he said quietly.

She rubbed her cheek against the back of his hand. "I've missed this," she said, an almost surprised look on her face.

"When you and Mirabella were taken from me," he began, his voice rough, "a part of me died. Short of actually killing myself, I did everything I could to drown my pain—to forget." He gently cupped her chin, his thumb brushing against her lips. "Losing you ended me, and I was more than happy for my life to be done with. But fate plays tricks, and we adapt. Somehow, someway, I came alive again, and I'm better for it. I'm a changed man, Therese. A lucky man. I want more than anything to be with you again, but I'm afraid I will not survive another death." He took in a ragged breath. "I've loved you since the day you walked into my bar, and I've never stopped, but I'm a man of reason, and I need to know. Where were you? Who took you? And why are you back?"

Therese stepped away like she'd been shocked. "I've told you everything. What else do you want?"

Scobert's apprehension was a wet blanket on an otherwise happy occasion, and while he regretted it, it was absolutely necessary. "I don't ask for much. Just your honesty. If there's something you don't want to tell me because you're afraid—or whatever it may be—we'll figure it out. You, me, and Mirabella. As a family, we'll figure it out."

Tears pooled in Therese's eyes, her expression hurt and insulted. "How could you doubt me so? I've told you everything. We don't remember. Somebody took us and stashed us away in a cabin in the middle of nowhere. We've lived our lives as best we could, never knowing what the future may bring. Fate brought us back to you. Whether you'll cherish it as gift or cast it away like garbage is entirely up to you. We don't *need* you in our lives, Scobert. We can manage on our own. But I do want us to be a family again. I want a second chance."

The gut-wrenching emotion evident on Therese's face melted away any remaining traces of doubt. Scobert let out a harried breath, wondering how he ever questioned her. In the next instant, he had her in his arms. "That's what I want, too," he breathed. "It's all I've ever wanted." Her journal landed on the stone floor as she lifted herself up on her toes and wrapped both arms around his neck. Scobert bent down to kiss her in earnest, casting inhibitions aside and allowing himself to enjoy his wife again. At that moment, all guilt and uncertainty faded away. Having Therese back in his arms felt exactly right.

"I'm never leaving your side again," she promised, breaking briefly from their kiss.

"I'm never letting you," he whispered back.

※

Clover and Button made their way through Market Square in relative anonymity. Disguised as Sinann, Clover was amazed at how openly men ogled at her. Catching her reflection on a storefront window, she wasn't so surprised.

"I guess this is how it feels to be a supermodel," she said, feeling herself blush.

"What's a *super model*?" Button asked, her brow knitted in confusion.

"It's like a regular model, only better," Clover said.

Button shook her head, looking just as confused as before. "Why did you have to disguise yourself as Sinann, anyway? It's a little disturbing. You could have just gone as me again."

"I can't very well *be* you if I'm *with you*."

"Oh, right," she said, thoughtful. "And why do you have to be in disguise?"

Clover took in a breath. Sometimes, being with Button was like chaperoning an easily distracted child, but for all her little quirks, she couldn't help but warm up to her. There was something so unapologetically simple and pure about Button that it was nearly impossible not to like her. If nothing else, it was refreshing. "Remember?" Clover said. "I told you about Alistair and how he tried to kill me. I have to be careful. Unseelies might be on the lookout."

Button let out a little shiver, as if the thought of Alistair gave her the creeps. "I'm sorry you have to hide so much," she said.

"Me, too," Clover agreed.

They evaded the crowds at Market Square and got on the grassy path that led to Anna's house. Clover relaxed a little as they walked in silence, the sun bright and warm on their faces, birds chirping nearby. After her argument with Finn last night, Clover had been restless, worried, and mostly remorseful that they'd parted the way they had. Apart from needing to see Momma Ruth to tell her about the rather disturbing news about her mortality, she was also hoping her early morning visit might lead her to Finn, and that they could sort things out before he left.

Button glanced at her and rubbed at her eyes. "Nobody's around anymore. Would you mind changing back to your regular self?"

Clover giggled. "It really bothers you, doesn't it?"

Button made a face. "Imagine if I were wearing a very convincing *Finn* costume, and every time you looked at me, you saw him. How would that make you feel?"

Just the mention of his name elicited a tightness in her chest and a quickening of her pulse. She licked her lips and suddenly wasn't feeling so relaxed anymore.

"I get it," Clover conceded. She channeled the power resting dormant within her and summoned her transformation. Heat pulsated throughout her every nerve ending, culminating in a sort of inner explosion that signified the change was complete. She knew without having to check that Button was not seeing her girlfriend anymore, but the real Clover. Not to toot her own horn or anything, but she was getting really good at shapeshifting.

"Happy now?" she teased.

Button smiled and nodded. After a few minutes of companionable silence, she turned to Clover. "I know you and Finn had a fight. I saw him leave with Ilbreac—I mean, Tony."

Clover didn't meet her gaze. Somehow, talking about their

argument made it seem more real, final. She kept on walking, hoping that Button would drop it.

"You can talk to me, you know? I know a little something about dating an outrageously good-looking faerie. Just saying. It's not always easy. But you do love him, right?"

"I'm pretty sure I do," Clover said. "But I'm afraid to." Her own honesty surprised her, and she had to admit: It felt pretty good to say it out loud. "Do you love Sinann?"

Without hesitation, she answered, "Of course. Why do you think I stayed?"

"I didn't realize you had a choice in the matter," Clover said.

"Tsk, tsk." Button wagged a finger at her. "A choice exists in *every* matter. You just have to be brave enough to make it, and strong enough to stand by it."

That was the thing with Button. Just a moment ago, she was as clueless as ever. The next moment, she was spouting Yoda-like nuggets of wisdom. Clover wondered whether she was ready to make the decision to choose Finn—everything about him, and all that implied. Even as she wanted desperately to be, she still wasn't so sure. Her life was complicated enough as it was.

The sight of Anna's house in the distance buoyed her spirits. "We're almost there," she said. "Thanks again for coming with me. I really appreciate it."

Button smiled wildly, picking up her pace. "Are you kidding? I haven't been *anywhere* in *forever.* I'm so excited to meet your family."

Button's lighthearted and positive attitude was infectious, forcing Clover to cast aside her own worries, even for a time. "Last one there's a rotten egg!" she called to Button before she set off on a run.

Peals of laughter followed closely behind her as Button quickly caught up. The frivolity of a little friendly competition had Clover's blood pumping as she sprinted up the hill to Anna's, her muscles welcoming the rush of adrenaline. Toe to toe, they reached the doorstep nearly at the same time, flushed and out of breath.

"Rotten egg," Button said, panting and pointing at Clover.

Clover was happy enough to claim defeat. "I was pacing myself."

Button gave a little silent victory dance on the doormat, waving her hands in the air as she circled in place. Clover giggled and rapped on the knocker, happy that she'd brought a friend.

Ruth stared open-mouthed at Clover's friend. She hadn't realized that when her granddaughter visited in disguise the last time, she had taken on somebody else's appearance, and that Adele was a real person. Looking at the original article, she marveled at the skill of Clover's transformation. She had altered herself into an exact replica of the girl that now stood before her.

"Adele, is it?"

"Yes, Ma'am, but everybody calls me Button. You must be Momma Ruth." She stepped closer and gave her a big hug. "I've heard so much about you. I feel like I know you."

Ruth hugged the sweet girl back. Any friend of Clover's was a friend of hers. "You darling little thing. I'm so pleased to meet you."

"Same here," Button said as she released Ruth from her tight bear hug.

"Where's Dad?" Clover asked.

"He's out running. I wish we'd known you were coming. We could have prepared brunch. Anna is in the backyard, tending to her vegetables. Oh, goodness, where are my manners? Ladies, sit." Ruth fluffed the pillows on the couch and motioned to the girls. "Let me get Anna, and perhaps Cordelia could whip something up for you girls to eat."

Clover plopped down on the couch the way teenagers did—as if their butts were weighted down by some gravitational sofa magnet. Button took a seat on the armchair, her hands folded on her lap.

"Did you say Dad was out running?" Clover asked, bewildered.

Ruth nodded. "He runs every morning now, but he should be back shortly."

Cordelia, and the cat, Diana, chose that moment to make their entrances—one buzzing overhead like a frazzled bumblebee, the other sauntering assuredly like someone owed her some money. The little faerie zoomed in on Clover, the incessant flapping of her little wings slowing incrementally as she lowered herself on the girl's lap.

"My faerie-in-training is all grown up," she gushed at Clover. "Look at you! So beautiful." Her voice was a crystal bell chime on a blustery day. "And who is this cherub-faced friend of yours?"

Button bent down and extended her hand to the tiny faerie. "My name is Button."

Cordelia extended both hands, clasping Button's finger. "Well met, pretty lady. Are you hungry?" she asked as her wings flapped in excitement. "Would you care for some flapjacks with honey and blueberries?"

"I would love some," Button beamed.

That was all it took for Cordelia to soar back up, her pink, translucent wings working overtime. "Done!" she said with a flourish. Then, to Clover, "and you and I will gossip later." She flew to the kitchen like a shrunken helicopter on a mission.

Diana pounced on the couch and settled herself beside Clover with the same aplomb as always, stretching on her side, exposing her belly. A satisfied purr reverberated throughout her feline form as Clover rubbed her down, playing close attention to that sweet spot behind her ears.

Anna walked in through the back door, probably disturbed from all the hubbub. "I thought I heard your voice," she exclaimed, clearly pleased to see Clover.

Clover got up and gave Anna a hug, disrupting Diana's belly rub and obviously irritating the cat to no end. Button stood back at first, then promptly introduced herself to Anna. What a pleasant young woman she was, Ruth thought.

"Is everything okay?" Anna asked, her brow knitting

infinitesimally. "We love having you here, but I worry when you travel around so much, dear."

"Blame Button," Clover joked. "She desperately wanted to meet you guys."

"Guilty," Button admitted sheepishly.

"Well, we're glad to have you," Anna said. "Come. My home is your home. There's a pot of coffee in the kitchen. Shall we?"

As they all moved to the airy kitchen, Button bumped Clover's shoulder and whispered, "Is she your future mother-in-law?"

Ruth chuckled to herself when Clover turned beet red as she shoved and shushed at Button. She was glad that her granddaughter had someone her age to hang out with. Having someone around to be silly with was just plain old good for the soul. They took their seats around the huge butcher-block-slash-table as Anna poured everyone a cup of coffee. Cordelia happily zipped around the room, dumping ladles-full of batter onto a large skillet while she fried up bacon on another one.

Anna found herself a vacant stool and took her seat, blowing on her coffee as she took little sips. "You just missed Finn," she said to Clover. "Did he know you were coming?"

Disappointment was evident on Clover's face even as she attempted to mask it. "No, actually. I hadn't mentioned it." She absent-mindedly traced the cup's brim with her finger. "We just missed him, huh?"

Anna nodded. "He was in quite the rush, but he wanted to make sure to give me this." She reached into her pocket to reveal the brass compass; the same one they'd used to contact Scobert only days ago. "So that we can keep in touch."

By the slump in her shoulders and the sudden resignation in her eyes, Ruth was certain something was bothering Clover, and it didn't take extraordinary sleuthing to infer what it was. She could sniff out a lover's quarrel even if she was gagged, blindfolded, and bound.

Just as Cordelia was laying the finishing touches on her pancakes, Ruth concocted a simple scheme to get a few minutes of alone time with Clover. "Sweetie, before I forget, I need to show you something," she said innocently. "Anna, Button, if you'll excuse us for a moment." She was smooth like that.

Clover shot her a dubious look, which she promptly ignored. She got up and left the room, expecting her granddaughter to follow right behind her.

※

Trailing Momma Ruth into the living room, Clover worried that something was horribly wrong. Why else would her grandmother set up a ruse to get her alone in the other room? Once they were out of earshot, she pulled her to the couch.

"What's the matter?" they asked each other in unison.

"I was worried about you," Momma Ruth confessed. "The look on your face when Anna mentioned Finn. Something awful. I figured you two had a fight, and you're here bright and early today because you hoped to see him before he left for Earth."

Clover let out a sigh. "You hit the nail on the head. Am I that obvious?"

"Only to me, sweetie. Tell me."

The concern on Momma Ruth's face shamed Clover and broke her heart. There she was, pining over Finn, when she should have been concentrating on how to tell her grandmother that she was now immortal. How self-centered could she be?

She took Momma Ruth's hand. "Don't worry about it. It was something silly. *I'm* silly. A shallow argument with Finn should be the least of my worries—"

"Shush. You're eighteen," Momma Ruth said as she squeezed her hand, "you had a fight with your boyfriend. Of course, you're going to fret. That's what teenagers do. Sure, big things are afoot, but that doesn't change the fact that you're a young woman in love. Go be a teenager. There's no shame in that."

Marveling at how lucky she was to have Momma Ruth in her life, she couldn't help but shed a tear. "Oh Momma," she sighed as she gave her a tight hug, "I don't know how I'd ever survive without you." Selfishly, she realized she'd never have to. She wiped a tear from cheek and steeled her nerves. "I have to tell you something important."

Momma Ruth inhaled, her expression turning grave. "It's about the effects of Finn's healing, isn't it?"

Clover nodded.

Momma Ruth brought both hands to her face. "I think I know what's happening to me."

"You do?"

"I'm turning into one of them, aren't I?"

"One of *who*?" Clover asked, genuinely perplexed.

"You know," she whispered. "One of them. One of *you*. A faerie. I realize Finn didn't bite me or anything, but I've seen enough movies to know how this works. He does this life-altering thing for me. All of a sudden, I'm changed. I look younger. I feel stronger. Next thing you know, I'm transforming pumpkins into coaches, and I've grown wings."

Clover laughed despite herself. "You think you're turning into a faerie godmother?"

Momma Ruth shrugged. "I'm not?"

"No, but something did happen to you. Or I guess I should say, something *won't* happen to you. Not without a great deal of trying, I suppose. I'm not sure—"

"Clover!" Momma Ruth bellowed with gritted teeth. "Just tell me."

"When you had a heart attack, and I wished for Finn to heal you, I wished that you wouldn't die. Finn thinks that by granting that wish, he may have inadvertently turned you—immortal."

Momma Ruth was silent for what felt like an eternity, her head titled to one side as if she didn't quite hear what was said. Finally, as if waking from a dream, she spoke. "I won't die?"

Clover shook her head sheepishly. "I don't think so."

"Will *you* die?"

"I think I'll be around for a while."

"So, I get to be around for the rest of your life," Momma Ruth mused, seemingly to herself. "I could work with that."

"You're not upset?" Clover asked.

"A little jarred, obviously, but not upset. No. I'm relieved. At least now I know what to expect—and I get to live this incredible journey with you. Can you imagine that? Sweetie, I wouldn't miss that for the world."

A huge weight lifted from Clover's shoulders. As she gave Momma Ruth a hug, the future didn't seem so bleak at all. No matter what happened from that point on, she knew she'd never have to face the prospect of losing the most important person in her life. *Incredible* didn't even begin to describe that journey.

The front door opened, and Nick walked in. Judging from the look on his face, it was safe to assume that she and Momma Ruth looked a total mess. Clover wiped away tears and sniffled loudly. Her grandmother was in the same exact state of disrepair.

"What? Tell me," Nick said, face ashen.

Kean entered the living room shortly after, his worried expression matching Nick's.

"It's nothing. We're fine," Clover reassured her dad as a giggle escaped her lips. They were more than fine.

"Are you sure?" Nick asked, still worried.

"Absolutely," Clover replied, happy to see her dad looking so vibrant and healthy, while also a little surprised to see he'd been hanging out with Kean again. She gave an awkward little wave to the handsome soldier.

Momma Ruth squeezed her hand and gave her a playful little wink before getting up to face Nick. "Settle down, son," she said as she patted down the pleats on her skirt. "Just a little bit of girl-talk here. Nothing to concern yourself about. We are *good*. Now, are you lads up for some blueberry pancakes?"

Her dad searched her face, a final attempt to verify if everything was indeed fine. Clover nodded resolutely. Nick's relaxed and unfurrowed countenance slowly returned, and Clover's heart nearly overflowed to see how much he'd actually cared.

"I'm in," Nick responded with a huge smile.

When Momma Ruth eyed Kean expectantly, he shrugged. "I could eat."

The four of them made their way to the kitchen, the enticing aromas of bacon and pancakes leading the way. Nick quietly took Clover's hand and brushed it against his lips. "Love you, kiddo," he said matter-of-factly. At that moment, she couldn't have stuffed more happiness into her bursting heart if she tried.

9

Helena stood in front of her full-length mirror, clutching her walking stick, and observing the reflection staring back at her. She looked so young, this woman with the steadfast gaze and apathetic face. What secrets was she hiding behind the unflinching set of her mouth and the confidence in her stance? With an innocence to her countenance, but a certain guile in her eyes, were the many wars she'd lived through and the countless deaths she'd ordered written on the planes of her face?

Would someone know, for instance, just by looking at her, the immeasurable feats she'd accomplished, the many times she'd survived the unthinkable and the multitude of ways she'd escaped death? Probably not, she decided. Most people don't bother to peer that closely. She tightened her grip on Scobert's *shillelagh* and considered leaving it all behind—the magnificent room she was in, the Seelie Court, the realm, and multiple lifetimes worth of victories and losses.

In the blink of an eye, she could disappear and never return. The prospect was so tempting that her heart fluttered in excitement. Her mind travelled to faraway, exotic locations; her imagination ignited. Would the realm suffer her loss? A queen can easily be replaced, she decided solemnly. As long as peace prevailed, mouths were fed, and battles were won, it mattered not who sat on the throne. *She* mattered not.

With one focused thought, it could all be over. She could finally be free. As she closed her eyes and gripped the handle of her walking stick, she sought to choose a location, a place where she could be herself, where she could experience true joy. A barrage of images and experiences filled her mind, like a catalogue of possible futures to sift through. The *shillelagh* fell limply to the ground when her thoughts conjured up a person, rather than a place. Her face contorted in pain as she cursed the irony of her predicament. She was given a gift that had the power to free her by the man who held her heart in chains.

Liz entered her rooms tentatively. "My Queen? Is everything all right?"

She straightened, almost welcoming the distraction. "Everything is just grand. What do you want?"

"Scobert is outside." Liz shifted nervously. "Will you see him in here or the throne room?"

Helena let out a breath. "Send him in." She picked up the walking stick and laid it on a nearby settee. She took one last glance at her reflection and turned to face the entrance.

Scobert walked in, looking as conspicuous as ever. With his large, muscular frame and bushy beard, he looked like a conquering barbarian, only a tad better groomed. The fact that his hair was still damp from a bath sent an irrational bolt of anger up Helena's spine. It wasn't the first time he'd spent the night in court. It was the first time he'd spent the night *with somebody else.*

"I trust you had a good evening," she said, hating the venom in her voice.

Scobert's gaze sought the ground briefly before his steady, brown eyes settled on Helena. "Are we going to talk about this or are we going to skirt around it for the rest of eternity? You have to understand how impossible this situation is. I never intended to hurt you. Helena, you know how much you mean to—"

"Stop. Don't say another word. There's nothing to discuss. Not anymore. You and I—you and I are no longer. Please don't concern yourself with my ruffled feelings because I am fine. Such is life. An endless chess match where everyone is a pawn. I can no sooner fault you for your moves than chastise myself for my countermoves. All is fair, Scobert. Let's leave it at that."

Scobert took in a breath like he wanted to say something, then shook his head, a look of defeat in his eyes. "Why have you asked to see me this morning? My Queen."

"The Unseelies. I will not wait for them to attack before I defend my throne. We've played that game already. I want you to coordinate with our top men and formulate strikes. I don't intend to charge their court. For now, I intend to weaken it. Find out who their best soldiers are and carry out the tasks. You are free to command my army as you see fit. That is, if you're still willing to defend the Seelie Court."

"My loyalty to you and the throne has not changed. I stand ready to do as you command. Do you wish for these attacks to be performed in stealth or overtly?"

Helena smiled, marveling at how quickly her greatest strategist donned his old hat. "Your thoughts?"

Scobert shrugged. "Either way, the message is clear: We're not taking this sitting down. Dealer's choice, I guess."

"Do you have a crew in mind?"

"I have a few lads in mind. Mackey, definitely. I could use Finn when he's back. By then, he'd have accomplished his mission and our army will be at full strength. The Unseelie King will not stand a chance."

"Good."

A tense silence filled the room, snaking between them like a raging river. Scobert rubbed the back of his neck, his gaze tracked on the ground once more. When he finally looked up, Helena thought she glimpsed his eyes water. "Is that all, Queen Helena?"

Helena considered his question, answering as honestly as she could. "Yes. I suppose that is all. You may go."

It had taken Finn nearly two weeks travelling via portals to round up about fifty of Queen Helena's soldiers, who were scattered worldwide. He made easy work of it. Scobert was right. When it came to a question of loyalty between him and Alistair, the soldiers unerringly chose Finn and were more than ready to heed Helena's battle call. Manhattan was his last stop, where a majority of Helena's semi-retired soldiers had taken residence. He had travelled from the *Pont Neuf* in Paris to the Manhattan Bridge in under two seconds flat. A convenient perk of travelling faerie-style were the thousands of portals connecting tunnels and bridges like a supernatural transit system across the globe. Working ahead of schedule and with plenty of time on his hands, Finn decided to take the evening off to catch up with an old friend.

Back in his old stomping grounds, walking the streets of the East Village, nostalgia hit hard. He'd spent the past two decades living in New York City and it had been some of the most memorable of his lifetime. It was the time he'd spent looking after Clover. He had no way of knowing then what he knew now: that obeying Alistair's order to grant the child luck for eighteen years would change his life irrevocably. Little did he know then that he would fall in love, or that he was even capable of real love. Now, he was in danger of losing the only girl he'd ever truly cared for, and he doubted whether a bigger knucklehead had ever walked the planet. His spirits lifted somewhat when he turned a corner and glimpsed the gaudy neon sign with the blinking shamrock: The Blarney Boulder.

Picking up his pace, Finn soon pushed open the door to the downtown dive and instantly took comfort in the dim lighting, the smells of pool cue chalk mixed with stale beer, and the familiar face who smiled widely at him from behind the bar. Finn chose a barstool and clasped hands with the clurichaun.

Shamus instantly started pouring him a pint, then leaned in and lowered his voice. "I was worried about you, mate. I've been hearing strange things. Is it true? Is *Alistair* the new Unseelie King?" he asked, sounding *Alistair* out like it was a bad word.

Finn nodded somberly and took a big gulp. "Yup."

"Unbelievable." Shamus shook his head and wiped the bar down. "And the girl? Is she really—"

"Half-Fae? Yes." Finn downed his beer and slid the empty glass forward. "Keep 'em coming." He rubbed a hand across his head. "Since last I saw you, things have been insane. Alistair almost succeeded in killing Clover and closing the portals between Earth and Faerie forever. King Boris unsuccessfully attempted to overthrow the queen. He got himself killed, and Alistair somehow managed to elect himself king. Clover's still in danger and I'm up here herding the queen's men when I should be down there protecting her—that is, if she'll ever speak to me again."

Shamus refilled the beer and took out two shot glasses. He poured tequila into both and raised one in a toast. "Cheers."

Finn raised his glass with a smirk. "Long live the queen."

Shamus gulped down the tequila like it was water and refilled both glasses. "I see you've taken my advice to heart."

Finn eyed him quizzically. "And what advice was that?"

"Last time you were here, I warned you not to start a war with Alistair McCabe. I also cautioned you against falling in love with a lackey. It appears you went ahead and did both." He raised his glass again. "Cheers, mate."

Finn burst out laughing. "Is this your not-so-subtle way of saying I've brought this upon myself?" He tipped his tequila back and coughed. "I suppose I deserved that."

Shamus refilled their glasses and offered up another toast. "Here lies Finn Ryan. Taken at the ripe, young age of several hundred and so-and-so. Death by lackey-lust and misplaced alliances. May the good Lord above have mercy on his wasted soul."

Finn laughed and picked up the shot glass. Before he could bring it to his mouth, he was in a headlock from behind, his bar stool nearly tipping from underneath him. A familiar voice spoke menacingly near his ear, "Didn't I tell you to be smart, alert, and fast? All you are is dim, daft, and dopey."

A huge smile broke out on Finn's face. "Garrett."

"The one. The only," his attacker acknowledged with a smile. The chokehold quickly turned into a hug between old friends.

"What are you doing here?" Finn asked, incredulous. The last time he'd seen his friend was at the battle with the Unseelies, when he'd shown up out of nowhere to rescue Clover's grandmother from one of Boris's minions. Garrett had an unusually handy talent of making appearances at the most opportune moments, saving the day, and leaving the scene even quicker than he'd arrived. Somewhat of a pariah, he lived by his own rules, not fully able to bow to anybody's power but his own—and boy, was he powerful. Pookas were considered the most feared of the supernatural creatures, and Garrett the most formidable of the lot.

He took the empty seat next to Finn. "You think you can go on a transatlantic crusade, sniffing the globe for errant Seelie soldiers, and I'm not going to hear about it? Please," Garrett scoffed. "You insult me." He turned to Shamus and pushed the tequila bottle in his direction. "Let's bring out the good stuff, shall we?"

Shamus bent to open a cabinet under the bar and brought out a crystal decanter half-filled with a rich mahogany liquid. "Irish single-malt. Sixty-five years." He unstoppered the bottle and poured them each a glass. "It's good to see you, Garrett. It's been too long."

"That it has." Garrett swirled his glass and took a sip. "This city is but a sanitized caricature of what it used to be. Unfortunately, when the hookers and the hustlers made their exits, so did I. Luckily for the natives, I've returned, daring New York to prove me wrong. Now, tell me. What sort of sappy drivel has this lovesick leprechaun been feeding you?"

Shamus wiped the bar down. "Usual stuff. Faerie wars. Lovers' quarrels."

Garrett clicked his glass with Finn's. "I see Clover finally came to her senses. It took her long enough."

"You're hilarious. You know that?" Finn mock-punched Garrett's shoulder, connecting a little harder than he'd intended.

"Nobody likes an angry drunk," Garrett shot back. He took another sip of his whiskey, then turned to Finn, a trace of seriousness on his face. "Is she all right?"

"Yeah. I mean, I think so. We haven't really spoken since I left."

Garrett rolled his eyes at Shamus. "Should I tell him, or will you?"

"What?" Finn asked, his hands in the air.

"You chose the futile pursuit of wooing, seducing, and ill-advisedly falling madly in love with this girl. The least you could do is be good at it. You wouldn't want a certain lurker of a soldier snatching her up while you're radio silent, now would you? Have you completely lost *all* your game?"

"It's not like I can text her or call. She's in another realm."

"Oh, please. You and I both know there are an infinite number of ways around that. We are supernatural creatures and magic courses through our veins. You're telling me you can't find a way to send a message to your girl?"

Shamus chuckled into his drink.

"You, too?" Finn spat. "First, you both discouraged me from getting involved with Clover. Now, you're a couple of Casanovas giving me love advice?"

"You've already gone off the deep end. The least we could do is throw you a dinghy," Shamus retorted, followed by another heartfelt chortle at Finn's expense.

"You don't see me interfering with your love lives," Finn joked as he grabbed a fistful of peanuts from a nearby bowl.

"Mate," Shamus said before Finn could pop one in his mouth, "I wouldn't."

Finn released the peanuts back into the bowl. "A fine establishment you're running here, old friend."

Garrett suddenly raised a finger, his expression cautious and serene. He closed his eyes as if listening to some faraway sound, his left palm flat on the table. Having seen it countless times before, Finn knew that face well. Garrett was tracking.

"What is it?" Finn whispered.

A devilish smile found its way to Garrett's lips. "Speaking of this establishment." He turned to Shamus. "How much do you value it?"

Shamus scanned the crowd and downed his whiskey. "Quite a bit, actually. Explain."

Garrett stretched his neck from left to right, as if limbering up for a fight. "Back booth. Four morons—Unseelies I presume. Heads bent low. Plotting an attack."

Shamus casually glanced in their direction while Finn scoped their reflections from the mirror on the wall.

"I'm about to *literally* rip some heads off and cause serious property damage. If you don't want that to happen in here, then we better take this fight elsewhere—quickly," Garrett said.

"Definitely not in here," Shamus confirmed.

Finn nodded. "Let's step outside then."

"Wait," Shamus said. "Outside isn't much better. A fight to the death in front of my bar? With who-knows-what type of animal our dear pooka here decides to morph into? No. The only reason this place has been around for so long is because I keep a low profile, and my guests feel safe—both supernaturals and lackeys. I can't have a massacre anywhere near here."

Garrett stretched his arms forward and cracked his knuckles. "This is going to happen no matter what. They followed Finn in here to kill him. If I have to drag them up the block before I beat them to a bloody pulp, then that's what's going down."

Shamus leaned forward and whispered, "There's an abandoned pub on the Upper West Side. Clurichaun-owned."

"And this information serves me how?" Garrett asked.

Finn had understood right away. "Pub crawl," he said with a lopsided grin. "Clurichauns are able to teleport to any pub in the world in an instant. As long as the pub is owned by another clurichaun."

"Crafty. So, we take this fight to an even lesser establishment. I'm all for it. Where's the portal and how do we get these four ninnies through?" Garrett asked.

Shamus grinned. "I'm the portal. I could teleport every single person in this pub in the blink of an eye."

"All I want is the booth in the back," Garrett said, chomping at the bit.

"Done," Shamus said, and all went dark.

In the next instant, they were in a similar looking pub with upturned tables and boarded-up windows. The air was dank and musty and discarded peanut shells lined the untrodden floor. Standing in the middle of the room with Shamus and Garrett, Finn was at the ready, scanning the abandoned pub for Unseelies.

"Where are they?" Garrett whined like a child pining for a toy.

The atmosphere sizzled and shifted before four men appeared out of thin air, looking disheveled and confused.

"Ah. Christmas came early," Garrett gloated.

Finn recognized one of them from battle. He was older and bigger than the others and was clad in the usual punk-rock motif Unseelies seemed to favor: A pair of plaid pants topped with a sleeveless mesh shirt. The younger guys, though similarly dressed, didn't look nearly as menacing as the one who now stepped forward, clearly the leader of the bunch. "Where are we? What have you done?"

"Does it really matter?" Garrett said as he took a step toward them. "You followed my friend into the bar with the intent to kill him." He motioned to Finn with his hands as if he was showcasing the prize at a gameshow. "Get to it, then."

The Unseelie twitched, then hesitated. "Who are you?" he asked Garrett.

"That you don't know who I am is the only reason you haven't run screaming out the door."

Clearly having no idea who or *what* Garrett was, the Unseelie lunged at Finn with a knife.

Scobert's days had become a surreal montage of unlikely scenarios and occurrences. His mornings were spent with Helena, where he'd report on any progress made in the war effort and strategize future moves. He and Kean had carried out a couple of hits on Alistair's soldiers and were now perennially alert and on the offensive. The Unseelies would no doubt strike back. The queen was pleased with their handiwork, intent on letting the enemy know how efficiently and lethally her army could strike.

Their daily briefings were an exercise in forced civility. After rekindling his relationship with Helena, he'd never imagined ever sharing an awkward moment with her, but lately he doubted if they'd ever enjoy familiarity again. He didn't blame her. He had neither the gall nor the right to reproach Helena for her behavior. Was he not the man who only a month ago professed his love to her and shared her bed? And was he not the same man who now shared a room with his wife under Helena's roof? As much as his current situation pained him, he was more than willing to endure whatever animosity Helena was doling out. He certainly deserved it.

The remainder of his days were usually spent with the troops, with Kean, or if he was free, with Mirabella. Those were the days he'd looked forward to the most. Getting to know his daughter was proving to be the greatest delight of his life. Fiercely independent and just about as stubborn as he was, Mirabella was a diamond in the rough. While marveling at her tenacity and biting sense of humor, Scobert was amazed at how well she turned out, considering her unusual upbringing. Most of all, he was heartbroken that he had missed so much of it.

Knife-throwing had become a favorite shared activity, and on the day that Mirabella hit the bullseye three times in a row, Scobert doubted that a greater pride could exist in one person's heart. They'd sometimes share a drink in the late afternoons, and Scobert would tell her of the bygone days of his service to Queen Helena's throne. Mirabella was an apt study, always eager to hear more stories and take instruction. Despite this, Scobert sensed a certain faraway and closed-off quality about her—as if she carried the weight of a concealed burden. Nonetheless, he was determined to break through every barrier to get closer to his daughter.

On one particularly special afternoon, he'd decided to introduce Mirabella to Mary, and the sight of his daughter and mother together in the same room nearly undid him. On that same day, they also happened upon Clover and her lackey friend, Button, and Scobert was delighted for Mirabella to meet girls her own age. The girls started to join them whenever they threw knives and it'd become an ongoing competition. Mirabella held the top spot, but Clover wasn't trailing far behind.

Being with Clover—another half-Fae—seemed to be doing Mirabella a world of good. Though not as powerful as Clover, his daughter displayed some aptitude in enchantment. One day, out of necessity or sheer boredom, Mirabella had inadvertently magicked a small rock to play a jovial melody. On impulse, she'd immediately kicked the stone away and cast Scobert a guilty look, as if expecting a reprimand. He had joked that the only thing wrong with her magic was that she should have chosen a bigger rock. Mirabella had laughed the incident off, but afterwards stood a little taller and prouder because of it. Like his daughter, Scobert had always displayed a proclivity to enchanting inanimate objects. One of his very first creations was the magical *shillelagh* that now belonged to the queen. Over the years, he had magicked countless more objects.

Not having grown up with other faeries, there was no way of fully knowing what other gifts Mirabella might possess, or how her magic would choose to manifest itself. Only time would tell. As most powers were passed on, it was no surprise that both he and Mirabella were enchanters. It also came as no surprise that both clurichauns enjoyed the same taste in drink. He couldn't think of a better use of a sunset than to experience it with his daughter, whiskeys in hand, at close of day.

His evenings were spent with Therese exclusively, and his wife seemed to relish their time together as much as he did. They'd reminisce about the early years of their marriage and share the ins and outs of their daily lives. His wife preferred to spend her days indoors, resting and writing in her journal, but was always eager to hear about his afternoons spent with Mirabella. On one occasion, she even made a special effort to meet her daughter's new friends and spent the day with them. Her interactions with Mary, on the other hand, were quite strained. Neither had quite warmed up to the other, something Scobert chalked up to the whole mother-in-law dynamic. They would thaw soon enough. Other than that, Scobert couldn't complain. Having his family back meant everything to him, and he was more than grateful for the happy mix of mundane and extraordinary in his day-to-day life.

This morning was no different from the one before it. After kissing his wife goodbye, he made his way to the plaza to see his queen. The two gigantic gnomes who guarded the door to Helena's lair greeted him in their usual cheerful way. While Archie and Alfred were two of the deadliest creatures in Helena's arsenal, they both had the air and bearing of two gentlehearted giants. Archie tugged at the knocker of the wooden trapdoor, and Scobert waved his goodbyes as he descended into the inner reaches of the Seelie Queen's sanctuary. He crossed the empty atrium toward the side of the raised dais where Helena's rooms were. Entering the receiving area, he craned his neck in search of Liz. At this hour, the queen's premier lady-in-waiting was usually found prepping Helena's breakfast tray and picking out the freshest flowers for the crystal vase that adorned her serving cart. Seeing that Liz was not in the receiving area, he cooled his heels—he wasn't exactly looking forward to the daily dose of awkwardness ahead of him. As he stood waiting, he heard voices coming from Helena's private quarters. Concluding that Liz was in there with her, he sat at a nearby bench and waited.

After a few idle minutes, Helena emerged from her quarters with Anna trailing behind her. Judging from the looks on both their faces, Scobert knew right away something was wrong. With her jaw set and her hazel eyes almost aglow, Helena had never looked angrier nor more exquisite at that moment. Instinctively, he reached out to her, caught himself, and took a step back. "What's happened?"

"There was an attempt at Finn's life last night in Manhattan," Helena declared without preamble.

Anna stepped forward. "We spoke using the compass. He is fine. Four Unseelies followed him into a bar late last night. Shamus and Garrett were with him."

"Garrett?" Scobert asked, surprised. Then he nodded with understanding. "I assume the four Unseelies are now dead?"

Anna nodded.

Already, the wheels were turning in Scobert's head. "Bold move. We took out two of his minions; Our best soldier's life in exchange is hardly reciprocal."

Helena paced the room with fists clenched, her fury seemingly emanating in waves. "There's more," she said before taking in a sharp breath. "They have Liz."

Anna held out a piece of parchment. "When I came this morning to deliver news of the attack, I found this pinned to one of Liz's flowerpots."

Scobert unfurled the piece of paper.

If you want Liz to live, call off your assassins.
  Alistair

10

A singsongy bell chimed, and for a moment, Finn wasn't quite sure where he was. He peeked from under incredibly cozy covers, unveiling his lavishly over-the-top surroundings. A hotel suite. New York City. The previous night's events came rushing back to him in a barrage of booze-fueled images of violence and decadence. If for a brief moment, he was unsure of where he was or what had happened to him, all uncertainty was now gone. *Garrett* happened to him.

"Ah. Room service," Garrett emerged from under a sea of blankets on a nearby couch and jogged to the door, wearing only a flimsy pair of boxer briefs.

Finn got up, grabbed a pillow, and flung it at him. "For Chrissake, man. Will you put some clothes on?"

Garrett deflected the pillow, ignoring Finn's advice. "Last time I checked; briefs were considered articles of clothing. Therefore, I'm more dressed than I ought to be. I'm practically dapper." He opened the door to a wide-eyed female server. "Come on in, love." The lady pushed the service cart in, eyeing the half-naked pooka incredulously. It wasn't uncommon for people to get overwhelmed by Garrett. He had the looks of a runway model and the confidence of a crown prince. It was often difficult not to get intimidated. He picked up his jeans off the floor and fished around in its pockets, taking out a hundred-dollar bill. "Thank you for your service," he said with a grin.

The girl saw the bill and waved him off. "That's way too much. The food isn't even worth that."

Garrett placed the bill on the girl's palm and closed her fingers around it. "I insist," he said with a wink.

The poor flabbergasted girl walked out ashen, muttering a silent thanks, looking like she wasn't quite sure what just happened to her. *Garrett happened to her.*

Finn shook his head. "Was that absolutely necessary?"

Garrett chomped on a piece of crispy bacon from the tray. "What?"

"It's called sexual harassment. Look it up." Finn grabbed a breakfast-laden plate and brought it to the small dining table by the window. The previous night's exertions had left him starving.

Garrett poured himself a cup of coffee and joined him. "Lighten up, leprechaun. I hardly think she'll file a complaint," he said with a wicked smile. "So," Garrett continued, "who's next on our hit list?"

A sound somewhere between a chortle and a cough escaped Finn's lips as he nearly choked on his English muffin. "Christ, you really enjoyed that, didn't you?"

"The carnage? Hell, yeah. Those morons had it coming. It was almost too easy; I didn't even have to change."

Finn couldn't argue that. Last night's opponents didn't merit tapping into Garrett's extraordinary abilities. When in the heat of battle, he usually chose to change into a leopard, but in the abandoned pub, he opted to fight in his true form, although the savagery wasn't any less intense. Garrett, in any form, would always be just a little more primal than most.

Finn eyed his friend curiously. "Are you saying you want back in the army?"

"When did you hear me say that? All I want is to have a little fun. A taste for battle has got me longing for the good ole days, that's all." Garrett grabbed a piece of bacon off Finn's plate. "To be clear, I do not want to rejoin the army, but I wouldn't mind pinch-hitting for the queen's team—a cameo, if you will, a special guest appearance. After heads have rolled and the battlefield is awash with the blood of our enemies, then I'll go on my merry way. What do you say, old friend? It'll be a blast."

Finn nodded his head in agreement, remembering the days of fighting side by side with Garrett. It would certainly be an honor and a treat to battle alongside him again. "The elusive pooka returns to fight again," he teased.

Garrett flashed him a menacing grin. "Hell, yeah, man." He got up and put his jeans on, instantly raring to go. "Let's round up the rest of the queen's stragglers and get this battle going then."

Finn remembered one more thing he needed to do in Manhattan. Before he and Clover quarreled, she had given him a letter, with a fervent request for its safe and speedy delivery. "Before we assemble the soldiers, I need to deliver a letter to Clover's best friend."

The slight detour seemed to buoy Garrett's spirits even higher. "Two mysterious faeries, one dashingly handsome, one slightly bedraggled, show up at a lackey's door with covert correspondence from the other realm. Will she invite them in? Or will absolute mayhem ensue? The suspense is killing me. What, pray tell, is the young lass's name?"

"Andie. She lives in Chelsea."

"She sounds delicious," Garrett said, clearly trying to get a rise from Finn.

"If you can't behave yourself, you can't come," Finn cautioned, dead serious.

Garrett held his hands up in mock surrender. "I'm teasing. Besides, I've already had breakfast."

Extra fortifications were put in place, and yet Helena couldn't find a calming breath as she paced anxiously in her rooms. Even as Scobert and Kean were by her side, and a dozen soldiers stood sentry outside her quarters, she felt exposed. For the Unseelies to snatch Liz right from under her nose was a brazen move, to say the least, and if she was being completely honest, a quite effective one. Helena was not only enraged but shaken—an unholy combination. In her current state, she was in no condition to make command decisions, and while her logical mind knew it, her anger prevailed. If it was an all-out war that Alistair wanted, then so be it.

As if responding to her very thoughts, Scobert placed a hand on her shoulder and whispered softy. "Helena, breathe. Let's try to approach this calmly."

As much as she resented Scobert for effortlessly reading her every emotion, she admittedly took comfort in his presence, an anchor keeping her afloat in the storm. She took a seat and attempted to slow her heartbeat. "This is impossible!" she proclaimed. "How am I to remain calm when Liz is held hostage and I'm beset with the knowledge that perhaps for the first time in millennia, the Seelie Queen's home has been breached? The gods help me Scobert, I will wipe them out."

"Alistair will not harm Liz. He's merely trying to rattle you, and succeeding," Scobert said.

Helena couldn't stay seated; it was as if her body wouldn't permit it. She got up and resumed pacing. "How were they able to get in here?" she almost screamed at Scobert and Kean, searching their faces for an answer. "We have multiple layers of security in place, and even if they were able to get through the most obvious ones—the gnomes, there still remains enchantments, censors, not to mention the fact that the entire Seelie Court is littered with soldiers."

Scobert shook his head, looking as perplexed as they all were. "Kean was the last to see Liz last night. I honestly don't see how somebody could have penetrated our defenses without sounding alarms. Even if Iekika abducted her and black magic was employed, we still would have known that magic was used. I hate to say it, but could we possibly be looking at an inside job?"

"Unlikely," Kean surmised, "because even if it were, the only way in and out of here is through the gnomes, which means if it were an inside job, they would have to have been in on it. That's simply not possible. Archie and Alfred are incorruptible, so are the other gnomes."

Helena nodded, resolute in her trust and confidence in the gnomes. "What time did you see Liz last night?"

"It was after I'd delivered my evening report to you—at about the twenty-second hour, maybe twenty-second and a quarter? She was tending to her flowers. I guess she was just waiting for me to leave before calling it a night herself. She seemed perfectly fine."

"And the gnomes attest that nobody else entered or left after you, not until the next morning when Anna called and discovered the note," Helena said to no one in particular.

A silence descended as Scobert and Kean awaited Helena's instructions.

"Finn should be back in about two days, correct?" Helena asked.

Scobert and Kean exchanged glances and nodded.

"The three of you will rescue her. You will go into their territories, breach their defenses the same way they did mine, and like a thief in the night, you will get Liz back. Do you understand me?"

"Understood," Scobert said.

"You will slay whoever stands in your way. And when Liz is safely returned, my army will mount an attack on the Seelie Court," Helena ordered with resolve.

Again, and again, the Unseelies had brought destruction to her court. Now she was inclined to unload her fury at their doorstep.

Garrett leaned against the wall, arms crossed with a roguish grin on his face, as Finn rang the buzzer to Andie's apartment. Even though he'd already checked countless times, Finn reached into his pocket to check for the letter. Folded up and creased beyond belief, Clover's note to her best friend had survived a trip around the world, a deadly bar brawl, and a night of heavy drinking in New York City. He'd be damned if it wasn't getting delivered to its rightful recipient. As he waited for Andie to get the door, he felt a nervousness settle at the pit of his stomach.

Buzz. Buzz. Buzz. Before Finn could swat Garrett's finger away, it had already inundated the doorbell with pesky insistence.

"Jaysus, Garrett. You'll wake the dead," Finn scolded. "I should have left you at the hotel."

"Oh, relax, will you? When did you become a freakin' schoolmarm?"

Finn heard the deadbolt unlock and in the next moment, Andie peeked out from a small opening; the door chain still fastened. "Yes?" she said, her voice groggy from sleep and her dark hair a tangled mess. She rubbed her eyes and looked expectantly at Finn for an answer. Then suddenly, as if realization and wakefulness dawned at the exact same second, her eyes widened and she jerked forward, her face filling the gap in the door. "You," she said accusingly. "I *know* you." She opened the door wide and stood there in her pajamas with her hands at her waist and a murderous look on her face. "Where is she? What have you done to her?"

"You know me," Finn said, both a query and a statement.

"Duh. I saw you that day at the park and I know that there's something going on between the two of you. And by the way, I never believed for one second that she just jetted away on holiday without telling me in person. She left me a stupid letter—which I've shown numerous times to the police, I'll have you know. And now *you* show up at my door, looking all guilty." She noticed Garrett standing by the side of the door and turned her nose up at him. "You better start talking or else I'm calling the cops," she said haughtily.

Finn pulled the letter out and waved it in the air like a white flag. "This will explain everything."

"Another letter? Are you kidding me?"

"With the truth this time, I promise," Finn said, placating. "Just read it."

Andie snatched the letter from Finn. "I hope you're aware that I know her handwriting well. If this is a forgery—"

Garrett interrupted. "A forensic examiner. How charming."

"Nobody was talking to you, pretty boy," Andie spat back. "I'm going to read this. You two can wait out here."

As the door slammed on their faces, Finn laughed inwardly at the assaulted expression on Garrett's face.

"What the hell?" Garrett said incredulously. "That girl has some personality on her."

"Get over yourself, *pretty boy*," Finn teased. "You're so used to women fawning over you that when someone doesn't fall over themselves admiring you, you assume they've got some kind of personality disorder."

"We're trapped in the dingy hallway of a fifth-floor walk-up in the sketchy outskirts of Chelsea. This is not an ego thing; It's a human dignity thing."

"Stop being so dramatic."

Garrett let out an exaggerated sigh. "The lengths I go to."

Finn did his best to ignore his theatrics. A few short minutes later, the door inched opened. Andie looked like she'd run a comb through her hair; her eyes were brighter and her expression keen.

"You read it?" Finn asked.

Andie nodded as her gaze shifted from Finn to Garrett, then back to Finn. "Clover trusts you, so I'm going to trust you. Are you —I can't believe these words are about to come out of my mouth—are you both *leprechauns*?"

"Hell, no," Garrett answered with disdain. "I'm much cooler than Finn will ever hope to be."

Finn continued to ignore Garrett. "I'm a leprechaun. Garrett is a good friend of mine. He's a pooka—a shapeshifter."

"Like a werewolf?" Andie asked, her eyes wide.

"No," snapped Garrett. "Not like a werewolf at all. Have we not been speaking English this whole time? Jaysus."

"Garrett, please," begged Finn. Then, he turned to Andie. "If you'll let us in, we'll explain everything. I'll answer any of your questions."

Andie seemed to consider the demerits of inviting two mythical creatures into her home, but her curiosity clearly got the better of her. She threw the door wide open. "Come in."

※

After two pots of coffee and the proffered remnants of day-old pizza, which they both politely declined but Andie devoured, Finn and Garrett found themselves at the tail end of what can only be described as *The Andie Inquisition*. The minutes had dragged on as Clover's best friend peppered them with endless questions—each one designed to catch them in a lie. When finally she seemed satisfied enough with their answers, she asked the same recurring question, "How come I can't go to Faerie-land to see her?"

Finn took in a breath to respond, but Garrett saved him the trouble.

"Doll-face, haven't we been through this already?" Garrett said, his voice tight with frustration. "It's not safe. Faerie is not like Disneyland, where every lackey so inclined can visit on a whim. Do you understand?" He asked, brimming with exasperation. "And it's not Faerie *land*—It's just Faerie."

Andie lifted her chin. "Yeah? How come Momma Ruth and Nick got a free pass?"

Garrett threw his arms up and paced the room, giving Finn a deadly look that clearly said, *you owe me one.*

Finn placed his coffee cup on the table and leaned toward Andie slowly, as if sudden movements might provoke another round of cross-examination. "Please believe me when I tell you that I won't let any harm come to Clover or her family. When all this is over and the danger has been taken care of, I promise you she'll come back to you safe." Finn decided to lay all his cards on the table. "I care about her. I'm going to make sure she's okay."

Andie glared at him. "Says the leprechaun who's out gallivanting in New York City with his pet pooka while his girlfriend is basically trapped in another dimension. Some Prince Charming you are."

Garrett looked ripe to strangle the poor girl. "You *did not* just refer to me as a pet. I vow to the Gods, woman—"

Before Garrett could complete his ominous oath, the doorbell rang, and the room went silent.

"Are you expecting anyone?" Finn whispered.

Andie got up to get the door. "Chill out. We *lackeys* do this thing called online shopping. It's a real wonder of the modern world."

Finn and Garrett situated themselves into Andie's small kitchen, hidden from sight, but ready in case of trouble. Andie rolled her eyes at them as she opened the door. Finn watched as she unlocked the deadbolt.

"Yes?" Andie kept the door chain fastened while her left hand grasped the doorknob. Then her finger slowly made its way to the side of the door and started tapping soundlessly–in quick succession to begin, then slower and more deliberate, then quickly again.

The voice from the hallway answered jovially. "I have a package for Noelle Estrada."

"She's in the apartment two doors down," Andie replied, her tone flat.

"Oh, pardon me. I must have gotten my numbers mixed up," the voice responded in the same cheery tone.

"Don't worry about it. Can I help you with anything else?"

"Well, if you wouldn't mind," the voice said sheepishly, "I've been driving since dawn, I could use a proper toilet."

Garrett nudged Finn and whispered, "What the hell?" but Finn's attention was still focused on Andie's twitchy finger.

"Sure," Andie said, her voice robotic while her finger continued to tap on the door.

Finn turned to Garrett, finally understanding. "SOS. When that door opens, get ready to attack."

"Abso-freakin-lutely" Garrett said as he shimmered, ready to change at a moment's notice.

Andie had never seen a gun in real life, but when she opened the door to the bogus delivery guy, she had known right away she was in big trouble. With a finger to his lips and a gun pointed directly at her, the man at the door mouthed the words *be quiet*. Andie had nodded imperceptibly at the same moment her finger found the door. *Tap-tap-tap. Tap. Tap. Tap. Tap-tap-tap.* While she played the totally unrealistic part of the clueless New York City girl who'd let a complete stranger use her bathroom, all she could really concentrate on were the little taps she made on her door and the all-consuming wish that faeries knew Morse code.

As she prepared to let the armed man into her house, three more emerged behind him, all of them looking like grunge delinquents out trick-or-treating. She'd wondered what they'd discover when they walked through her door. With her luck, probably two insanely handsome faeries eating cold pizza. Her heart hammered in her chest as her fingers fumbled at the door chain. As she invited danger in, she hoped against hope that her two guests were armed and prayed to any god who would listen to spare her life.

She opened the door and dropped to the floor. "Help!" she finally screamed as she covered her head with her hands, in total cowering-in-a-foxhole mode. What happened next was hard to determine with her face pressed against the parquet and her eyes barely open, but it sure sounded like the faeries had been ready, she thought triumphantly. Someone had dragged the trespassers in and somehow launched them like sacks of flour into her living room. *Thud, thud, thud, thud.* She dared a peek and witnessed absolute mayhem unfolding; her bargain furniture taking the brunt of the commotion. Two apiece, Finn and Garrett battled the now disarmed punk posse with awe-inspiring grace and skill. Crouched on the ground as she was, she couldn't help but watch and marvel. It was like watching those old Kung-Fu movies, but way cooler. Despite the danger she was in, an errant thought zipped through her traumatized brain—No wonder Clover fell for Finn. Hot *and* deadly.

The punk posse, though not as quick as Finn and Garrett, were holding their own. They seemed intent on getting at Finn and seemed willing to take however many punches to succeed. In the heat of the melee, it was hard to tell whose fist was obliterating whose nose or which guy had a shoe up whose mouth. Suddenly a gun fired, loud and all-encompassing; Andie felt like her heart had exploded in her chest.

The fighting stopped, a chaotic freeze-frame of sorts. The one thing that caught Andie's eye was the patch of blood blossoming in Garrett's pristine white shirt and the look of pure and utter rage on his handsome face. Then the impossible happened. A leopard, huge and menacing, appeared in the middle of her studio apartment in the spot where Garrett had stood only a few moments ago.

It paced amidst the broken furniture scattered all over her faux Persian rug and gave out a deafening roar. As if her body had a mind of its own, Andie crawled into the kitchen, squished herself under the kitchen sink, and listened in horror as all hell broke loose.

༺༻

Anna replaced the sheets in Clover's bedroom and caught herself marveling at how quickly she'd started to call her guest bedroom *Clover's room*. She'd only had her stay for a short while, before she was forced to spend most of her time in the Otherworld, and yet she could honestly say she missed having the girl around. With Ruth and Nick staying at her home, too, it seemed the group was not complete without her. As she puttered around the bedroom, she reflected on the complicated relationship brewing between Finn and Clover. The day would come when the girl would need to go back to Earth; she wondered whether her son loved her enough to call her home his. She hated the idea of losing Finn again, of having him live so far away. She secretly hoped Clover might decide to stay permanently in Faerie after the whole Alistair mess was all sorted out. Then she quickly decided it was none of her business and that she shouldn't be sticking her nose in other people's business.

Anna opened the armoire and gasped. Embarrassed at its untidy state, she started emptying its contents to make more space for Clover's belongings. Dresses, parasols, and slippers that hadn't been worn in perhaps a century were stacked upon old dusty boxes and long forgotten knick-knacks. She smiled when she spied a wooden makeshift sword that Scobert had carved long ago for a young Finn. As her son's very first sparring partner, she recalled with fondness how, even at a very young age, Finn had displayed such a natural talent for the warrior arts.

She blew at the dust that coated the items at the bottom of the wardrobe. Tin sewing kits, all rusted from disuse, piled haphazardly atop old scarves and sweaters. As her tidying progressed into a full-blown project, Anna plopped down on the floor, now sorting through the junk in earnest. Rummaging through long discarded possessions and tchotchkes, Anna silently scolded herself for being such a packrat. She sorted the items into two piles: keep and toss. Finn's old play sword unerringly found its way to the keep pile. Underneath an old, tarnished jewelry box that was headed for the toss pile, Anna saw something that caught her eye—a red leather satchel, hardened and brittle from countless years of neglect.

A lump caught in her throat as she realized it had belonged to a good friend, an old friend. She'd almost forgotten she had it. When Finn's real mother died, Anna had put away all her belongings, the sight of them causing too much pain. She gingerly picked it up, turned the bronze clasp that served as its lock, and looked inside. A length of cloth so old and moth-ridden fell apart in her hand as she reached for it. Tears fell silently down her cheek as she realized what it was. It was the baby smock that Brielle had sewn for her son; he was to wear it to his very first Midsummer's Eve celebration, which never came to pass. The Queen's Army had gone to war and Brielle with it. She never came back, dying in battle in defense of her queen. So revolted was the queen of the notion of a new mother dying in battle, she had thenceforth banned women from joining the army. Anna had lost her best friend that day, but she had also gained a son.

Seeing and touching her friend's timeworn belongings tore old wounds wide open. While raising Finn had been the greatest joy of her life, losing Brielle had been its most significant loss. They had trained for the army together, she a year older than Anna and more experienced. Anna would have joined the army the following year, but fate had other plans.

Remembering the fiercest and most honorable woman she had ever known; it became no surprise that Finn was who he was. Born of such mighty stock, the boy was bound for greatness from the beginning. His father had been a soldier, too—a nameless liaison Brielle was happy to have nothing further to do with. She had planned from the start to raise the child by herself. When Brielle passed, Anna vowed to do right by her and raise Finn the way she imagined Brielle would have. She could only hope she'd done nearly as good a job.

A small notebook lay at the bottom of the satchel, the parchment so frayed and fragile that Anna was afraid it might disintegrate in her hands. Having never seen it before, she picked it up and slowly leafed through its pages, deciphering the small scrawl within, smiling to herself. Brielle's journal was like a little manual to the warrior arts, filled with her own drawings and step-by-step instructions. *Most effective disarming techniques. The virtues of a battle-axe vs. a longsword.* She chuckled when she turned a page and found recipes for *curiously strong mead* and *not so special barley bread.*

Suddenly, she missed her friend with a longing so intense it nearly broke her heart. She continued flipping through the book's pages, savoring all the little bits within, feeling as close as she'd ever been to her friend in years. Toward the end, Brielle had jotted less about fighting techniques and recipes, and more about her own life.

She wrote about the baby that kicked ferociously inside her and how she'd known right away he would one day grow up to be a great warrior. Anna touched that page fondly, imagining where Brielle might have been when she wrote that. Had she started sewing Finn's smock by then?

Anna wiped another tear from her eye as she flipped through the journal's pages. She settled on one particularly long entry, simply titled, *My reasons.* As she began to read her friend's words, her heart fluttered in her chest and a cold sense of foreboding settled at the pit of her stomach. Her eyes quickly scanned through Brielle's musings and when she finished, she went back and reread every word. Anna dropped the journal as she put a hand to her mouth, feeling like her very life was being sucked out of her. In an old, crumbling journal beneath moth-ridden piles of rubbish, Anna had uncovered the truth about Finn's lineage. Without further hesitation, she reached into her pocket and pulled out the magical compass.

11

Finn found Andie crouched under the kitchen sink in a panicked state; the frightened girl cowering amidst dish soap, bleach, and scrub brushes.

"Take my hand," Finn said.

Andie looked at him wearily, extended her hand, then pulled it back. "Why?"

"Because we need to get out of here before the cops arrive and you'll be needing all the luck you can get. I can help with that. Just trust me and stay close."

Her hand shook as she reached for Finn's. He had to give it to her—the girl had been through a lot in one morning. All things considered; she was handling everything like a champ. Finn pulled her up from her clever hiding place and placed a reassuring hand on her shoulder when she started to tremble.

"I'm okay," she said, lifting her chin up. "I'm going to be okay."

From her little kitchen alcove, they walked into the living room together.

Andie brought both hands to her mouth and shrieked. Finn couldn't blame her. The place was a mess. He made a mental note to reimburse her for all the damage.

"Are you wearing my sweatpants?" she asked Garrett in disbelief.

Garrett, who stood in the middle of her destroyed apartment looking markedly pleased with himself, was indeed wearing her sweatpants. Loss of clothing was one of the cons of being a shapeshifter. Despite the gunshot wound that was already starting to heal and his rather questionable attire, Garrett still managed to look perfectly at ease.

"Would you rather I be naked? While I'm more than happy to accommodate, we are in a bit of a rush," Garrett said as he grabbed Andie's purse from the floor. "Time to go, sweetcakes. Your local authorities should be arriving soon."

"Where are we going?" Andie asked, her panic clearly returning. "And what happened to those men? Where are they?"

"Oh, they're here. They're just invisible for the moment. But don't you worry—they're all quite assuredly dead." Garrett said.

Andie paled and inadvertently squeezed Finn's hand until it started to hurt. "Okay. I can handle this," she said, seemingly to convince herself. "Where are we going?"

"A safe house," Finn said. "Don't let go of me, okay? Garrett and I will go unseen, just in case. The Unseelies don't really know your face, but when they realize these guys are missing, they'll soon find their way here. We'll get a cab, and we'll show you the way. We need to leave now, but everything should go without a hitch. You'll be fine."

"Because you're my lucky charm?" Andie asked after taking a long breath.

Finn nodded. She was obviously trying her best to keep it together, but Finn could see the cracks through her veneer.

Andie took her purse from Garrett and reached for the house keys that were hanging by the door. "Let's go. I'm ready."

As they prepared to leave, Finn felt the compass vibrate in his pocket.

Nothing ever got past Garrett and his exceptional hearing. "Aren't you going to get that?" he asked.

Finn shook his head. "Not until Andie is safe. I'll contact Anna later. Let's get out of here."

※

The safe house was a large Dutch colonial in a non-descript suburb of New York, an hour away from the city by cab. From the outside, it looked like every other house on the sleepy block, but inside it was a fortress, with galvanized steel doors, reinforced window grates, and the most sophisticated security system Andie had ever seen. Once they were all safely ensconced in this secret suburban stronghold, the faeries finally dropped their invisibility cloaks—or whatever it was that kept them unseen.

"There you are," Andie said, as she let out a sigh of relief. "It was getting weird sitting in the cab, not seeing either of you, but feeling like I was being squished between two boulders. Did I have to sit in the middle seat? I looked absurd. The cabbie must have thought I was some kind of weirdo."

Garrett laughed unreservedly. "We've just fled a fatal crime scene—your apartment, by the way—and you're worried what the cabbie thinks?"

The sight of Garrett, bare-chested and in her sweatpants, was disconcerting to say the least but try as she might, Andie could not look away. "Maybe you should go find something to wear. You look ridiculous."

"And yet you haven't stopped staring, sweetheart," Garrett said with a wink.

Andie immediately looked away, infuriated. She'd thought she was being a lot less obvious than that.

Finn started rummaging through the kitchen cabinets and the fridge, and took out some deli ham, a jar of mayonnaise, and a loaf of bread. "Are you hungry? You should eat."

Andie's appetite had gone the way of the four dead faeries in her apartment. "I can't eat right now, but thanks. I'm surprised there's food here. It doesn't look like anybody's been in here in ages."

"Somebody comes twice a month to restock the fridge. Just in case," Finn explained. "Garrett, help yourself to my closet. While you're at it, grab me a fresh shirt, will you?"

"I'm in fervent need of a shower. I may have bits of brain matter in my hair," Garrett said matter-of-factly.

"That's disgusting," Andie said.

"Care to join me?" retorted Garrett.

"In your dreams."

"I'm pretty sure, in yours," Garrett said with a self-possessed grin.

"If it were a nightmare," Andie countered. She rolled her eyes as the pooka pranced out of the room like a model on a runway.

Andie turned to Finn. "Is he always like that?"

"You mean irritating as all hell?"

"Yes."

Finn nodded. "But I'd lay my life down for that guy, and he'd do the same for me in a heartbeat. Garrett is the type of man you *always* want on your side."

Andie plopped down on the plush sofa in the living room. "I guess."

"Don't let him get to you," Finn said as he sat next to her, two cans of soda in hand. "He makes light of everything. It's just his way," Finn explained as he popped open a can and offered the other one to her.

Andie took a big gulp, suddenly feeling the day get the better of her. Adrenaline was quickly replaced by exhaustion as she pondered her next step. Where would she go and what would happen if somebody discovered the dead bodies in her apartment? She worried about Clover, too. How safe was she really when thugs like that were out to get her? Andie pinched her brow and wondered how one perfectly normal day could go so horribly wrong.

"Hey," Finn said as he bumped shoulders with her. "I'm really sorry you got messed up in all of this. I should have known better than to endanger you like that. Clover might literally kill me for this."

Eyeing the handsome leprechaun sitting beside her, Andie couldn't help but smile. "You're a good guy. And you really like her, don't you?"

Finn slumped lower in the couch and exhaled in one long breath. "You have no idea."

She nudged his shoulder right back. "I'll put in a good word for you."

A welcome silence filled the space between them, both seemingly engrossed in their own thoughts. Despite the uncertainty of what lay ahead and the prospect of danger at every turn, Andie felt surprisingly safe, hiding out as she was with a couple of supernatural creatures.

Garrett walked in, looking disturbingly dapper. The boy had flair; Andie had to give him that. In a plain gray shirt, a pair of vintage-looking designer jeans, and white sneakers, he looked like he'd just stepped off the pages of a magazine. The effortless pizzazz in which he carried himself was so maddening in its perfection that Andie sighed despite herself.

"Has our dear leprechaun been boring you with inane lamentations to do with his weepy heart?" Garrett went straight to the fridge and grabbed a beer. He flashed them a well-rehearsed grin like he was posing for a print ad, then threw a balled-up shirt at Finn.

Finn caught the shirt then sidled close to Andie, whispering, "Pay him no mind." He got up and changed his shirt. "I need to get in touch with Anna and make a few other calls. I'll have some clothes brought for you. Take a nap if you'd like. First bedroom to the right on the second floor. I'll have someone take care of the situation in your apartment and then later, after you're well rested, we can discuss the next steps."

It had all sounded so reasonable and mundane. No big deal—fresh clothes, dead body clean-up, a nap. "Actually, a bed does sound inviting right now." Realizing she'd just left herself wide-open for a jibe from Garrett, she shot him a preemptive cautioning look.

He flashed her the most wicked of smiles. "What? I didn't even *say* anything."

She got up and made her way to the stairs. "We'll figure this all out later?" she asked Finn.

Finn nodded reassuringly.

"Keep the bed warm for me, all right?" Garrett teased.

"Oh, shut up," Andie retorted as she ascended the stairs, hating that she blushed like a schoolgirl and flattered that the obnoxiously irresistible pooka couldn't take his eyes off her. She'd encountered her fair share of men to know that—faerie or otherwise—Garrett was trouble. If she knew what was good for her, she'd stay away. She bit her lower lip as she realized making wise decisions was never her strong suit.

After what felt like hours of restless sleep, Andie was softly nudged awake. The room had gone completely dark, illuminated only by the small lamp on the bedside table. Rubbing at her eyes, a little bit of the panic she'd stashed away and suppressed began to burble back to the surface. In the dark, somebody was sitting on the bed beside her.

Garrett softly shook her again. "You awake? We've got a situation."

Garrett's tone and the lack of his usual playful innuendos told Andie something was definitely wrong. She bolted right up, suddenly as wired as if she'd taken two shots of espresso. "Tell me."

"Finn's gone," Garrett said, his tone almost disbelieving.

"What do you mean, *gone*?"

"He's not dead, if that's what you're asking," Garrett said as he got up to turn the light on. "He left. After you went up to nap, Finn had gone into the den to make some calls. I had laid on the couch and dozed off. When I woke up, he was gone."

"He probably got take-out or something. He'll be back, right?" Andie asked.

Garrett half shrugged, half shook his head, then pulled out a Post-it from his pocket. He sat back down on the bed and handed the note to Andie.

Garrett,
  Keep Andie and Clover safe.
  I owe you one, old friend.

Finn

Andie examined the sticky note like it was some relic from the past; rereading Finn's words as if they'd somehow magically reveal some cryptic coded message. "What the hell is this supposed to mean?"

"Listen, I'm as flabbergasted as you are," Garrett said, keeping his tone light, but clearly bothered by the unexpected turn of events.

"He said we'd figure this out after I took a nap. Why would he —I don't understand. What are we going to do now?" Andie asked, her panic now pouring forth in waves.

Garrett flashed her a sideways grin, his usual charisma making a comeback. "Good news, sweetheart. You're going to Disneyland."

※

Clover's days had started to blend together, composed of the same dependable company and predictable routines. Her training with Meara had been going splendidly; her magic flowing more freely and almost every day, a new skill uncovered. As her confidence grew, so did her worry and longing for Finn. Not having parted on the best of terms, every day that passed without a word from him compounded the growing uneasiness in her gut.

Hanging out with Button and Mirabella certainly helped lift her spirits. The stronger she became, the slacker her tether was to the Otherworld. Meara had let her visit with her friends and family more often—something Clover had appreciated and looked forward to. Throwing knives and visiting with Anna had become their unusual yet enjoyable routine. Mirabella was as fierce with a blade as her father and seeing Scobert with her warmed Clover's heart. She couldn't even begin to imagine Scobert's inner turmoil over the whole Helena-Therese situation, but it was evident to all that spending time with Mirabella had become the clurichaun's favorite pastime.

Button, too, seemed to enjoy their company immensely. Even Sinann seemed to embrace her girlfriend's small yet burgeoning social life. She'd happily see Button off to her adventures above the sea, always making her promise to take good care of herself and return safely to her. Clover had admittedly judged their relationship in the beginning but had since come to understand its complexities. Faerie and human relationships were difficult enough without having peering eyes and rubberneckers cast judgement. How different was Button and Sinann's relationship to her and Finn's? Hadn't she agreed to travel to another realm with a leprechaun who'd known her all her life, but she'd barely just met? Talk about complicated.

Clover's thoughts were interrupted when her mother walked into her bedroom—more accurately, the huge one-bedroom suite in Lir's castle that could easily have housed a family of five.

"Get dressed," Meara said without preamble.

Even though she saw Meara every day, her presence still elicited in her a sense of awe. That her mother was an honest-to-goodness merrow and a total goddess was still hard to fathom sometimes. If it weren't for the magic that undoubtedly coursed through her own veins, she would have easily wagered she was adopted.

"Where are we going?" Clover asked.

"I've received word that Anna requests our company at her cottage."

The resident butterflies resting dormant in Clover's belly stirred. "Do you think Finn is back?"

"Quite possibly," Meara replied. "A sizable contingent of Queen Helena's men has slowly been trickling back to the realm in the past few weeks. I would surmise Finn's work is done."

Suddenly, the moment she'd been waiting for seemed daunting. She wondered whether Finn had thought of her in the past weeks and if their silly argument was for him long forgotten as well. Whatever the outcome of their impending reunion, she was just happy to have him safely back. What with the escalated skirmishes with the Unseelies and Liz's recent abduction, she needed more than ever to have loved ones close by.

"Give me a second to get ready," she said as her heart hammered in her chest.

༺༻

Before she could even get a toe past the door, Momma Ruth had enveloped Clover in the tightest of hugs and she hugged her back with equal intensity. Her grandmother would always be her calming security blanket in every situation. When finally they released each other, she saw that Anna's house was packed with the usual suspects: Her dad, Scobert, Mary, Anna, Cordelia, and even Kean. No sign of Finn.

She greeted everyone and found a seat next to her dad on the sofa. She gave him a peck on the cheek as he ruffled her hair as usual. "Everything all right?" Clover asked, sensing a tense undercurrent in the room.

Nick squeezed her hand as everybody sort of corralled themselves in the small living room—Scobert in a chaise meant for two, Anna and Mary on the sofa across the coffee table with Cordelia hovering overhead, Kean standing behind them, Momma

Ruth sitting beside her, and Meara, perhaps unsure where to situate herself, perched on the arm of Scobert's chaise. The scene had the feel of a badly choreographed intervention.

"Somebody say something," Clover blurted out.

Scobert shifted in his chair and cleared his throat. "We've received word from Garrett. He and Finn had delivered your letter to your friend, Andie, when they were attacked by four Unseelie soldiers."

Clover brought a hand to her mouth, fearing the worst.

"She's fine," Scobert assured. "Your friend is unharmed."

"Is Finn—"

"Nobody was harmed," Scobert clarified. "They bested the Unseelies and brought Andie to a safe house, but Garrett felt Andie would be safest here for the time being, so she and Garrett are on their way. The journey, as you know, will take a few days. They were already in Limerick as of last night."

Clover let out a sigh, relieved nobody was hurt, and equal parts thrilled and anxious to have her best friend in the faerie realm. Her two worlds were slowly merging and messy as it was, she was happy not to have to hide from Andie anymore. Soon enough, Finn would complete his mission and be back, too. Sinking into her seat, she started to relax; everybody was safe. There was nothing to worry about.

With a pained expression on her face, Anna edged forward in her seat, opened her mouth to speak, then closed it, hesitating. Clover hadn't really noticed when she first walked in, but now that she got a better look, realized Anna looked absolutely distraught. She steeled herself for what would certainly be bad news.

"Yesterday, I uncovered some rather distressing information when I was going through some of Finn's mother's old things," Anna said, her voice shaky.

Clover knew practically nothing about Finn's mother; only that she passed when he was a baby and Anna had cared for him ever since. Whatever it was that Anna discovered, she doubted it could be all that bad, but judging from the look on her face, Clover had to reconsider.

"I realize perhaps I shouldn't have contacted Finn right away—"

"You think?" Scobert interrupted.

Completely taken aback by Scobert's tone, Clover shot him a look and turned to Anna encouragingly. "Go on, please."

"He's my son, and he deserved to know," Anna said to the whole room.

"What exactly did you tell him?" Clover asked, trying not to lose her patience.

"The identity of his father."

Clover swallowed. "His father?"

Anna fidgeted with the hem of her skirt, plucking at loose threads, and avoiding everybody's gaze.

"Go on and tell them," Scobert said.

"You see," Anna started, "Brielle—Finn's real mom, was my best friend, but she'd never told me who her babe's father was. She never wanted him in the picture, and I'd respected that." Anna paused and took in a deep breath. "In the old journal I found yesterday, she'd written about him and all her reasons for not wanting this man to be a part of their lives."

Clover searched the faces of those gathered in Anna's living room, and with the exception of Scobert who no doubt already knew the answer, found the same question evident on all their expressions—who was Finn's father?

"Alistair McCabe is Finn's father," Anna said before she cast her gaze to the floor.

As a cacophony of raised voices filled the room, Clover's heart caved in on itself even as it went out to the leprechaun who would have done anything to protect her, the boy she'd fallen in love with, the same man who'd unknowingly vowed to kill his own father.

Everybody had something to say—thoughtful advice, a strategic ploy, cautioning words—but amidst the din, Anna sought Clover out. The girl had escaped to the kitchen after the proverbial cat was let out of the bag. Even though every soul in the house cared for Finn one way or the other, Clover had been the center of Finn's life for so many years and she was also the girl who now owned his heart. Anna owed her the rest of the story.

Clover sat by the butcher block that doubled as the kitchen table, her gaze fixed on Anna as she walked in the room.

"What did he say?" Clover asked. "After you told him."

Anna's heart bled for her son as she recalled the pain in his voice. "He was quiet for a long while, and then he said he needed to see him."

"That's it?" Clover asked, her face etched with worry.

Anna nodded. "He'd abruptly ended our communication. Later, we found out he'd left Garrett a note. He asked him to keep you and Andie safe but mentioned nothing else."

"Does Alistair know about him?"

"No. Brielle had intentionally kept him in the dark. She didn't want Alistair to have anything to do with Finn's upbringing. I wish she would have told me," Anna said, her voice breaking despite herself. "I had no idea. When Finn came of age, I had intentionally sought Alistair out so he could train him. He was the best in the army. How was I to know—how was I to know that I'd pushed for my son to be mentored by the very man his real mother had despised?"

Clover caught her in an embrace as her tears flowed freely. "What have I done? I can't lose Finn to Alistair. I just can't."

"You won't. Look at me," Clover said as she gently lifted Anna's chin. "Finn will come back to you—to us. We just need to have faith."

Anna shook her head, completely deflated. "I just don't know. I've been trying to make contact using the compass, but he's been ignoring me. Trying to reach his mind proved even more futile. If I were his real mother, it would be easier. Faeries who are related can almost always seamlessly communicate with each other telepathically. Look at you and Meara. Remember how effortless it was when she first breached your mind?"

"But some faeries can reach other's minds, even though they're not related, right? Alistair controlled mine when he pretended to be Finn," Clover said.

"Yes. Some very powerful faeries can. Also, don't forget. In Alistair's case, he'd already had a magical connection to you from the beginning. In a way, he'd been breaching your mind since your birth."

Clover bit her lower lip, seemingly lost in thought. "Maybe my mom can try. Or Scobert—after all, they're cousins, right?"

"Not real cousins, dear. Mary and I are related, but since I'm not Finn's real mother..." Anna shrugged.

When Diana padded in and nestled at her feet, Clover absentmindedly picked the cat up, gently petting her. Suddenly, her face lit up. "I have an idea. Diana and Finn have been able to communicate with each other even through long distances. Do you think perhaps—"

"We could try," Anna agreed. "And since all faeries can pretty much understand animals, Diana could, in theory, pass a message on to me."

"*Pretty much* understand animals?"

"You have to have a close connection to an animal to thoroughly understand it. For instance, when I try to breach Diana's mind, I see images and memories, but not necessarily words and ideas."

"It's worth a shot." Clover looked Diana in the eye. "Please tell Finn I really need to speak to him and that I'm worried about him. We just want to make sure he's okay."

Dianna purred and lightly butted her head against Clover's chin, a clear acquiescence. The cat squeezed her eyes shut, as if working out a puzzle. Then she opened her eyes and meowed. Reaching out to the cat's mind, Anna saw fragmented images of Finn and a large wooden door shutting firmly closed.

Her shoulders slumped. Finn was blocking Diana out. He wasn't letting anybody in.

Clover instantly picked up on the disappointment on Anna's face. "What do we do now?" she asked.

"I'm afraid it's up to Finn now. All we can do is hope he finds his way back home."

Liz's hands and feet were bound and shackled to a stone wall in what looked to be a dark medieval prison, except there were no cells, just one cavernous room with chains and restraints screwed into the walls. There was hardly any illumination except for sparse sunlight that streamed in through a small window overhead. A basin of water and a hard loaf of bread lay barely within arm's reach. She blew at the errant strand of hair that maddeningly fell across her sweaty face and swore an oath of revenge against whomever it was that did this to her.

Hearing the shuffle of footsteps approaching, she braced for the worst.

"Why haven't you eaten?" A kindly female voice asked.

When her captor came into the light, Liz found herself staring at the familiar ruby-red eyes of Iekika, the sorceress. "You," Liz spat. "Traitorous leech. This is how you repay me after I saved your miserable little life?"

"There, there, now. Don't take it personally," Iekika said in the same cheerfully creepy voice.

"I never should have helped you. You promised me you'd get rid of Clover, but all you did was murder Boris and frame the Seelie Queen for his death. How did you even take me? The queen's lair is impenetrable. The last thing I remember was tending to my freesias, the next thing I know I'm in this godforsaken hell hole."

Iekika squatted so they were eye to eye. "I barely lifted a finger. It was all you. You wrote the letter, made yourself invisible, snuck out when the soldier left, trekked across the faerie realm, and delivered yourself trussed and bound at my dungeon door." She wagged a bony finger at Liz's face. "Don't underestimate the power of suggestion."

Dehydrated as she was, Liz hocked up all the spit she could muster and propelled it at Iekika's face. The profound satisfaction she got from the look of absolute disgust on the sorceress's face was short lived. In the next moment, she was engulfed in searing and agonizing pain. From the tops of her skull to the very tips of her toes, hot lava seemed to rapidly flow forth. Try as she might to mask her suffering, she let out an ear-splitting cry.

"I urge you not to test me," Iekika said, her voice sweet and amicable. "Alistair wants you alive, but frankly, I don't give a crap if you live or die."

When Iekika allowed her a brief reprieve from her mental assault, Liz dared a retort. "Mark my words. The Seelies will come for me and they will kill each and every one of you. Now, get those disgustingly diseased eyes away from my face before I catch whatever repulsive fungus you've got."

Liz's body contorted in pain and a whimper escaped her lips before everything went black.

12

Jet lag had taken on a whole new meaning. From New York, Garrett had called a cab that somehow had the extraordinary ability to travel between any bridge or tunnel in the world in under a second. The driver, Willie, had been a hoot, regaling her with tales of worldwide escapades, and confiding that she was the second lackey he'd ever driven in his cab, Clover being the first. The cab itself was another story all together. A nondescript sedan from the outside, it was opulence on four wheels on the inside. Miraculously large enough to fit at least twenty people, it had plush velvety seats and a curious serving table that mysteriously dished out an assortment of goodies, the aroma of freshly baked brownies filling the space like car freshener. Andie's only complaint was that the ride was too short. One minute they were at the Tappan Zee Bridge, the next moment, they were emerging from a tunnel in Limerick. From there, they'd travelled on foot through the backwoods of Ireland on a faerie path, of all things.

Now on the final leg of their journey, Andie's anxiety was at fever pitch. Garrett had been as much of a gentleman as he could be as they'd navigated through hills, streams, dense thickets, and bogs. According to Garrett, there was only one way for a first-time human guest of the Seelie Court to enter the other realm—through a portal on an island in the middle of a lake in County Donegal, but only after a long journey—an epic runaround if she ever saw one.

To say that they'd *camped* overnight was using the term loosely. There was a campfire, a can of beans, and roasted squirrel, but not much else. They'd slept on the hard, cold forest ground with only a stolen blanket from Finn's safe house to keep them warm. Garrett was a most eager provider of body warmth, and admittedly, Andie had welcomed lying next to the pooka late at night—not for the obvious reasons that would pop to mind, but because he did have a satisfyingly warm body. Hot, even.

As they prepared to leave their campsite that morning, a thousand questions buzzed through Andie's mind. Fear of the unknown, anxiety over seeing Clover again, topped off with a growing attraction to her gorgeous travelling partner created a dangerous cocktail of apprehension in her head.

"Don't think too hard, doll face. You might hurt yourself," Garrett quipped.

"Run it by me again, will you? I'm supposed to jump into some kind of wormhole, but only after performing a particular task—and there's no way of knowing what the task may be until the moment before I'm about to jump?"

"You're so adorable when you pester me with silly questions. We've been through this countless times. We'll know what the portal wants when we get there. It's usually some ridiculous thing, like reciting a poem or solving a riddle. Faerie portals are absurdly bored; they are entertained by the most mundane things."

"And we're supposed to fly over a lake to get to an island that houses the portal? Couldn't we just take a boat? What if those Unseelies are still after us? What will we do then?"

"Unless you've packed an inflatable raft in your purse, I'm afraid paddling to the island is out of the question. We could swim, but I'd rather stay dry, so levitation is really the only plausible option," Garrett explained. "Do you think you could break character for one second and just trust that I won't let anything bad happen to you? There's nothing out there I can't defend you from. Not to brag or anything, but I'm kind of a big deal."

Andie had to laugh. "You can't say *not to brag or anything*, then literally brag about something in the next breath."

Garrett extended his hand and offered up one of his trademark smiles. "Trust me?"

Andie didn't really have much of a choice. She took Garrett's hand and trekked on, hoping he was really as big of a deal as he claimed to be.

※

Hours later and after irreparable damage to the soles of her feet, they were almost at their destination. As the miles piled on, Garrett had become progressively quieter and more pensive, and much to her surprise, Andie had actually started to miss his wisecracks.

"Hey," she finally prodded, not able to help herself. "You all right?"

"Tippy-top," said Garrett.

Andie peered at him sideways, not buying it at all. "Don't lie. Something's up. You're not your usual self."

"And what, pray tell, is my usual self like?"

"Absurdly narcissistic and incessantly flirty?"

When he really found something funny, Garrett had one of those deep, spontaneous laughs that were so unapologetically mirthful they were downright contagious. It had quickly become one of Andie's favorite things about him.

"You are such a nag. Do you know that?" Garrett said between snickers.

While some may call it nagging, Andie labeled it persistence. "Seriously, though. What's up?"

Garrett rolled his eyes and exhaled—a clear sign of caving in. "If you must know, I'm feeling a little antsy," Garrett said, as he shot her an uncharacteristically sheepish look. "Being in the woods this whole time. It's like a trigger, you know?"

Andie tried to puzzle through what Garrett was saying.

"You have no idea what I'm talking about, do you?"

She raised a finger. "Give me a minute."

"Let's just say that my current form, though flawless, is wanting. To be honest," he shrugged, "I miss walking on all fours."

Andie burst out laughing. "You want to shapeshift?"

"I didn't bring a change of clothes, so I'll just have to hold off until we get to the other side."

Comical though it seemed on the surface, it made Andie wonder. How much of this gorgeously handsome man was even close to human at all? As if it wasn't bizarre enough that he was a faerie, he preferred to be one in the body of a leopard. A tiny shiver went up her spine as a time-worn adage suddenly came to mind: Beware of the company you keep.

"You're not afraid of me now, are you?" Garrett asked.

Andie shook her head and forced a smile on her face. "Nah."

Her response was met with another heart-stopping smile. "Good, because we're here."

They emerged from a clearing onto the sandy shore of a pristine lake, their small island destination at its center. In a few short minutes, Andie would be crossing over into another dimension. There was no turning back now.

"What now?" she asked.

"Now, you hold on tight," Garrett said as he closed the distance between them. "Put your arms around my neck."

Standing face to face with her arms around him and his hands at the small of her back, they looked like they were about to dance. Instead, they flew. She gripped him tighter as they crossed the lake, unintentionally digging her nails into his back.

"Ouch," Garrett said playfully, his face only inches from hers as they glided just above the surface of the clear blue water.

Before she knew it, they landed on the island and Garrett let her go. She righted herself and evoked a modicum of composure. She wasn't sure what gave her the greater high—flying or being in Garrett's arms. When she regained her bearings, she noticed they were standing next to what looked like an old well that had been filled in with stones.

"Is this the portal?"

Garrett nodded. "You're up," he said as he stood aside so she could come closer. Then he leaned forward like he was straining to hear something emanating from the portal.

"What's going on?" she asked, not being able to stand the suspense.

Garrett put a finger to his lips. "It's telling me what you need to do." He bent forward again, then nodded sagely. "It seems you are to solve a riddle."

Panic gripped her. She'd never been great at tests. She wondered if she could use the search function on her mobile phone, but quickly conceded the portal would probably consider that cheating. "Let's do this."

Garrett cleared his throat. "Used to bid goodbye or to say hello. Better wet than dry. Some are quick, some are slow. What am I?"

An imaginary clock counted down in Andie's head as she quickly deciphered the clues. She repeated the riddle to herself, and then there it was—the answer, plain and clear. "A kiss. You are a kiss!"

"Indeed, I am," Garrett said. Then he leaned forward and brought his lips down to hers in a slow, tender kiss.

As Andie's knees buckled from under her, she gently pushed the pooka away, afraid she wouldn't be able to stop.

"You did great," Garrett said, a mischievous twinkle in his eye.

Andie blushed to high heavens and turned her attention on the portal. Nothing happened. "What's going on? How come it didn't work?"

"Oh, the portal said wiggle your nose and touch your toes. I threw the riddle in because I wanted to kiss you."

For a brief second, she equal parts wanted to kill him and kiss him. She tugged at his shirt, bringing his face level with hers. "You could have just asked."

Finn was proving harder to kill than Alistair had initially thought. Admittedly, he was an excellent soldier. It was, after all, Alistair himself who'd molded him into the fine warrior that he was today. He'd known it wouldn't be an easy task, which is why he'd sent some of his finest soldiers to carry out the deed. What he hadn't counted on was Garrett. Finn alone was a hard target. The two of them together were practically invincible. Alistair quickly realized some jobs were too important to delegate; to get it done right, he'd have to do it himself.

He went to his desk and opened the journal. His daily missives from his pliable marionette had been ever so informative. Therese was the ideal operative—completely devoid of moral fiber and servile to a fault. The years it took to break her in had definitely paid off. He dipped the quill in ink and asked his question.

Has Finn returned to the realm?

He laid his quill down and waited. As the minutes ticked on, he silently cursed Therese for being unresponsive. Alas, even the seemingly perfect minion had her faults. He closed the journal and decided to give his newly acquired captive a visit. He always did enjoy seeing Liz. Now that Finn was otherwise enamored, Liz was essentially unattached. Toying with the idea of a romantic alliance with the spirited beauty got Alistair's blood pumping. He admittedly found great amusement in claiming for himself what belonged to others.

As he crossed his chamber to leave, a distinct presentiment tugged at the edges of his awareness. Like a familiar scent or a remembered task, something made him stop and take in his surroundings. No sound alerted his senses, but a presence. Moving silently to the fireplace, he recognized a singular aura, akin to a soul's fingerprint. When he realized he had an intruder, Alistair brought his hands together in applause.

"Well done, soldier. I'm impressed," Alistair announced to the empty room.

Barely making a sound, Finn rappelled down the chimney and entered the room through the fireplace.

"I knew it was you," Alistair said as he faced-off with his onetime prodigy and friend. "It's quite serendipitous, actually. I had just a few moments ago decided to end your life with my bare hands, and like magic, here you are. Talk about luck."

"Did you know?" Finn asked, his voice cold as ice.

"That you would slither in here like a rabid raccoon and attempt to murder me? No. I did not know. Neither did I expect it, but a leprechaun can hope. Now that you're here, let's begin, shall we?"

Alistair assumed a fighting stance. While he'd never intended to kill the lad, like a rolling stone gathering speed, their present circumstances have inescapably led to this moment. One of them had to go, and it sure as hell wasn't going to be him. He delivered a low roundhouse kick, knocking Finn off his feet. In the next second, Alistair was on top of him, ready to deliver a deadly blow to his neck. Instead, he slapped him across the face. "Defend yourself, soldier. You're making this too easy to be enjoyable. What the hell's wrong with you?"

"Have you known all this time that I'm your son?" Finn shouted.

Alistair let him go. "What are you talking about?"

Finn sat up and raked his fingers through his head like he meant to draw blood. He blew out a long breath, his steely gray eyes intent on Alistair. "Anna told me. She was going through my mother's old things and found a journal."

Alistair shook his head. "I am not your father. I knew Brielle, yes, but she would have told me if we had sired a child together. We were barely together, a passing fancy."

"Are you sure about that?"

Sifting through the memories of numerous lifetimes spent with Finn by his side, Alistair sought to discover if there'd been any indication that he was more than just a trusted soldier and right-hand. He recalled how he'd despised him when they'd first met—something about his irreverent confidence had reminded him too much of his own arrogance. Still, he'd given him a chance and trained him, paying more attention to the lad over any other in the Queen's Army. The years under his tutelage soon shaped Finn into the best soldier in the realm; and fighting side by side, they'd been unbeatable. Although they'd always shared a strong connection, Alistair had never attempted to breach his mind, the act unacceptable amongst comrades.

Morbid curiosity got the better of him when he placed both hands on Finn's shoulders. Upon contact, an electrifying sense of clarity engulfed Alistair's senses. Finn's thoughts and feelings were crystal clear, not the usual murky meanderings into someone else's mind, but a patent and powerful connection, as if barriers didn't exist between them. With one touch, what he'd always suspected but never entertained was confirmed: Not only was Finn a purer, stronger, nobler version of what he could only ever hope to be, he was also undoubtedly his son. A searing sense of obligation overcame him as the gravity of his realization hit home. Alistair released him as if burned, his mind reeling.

Finn gasped for air; no doubt having experienced his own jarring insights into the inner workings of Alistair's mind. Evidently, he didn't like what he saw. In the next instant, he was pummeling Alistair with wrathful, debilitating punches—blows that more than made up for in torque what they lacked in technique. Finn wasn't conserving energy for a drawn-out fight. He was giving his all to end it right then and there.

Alistair tried to deflect Finn's onslaught, even as he resisted the compelling urge to fight back. His son was not going to die by his hands. The tip of a knife pierced his jugular as Finn hovered above him, incensed.

"Would you kill your own father?" Alistair shouted as the knife dug deeper into his skin, drawing blood. "For what? A girl? I trained you. Hell, I practically raised you. I held your life in my hands countless times and defended it at every turn, stood back-to-back with you in battle and trusted my life to you, taken innumerable lives to save your own. Is this how you want this journey to end? With my blood on your hands and our legacy forgotten?"

The knife stilled as Finn hesitated, his expression unreadable.

"I didn't know you were my son," Alistair said. "If I had known—"

"If you had known, what?" Finn yelled, his anger resurfacing. "Would you have done things differently?"

"I would have tried to be your father."

Finn let out a primal yelp as he grabbed Alistair by the collar and pounded his head fiercely against the stone floor underneath. Then he got up, muttered a curse, and kicked the knife away.

Every last inch of Liz's body throbbed in pain—even her skin was raw and tender to the touch. In the grips of Iekika's torture session, she'd almost wished for death. Again and again, the murderous sorceress had ordered her to claim Alistair as her king. *Just say the words,* she had cooed, with a promise to stop her suffering. *Just admit that Queen Helena is an unworthy, opportunistic hussy, and I'll let you rest.* Liz was not accustomed to discomfort, let alone mind-shattering pain, but even at the precipice of her most abject horrors, she couldn't make herself say the words. Eventually her tormentor grew tired and took leave, with a cheery promise to return shortly.

In the dark, dank confines of the dungeons, Liz sobbed as she lay crumpled on the floor, wishing to be anywhere else. Desperately, she attempted to heal herself, but her wounds were inflicted with witch magic, which her own healing powers were ineffectual against. The fabric of her beautiful blue dress had stuck to the bloody claw marks that lined her back and every tiny movement induced a fresh torture. Her throat was parched and sore from screaming, and her head felt like it'd been hit with an anvil. A hysterical laugh escaped her lips as she tried to imagine how she looked at that moment. Unapologetically vain and finicky with her surroundings, Liz was no doubt living her absolute worst nightmare. She quietly moaned in utter defeat, hoping to pass out and find some reprieve.

When she heard quiet footsteps approach, she frantically sought a way to knock herself out before Iekika could inflict a new round of suffering. A futile attempt to bang her head against the wall quickly proved her ineptitude for self-flagellation. Squeezing her eyes shut, she steeled herself and braced for the worst.

A hand clamped down on her mouth, muffling her screams. She opened her eyes expecting to see Iekika's scarlet ones staring back at her. Instead, she found herself gazing into familiar warm gray eyes.

"Finn?" Liz croaked, almost disbelieving.

Finn gently pressed his mouth against her forehead, supporting her head with his hand. "You're safe now. I'm here."

Clutching at Finn for dear life, Liz finally allowed herself to hope. "I didn't say what she wanted me to, Finn. I stayed strong," she mumbled, close to hysterics.

Finn gently cradled her in his arms. "I know you did. I'm so sorry this happened to you. Let's get you home."

"Home?" Liz asked as a small smile found its way to her cracked, dry lips.

Finn gingerly picked her up, placing her arms around his neck. "Rest now, Liz. I've got you."

It had all felt like a dream, seemingly too good to be true. Liz didn't care. For the first time in what felt like forever, she finally felt safe. She let go of her fear and trusted Finn to see her safely home.

※

In the weeks since Liz was returned to the Seelie Court, nobody had seen or heard from Finn. A bedraggled and injured Liz awoke in Anna's living room in the middle night, with no concrete memory of how she got there. All she knew was Finn rescued her from Iekika's dungeon and brought her back. The queen herself, with a handful of her best soldiers, picked Liz up and saw to her safe return to the court.

Not to be a total child about it, but Clover was secretly miffed that Finn would go out of his way to rescue Liz, then promptly disappear again without even a word to her or his family. With his continued absence, assumptions were bandied about left and right. That he'd sided with Alistair and the Unseelie Court was a common refrain, punctuated with sanctimonious tongue-wagging at his swift betrayal. The handful of them who were closest to Finn kept the faith, Queen Helena chief among them. She'd let it be known that anybody who had accusations to fling at Finn better address them to her face, or else keep their opinions to themselves.

As the weeks dragged on, even Clover became beset with not only worry, but doubt. Horrid though Alistair was, he was still Finn's father. Her own tumultuous relationship with her dad proved that blood was thicker than water. No matter what happened in the past, he was still her father. Of course, Nick wasn't a murderous sociopath, and Alistair most certainly was.

The silver lining amidst all the uncertainty was having her best friend by her side. Andie had adjusted superbly to life in Faerie, making fast friends with Button and Mirabella and settling into Anna's house with ease. The budding romance with Garrett no doubt contributed to her seamless transition into all things supernatural. To the surprise of many, when Garrett wasn't aiding in the war effort or disappearing into the woods for days, he was spending an inordinate bulk of his time with Andie. Although Clover was delighted that he and Andie were getting along, she couldn't help but worry. Garrett was fiercely independent and a self-professed nomad. There was no way of knowing when he'd leave again. On the other hand, at least Garrett was there now, while her supposed boyfriend was still nowhere to be found.

Anna's house had quickly become the group's clubhouse and headquarters of sorts. Scobert, Garrett, and Kean would routinely drop by, updating them on the strengthening of the Queen's Army and the planned attacks on the Unseelie Court. At an attempt at normalcy, they'd all sit down to meals or share a few bottles of wine in the cozy living room. Mostly, everyone was just hoping to hear from Finn, but despite their combined hopes, the magical compass remained quiet and still.

Today, Garrett and Kean had come bearing gifts—a couple of bottles of good mead and four pheasants care of Garrett's unrivaled hunting skills. As Anna and Cordelia prepped the fowl for dinner, Clover, Button, Mirabella, Andie, Kean, and Garrett hung out in the kitchen doing shots of mead. Despite the peculiar composition of their small group, they'd managed an easy camaraderie: faeries, humans, and half-breeds alike—a veritable United Nations of the supernatural world.

"Anna, your turn," Garrett proclaimed as he refilled a glass.

Anna graciously reached for the glass and downed the drink, shoving the glass back on the table with a challenging smile on her face. "Clover, you're up."

Kean refilled the cup and handed it to Clover. As she chuckled and took the mead, she and Anna locked gazes, both knowing participants in a charade. Since Finn's disappearance, neither of them had been able to don a genuine smile on their faces.

The cup got passed around—to Button, who pinched her nose, made a face, and swallowed the mead like it was poison, to Mirabella, who took her shot, rapped the cup on the table and swiftly demanded another one.

Garrett poured himself a drink and downed it. Draping his arm over Andie's shoulder, he deftly snaked his way to the hollow of her neck and inhaled. "Gods, you smell delectable."

"You're in a good mood," Andie shot back, clearly attempting nonchalance.

"Garrett is psyched for tomorrow's mission," Kean explained.

"You bet your ass I am. We're going to kill Vincent," Garrett said plainly.

Clover went cold. Vincent was the Unseelie soldier who'd shot an arrow at Finn and slapped her so hard across the face, her ears rang for days. She'd also bitten him, kneed him in the groin, and during the battle with the Unseelies, Nick had beaten him to a bloody pulp. There was history with Vincent.

"We've received intelligence that he's near the Unseelie border with a handful of soldiers, building an outpost," Kean said. "Garrett and I are paying them a little visit."

"Just the two of you?" Clover asked, worried.

"A bigger contingent will arouse attention," Kean said. "We'll be fine. It should be a walk in the park."

A silence descended upon Anna's kitchen, even the incessant flapping of Cordelia's tiny wings quieting as she settled on an empty stool. Despite their efforts at normalcy, the reality was they were at war and the danger was real. There were no guarantees they'd all make it out alive.

"Do be careful," Anna finally said, somber.

"Give me some credit here," Garrett scoffed. "They won't know what hit them."

13

Garrett and Kean trekked through the woods in silence, slowly and stealthily making their way to the Unseelie outpost. Though he hated to admit it, Garrett was finding himself most impressed with the rookie soldier's skills. Not only was he cautious and strategic, but he was also a highly accomplished fighter. It was no wonder Queen Helena favored the lad. Only very slightly annoying, he wasn't horrible company either. The only thing that bothered Garrett—what really got his goat—was the fact that Kean obviously still had the hots for Clover.

"You know you don't stand a chance, right?" Garrett asked.

"Excuse me?"

Garrett shrugged. "Fact of the matter is, you're no Finn. The odds aren't exactly stacked in your favor. I'd fold now before you make a damn fool of yourself."

Kean laughed. "Thanks, man. Good to know."

"Look, I get it. She's a cutie, but Finn asked me to look out for her. If you make a move, I'll have to kill you. It'll be fun and all, but good soldiers are hard to come by."

"I'm flattered," Kean scoffed. "The truth is, I like being around her. I don't think I'm breaking any rules by doing so. Finn's not exactly here to say otherwise."

"Watch yourself, soldier," Garrett warned.

"What about you?" Kean asked.

"What *about* me?"

"You and the lackey. What's the story there?"

"The story there is mind your own goddamn business. Got that?"

Kean laughed heartily. "Sir, yes, sir."

Suddenly Garrett stilled, put a finger to his lips, and signaled for Kean to get down. From roughly half a mile northwest of them, he tracked the scents and movements of about six Fae. He kept low to the ground and took out a knife as he started crawling in that direction. Kean followed closely behind.

As they approached surreptitiously, a familiar yet coveted sensation filled Garrett's senses. As his heart ferociously pumped blood throughout his body, his vision became even clearer and his hearing keener. It was as if his whole being came alive and existed only for one thing—the kill. Their targets now merely a few yards away, Garrett could pinpoint their exact locations even with his eyes closed. He knew their breaths and beating hearts, recognizing by instinct exactly where to strike to inflict the most harm. Already a well-oiled killing machine; and he hadn't even changed yet. It hardly seemed fair.

Garrett and Kean crouched by the outpost's perimeter, surveying the scene. The Unseelies were building a rudimentary watchtower and not doing a very good job at it. Four of them milled around the foot of the lookout, passing around a small flask.

"Four targets?" Kean asked in a whisper.

Garrett shook his hand and pointed to a wooden shanty west of the tower and lifted two fingers. Seeing Vincent wasn't among the four builders, he surmised their main target was in the shanty.

"You take the two in the shed, I'll take the rest," Garrett mouthed.

Kean nodded, and they split up. Garrett headed toward the tower and Kean in the opposite direction. When he was close enough to his prey that he could count the stubbles on their sweaty faces, Garrett emerged from the cover of the forest to face them head on.

Four pairs of Unseelie eyes focused on him as he made his entrance. "Gentlemen," he said in greeting.

Before the one closest to him could reach for his knife, Garrett dove as if stealing second base and snapped his neck in one quick motion. The remaining Unseelies attacked at once, showering Garrett with a threesome of soon-to-be dead bodies. In the scrimmage, he sought the closest appendage and with a strategic twist, shattered bone. The guy with the flailing arm soon became an easy target. With a targeted blow to the back of his neck, the second Unseelie went down with a thud. Two more, Garrett thought with eager anticipation.

As he tried to decide which one to kill first, a familiar scent wafted through the air, momentarily breaking his concentration. Even as he tracked and identified its source, his knife unerringly found the heart of his third target. He threw a hook to the fourth guy's jaw, killing him instantly. He turned around and braced himself for what he knew he was about to see.

Finn walked toward him, slowly raising both hands in the air, Vincent trailing behind him looking absurd with his blue mohawk and acid-washed jeans. Kean stood a distance away, looking like he'd seen a ghost—a ghost he wanted to tear apart limb from limb.

"Stop, Garrett. Let's talk," Finn said.

Vincent stood beside him with a smug look on his face.

An unfamiliar rage overtook Garrett as he watched Finn stand alongside one of their worst enemies. "You have got to be kidding me."

"We offer a truce. I don't want to fight, but I will if I have to," Finn said.

"*We?*" Garrett yelled. "You and that dipwad are now a we?"

Finn's expression was pleading, yet resolute.

Garrett shimmered with rage and feared what was about to happen next. He knew his unsuppressed warring emotions would trigger him to change. He also knew that if he did, he was going to kill his best friend.

※

Kean had seen his fair share of gruesome or troubling sights, but never in his life had he witnessed something quite so frightening and bizarre. Garrett was an angel of death, seething with rage as he glimmered in a surge of power and erupted in the next moment into a massive leopard's body. The fearsome cat charged with feral precision, barreling its claws down on its prey with frightening intensity. Vincent lay on the dirt drenched in his own blood, a deep gory gash stretching from his brow to his bellybutton.

Garrett, or the leopard who used to be Garrett, turned away, pranced about, and primed for another attack. Before the cat pounced anew, Finn threw himself in the leopard's path, halting the attack. A deafening roar filled the forest and Kean instinctively reached for his knife. With a deadly animal in such close proximity, one's survival instincts were bound to kick in. If it weren't for his own grisly curiosity over the scene unfolding before him, Kean would have definitely taken cover.

Finn was now on the ground with his hands in the air in what looked to be a misguided attempt to mollify the bloodthirsty jungle cat. Garrett showed no signs of letting up. In one swift, graceful movement, he pounced and zeroed in on Finn's neck, going for the obvious kill. Finn's attempts to push the leopard away proved futile. The animal was just too ferocious.

Just when Kean braced himself to witness Garrett rip Finn's throat out, the cat gave another loud roar, then a less menacing sound, close to a whimper. Its large head loomed over Finn's, its fangs sharp and deadly. The cat placed two front paws on Finn's chest and bore down hard, almost the feline equivalent of a shove. Another whimper. Then it turned its sights on Kean and jerked its head to the left, as if to say, *let's go*. The leopard ran off into the woods, with Kean fast on its heels.

Not for lack of trying, but Kean simply could not keep up with the leopard. Focusing on the yellowish blur that blazed through the trees, he ran until his legs felt as if they might fall off. After several miles in hot pursuit, a disturbing thought flittered into Kean's head. Shouldn't he be running away from the leopard instead of sprinting toward it? As he considered his alternatives, he lost track of the cat and slowed his pace.

"Garrett!" Kean shouted as he jogged through the woods. "Where are you, man? Garrett!" Keeping on the path he thought the leopard ran toward, he continued his search.

From a spot unseen in a dense copse ahead came a voice. "Seriously? Could you *be* more conspicuous? Sound a foghorn while you're at it. I don't think all the woodland creatures got the memo."

Kean breathed a sigh of relief. Lounging on the forest floor with his head against a tall oak was Garrett in full birthday suite regalia.

"What the hell just happened?" Kean asked, breathless.

Garrett shook his head, the same feral look still lingering in his eyes. "Don't breathe a word to anybody until I've briefed the queen. Do you understand?"

Kean understood full well. A betrayal from Finn Ryan was a horrible blow to the Seelie Army, to the realm, and to Queen Helena herself. This was not news to be thrown around lightly.

Kean nodded. "Understood."

※

When Garrett and Kean delivered their report to the queen, for the life of him, Scobert could not believe it to be true. If he hadn't trusted both lads with his very life, he would have easily dismissed the news as hearsay, trickery, or downright black magic. Perhaps it wasn't Finn at all, but a changeling in disguise, he'd countered. Garrett, on the other hand, was quite certain it was him, and there was no questioning the pooka when it came to tracking.

Perhaps Finn was merely infiltrating the Unseelie Court and pretending to have switched alliances, the queen proffered. It was a likely scenario they'd all wished were true, but if it were the case, Finn would have made contact and briefed them of his plan. Long into the night, the four of them argued stances and pursued possible scenarios. In the end, there was one obvious possibility neither one dared broach—that Finn had chosen his own flesh and blood over his loyalty to the Seelie Court. While the premise remained unspoken, it had been on everybody's mind.

Before their meeting broke, Garrett thanked the queen for her hospitality, promised his eternal loyalty, but offered his farewells. A war against Finn was not a war he'd come prepared to fight. Helena urged him to stay on, beseeching now more than ever. She'd need dependable soldiers at her side. It was a plea no true Seelie soldier could refuse. Though his heart wasn't quite in it, the pooka agreed to stay for his queen.

Several days had passed since and Scobert's heart wasn't in anything, it seemed. With the prospect of potentially battling Finn looming heavily on his mind, everything had lost its luster. Even the joy of his life, his daughter, couldn't get him out of his funk.

Mirabella passed him a flask as they sat side by side watching the sun set from the gardens of the Seelie Court. "Are you going to be okay?"

Scobert shrugged and realized he didn't know the answer. Somehow, he was convinced that if he could just talk to the lad, everything would be explained—that the impending war with the Unseelies did not have to entail potentially killing his cousin. He took a long swig of whiskey, then passed the flask back to his daughter. "I hope so," he said.

Mirabella took a sip and stared out at the horizon, seemingly deep in thought. "Maybe he has his reasons," she said, her voice low. "Perhaps he's doing this not out of allegiance, but to protect someone he loves. Possibly he's sacrificing himself to save someone else."

"Perhaps," Scobert conceded, as his thoughts reached out to

Finn. Then he peered at Mirabella. "What do you know of sacrifice?"

His usually fiery daughter remained quiet for a time, as if a light inside of her was slowly extinguishing.

"What's the matter, Bella?" Scobert asked.

Mirabella smiled softly. "You're the only one who's ever called me Bella."

Scobert laughed heartily, recalling a memory. "When you were just a wee babe, I used to say 'Ciao, Bella' whenever I left your side." The fake Italian accent he'd just affected made him snigger even more—the first time he'd laughed in days.

Mirabella threw her head back and giggled uninhibitedly. "I wish I'd been old enough to remember that."

"I wish I didn't lose you so soon," Scobert said, growing somber. "I'm so happy to have you back in my life. You know you can talk to me, right? If you need help with anything at all; if something is bothering you, you can come to me."

"I know," Mirabella said as she passed the flask back to Scobert.

Taking another sip, he silently wished he were a better father—the kind of father who knew how to talk to his daughter. Instead, he sat there without saying another word, even though deep inside he sensed Mirabella had something on her mind. At that moment, he would have given his right thumb for a manual on sensible parenthood. He was quite certain getting drunk while avoiding meaningful conversation would not be in there.

"Dad?"

"Yes?"

"How are things with Mom?"

Scobert blew out an uneasy breath, having no real desire to discuss his love life with his daughter. "Relationships are complicated. I care for your mother a lot, but I would be lying if I told you things haven't changed. We're not the same couple we used to be, but we try every day to get to know each other again, to treasure each other like we used to."

The setting sun cast an auburn shade over their shared space and Mirabella was an angel sitting next to him in the fading light. When she knitted her brows and wiped a tear from her eye, Scobert swore he heard his own heart break in two. Out of sheer instinct, he took his daughter in his arms, stroking her gently as her sobs flowed more freely. Completely out of his element, all he could think of was taking whatever pain she was suffering and make it his own.

When her tears subsided, Mirabella straightened and looked Scobert in the eye, a trace of her usual fierceness reclaimed. "If I ever disappoint you, just remember I love you."

Scobert found it impossible to envision a scenario wherein his daughter would be a disappointment. "Let's make two things absolutely clear, young lady. One: you will *never* disappoint me, two: I love you more than you'll ever know."

Mirabella rested her head on his shoulder. As twilight enveloped father and daughter and another tumultuous day neared its end, a thought arose. Perhaps he had it in him to be a good father, after all.

※

Fall Valley had been Clover and Finn's special place. A magical spot in the faerie realm, every morning when the sun rose, the colors in the valley changed from summer greens to radiant fall hues in the blink of an eye. From the leaves in the trees to the grass on the ground, every surface transformed.

They'd had their first date there. It was where Finn first told Clover he loved her. Ever since she'd found out Finn was with the Unseelies, Clover had been in a sort of limbo, unable to move forward and incapable of accomplishing anything in the present. It wasn't just the fact that she'd lost her boyfriend that plagued her, it was the heart-wrenching doubt that perhaps she never really knew him at all.

Despite all her misgivings, a part of her still had faith. Surely, she hadn't been wrong to trust him. To remind herself of what she'd seen in him—the reasons she'd fallen in love with him—she decided to go to the one place that to her, was all about Finn.

The rising sun blanketed the field in warmth and light, magical in its ability to prompt the changing of seasons. As verdant plains transformed to vibrant oranges, pinks, and reds, Clover traipsed down the valley with a trace of hope in her heart. If the rising and setting of the sun could evoke such a dramatic change in any one place or time, then perhaps the new day might also evoke a change in Finn's heart.

She sat on the coral grass and lifted her face to the sun, willing Finn to reach out to her, to explain himself, or at the very least, to say goodbye. The harder she tried to feel closer to him, the farther away he seemed. Don't let go, Clover pleaded in her mind. Whether her plea was to Finn or to herself, she wasn't certain. Either way, holding on was all they had left.

❦

Clover made her way back to Anna's and was surprised to find Button and Mirabella waiting for her at the door. She didn't expect to see them so early in the morning.

"What's going on?" Clover asked.

"We're on a mission," Button whispered, all cloak and dagger. "Destination: Brooklyn." She motioned for both girls to follow her into a nearby thicket of trees.

Clover obliged, but suspected Button may have lost her mind. When they were far enough away from Anna's door, she asked, "Are you crazy? We can't go to Earth right now."

"Button found an old relative," Mirabella explained. "Like literally, she's in her nineties. She thought all her family had died, but we did some digging and found out her second cousin on her father's side, Constance, is alive and living in Brighton Beach."

"That's awesome news," Clover gushed and meant it, but although she knew how important this was to Button, she couldn't get on board with their plan. "It's just too dangerous right now. I think we should wait."

"Willie has agreed to help us," Button replied, wide-eyed and giddy.

Willie was one of the realm's resident taxi drivers, who had the magical ability to teleport to and from all bridges and tunnels anywhere in the world in the blink of an eye. Clover worried at her lower lip and thought things through. Having Willie sure would help.

"There's an abandoned bridge not too far from the portal. We can be in Brooklyn in less than five minutes. What possible harm could come to us in that time? We'll be back before anybody even realizes we left. C'mon, Clover. I need this."

Though her heart went out to Button, her gut tightened into a ball. "I just don't know—"

"Since you and Mirabella are half-Fae, you can safely get me and Andie back through the portal."

When Mirabella nodded encouragingly, Clover felt ganged up on. "Clearly you two have already worked out the logistics—without consulting me. I see you've included Andie, too."

Button rolled her eyes and sighed dramatically. "As if she'd let us leave without her."

"Plus, we need you guys. Button hasn't been in Brooklyn in ages, and I've never been in a big city. We'd be totally lost," Mirabella entreated.

"We'd have to be really quick about it," Clover said, her resolve crumbling. "No lengthy reminiscences while poring over old albums. In and out."

"Yes, yes, of course," Button exclaimed, practically bouncing from excitement.

"All right," Clover said, completely caving in. "I'll wake Andie up and feed Anna a story about where we'll be all morning. Let's meet by the Enchanted Pond in an hour."

Three-quarters of an hour later, Clover and Andie were making their way through the wooded path that led to Market Square, a short trek away from the Enchanted Pond.

"Hurry," Clover said. "I want to get this over with."

"I'm surprised you even agreed," Andie said, still slow-moving and groggy from sleep. "I mean, I'm all for an adventure, but even *I'm* a little iffy about this ill-conceived plan. Shouldn't we at least tell someone where we're going? Just in case?"

"Like who, Garrett?" Clover blurted out, quickly regretting it. Though she'd never meant it to, it made her sound petty and accusatory. Just because she'd lost Finn, it didn't mean everybody else had to be miserable, too.

Andie's face fell. "I haven't seen him in days. He hasn't been taking the whole Finn thing well."

By *Finn thing*, Andie meant the horrible betrayal that had almost led Garrett to rip his dearest friend to shreds. "I'm sorry," Clover said. "I didn't mean to—I just want to be part of something good, you know? This thing for Button, I think we all need this right now."

"I hear you," Andie said. "We could all use a little lift."

The path in the woods forked to the right onto Market Square. Early in the morning, the market was humming with activity—bakeries hawking their first batch of goodies, local florists unloading carts of fresh flowers, and pubs serving up breakfast by the trays-full. If they didn't have somewhere to be, Clover would have loved spending a leisurely morning sampling pastries and window-shopping.

Andie tugged at her shirt and gestured to the right. She hadn't even noticed Kean walking toward them holding a brown paper bag, a big smile on his face.

"Hey," Clover said. "What are you doing here so early?"

Kean held up a steaming brown bag that smelled mouth-watering. "I have a serious pasty problem. I like to get my stash first thing."

"What's a pasty?" Andie asked.

"A handheld meat pie," Kean explained. He opened up the bag. "Please, help yourselves. It'll change your lives."

Without hesitation, Andie reached into the bag, pulled out a hot pasty and took a big bite. "Ohmmgod," she said, her mouth bursting, "yougadda habwan, Clober."

She couldn't help but laugh as she picked a pasty and tried it. It was absolutely delicious. "Mmm," was all she could say.

Kean beamed, looking as relaxed as Clover had ever seen him. "Take the whole bag," he said as he patted his exceptionally flat belly. "I should really watch what I eat."

Andie grabbed the paper bag. "Yeah, you really should. Let me take these off your hands."

Clover stifled her laughter. "We really should get going."

"Where are you off to?" Kean asked.

"We're meeting the girls—for breakfast."

"Oh," Kean said. "Well, I hope I didn't ruin your appetites. I'll let you go, then. Take care of yourself," he said, looking only at Clover.

Clover nodded, and they said their goodbyes. When they were out of earshot, Andie grabbed her by the shoulders. "You should have told Kean where we were going."

"No. He wouldn't have let us go."

Andie huffed. "In case you haven't noticed, that faerie boy is totally into you. He would have let you do anything you wanted; not a bad guy to have around."

Clover's eyes widened.

"I'm not saying as a replacement to Finn, but don't close yourself off to possibilities. There's nothing wrong with making friends. He's not exactly hard on the eyes either, and he's a total gentleman. You're eighteen. Be eighteen."

"Fine," Clover conceded, "but right now, we're running late. Let's get to the pond. I can *be eighteen* some other time."

Andie mused that the most exciting part of using the portal the first time was what had happened right before it—kissing Garrett. Her second passage through the portal in the Enchanted Pond was not quite as exhilarating. One moment they were all jumping into the fake pond, and in the next instant they were emerging from the old well on Station Island.

Willie, the taxi driver, met them at the island and happily levitated them over the lake two at a clip, fancying himself quite the ladies' man. Clover had attempted to levitate on her own but gave up on the pursuit after a few botched tries. While she would have loved to see her friend fly, it seemed levitating was not a skill Clover had yet mastered. After a short trek, they found their ride on an old, abandoned bridge and Andie couldn't wait to get on the magical cab again. She'd been in her fair share of taxis, but Willie's was out-of-this-world spectacular. Mirabella's eyes nearly popped out of their sockets admiring its richly upholstered interiors and fully stocked bar, while Button shrieked with delight as the magical mahogany table at its center started doling out croissants and crumpets. For a few precious moments, they were just girlfriends out on the town being silly and Andie didn't want it to end, but soon enough they'd arrived at their destination.

Button's cousin lived in an old detached house on a quiet block. A bunch of retro-looking folding lawn chairs littered the semi-dilapidated front porch, looking like nobody'd used them in ages. The day's mail was inserted through a gaping hole in the screen door and a soft jazz melody drifted from inside. As Button gathered the nerve to ring the doorbell, Andie, Clover, and Mirabella stood behind her, ready to offer up any kind of support for what was sure to be an emotional reunion. When she finally rang the bell, they all held their breaths in anticipation.

Nothing.

"Maybe she didn't hear it," Andie offered. "She *is* in her nineties and the radio is on."

"You're right," Button agreed. She knocked three times, but

when still nobody answered, she tried the door and it creaked open. "Should we go in?"

"Might as well," said Mirabella. Andie and Clover both nodded in agreement. This was Button's party; they were just in it for the ride.

Button stepped in tentatively. "Hello. Anybody home?"

The inside of Constance's house was nowhere near as shabby as the front porch. It was one of those well-preserved old-fashioned homes that made you feel like you were walking into a staged exhibit at a museum—old record player, wooden rocking chair, richly upholstered chairs, and thick curtains held up together with tasseled golden rope. The smell of mothballs was almost as pervading as the scent of furniture polish.

"Hello?" Button called again as they all sort of stood around by the foyer.

A sound like a kitchen door swinging open alerted them of somebody's presence, and they all turned their heads toward the sound. Expecting to see an elderly woman emerge, Andie was flabbergasted at the sight that greeted them instead. A blond man—an exceptionally handsome blond man—in a three-piece-suit was standing there smiling at them. If she'd been surprised to see that, then what happened next totally knocked her socks off. Without hesitation, Clover extended her right arm like Spidey casting a web and a torrent of water gushed forth from her fingertips, knocking the guy off his feet.

"What the hell?" Andie screamed.

The guy was soaked to the bone but was soon back on his feet, looking pretty incensed. "I see my wife's powers have grown," he said.

In response, a glass candelabra flew from a nearby table and struck him hard on the head, making Andie's jaw drop. She'd known Clover had powers but seeing her in action was without a doubt impressive.

"Enough!" the man commanded.

"Where's Finn?" Clover asked.

"Don't concern yourself with my son," the man replied.

"What do you want, Alistair?" Clover screamed.

"You," he said, then disappeared.

A moment later, he was standing behind Clover with a sharp knife pointed at her throat.

"Let her go!" yelled Mirabella.

Alistair sneered. "Drop the charade, Mirabella. It's time for your true alliances to be known. Tell them how you helped lure them here, lied to them, pretended to be their friend, so I could get Clover back."

A fly could've happily flown right into Andie's gaping mouth and taken residence there. The growing list of surprising twists and turns had left her momentarily catatonic it seemed.

"Is that true?" Clover asked Mirabella, hurt and anger in her eyes.

Tears welled up in Mirabella's eyes, but she didn't say a word. Instead, she focused her attention on the tall coat rack behind Alistair. Suddenly the wrought-iron piece of furniture shook itself, like a person might from the cold. The scarves and jackets hanging on it dropped to the floor. In the next fluid motion, like a fencer delivering a killing blow, it pierced one of its arms into Alistair's side. Then it took its other arm, skewered him from the left, and pulled both arms out at the same time.

Alistair yelled in pain and dropped to the ground, two wounds on either side of him gushing blood.

"Run!" Mirabella pleaded with Clover. "I can take your place. Just go, please."

Even as he crouched over, attempting to heal himself, Alistair made a grab for Clover as she stepped away in the nick of time. "You stupid little whore. I'll make you pay for this!" he screamed. Andie wasn't sure whether his threat was directed to Clover or Mirabella.

The animated coat rack motioned like it was teeing off, then swung hard, hitting Alistair across the face with one of its many arms brought to life. With Alistair momentarily incapacitated, Mirabella approached Clover.

"I hope you'll someday find it in your heart to forgive me. Tell my father the woman he once loved is gone. He should let Therese go." Mirabella's eyes darted to Alistair, who was struggling to get up. "There's not much time. Go!"

Clover hesitated, but eventually nodded. She called to Andie, "Where's Button?"

Andie looked around for Button, but in all the excitement, she'd lost track of her.

"I'm out here," she heard her call out.

They ran out to the front porch toward the sound of Button's voice.

Of all the astonishing things Andie had seen that day, nothing could have prepared her for the sight that greeted her then. An old woman, wrinkled and gray, stood before them, wearing the same white tunic Button was wearing that morning. Once again, Andie's jaw dropped right to the floor.

"Button?" Clover asked, disbelieving.

The old lady nodded. "I got old."

14

In the days following their return to the realm, Clover had a lot of explaining to do. Their last-minute sojourn onto Earth hadn't exactly gone as planned. Not only did they discover Mirabella's betrayal and lose her to Alistair, but they'd also returned with a much-aged Button. She wasn't sure which was worse—Button's heartbreaking reunion with Sinann or Scobert's utter anguish over the news about Mirabella. If she had to choose, her heart bled doubly for Scobert. Not only did he lose Mirabella again, but his wife, too. When she'd learned that Alistair had Mirabella, Therese had quickly dropped the act and admitted her treachery, spouting praise and adulation for Alistair like some kind of crazed cult member. Queen Helena quickly saw her to the dungeons, and Scobert had been a wreck ever since.

Even Momma Ruth was quick to point out how foolish their secret excursion had been. "I love you, sweetie," she said as she poured them tea in Anna's living room, "but what were you thinking?"

Clover's shoulders slumped. "There was no way of knowing everything would go horribly wrong."

Andie grabbed a biscuit from the serving tray and nibbled at it. "I had a bad feeling from the start."

"Gee, thanks," Clover shot back.

Anna, ever the diplomat, chimed in. "There's no use pointing fingers now." Then, she sighed heavily. "Such a shame, though. Any faerie could have told you that returning Button to Earth after all these years would undoubtedly trigger a hastened aging process. She is, after all, a human."

"If only we'd told Kean like I suggested," Andie offered up.

"I swear to God, Andie—" Clover started.

"Sorry. Just saying." Andie held her hands up in mock surrender.

Burying her face in her hands, Clover let out a frustrated sigh. "You're right, though. This was all my fault. We shouldn't have left."

"Like I said," Anna chimed in, "assigning blame doesn't do us any good right now. This was nobody's fault."

Clover had to admire Anna's grit and resilience. Despite having to deal with the extant possibility she'd lost her son to the Unseelie King, she still managed to hold her chin up and keep it together, a true class act.

"I still can't believe Mirabella was in cahoots with Alistair," Momma Ruth mused, shaking her head. "She seemed like such a sweet girl."

"I hardly think the girl had a choice," Anna said. "She and her mother disappeared so many years ago. It's clear now that Alistair was the culprit, which means he'd had all this time to get his hooks in them. I wouldn't be surprised if they'd been completely brainwashed. I just hope they didn't gather too much intelligence while they were spying for him."

Close to tears, Clover gave herself a little shake, attempting to regain some composure. She still couldn't believe Mirabella had lied to them. Every time she thought about it, a lump formed in her throat and her hurt rippled to the surface.

As if reading her thoughts, Andie reached for her hand and said, "I know. I still can't believe it, either. Floors me every time. I really liked her, too. You couldn't have predicted she'd do that."

"She did help us escape," Clover said.

"That's true," Andie conceded. "Buyer's remorse. She probably realized too late she'd sided with the wrong faerie."

"In the end, she sacrificed herself for us."

"Don't you do that," Andie said, chastising. "You are not going to feel guilty about Mirabella. You did what you had to do to survive."

Despite her oftentimes happy-go-lucky attitude, Andie possessed a practical, no-nonsense world view which never failed to set Clover to rights. She inwardly appreciated the random series of unfortunate events that brought Andie to the faerie realm. She wasn't sure how she'd cope without her.

"You're right," Clover conceded.

Momma Ruth gently cupped Clover's cheek with her palm. "No matter how many road bumps we encounter and no matter how far we veer from the path, all we can do is keep on going."

Clover nodded, silently vowing to dust herself off and, like Momma Ruth said, to keep on going. What choice did she have?

"It's been tough going for all of us," Anna said. "Tomorrow, the Seelie Court celebrates *Lughnasadh*, the Harvest Festival. I believe we could all welcome a little distraction. I've been enlisted to prepare a dish for the evening's festivities. Anybody care to help me roast a calf on an open spit?"

"I'm in," they all replied in unison.

In the many lifetimes Helena had known Scobert, she'd seen every side of him—from the downright silly to the unequivocally frightening—but in all those years, she hadn't seen him quite so broken. The first time he'd lost his family, he'd gone on an angry rampage for nearly two decades, ostracizing everyone, including Helena. When his family returned, a long-ago extinguished light had turned on inside him, and much as it pained Helena to let go of what they'd shared, she couldn't deny him a chance at happiness.

Now that he'd lost them again, this time to betrayal, the wounds inflicted seemed too deep to heal.

Alone with him in her private quarters, Helena sought to find soothing words, but failed. She reverted instead to the one topic they'd always found common ground on—war.

"*Lughnasadh* befalls us and while the Court celebrates, our forces should be on high-alert. I wouldn't put it past Alistair to try something," Helena said, pacing the room.

Scobert was sprawled in one of Helena's ancient armchairs. He exhaled, his jaw set. "I can almost guarantee he has something up his sleeve. He attempted to close the portals on Midsummer's Eve, one of the great festivals of the *Daoine Sidhe*—an auspicious day, where magic is at its strongest and the walls that divide the worlds at their weakest. Harvest Festival is perhaps not quite as magical as Midsummer's, but propitious, nonetheless. A perfect opportunity to complete the spell he'd botched when he failed to offer up Clover's life to close the portals forever."

"We'll have Clover guarded and increase the fortifications on all the portals to the realm," Helena said.

"He hardly needs Clover now, does he?"

Helena's brow furrowed. "Of course, he does. He needs a half-blood to complete the spell."

"Don't you see?" Scobert almost shouted. "He has Mirabella. My daughter is half-Fae."

As realization hit Helena, she instinctively found the closest chair and slumped down, ashen.

Scobert got up and paced the room. "It was his plan from the start—the reason he'd snatched my family. He'd groomed Mirabella to be his back-up and my wife a weapon used against me!"

"We won't let him succeed," Helena vowed.

A bevy of conflicting emotions seemed to plague Scobert at once. The expression on his face vacillated from anger to remorse and back to fury within seconds. The more he paced the room, the more emotions seemed to find their way to the surface. Finally, he stopped in front of Helena and knelt before her, his head resting on her knees.

"Helena, I hope someday you'll forgive me for hurting you," he said, his voice rough. Then he raised his head to look up at her. "However many lifetimes it may take, I will make it my mission to regain your trust. I recognize the value you place on allegiance and honor—notions that I similarly take to heart. But know this: I *will* kill Alistair McCabe and if Finn gets in my way, I will do what needs to be done."

※

Andie tossed and turned in Anna's guest bedroom, her anxiety getting the best of her. Ever since Finn and Garrett had shown up at her doorstep on that fateful, yet otherwise ordinary morning, her life had become some sort of prolonged hallucination. Like Alice down the proverbial rabbit hole, she wondered if she'd perhaps descended too far and whether she'd still be able to find her way out. The longer she stayed in the realm, the farther the real world seemed, and as much as she enjoyed being there with Clover, she had no intention of becoming another Button, unaged and unchanged forever—that is until she returned to Earth and became an instant senior citizen.

At some point, she'd have to go back home and hopefully, Clover would return with her. The thought of life in New York without with her best friend was just too stressful to fathom. She'd probably have to move apartments, she decided. The ghosts of four dead faeries didn't exactly bode well for a homey living environment. As she tried to foresee the possible twists and turns her life was about to take, a soft breeze wafted in through an open window. She turned to her side, then pulled the covers up to her chin. Next thing she knew, she was enveloped in a warm embrace. *Garrett.*

"God, you're sneaky," Andie teased, feeling Garrett's cool breath on the back of her neck; not yet daring to turn and face him.

Garrett muffled a laugh. "You still don't fully appreciate the whole *pooka* thing, do you?"

What Andie fully appreciated was the fact that letting go of Garrett would be one of the toughest parts about leaving the faerie realm. She nestled against him, feeling safe in his arms. "I haven't seen you in a while," she whispered into the darkness.

A tender kiss landed on her nape. "You still haven't," Garrett breathed.

For what seemed like a very long time, they stayed like that—Garrett with his arms around her and Andie treasuring the priceless moment of just being, not wanting to say a word lest the spell be broken.

Finally, Garrett disturbed their tenuous calm. "I heard what happened in Brooklyn. I'm really sorry I wasn't there to rip his freakin' head off."

Andie breathed a long sigh. "Everything is so messed up."

"That it is," Garrett agreed.

Andie reached for Garrett's hand, interlocking her fingers with his. "What's going to happen now?" she asked, sounding like a frightened child to her own ears.

"I don't know," Garrett admitted, and for the first time since she'd known him, Andie sensed a fissuring in his usual unshakeable façade.

"Will you stay?" Andie asked, then held her breath, fearing his answer.

"Not going anywhere, doll face," Garrett said as he nuzzled in closer. "Not tonight."

Andie closed her eyes and relaxed against him, knowing full well he'd probably be gone by morning.

⁂

Anna had always enjoyed the festivals of the *Daoine Sidhe,* the faerie-folk's time-honored celebrations meant to mark the passing of the seasons. Whether in peace time or at the grips of war, Queen

Helena and her Court had always upheld the realm's traditions. This year, no matter how hard she tried to plaster a smile on her face and carry on as usual, she couldn't quite get into the spirit of things; recent events making it virtually impossible. With Finn gone and Scobert in a state, every passing hour seemed to lead closer to disaster, as if they were all just bracing for yet another catastrophic train wreck.

Even when the usually comforting activity of prepping for an outdoor roast failed to lift Anna's spirits, she donned the most believable happy face she could muster for the sake of her guests.

Mary was the first to arrive with a plate of pigeon pies. Anna laid the plate on a nearby table and gave her sister a tight hug. They regarded each other with the same concerned looks—they were both, after all, grieving for their sons.

"Is Scobert coming?" Anna asked.

Mary shook her head. "He'll need some time."

"Of course," Anna said, understanding completely. Losing his family the first time had almost damaged Scobert irreparably. She couldn't even imagine how hard he was taking this second blow.

A group of Anna's neighbors arrived bearing crates of food, booze, and lawn chairs. It was tradition—every time Anna roasted meat on a spit, the whole block came to celebrate. She spotted Clover and Meara arrive with the crowd and waved them over.

They both had the same manufactured looks on their faces—shallow smiles that never quite reached their eyes. Anna almost laughed out loud. Her contrived block party was fast resembling a funeral rather than a feast.

Noticing Button's absence, Anna shot Clover a quick inquiring look.

Clover cast her gaze downwards before meeting Anna's eyes. "She didn't feel like coming, but she sends her love."

Her heart breaking for the poor girl, Anna simply nodded. "Come, the gang's in the kitchen helping Ruth bake a cake."

The mention of cake seemed to genuinely perk everybody up a tad. Anna rubbed her hands together and stood a little taller. No matter the present circumstances, she was going to try her darndest to enjoy the Harvest Festival and she'd be damned if she didn't get everybody else to give it their best shot.

※

Button certainly didn't feel like partying. Already self-conscious as a seventeen-year-old, morphing into a geriatric in the blink of an eye didn't exactly help boost her self-esteem, especially since her girlfriend was drop-dead gorgeous—in Clover's words, *a supermodel*—and now she looked old enough to be her grandmother. *No sirree.* She was fine on her own. Begging off of all Harvest Festival invites, she decided to take a long walk in the land where she grew up, the place she called home—the Land Beneath the Waves—the Otherworld.

As she traversed the extraordinarily beautiful walkways that miraculously meandered lazily through interconnected ponds, lakes, oceans, and rivers, she sighed contently. What business did she have inserting herself back in Brooklyn when she'd had a home all this time? When they'd returned beneath the waves that night and Sinann had seen her for the first time, she'd cried. Button had averted her gaze and shrunk from her touch, not even wanting to be in her presence, utterly mortified. Her stunning, statuesque girlfriend had gently cupped Button's withered face in her delicate hands and whispered, "To me, you are eternally beautiful."

The memory brought tears to her eyes and every step she took brought back more remembrances of her time in this other realm—the loving acceptance from Lir and Sinann's whole clan, the friendships she'd forged, the extraordinary life she'd gotten to live. If she had wanted to return to Earth, all she needed to do was ask. In all those years, she never had. She wondered at whatever possessed her to try such a stunt without expecting consequences. Blood rushed to her face as she recalled Mirabella's continuous prodding. She had been the one to plant the seed about attempting to find living relatives. Whatever her reasons may have been for deceiving them, Button doubted she had it in her heart to forgive her.

Walking past the city limits, Button made it to one of the largest ocean formations in the Otherworld, the one that connected to the Atlantic Ocean. A light mist enveloped the beach, the sea surging beyond it, prompting the most remarkable of Button's memories. This was where she'd first crossed over from her world to Sinann's: The Ninth Wave, one of the rarest portals into the Otherworld, existing only when the sea was ferocious, and the swells were majestic; its existence known only to the merrow-folk.

A lifetime ago, hand in hand with a beautiful, mysterious merrow, she had swum out to sea, meeting oncoming waves head-on, half elated, half-terrified. Each new wave was bigger than its predecessor, seemingly saturating her whole being. When she felt she couldn't go any further, Sinann's voice was in her head. *The Ninth Wave will carry us to a new world. We're almost there.* She swam on, the Ninth Wave looming like a tsunami in the distance. When finally the surge was upon them, they dove and were lost to that world. They'd emerged on the other side, on a different sea.

Countless years after that life-altering day, Button gazed out to sea, her eyes tracked on the burgeoning crest in the distance, bigger than any wave ought to be, the Ninth Wave. She gingerly jogged along the rocky sea wall, passing each amplifying wave, reliving the journey those many years ago that had changed her life forevermore. Now completely soaked from the spray of the sea and the crashing waves, Button felt the same heart-pounding excitement she'd felt that day. Standing on edge of the jetty, she closed her eyes as the Ninth Wave swelled and crashed upon the angry sea, drenching her from head to toe, nearly carrying her out to the water.

With a smile on her lips, she opened her eyes and was greeted by a most surprising sight. Three heads bobbed in the water, rocking with the ocean's ebb and flow. Button crouched low and watched intently as the tides carried the mysterious travelers to shore, her curiosity peaking. She squinted as their silhouettes reached the shore, two of them clearly recognizable despite their soaked and bedraggled appearance. The third was someone she'd never seen before but whose identity she easily guessed at. A petite woman with rich mahogany skin. She would have bet her bottom dollar that if the lady turned around, she'd be greeted by blood-red eyes. Even though her advanced age had affected her eyesight, she was pretty darn sure. Alistair, Mirabella, and Iekika had just entered the Otherworld.

※

Alistair watched a contingent of Unseelie soldiers swim to shore while Iekika prepped for the sacrifice like a suburban housewife would for a tea party, with pep and precision. Since *Lughnasadh* wasn't quite as magical as the summer solstice, the sorceress needed to make a few adjustments to amplify the magical field. After laying a blanket on the beach, she dragged Mirabella and unceremoniously plopped her down, and with a few flicks of her wrist, performed a binding spell. When the girl was safely contained within its four imaginary walls, Iekika drew an inverted triangle on the sand around the blanket, stepping aside every now and then to admire her handiwork. She clapped her hands together eagerly.

Of all the women Alistair had been involved with, Iekika was fast becoming the most useful, yet the most bizarre. Her allegiance to him was only bested by her own uncanny abilities to inflict harm on others.

"How much longer?" Alistair asked.

"Almost," Iekika replied while she drew another line on the sand, this one inside the triangle, parallel to the bottom.

Mirabella sat on the blanket, still as a statue, her fierce, emerald eyes shooting daggers at Alistair.

"Spare me the attitude, mutt. You knew this was coming," Alistair mocked.

She held her chin up. "I'm keeping my end of the bargain. You better keep yours."

Alistair laughed, marveling at the girl's audacity to make demands while facing her impending death. "And if I don't?"

Mirabella charged at Alistair but was held back by magical restraints. "You promised me you'd keep my mother alive!"

"Relax, child. Your mother is no good to me dead. If I ever break her free from Helena's dungeons, she will live."

The Unseelie soldiers made their way to shore, all heavily armed and foul tempered.

"Iekika, I don't have all day," Alistair admonished. "Are we ready?"

The sorceress beamed at him, and the effect, quite frankly, was frightening. "We are ready. Do you recall the spell?"

Alistair nodded. Every word of that spell had been faithfully etched into his brain, waiting for this moment. He'd failed to offer Clover up as sacrifice at Midsummer; there was no way he was making the same mistake again. A half-Fae bride would die by his hands tonight. Knowing that all the portals to Faerie would be monitored by Helena's men, he chose the most obscure portal in the realm, one very few knew of: The Ninth Wave, a rare phenomenon and closely guarded secret by the merrow-folk. He had his love-affair with Meara to thank for that bit of useful inside information. Especially in matters of the heart, he was nothing if not resourceful.

He walked over to Mirabella and pulled her up. "Are you ready for marriage and death?"

"Death would be a welcome reprieve after being married to you," Mirabella hissed.

Alistair traced a finger from her temple to her collar bone, admiring her hutzpah. "You *are* a beautiful woman." He leaned in until their lips were barely touching. "Soon to be a beautiful corpse."

He turned to Iekika. "Perform the ceremony. Quickly."

The sorceress raised both hands upright like she was declaring a touchdown. The sky turned dark, and the sea raged. Alistair smiled to himself.

※

Usually always at Queen Helena's side, Liz opted to forego *Lughnasadh* festivities for the first time in centuries. She stayed behind in the queen's private quarters, under the pretense of tidying up. Helena, ever pragmatic, had allowed her the charade, fully understanding her predicament. Although her physical wounds had mostly healed, she still carried emotional traumas that, while invisible on the surface, were nonetheless devastating. A tightly strung ball of anger and hate, when she closed her own eyes at night, Iekika's crimson unfeeling ones greeted her in the dark, the image seemingly burned into her retinas. She longed for the time when she didn't jump at the most innocuous of sounds or whimper like a child at the most gruesome of nightmares. The thought that even her mind wasn't safe from Iekika's sinister intrusions was enough to give any girl serious trust issues. Mostly, she longed to be with Finn. The last time she'd felt any degree of safety was in his arms.

When she'd found out Finn had sided with the Unseelies, she hadn't believed it then—and still couldn't. Knowing somebody for as long as she'd known Finn, it gave one an up-close look into a person's soul. He was the most honorable man Liz had ever known, and it would take a hell of a lot more than hearsay to convince her of his betrayal. Blood be damned. The Finn she knew would never turn his back on the Seelie Court.

Liz sighed, hoping against hope that her faith in him was not misplaced.

A strange sound coming from the queen's bedroom made her jump. Silently she berated herself for being such a nervous wreck. When she got her heart to stop hammering in her chest, she listened intently for the sound, trying to find its source. The queen's quarters was home to countless curios, priceless and oftentimes magical objects that were known on occasion to buzz, chime, or even speak.

Plop. Plop. Plop.

It was the sound of amplified waterdrops. Her curiosity getting the better of her, Liz searched the queen's bedroom frantically, pushing rubies, ornate boxes, and other unidentifiable knick-knacks aside to locate the source of the strange sound.

Then she saw it. An ancient barnacle-ridden conch shell—one of the oldest treasures in Queen Helena's cove. It had been a gift from the God of the Sea, with a promise that if Helena ever needed help from the Otherworld, all she need do was pick up the conch and call. Helena, in turn, had extended the same offer of assistance. In all the years it'd gathered dust among the queen's riches, it had never once moved or made a sound. Until now.

※

"You are wed," proclaimed the red-eyed witch with a genial smile on her face. Mirabella had to look away. Everything about the woman gave her the creeps. Now, she was face to face with Alistair —the evil leprechaun who'd abducted her when she was a baby, groomed her for sacrifice, married her, and was now about to kill her. She almost vomited in her mouth just looking at him. Disgusted though she was, she wasn't backing off. She'd barely had a life, with no one for company except her brainwashed mother, basically just waiting for something—*anything*—to happen. Then she'd met her father, Clover, Button, and so many other wonderful people. She'd be damned if she was going to let anybody take their lives, even if it meant sacrificing hers.

"Let's get this over with," she said, willing herself to look Alistair in the eye.

"Very well," Alistair said, all smug and prissy-like. He pulled a short sword from a sheath that hung by his side. It looked like some kind of ceremonial knife with an exceptionally sharp tip. He took in a breath to speak. "On this August eve, a spell I weave to summon forces dark and light, that earthly plights and faerie nights need never be as one tonight. A virgin bride, two worlds collide. A mongrel sacrifice. Of unions cursed, such was foretold, a new day to behold. With tainted blood and might of lore, *Daoine Sidhe's* door shall be no more…"

Mirabella braced herself. She wasn't about to die with her eyes squeezed shut and her head bowed low. Squaring her shoulders, she returned Alistair's gaze.

A gilded arrow zipped through the air, almost nipping Mirabella's ear, piercing straight through Alistair's wrist. The sword dropped, and Alistair turned in the shooter's direction.

Mirabella swung around to see an imposing man holding a golden bow and arrow, his torso covered in the most exquisite looking tattoos, his eyes as deep as the sea.

Alistair pulled the arrow from his wrist with a wince. "Lir, this is not your fight. Stay out of it."

"When a young girl is harmed in my kingdom, the fight is laid at my door. When that same girl happens to be a good friend of someone I love dearly, then I bring the fight to you." Lir nocked another arrow and aimed it at Alistair, this time, at his heart. Mirabella spied Button and Sinann standing behind Lir, along with a cavalry of the sea god's forces, mounted on animals that looked to be half steed, half seahorse.

Iekika raised a hand in Lir's direction, clearly conjuring a spell. Sinann wasn't having it. With a lazy flick of her finger, a powerful jolt of energy propelled Iekika backwards into the foamy waves. A whispered incantation from Sinann's lips soon bound the witch's hands and feet with unseen restraints. Mirabella tried not to laugh as Iekika tumbled around in the surf like an irate beach ball.

"Don't make the mistake of underestimating my kind," Sinann said to Alistair. "You've been warned."

Lir's cavalry aimed their arrows at Alistair and the Unseelies.

"If it's a battle you want, *sea god,* so be it. My troops are prepared to fight."

Mirabella slowly moved away, not wanting to be caught in the middle of an impending skirmish. When the restraints cast by Iekika prevented further movement, a quick pleading look sent in Sinann's direction soon found her freed from her magical fetters.

"Alistair!" boomed a voice from a distance. Mirabella turned, recognizing it instantly.

Scobert barreled toward them, Queen Helena at his side, and a large contingent of Seelie soldiers at their heels. Mirabella wasn't quite certain which was more frightening—the look of utter bloodlust on Scobert's face or the same look mirrored on Queen Helena's. She shivered despite herself.

Alistair's expression bordered somewhere between annoyance and fear. Despite being now outnumbered, he stood his ground.

When Scobert screamed, "Charge!" Lir's and the queen's army attacked, and it was as if the beach exploded on itself. Mirabella cowered in the sand, trying to crawl to safety. Arrows swooshed by in fast succession, the smell of magic permeated, and the clash of swords and the ring of gunfire filled the air.

When she was safely out of reach, Mirabella searched the melee for Button. Despite her acts of betrayal, Button had shown up for her. She owed her friend an apology. Amidst the chaos, she spotted Button crouching by a tree in the distance. As she made her way toward her, she saw something that made her heart drop. As Scobert battled Alistair, from a short distance away, an Unseelie soldier with a blue mohawk pulled out a gun and aimed it at her father. As the Unseelie punk adjusted his sights, out of sheer instinct, Mirabella ran.

The next thing she knew, she was leaping toward Scobert, then she was down on the sand. When her hand went to her rib cage, it came back covered in blood. The world became a blur as coldness gripped her, her breath coming out in frantic spurts. She saw her father's face contorted in fear, perhaps anger.

Then she heard Alistair's voice. "With tainted blood and might of lore, *Daoine Sidhe's* door shall be no more! And what once was shall never be. All of this, I implore of thee!"

The spell. He completed his spell. Realization hit Mirabella like a cruel joke. As she gasped for a breath, a booming sound enveloped the realm, louder than anything she'd ever heard before. Another gunshot? She wondered, half delirious. Then, with an ironic clarity that perhaps came with impending death, she realized what it was: the sound of portals closing.

15

In an unmarked crypt in the most hidden depths of Faerie lay the remains of the greatest warrior known to have existed, the Great Berserker, once a god among the Fae, revered and feared across the realms. Laid to rest with his mythical Red Branch Knights, Cuchulainn was fabled to return when beseeched by a faerie warrior of his equal. Having determined the warrior's worth, he would once again lead the legendary knights of the Ulster Cycle into battle.

A romantic and noble tale though it was, Cuchulainn himself doubted it would ever come to pass—which would explain the demi-god's utter astonishment when millennia after being laid to rest, his warrior's heart once again beat strong against his chest and his Red Branch Knights finally rose from their long, deep slumber.

The months following Mirabella's death were the hardest in Clover's young life. Not only had she never lost a friend before, she was also ridden with guilt. "I can take your place," Mirabella had said when they'd escaped from Alistair in Brooklyn. She hadn't realized at the time how literal her statement had been. She'd been willing to offer herself up to spare Clover.

The battle in the Otherworld had occurred so suddenly that Clover and many others hadn't even been aware of it. While she sipped wine and ate pigeon pies at Anna's, her friend was being offered up as a sacrifice and a war was brewing. When the queen received the message from Lir, she'd wasted no time in mobilizing whomever she could for the strike. Even Meara had no idea her own family and her father's cavalry had mounted an attack on the Unseelies. Only when the realm was engulfed in a deafening roar did they get their first clue of the magnitude of what had transpired.

Later, Button had recounted everything to her—how she'd spotted Alistair, Iekika, and Mirabella crossing the Ninth Wave, the ensuing battle, and Mirabella's tragic death. She'd described how even as Scobert's deafening cry was drowned out by the roar of the portals, his utter anguish had been unmistakable. Soldiers from all sides had laid down their weapons out of respect. In the chaos that followed, the Unseelies collected their dead, went unseen, and made their exits. A handful of Seelie soldiers had sustained non-fatal injuries, including Kean.

Mirabella was laid to rest in the Seelie Court after a beautiful, yet somber service. Seemingly the entire realm had wept for the half-Fae girl who'd lived an unfinished and uncelebrated life spent mostly in the shadows. Those who had the privilege of knowing her, albeit briefly, suffered a more profound grief.

As an act of kindness, Helena had permitted Therese to attend the service, but the woman was so out of it, Clover doubted if she even realized what was happening. So thoroughly under Alistair's thumb, Therese was akin to a dummy who'd lost its puppeteer. Deprived of constant instruction and tutelage from her captor, Mirabella's mother seemed incapable of holding a coherent thought in her head. Clover's heart went out to her. Therese was as much a victim of Alistair's evildoing as Mirabella was.

Following the burial, everyone had been in a sort of daze—Momma Ruth, Nick, and Andie especially. All of them had basically followed Clover into another realm and now had no way to return to Earth. With Button's fate as a cautionary tale, all the humans in the faerie realm were on edge. Clover couldn't blame them. Even though she'd embraced her faerie side and found herself a home in this other world, she still couldn't say she fully belonged there. Giving up her true home was not something she'd been prepared to do.

On top of the growing anxiety over being stuck in Faerie forever, Clover still had lingering questions about Finn and his involvement with the Unseelies. Had he known of Alistair's plans to sacrifice Mirabella on *Lughnasadh*? It dawned on her that she didn't know which was worse—discovering that Finn had known about it or that he'd done absolutely nothing to prevent it.

Days had turned into weeks and weeks into months, everyone seemingly existing in their own uncertain limbos. Queen Helena had assembled a council of knowledgeable faeries, witches, mages, and warlocks to puzzle through the portal situation affecting the entire realm. Not only were humans prevented passage back to Earth, but a sizeable group of Fae were now also trapped on the other side, separated indefinitely from their homes and families. With tales of betrayal being whispered about and Mirabella's untimely death still fresh in every body's mind, the Seelie Court was thrust into very troubling times.

A more somber version though it was, life went on, all of them falling into their own new norms. Scobert spent most of his time in court with the queen, heavily involved in the pursuit of re-opening the portals and the war effort. He rarely visited Mary or Anna, and even when he did, he seemed a shell of his former self. Completely hardened and deadened, it was as if he'd permanently closed off his heart.

Button, although having adjusted somewhat to her new physique, didn't venture out as much to spend time with Clover and Andie. She mostly kept to the Otherworld, finding comfort and safety with Sinann. On the rare occasions when they did hang out, it seemed their old camaraderie was never quite rekindled. Clover felt responsible for what had happened to her and even though Button assured her nobody was to blame, she felt guilty, nonetheless.

Momma Ruth, ever the survivor, was taking everything in stride. Although the anxiety of never returning home plagued her, she didn't let it control her life. Her days were spent with Anna and Mary, concocting recipes in the kitchen or out exploring the faerie realm. It seemed the three ladies had learned to lean on each other for support, each of them going through their own personal upheavals, but striving with each new day to carry on.

Nick divided his time between his werewolf friends, training with Kean, and occasionally going out with Meara. Truth to be told, compared to the alternative—which had been prison—her father was living his best life.

Clover couldn't say the same for herself. Although she treasured every moment with her friends and family, Finn's alleged betrayal and unexplained disappearance had created an ever-deepening fracture in her troubled heart.

She sensed the same disquiet in Garrett, who was withdrawing into the woods more often and for longer periods of time. Even when he was with Andie and Clover, a faraway look would often cross his face. Clover feared that despite his pledge to Queen Helena and his obvious attachment to Andie, their days with the powerful pooka were numbered. Garrett was a true free spirit; his friendship with Finn seemingly his only anchor to the realm of courts, armies, and civilizations.

Kean, on the other hand, had become a new constant in Clover's life, and she'd be lying if she said she didn't enjoy his company. After the battle in the Otherworld, Kean's right arm was almost ripped from its socket. While he recuperated from multiple healing sessions, Anna had insisted on having him stay at her house. During that vulnerable time in both their lives, they'd formed a fragile connection that soon morphed into real friendship.

On one brisk, late fall afternoon, Clover and Kean enjoyed a leisurely walk near Anna's property. Autumn in Faerie was a sight to behold—the entire realm was blanketed in the crisp, vibrant colors that signaled the passing of another season, a harbinger of change; maybe even hope. She marveled at the beautiful sights and took in a breath of fresh, cool air. For the first time in what seemed like forever, she was actually feeling pretty good.

"Are you going to the queen's dinner?" Kean asked as he caught a falling maple leaf in the palm of his hand.

It was Helena's birthday, and after a long reprieve from any form of merry-making or celebration, she'd decided to host a small dinner party, a seemingly commonplace gesture that actually spoke volumes; an indication that the queen and perhaps the realm were ready to move on, despite their losses.

Clover shrugged. "I suppose so. Andie's looking forward to it. She's never been to the court."

Kean kept on walking, shooting a sideways glance at Clover. "Is she going with Garrett?"

Clover hadn't really considered it a *date* type of event, but now that she'd thought about it, realized she was being obtuse. "Yeah, I'm pretty sure."

Kean stopped at the top of a sloping mountain ridge and faced Clover, his unruly blond hair catching the sunlight in a way that made it almost sparkle. "Would you like to go with me?"

Clover opened her mouth to say something, then thought better of it. She had no idea what *to* say. As much as she'd enjoyed being with Kean, it wasn't like she wanted to date him. Or at least, she hadn't really considered it.

"Would a maple leaf do the trick?" Kean asked stone-faced as he extended a leaf in offering.

Not able to help herself, she burst out laughing. Kean always had a way of defusing potentially serious situations, and considering recent events, it was a most valuable talent.

He really looked at her then, his light blue eyes penetrating. "It's not like I'm asking you to walk the plank here," he said, then chuckled softly. "Would going out with me really be the most awful thing ever?"

Clover quickly looked away, feeling self-conscious. When her gaze nestled on the valley behind them, she realized with a start that she knew it well—Fall Valley. She couldn't believe she hadn't noticed before. Since the rest of the world had also changed colors, her special place now seemed a lot less magical. Her heart twitched in pain as she took in a breath and faced Kean.

"No," she said, poker-faced.

Kean shifted uncomfortably. "No?"

"No, it wouldn't be awful at all. Kean, I'd love to."

***

Helena held the magical *shillelagh* in her hand and allowed herself to dream. With her eyes closed and her hand wrapped tightly around the walking stick, once again she fantasized about leaving it all behind. A sound by the entrance to her private quarters broke her reverie.

Scobert cleared this throat. "Didn't mean to disturb you." He paused awkwardly. "May I?"

"Of course. Come in," Helena said as she motioned to the settee. She placed the walking stick in a corner, then took a seat.

Scobert sat beside her, looking uncomfortable in his ratty dinner jacket. Helena stifled a laugh; the man hated to dress up.

"What?" Scobert asked.

Helena evened out the lapels on his jacket and smiled. "Nothing. You look particularly refined tonight, that's all."

Scobert chuckled, his cheeks turning just a tad pink. "You always were an accomplished liar."

"Tools of the trade," Helena said with a resigned shrug.

When Scobert laughed heartily, she realized it was the first time she'd heard the sound in months. His eyes found the *shillelagh*. "Were you planning on going somewhere?"

She feigned shock. "And miss my dinner party? Not in a million years. In fact, I am told my guests are arriving as we speak. Shall we?" she said as she stood to go.

Scobert reached for her hand. "Wait. Could we stay and talk a moment longer?"

Taken aback by the seriousness in Scobert's tone, Helena sat back down, her hand still in his. "What's the matter?"

Scobert inhaled to speak. "I want to apologize for being a surly pain in the neck these past few months. You've been more than patient with me."

"After what you've been through, I hardly think that—"

He took both of her hands in his. "Helena, please let me get this apology out before I lose my words."

She simply nodded, the warmth of his touch fueling an avalanche of bottled-up emotions to stir anew.

"I haven't been fair to you, yet you've never once let me down or left my side—throughout everything. I wanted to let you know how much I appreciate that. Turns out making a complete mess of things is something I'm profoundly good at, but I'd hate to ruin *this*. I know these are difficult times and that there are harder times ahead. I also know how much you long for a chance at a different life, a normal life. I see it when you look at the *shillelagh* and even now, I feel it in the quickening of your pulse."

Helena's breath hitched in her throat. Still not quite sure what Scobert was getting it, she stayed still, allowing him to finish.

Scobert released her hands and pulled something out of his breast pocket. "I made you something for your birthday." He held a small ring made of wood, beautifully carved to depict two small hands clasping a crowned heart. "The hands represent friendship, the heart love, and the crown loyalty. The Irish Claddagh ring. I thought it described what you and I have shared through the years. What we still share."

Helena teared up as he placed the ring on her finger. Friendship, love, and loyalty encapsulated their relationship perfectly. Admiring its intricate design, a thought popped to mind. Most of Scobert's creations concealed some form of enchantment. "Is it magical?" she couldn't resist asking.

"Nah," Scobert said with a slight shake of his head. "The ring contains no magic. Just a promise," he added sheepishly. "A promise that from this day onward, I will be there for you in any way you will have me, whether it be a friend, a loyal subject, or a partner. If I ever come to deserve it again, I hope to be all three. And if the day should ever come when you'd choose to leave all of this behind, I will follow you to the ends of the earth and back."

She brought their clasped hands to her lips and planted a soft kiss on his knuckles. Looking into the eyes of her lifelong friend, all her burdens suddenly seemed easier to bear. Through ups and downs, and stops and starts, their partnership had certainly stood the test of time. She looked again at the ring that graced her finger. If what she and Scobert shared wasn't magical, then she wasn't sure what was.

***

The atrium in the Queen's Court was elegantly decked out with the finest table settings, freshest flowers, and most enchanting twinkling lights seemingly powered by fireflies, if not pixie dust. Looking around her, Clover felt like she was in a dream. Subtle melodies from miniature floating harps wafted through the air, along with the sweet scents of freesia and the smells of baked delicacies. A gathering of about thirty of those closest to Queen Helena socialized and enjoyed cocktails and appetizers, while they waited for the guest of honor. Clover had only been to a handful of formal events in her life; prom at the gymnasium among them, so this one definitely took the cake.

She, Kean, Garrett, and Andie were raiding the cheese buffet when Meara and Nick approached. Her father was dressed elegantly in a three-piece suit, clearly channeling the Great Gatsby, while her mother glowed in a figure-hugging ecru beaded gown. Nick had the look of someone who'd been picked to dance by the most beautiful girl in the room. Seeing her parents dressed to the nines and on a date almost had Clover bawling in a sentimental meltdown.

"You look gorgeous, sweetie," Nick said as he kissed her cheek.

Suddenly feeling bashful, she silently wished Cordelia hadn't convinced her to wear the red dress. It was just a little too *look at me* for her taste. It was made of some kind of shimmering fabric she'd never seen before and was cut pretty short. She'd worn heels, too, completing the sultry look and making her feel like she was at a costume party.

"You two look great together," she whispered while she hugged her dad.

"Ditto," Nick replied with a wink and a quick glance in Kean's direction.

Kean obviously overheard and excused himself to get drinks, looking equal parts pleased and embarrassed.

Clover rolled her eyes. Everybody seemed to be making a big deal of the fact that she'd come to the dinner with Kean. Momma Ruth had shed tears—of joy or remorse, she wasn't sure—and ordered her to have a good time. Anna had given her a knowing look and said there was no shame in moving on and Kean was a *good lad*, winning the award for the most awkward words ever spoken by an ex-boyfriend's mother. Andie had been psyched, but she'd also understood Clover's apprehension. She'd counselled that it wasn't about Finn; it was simply about *being eighteen* and enjoying herself. Only Garrett seemed to have strong opinions about the whole thing, but despite the fact that he'd threatened to rip Kean's heart out of his chest and feed it to him on a skewer, he'd eventually calmed down. Even now, Garrett and Kean were laughing it up by the bar, no doubt over one of Garrett's signature wisecracks.

That was one of the most endearing yet slightly infuriating things about Kean. Everybody just loved him. Deep inside, she hoped more people would be up in arms about the fact that she was letting Finn go, but in reality, it seemed she was the only one.

Kean and Garrett returned with drinks, looking like a couple of male models. Briefly, she wondered what she'd been stressing about. A girl could do worse. Garrett put a finger to his lips as he walked toward Andie, who had her back turned. Quiet as a mouse and quick as viper, he crept up behind her and mock-bit her neck, causing Andie to shriek like a banshee and amusing Garrett to no end. She punched him in the gut and brought her lips to his in a slow, passionate kiss, oblivious to everyone.

Now awkward spectators to this fiery little display of affection, Kean and Clover stood quietly side by side like suspects at a lineup.

Kean shrugged. "Hey. I'll take a happy Garrett over a homicidal one every time. At least he's not trying to kill me."

Clover giggled. "Well, there's that."

Kean raised his drink in a toast. "To not getting my heart ripped out of my chest."

Laughing unreservedly, Clover clicked her glass with his. In such a beautiful place, with awesome company, and the promise of an enchanting evening ahead, she'd run out of reasons not to enjoy herself.

※

Helena arrived, looking resplendent in a simple silver gown. She donned a small tiara on her pale blonde pixie cut and a genuine smile on her face. Anna remarked to Mary and Ruth that she couldn't recall ever seeing the queen so happy. A glance in Clover's direction found her sharing a giggle with Kean, their heads bent low. Anna smiled. She would never deny the girl a chance at happiness; the gods knew she deserved it. Seemingly everyone was bent on moving on; if only she had it in her to do the same.

Scobert took the empty seat at their table, breaking Anna's reverie. He was dressed as elegantly as Anna had ever seen him, which was to say he had a jacket on.

Mary took one look at her son and gushed. "Aren't you Mr. Dapper!"

Scobert blushed slightly. "Sure—about as dapper as a dime-store dunce."

"It's good to see you, son," Mary replied, turning serious. "You really do look good."

Anna couldn't have agreed more. After the past few months of abject sorrow, it really did seem like Scobert had turned a corner. She reached over and gave his hand a gentle squeeze, which Scobert reciprocated. He smiled self-consciously at Anna. Though no words were spoken, Anna could tell he was at peace. When he looked away, his gaze found Helena and suddenly it was clear to Anna that they'd inevitably found their way back to each other again. If she had the queen to thank for putting a smile back on Scobert's face, then so be it. She was eternally beholden.

Just as dinner was about to be served, Helena stood before her throne on the raised dais, and everybody raised their glasses in a toast. Liz handed her a glass flute of champagne. "Thank you, dear friends," Helena said as she raised her own glass. She took a sip and addressed her guests again, turning somber. "The Seelie Court has experienced several losses of late and we continue to face obstacles, still." She paused and scanned the room. "In our grand and extensive history, this is not the first time we've seen troubled times. Nor will it be the last. As your queen, I guarantee we'll see this through. Years from now, these brief, dark times will be but a smudge on the history of our people and of the Seelie Court, and no matter what happens, we will thrive."

Her statement was greeted by thunderous applause. Helena raised and lowered her hands, drawing the ovation to a close. "The half a millennium I've served as your queen and the many victories we've shared, big and small, will forever be my greatest of treasures—ones that I will take with me wherever I go, and ultimately to my grave. No greater honor exists than to lead, protect, and serve my people, and I thank you, my friends, and each and every subject in my court for that privilege." Helena caught her breath and uncharacteristically fidgeted with a ring on her finger. "I think the time for that privilege to pass on to somebody else has come. I have decided to step down at year's end. Seeing that I have no heirs, according to Seelie Law, I have the right to nominate my successor. If my choice is deemed acceptable by my people, then come January of next year, a new monarch will sit the throne."

Anna instinctively grabbed Scobert's hand. "Did you know about this?"

Scobert simply shook his head while a small smile played on his lips, his eyes still trained on Queen Helena.

A hush cut through the crowd like a scythe, Helena's guests seemingly stunned into silence. She raised her glass again in a toast. "Thank you for coming to my party, and bon appetite!"

❧

"Wow," Clover said as Kean walked her back to Anna's house later that evening. "I did not see that coming at all."

Kean shook his head. "I can't even imagine having somebody else sit on the throne. It's always been Queen Helena."

"Who do you think she'll pick?" Clover asked.

"Absolutely no idea. I mean, hers are pretty tough shoes to fill. I don't see anybody being up to the task, to be honest." Kean shrugged. "I guess I never imagined serving under a different monarch in my lifetime. It never even crossed my mind."

Clover tried to put herself in Helena's shoes and guessed at her reasons. "I think it's romantic. After all, she's really just a girl who probably wants to live a normal life." She imagined what her whole life must have been like—always having to put duty before anything else. "I'm happy for her," she declared before wobbling and almost falling over. High heels and expensive champagne were a dangerous mix.

Kean placed a steadying hand on the small of her back. "You okay?"

"Uh-huh. I'll be fine," she assured, delightfully buzzed.

Kean laughed. "Maybe you should take those shoes off."

"I'd love nothing more," Clover conceded as she removed the dreadfully uncomfortable things. "Ah. Much better."

"Did you have a good time?" Kean asked, as he took her hand and resumed walking.

A jolt went through Clover at the feel of Kean's hand intertwined with hers, not quite sure if it was from delight or self-reproach. Her worries on the verge of a total tailspin, Clover bit her lip and looked away.

"Yes, no, maybe?" Kean teased.

It was admittedly a simple question, and Clover already knew the answer. She felt silly for being so evasive. "Yes. Absolutely. I had a wonderful time."

"Cool," Kean replied simply. They walked hand in hand in silence, the luminescent glow from a giant Faerie moon lighting their way, a perfect close to a magical evening. Before she knew it, they were at Anna's door. She'd decided to crash there instead of heading back beneath the waves. Drunken deep-sea diving didn't seem like a bright idea.

"Drink a glass of water and eat a banana before going to bed," Kean said.

"Excuse me?"

"All-natural hangover remedy," he answered with a smile.

Clover giggled. "Yes, doc." His hand still in hers, she realized she wasn't ready to let go just yet.

Kean's pale-blue eyes were mesmerizing as he leaned in closer. "I want to kiss you so badly," he breathed, then looked down. "Only if you don't mind."

Clover paled as he looked up at him, her heart hammering against her chest. "No."

Kean straightened, a hurt look in his eyes. "I understand."

"No. I don't mind," she clarified.

A smile formed on Kean's lips. "Cool," he said simply, before bringing his mouth down to hers in a sweet, lingering kiss.

16

News of Queen Helena's impending retirement soon spread far and wide. As someone well-known throughout the realm as Helena's closest confidante, many were eager to hear Scobert's take on the big announcement. Tight-lipped and restrained, he'd simply brushed the gossipmongers off, assuring them the queen would no doubt nominate a most suitable successor and that the Seelie Court would continue to prosper for millennia to come. Deep inside, he was awash with conflicting emotions.

On the one hand, he feared for the future of the court. Helena commanded loyalty and allegiance not only by virtue of her title, but because of *who* she was and what she'd accomplished for the Fae. It was difficult for him to imagine bowing to anyone other than Helena. On the other hand, he was eager for the possibilities ahead. Perhaps a quiet life was in the cards for them yet. After all the betrayals and losses he'd gone through, a calm and peaceful existence seemed something to aspire for.

Headed this morning to his daily meeting with the queen and her advisers, Scobert pushed daydreams and aspirations aside. For now, Helena remained the queen, and there were still numerous pressing matters to deal with. A possible future with Helena would have to wait.

Liz greeted him as he entered the receiving area to the queen's private quarters. Since her recent liberation from Alistair's dungeons, he hadn't really had the chance to talk to the queen's premier lady-in-waiting. Despite the smile she now wore, it seemed Liz had never quite recovered. "How are you?" he asked.

"As good as can be expected."

"If you need someone to talk to…"

Her voice cracked when she responded, "Do you believe what they say about Finn?"

Scobert searched deep into his heart for an answer. "I don't want to, but—"

"He would never betray the queen," Liz argued.

"I think it's obvious the lad's made his choice," Scobert said.

Liz looked away. "They're waiting for you. You should get in there."

Scobert wanted to say more, but he couldn't form the words. He'd wanted to say he was sorry she was hurting, and the thought of Finn's betrayal was a perennial torment he bore, and as much as he'd like to give him the benefit of the doubt, it was a gamble he wasn't prepared to make at wartime. Instead, he said nothing.

Raised voices greeted him when he walked into Helena's rooms.

"Are you telling me that an assemblage of the greatest magical minds in this realm cannot figure out a solution to this problem?" Helena raged.

"The spell is too powerful," the warlock countered. "We've tried from every angle. It cannot be undone."

The other creatures in Helena's council nodded sagely.

"Where does that leave us?" Helena demanded.

"The sorceress. She wove the spell; therefore, the magic is linked to her. She must die, and so must Alistair."

"All's we have to do is kill them?" Scobert asked in frustration. "What have we been waiting for all this time?"

The warlock placed a dagger on the table. "This." Its gleaming blade glittered scarlet at the tip; the handle a rich emerald. "Infused with our combined magic, this weapon when thrust into their hearts will extinguish not only their lives, but any and all magic associated with it."

Scobert rolled his eyes. "And you couldn't be bothered to make two daggers?"

"Splitting the magic up would have weakened its efficacy," the warlock responded. "You will have to use the same dagger to eliminate both."

When Helena's gaze sought Scobert, he gave her a resigned look. "I suppose we haven't got much of a choice, now do we?"

※

With air in his lungs and returned vigor pulsing through his veins, Cuchulainn was once again ready for battle. Only partly recovered from the utter disbelief that a worthy warrior faerie was able to wake him from his endless slumber, the Great Berserker now roared in glory, thumping his fists against his chest like a conquering Hun. Surrounded by his longtime comrades, he once again relished in the dormant strength in his physical body and the undeniable power contained within.

Conall Kernach, Laery the Victorious, Keltar of the Battles, and the infamous Fergus Mac Roy—the greatest Irish warriors ever to have existed, all awoken from death and primed to battle another day. Soon they would be at their strongest, on the night when the barriers that divided the physical and the spirit worlds were down, when the Great Berserker and his Red Branch Knights would rule the battlefield once more.

※

"You kissed him?" Andie asked in disbelief. She grabbed a pillow and flung it at Clover. "You little minx."

Feeling her cheeks warm, Clover brought both hands to her

face. "I don't know what got into me. It must have been the champagne."

"Don't go blaming the booze. Besides, it was just a kiss. There's nothing wrong with that."

"But—"

"But what about Finn?" Andie interrupted. "Listen, I get that you feel guilty, but Finn—we may never see him again. Don't get me wrong, I love Finn, but it' not like you and Kean are getting hitched. It was just a smooch. No biggie."

Thoughts of Finn still elicited a tightening in her chest she still hadn't gotten used to. If only she could somehow speak to him, she wondered, perhaps there'd be a perfectly reasonable explanation for his disappearance—aside from the one inferred by most, that he'd sided with his father and abandoned everyone in his life without a backward glance. If only she could be with him again, perhaps everything could still be as it was.

"Earth to Clover," Andie teased. "Are you even listening?"

Clover snapped back to the present. "Sorry. What were you saying?

"How was it?"

"How was what?"

Andie reclaimed her weapon and attacked, causing an explosion of goose feathers and fluff. "The kiss!"

"It was…sweet." Clover admitted.

"Seriously? I ran in here the moment I woke up to get the lowdown and that's all you're giving me?"

Clover ignored her best friend's protestations and got out of bed. "I need to get ready. Lunch at Lir's today. Do you want to come?"

"Raincheck. I have brunch at Zeus's but give the sea god my best."

Clover doubled over in laughter. "I know, it's weird, right? That my grandfather's like a god?"

"You cheated on your leprechaun boyfriend with a faerie

soldier last night. I'm dating a powerful shapeshifter with commitment issues. Weird is so six months ago."

Not quite Zeus, but formidable nonetheless, Andie's real brunch date was Garrett. She'd convinced him to venture to Market Square for the famous Irish breakfasts served at the many pubs in the area. He'd acceded and chosen a place called the Gentle Stove, a bit off the beaten path, but heralded as the best purveyor of Bubble and Squeak, the quintessential morning meal.

Looking across the table at the disturbingly handsome pooka, the term *weird* again took on new meaning.

"I realize it's a struggle for you, but will you quit ogling?" Garrett joshed. "At least until after we've eaten, then you can have your way with me."

"God, you're conceited." Andie shook her head. "And I wasn't ogling. I was just sitting here thinking."

"Thinking of *how* you'll have your way with me?"

"Actually, I was thinking that I'm not sure which is stranger, the fact that I'm here with a pooka or the fact that you even agreed to breakfast at all."

"The breakfast thing, hands down. Literally everyone in here is a supernatural creature—except you that is—so that part's perfectly normal."

Andie cradled her coffee cup. "You've been pretty scarce for a while, then all of a sudden, you're Mr. Available. Quite honestly, it's giving me whiplash."

The food arrived, looking absolutely delicious. Served in a skillet, it was a cross between a potato latke and corned beef hash. On a separate plate were two fried eggs, a rasher of bacon, and buttered toast. Andie's stomach grumbled. Garrett momentarily forgotten, she dug in.

"You're so sexy when you're ravenously hungry," Garrett said before taking a bite.

"Shut up," Andie grumbled between mouthfuls.

They continued to devour their meals until Andie finally felt like she'd had enough and put her fork down, a half-eaten platter before her.

Garrett watched her intently, a small smile on his lips. "Doggie bag?"

"Absolutely," she said, and wiped her mouth with a napkin. "No way I'm letting that delicious food go to waste."

Garrett's lingering stare did not let up, making Andie feel equally flattered and self-conscious. "Looks who's ogling now."

The sound of Garrett's earnest laughter never failed to pull at Andie's heart strings. Something about his unapologetic amusement was so endearing, if not downright sexy.

"What?" Andie prodded. "Stop staring."

Garrett leaned forward, his voice low. "What do you see happening between us?"

Completely caught off guard, she reached for a glass of water and took a sip. "What do you mean?"

"You know what I mean," Garrett replied, uncharacteristically serious.

"Hard to say," Andie replied. "I've never dated a pooka before."

"Is that what we're doing—dating?" Garrett asked, a trace of playfulness back in his voice.

"I'm not sure," she answered honestly.

After a brief silence, Garrett said, "I'm afraid I'm about to be pretty *scarce* again," not quite meeting her eye.

"Oh," Andie replied, hiding her disappointment.

"October's upon us and it's a pretty unusual time for me. The month of the pooka, some call it," Garrett explained. "It's when I'm most powerful—even more so, if you can imagine that. I get progressively stronger, more *magical*, culminating in *Samhain*, Halloween to you, when I'm at my fiercest." He took in a breath. "I'm not exactly safe to be around when I get like that, when I'm more animal than man. I don't want you to get hurt."

Andie nodded, this time not letting on how freaked out she was. "So, you'll be scarce."

"Yeah," Garrett said, then he looked down and fiddled at his napkin.

"I'm not going to see you again, am I?"

Garrett flinched. "I didn't say that."

"It's okay," Andie said, realizing she meant it. "Soon the portal thing will be sorted, and I'll be heading home. We both knew *this*," she gestured to both of them, "wasn't going to last."

Without much ado, Garrett stood and offered his hand to her. He pulled her up and held her tight, nestling his face near her collarbone and taking a big whiff, like he was somehow committing her scent to memory. Andie hugged him back. It was hard to imagine that this sweet, handsome boy was as deadly as he claimed to be, but logic prevailed, assuring that he was.

"*This* is the closest I've ever gotten," he breathed into her neck, "to anything even resembling a relationship, but I can't change who I am."

"I know," Andie whispered back as she looked into his eyes, the busy pub and its rush-hour hubbub melting around them.

Garrett cradled her face and gave her the Rolls Royce of kisses, turning every bit of her body into Jell-O. "Don't forget about me," he said.

Not likely, Andie thought. As she kissed her gorgeous pooka back, possibly for the last time, she knew she'd entered a new level of weird. With a belly full of Bubble and Squeak in an out of the way pub in the faerie realm, Andie was simultaneously experiencing the best kiss and the most surreal, yet amicable breakup of her life, and with absolutely no regrets. If she had to do everything all over again, she wouldn't pass up *weird* for anything.

※

"I've missed you, girl," Button said as she hugged Clover.

It was still a little unnerving to see her friend aged at least seventy years. She still had the same innocent and childlike demeanor, only now she looked older than Momma Ruth.

"Me, too," Clover admitted.

"Come," Button said as she led her to the great dining room in Lir's castle. "Everyone's here."

By everyone, she meant Clover's merrow family. She walked in and was greeted by the smiling faces of Boann, Sinann, Lir, Meara, and Tony.

She immediately ran to Tony and gave him a hug. "I haven't seen you in so long!"

"I've missed you, too, kid."

"What have you been up to?"

"The usual. I'm the eyes and ears of the family, here and in the other realm. It was lucky I wasn't on the other side when the portals closed."

"That was months ago," Clover said. "Where have you been since?"

Tony cast a sideways glance at Meara, as if he wasn't sure if he should say anything.

"Lunch is served!" proclaimed Sinann, interrupting their conversation.

They all took their seats at the massive dining table, Lir at the head. "I'm so pleased to have all of you here this morning. Please, dig in," he said with a charismatic wink, proving that gods were actually pretty laid back.

After platters of cured meats, eggs, grilled seafood, potatoes, and bread were passed around and everyone filled their plates, Clover turned to Tony, who was seated beside her. "So, where have you been?"

Tony was methodically removing the top of his soft-boiled egg, revealing a gooey, orange yolk. He gingerly dipped a piece of toast in and took a bite. He'd always been very meticulous with his food. "Just sniffing around. Gathering intelligence."

"And?" Clover asked, dying of curiosity.

Sitting across from them, Meara spoke up. "Clover, I asked

Tony to look into Finn's whereabouts and to find out whatever he could."

Her heart racing, Clover grabbed Tony by the arm. "Tell me, please."

Tony seemed to scan the table. Everybody was rapt and eager to hear what he had to say.

"After the incident with Garrett at the Unseelie border, Finn seemed to have disappeared," Tony said. "He wasn't at the Unseelie Court with Alistair, nor was he with the soldiers at post. Nobody seemed to know where he was, not even those in Alistair's inner circle like Vincent. With no trace of him anywhere, I'd begun to suspect foul play."

Clover's heart stopped. "No."

Tony squeezed her hand. "He's alive, don't worry." He looked to Meara, then to Lir, seemingly intent on delivering his report. "After months of silence, both in this realm and above, I was starting to think the leprechaun had fallen off the face of the universe. Then a few days ago, there'd been a sighting. Someone who looked like Finn travelling with a small and unknown group of what looked to be warriors. Shortly thereafter, he was back at the Unseelie Court."

Meara's shoulder slumped. "I'm sorry, sweetie."

"What does this all mean?" Clover asked.

"We had hoped to find a definitive answer on what had happened to Finn, and if indeed, he'd flipped to the other side," Tony explained. "Meara felt you would never find peace without knowing the truth. For a while, I'd suspected maybe he was held captive, or worst case, that he was dead. It turns out he was gone because he was recruiting fighters to the Unseelie Army. That's what Finn does. No doubt Alistair was counting on his proven ability to round up troops and rally them for the king."

"It means he's definitely serving Alistair," Meara said sadly.

Clover felt like she had the wind knocked out of her. Hearing her worst suspicions confirmed was so much more painful than she'd imagined. Button shot her a sympathetic look, as did everyone around the table, it seemed.

"It's okay," she assured them, not sure if she believed it herself. "At least we know he's alive. I appreciate that you went looking for him," she said to Tony. "Now it's clear he's made his choice."

The awkward silence that descended on their family feast was quelled when Lir spoke, diverting to a different, yet much *related* topic. "On the subject of the King of the Unseelies, our battle with him is not done. If not for the distraction caused by Mirabella's tragic death, Alistair and his Unseelies would never have escaped our territories alive. I take great offense at his audacity to breach my lands without permission and shed faerie blood on my shores."

"Father, although I understand your sentiments, I cannot in good conscience abide by a pointless war with one as unhinged as Alistair," Meara reasoned. "I've said it before, and I'll say it again: Please don't let my fight be yours. Our clan has managed to stay out of these futile pursuits for centuries, living in peace. Why meddle in court politics now?"

"Daughter, your fight will always be mine. Make no mistake about that. Especially against a loathsome scoundrel who tried to kill my granddaughter. In her war against the Unseelies, Queen Helena has my full support. This is my final word on the matter," Lir said, his voice calm yet commanding.

Meara inclined her head but said nothing.

"I agree with Grandfather," Sinann chimed in. "Alistair's comeuppance is long overdue. I never liked him when he was with Meara, and I detest him still. His demise is one I'll relish."

Her appetite now a lost cause, Clover wondered whether Sinann would feel the same way about Finn's demise. Pouring herself a glass of wine, she soon became a fly-on-the-wall in a seemingly spirited discussion to end Alistair, and possibly by extension, her onetime love.

"I believe the clurichaun will want that honor for himself," Boann mused. "I'm afraid you'll need to get in line, sister."

Tony sniggered. "At this point, there's no shortage of souls who've been wronged by Alistair. It's just a matter of who gets to him first."

"Remember," Meara cautioned, "we may need him alive to reverse the portal spell, depending on what the Queen's Council comes up with."

"Good point," Tony conceded. "But one way or another, in the end, he'll get what's coming to him."

"Cheers to that," offered Sinann as she raised her glass. "May he soon be an unpleasant memory; a ghost never to be seen or dealt with again."

Clover robotically lifted her own glass, all the while hoping that when the time came, they'd spare Finn the same fate.

"Hear, hear!" Lir exclaimed. "Speaking of ghosts," he segued rather oddly, "November eve fast approaches and we may once again be blessed with the company of long-gone loved ones."

This caught Clover's attention. "You mean blessed with their *memory*, right? You don't mean actual ghosts."

When Lir laughed, it was a booming, wondrous thing. "Perhaps someone should explain *Samhain* to my granddaughter."

"It's pretty cool, actually," Button eagerly contributed. "Halloween is very different here than it is on Earth. In the faerie realm, it's a somber, gloomy time, which holds the promise of possibly reconnecting with the dead." She brought a fork-full of quiche to her mouth and continued, wide-eyed and animated. "Not all the dead come back. They say that those who still have ties to this world—those who are still mourned—are more likely to make an appearance. Also, ghosts who may have unfinished business or a message to deliver. There's really no way of knowing who might come back. It's different every time. Last year, Queen Fand was here. Isn't that cool? It's my personal favorite of all the great faerie festivals."

Lir's eyes watered at the memory. "That's right, my lovely wife graced us with her presence, and it was a night not ever to be forgotten."

Clover was floored. Just when she thought she'd figured out the faerie realm, a new discovery had her once more in awe. The thought of reconnecting with ghosts on Halloween was at once morbid and meaningful. "Do you think perhaps—Mirabella?"

Button shrugged. "That's the thing with *Samhain*. You never know *who* you're going to get. It'd be nice to see her again, though."

Thoughts of love, loss, and second chances filled Clover's mind. In a place where even the dead were still awarded opportunities, perhaps Finn had yet to right his journey. There was a certain death in broken promises and swapped alliances. Losing someone to the *other side* was tantamount to losing someone in its realest sense. She could only hope that one day, *Samhain* or any ordinary day, she and Finn would find their own reunion. If unfinished business kept a lost love alive in one's life, then certainly Finn would live in hers for years to come.

17

The days leading up to *Samhain* held a strange mix of apprehension and inevitability. The Queen's Army had agreed on a plan of attack and set the date. Like a trebuchet primed for launch, the realm was taut with anticipation. On the first day of winter, the Seelie Army would breach the Unseelie territories and take the king down. Armed with a magical weapon that could vanquish Alistair and Iekika while simultaneously re-opening the portals between the realms, the Queen's Army was eager for retribution, and yet Clover's anxiety multiplied with every day that brought them closer to war.

The first of November represented the beginning of a new year in the faerie realm; a time for fresh starts and auspicious beginnings. To mark the occasion, the queen would set her kingdom to rights, getting rid of Alistair once and for all. If their grandiose plans hadn't potentially involved killing Finn in the process, Clover would have been all for them, but as much as she hated Alistair, she couldn't even imagine painting Finn with that same brush.

To make matters worse, even though her merrow family intended to join the offensive, she'd been asked to stand down—reasoning that her connection to Alistair made her an easy target and a likely distraction. Unspoken, but clearly on everybody's mind was her complicated connection to Finn as well.

Even her easy friendship and budding romance with Kean was on shaky ground. During the handful of times she'd seen him, she'd been inordinately pissed every time Kean mentioned anything to do with the upcoming siege. Like an avalanche she was powerless to prevent nor escape, the war was proceeding full speed ahead despite her inner turmoil.

Only Anna seemed to share her gloom, but was handling it with far more pragmatism, even in the face of the would-be target on her son's back. With the strike commencing at daybreak, *Samhain* aptly took on the feel of an impending funeral.

Gathered first at Anna's house, their small group slowly made their way to Market Square for the time-honored tradition of lighting candles for the dead. Anna placed a hand on her shoulder, keeping pace. "I know you worry, as do I, but this battle was written in stone the moment King Boris attempted to overthrow Queen Helena's reign. While Finn's altered allegiance is disappointing, I cannot fault him for it. I suppose blood trumps all in this case."

"How are you not freaking out?" she asked incredulously.

Anna seemed to carefully consider her answer, her creased brow evident under the bright, full moon. "I trust him completely. Even though I may not understand his choices, my faith in him ensures that I abide by them."

Once again, Clover was awed by Anna's resolute confidence and steely composure. Through everything they'd endured, she couldn't recall ever seeing her lose her calm. "Thank you, Anna," she said.

"For what, dear?"

"For being who you are," Clover said without hesitation.

When Anna hugged her, she realized how decidedly lucky she was, despite everything. She'd been raised knowing only one true parent—Momma Ruth. Now, she was surrounded by people and faeries who cared and looked out for her, each and every one of them, she'd fight to the death to protect. She glanced back at their ragtag group, brought together by chance and fate. Momma Ruth, looking as vibrant as she'd ever seen her, Nick, finally getting his old swagger back and looking forward to a brighter future, Mary, with her quiet surety and cheerful demeanor, and Andie, ever resilient and adaptable, expertly taking the good with the bad and coming out smiling on the other side. She really couldn't wish for better company.

The scene that greeted them at Market Square was a stark departure from the plaza's usual chaotic and lively vibe. Gone were the numerous kiosks selling every type of knick-knack imaginable. The square was emptied out, with only what looked to be a dance floor in the middle, bystanders milling about lighting candles and lanterns, and only the sounds from a distant piano filling the air.

When Anna saw her take in the unusual sight, she explained, "It's for the Dance of the Dead—an age-old if not perhaps macabre tradition during *Samhain*. For those lucky enough to have their departed loved ones visit, a priceless opportunity to bring some joviality into an otherwise somber occasion."

Her thoughts intuitively went to Mirabella. As much as she would have loved a chance to see her again, the idea of mingling with ghosts on Halloween still admittedly gave her the creeps. She doubted she'd be able to keep a straight face. Just as memories of her friend flashed in her mind, she scanned the crowd and was instantly chastened when she spotted Scobert. Her childish fear of ghosts was soon dwarfed by her fervent hope that Scobert might get a chance to see his daughter again.

Making their way through the crowd to Scobert and his group, Clover was astonished to discover that they were already in the presence of guests from the spirit world. Like extremely lifelike holograms, a handful of ghostly apparitions had blended in with the crowd—some of them now being welcomed by loved ones; others still searching for family and friends. Trying her hardest not to point and stare, she was relieved when Scobert handed her a mug of cider.

"A blessed *Samhain* to you and yours," Scobert said as he started passing out more drinks. Accompanied by a small contingent of the queen's soldiers, it looked like they'd set up shop and had been there for a while. After everybody had been given a drink, tapered candles were distributed, with a whispered incantation— "To our dearly departed."

With a candle in one hand and a mug in the other, Clover looked around to see if anybody had matches. Not expecting to see Kean there, she was surprised when he walked toward her, an easy smile on his face.

"It sure is good to see you," he said.

"Aren't you supposed to be with the queen?" Clover asked without preamble. Helena hardly went anywhere outside of her court without Kean by her side.

"Soon. She's to make an appearance in about an hour. Let me get that for you," he said as he bent to whisper something at Clover's candle, lighting it up with a pretty orange flame.

"Cool," Clover said, feeling like a dork.

"They're enchanted," Kean said then he pointed to a nearby rustic altar with candleholders. Faeries were already setting their lit candles on its cascading shelves, creating a sort of flaming installation art.

Clover walked over and placed her candle on an empty votive, saying a silent prayer for Mirabella.

Kean stood beside her as they looked out at the makeshift dancefloor; a slow trickle of Fae and ghost alike already congregating for the Dance of the Dead. "Would you like to dance?" he asked.

"Isn't it just for the dead?"

Kean laughed and offered his hand. "I mean, there's no guest list or anything. I think we should be all right."

Clover put her hand in his and let him lead her to the dance floor, all the while shooting furtive glances at the ghosts among them. "It's impolite to stare," Kean whispered as he placed her arms around his neck then rested his hands at the small of her back.

"I'm sorry. This is just so—"

"Bizarre? Morbid? Creepy?"

"Yes," Clover admitted as they swayed in time to the slow melody.

"Listen, Clover. I'm sorry if I'd been insensitive before—about the war with the Unseelies. I realize how hard this must be for you. If it's any consolation, I don't want to fight Finn. Believe me, none of us do."

It was hardly any consolation at all. "I know," Clover said instead, focused on the slow shuffle of their feet on the dance floor.

Kean tilted her chin up. "You and me. Are we okay?"

Looking into Kean's pale-blue earnest eyes, she couldn't form the words. Yes, she liked him and enjoyed being him, but was it anything like what she'd felt for Finn? Not even close. *Were they okay*? And could they ever really be when her heart still obviously bled for someone else?

"Oh, Kean," she said, resting her cheek upon his chest, realizing just then that somewhere along the way, they'd stopped dancing.

"Shhh," he breathed into her hair. "Please don't say it."

She didn't—at least not yet. For a moment, they were still amidst the ghostly revelry, taking comfort in each other yet knowing they'd soon have to let go. The unavoidable came sooner than expected when Clover saw Anna approach, bright-eyed and slightly distraught, accompanied by an obvious ghost.

"Clover," Anna said, "I'd like you to meet someone very special. This is Brielle."

The apparition that stood before her, while elegant and beautiful, was also fierce and distinctly intimidating. When the ghost smiled at her, Clover wasn't sure if she was meant to recognize this woman or the name Brielle. She smiled back tentatively. Only when she noticed her piercing gray eyes did realization dawn on her. Of course. Brielle was Finn's mother.

"Hello, Clover," Brielle said.

"Hi," she said, instinctively reaching out to shake Brielle's hand, pulling it back when she remembered she was a ghost, then ultimately just hiding both hands behind her back. Meeting her ex-boyfriend's dead birth mother was so far going as awkwardly as expected.

Brielle turned to Anna, then to Kean. "I hope you do not mind if Clover and I had a private word."

"Not at all, Ma'am," Kean said as he gave Clover's hand a quick squeeze and left with Anna.

Alone with the imposing spirit of Finn's mother, Clover hardly knew what to do with herself. When Brielle pointed to a less crowded spot off the dancefloor and sort of floated over there, she obediently followed.

Brielle got right to it. "I am sure you have guessed at why I am here tonight."

Clover had no idea. "Well—"

"To deliver a message," Brielle interrupted. Then she peered at Clover, as if trying to puzzle something out. "You love my son. Yes?"

She opened her mouth to provide a long-winded retelling of their tragic tale of star-crossed lovers, but something about Brielle's direct manner demanded candor. "Yes," she admitted. She was already on a roll with mono-syllabic answers, why stop now?

Brielle nodded. "But you are stung by his betrayal."

Clover looked away, fighting to keep tears in. "Yes."

"Fall Valley," Brielle said.

"What?" Clover snapped her head back and was greeted by a knowing look in Brielle's steel-gray eyes. "Is Finn there?" she dared whisper.

"You must go," Brielle replied softly. Then her eyes scanned the crowd. "Anna and I have a lot of catching up to do."

"Thank you," Clover said, her heart hammering in her chest. Without another thought, she raced out of Market Square, her legs pumping as fast as her body would let them. With the cool night wind in her face, she was exhilarated. If Fall Valley held the promise of Finn, she wasn't about to waste any time getting there.

With that thought in mind and a desire for resolution filling her veins, Clover's feet left the ground. Caught off guard, she wobbled slightly but quickly reclaimed her balance. Soaring higher, she squealed into the night sky, another magical skill mastered and hope for a reunion underway.

※

Kean and a handful of Seelie soldiers had left to fetch the queen, but Scobert stayed behind. If there was even the slightest chance he'd get to dance with his daughter again, he wasn't going anywhere. Scanning the crowd at Market Square, he noticed the once-solemn vibe quickly morph into something more jovial and celebratory as dead loved ones were reunited with their families. He recognized some of tonight's ghostly visitors—soldiers he'd fought alongside with, long-gone faerie matriarchs, and even the occasional faerie child taken too soon. A sharp twinge in his heart cautioned him not to get his hopes up. It was a well-known fact that not all the dead come back.

Scobert took a sip of the cider and wished he'd packed something stronger. With every thought in his head unerringly revolving around the hope of seeing his dead daughter, fermented apples didn't quite carry the punch he needed. Still, he skimmed through the now thickening crowd, his fragile sense of hope betrayed by the slight shaking of his hand. When he spotted Manannán mac Lir arrive with his merrow clan, his eyebrows rose in surprise. They rarely ever celebrated *Samhain* on the other side, and it had been many years since the sea god graced any of Queen Helena's events, choosing always to send an emissary to represent the family. It was an unmistakable show of support. He made a mental note to alert Helena of his presence the moment she arrived.

The more ghosts he glimpsed among the crowd; the more his own spirits plummeted. No sign of her anywhere. He decided then to brush foolhardy dreams under the carpet. With a realm on the verge of war and a queen at the brink of abdication, he had more important things to worry about. A low hum of activity off the side of the square alerted him to the arrival of Helena's carriage. Good. Looking after Helena, while a noble pursuit that gave him great joy, was also a welcome distraction.

As he made his way to Helena, he noticed Anna speaking animatedly with a ghost who at first glance, looked vaguely familiar. Peering closer, he realized with a start that it was Brielle. Ironic, he mused, that on the very night that Finn was otherwise engaged, she'd chosen to make her appearance. Thoughts of Finn further dampening his already sour mood, he reminded himself that it was none of his business.

Just as he was turning in the opposite direction, Anna met his gaze and immediately went to him, her expression anxious yet guarded. Knowing her for as long as he had, he knew right away from the look on her face that something big was brewing and braced himself.

When Anna approached, she leaned in and whispered. "I may have some rather urgent information that demands the queen's attention."

"Tell me."

Just as Anna caught a breath to speak, a shocked, almost harried expression crossed her face. Then she reached into her skirt pocket and pulled out a vibrating magical compass.

"Jaysus," Scobert said. "It's Finn."

<hr />

The thrill of levitating was only rivaled by the prospect of seeing Finn again. Whether it was for a long overdue goodbye and or a much-coveted reunion, it didn't matter. Just to see him alive and well after all these months was prize enough. The rest of the drama involving their impossible situation, they could figure out later. Her heart jumped in her chest as she spotted Fall Valley beneath her. The fleeting panic that filled her when she realized she didn't know how to land was quickly replaced with relief when she slowly descended, and her feet touched the ground without incident. She jogged to the small meadow by the babbling brook—their special spot.

Short of breath, faced-flushed, and flustered, she searched for him, her eyes scanning the moonlit landscape. With Finn nowhere in sight, her powers suddenly burbled inside of her, a supernatural survival instinct. Suspecting she'd been lured into a trap, she had to admit that using Finn as bait was a surefire way to get her attention.

Feeling the confident crackle of magic in her fingertips, she called out to the night. "Who's out there?"

As true as the power coursing through her veins, she knew that except for a few errant fireflies and a handful of symphonic toads, she was without a doubt alone in Fall Valley. She wondered at the kind of sick sense of humor that would send someone on a disappointing wild goose chase and wished she could give Brielle a piece of her mind. When she realized the absurdity of having words with the ghost of Finn's long-dead mother, a cackle escaped her lips and her legs folded under her. On the crimson-colored grass, she brought her hands to her face. What was she doing? Was she that desperate to see Finn that when a ghost whispered, "Fall Valley," she literally flew there without question? She pulled at the grass in frustration, her fingers grasping at the turf even as she struggled to get her own grip on things. When she touched something that neither felt like grass or soil, she bent to investigate. Under a layer of fallen leaves and almost crusted to the ground was a yellowing piece of parchment folded up in a small square. Peering closer, she tried to read the rain-smudged scrawl on its surface. Her breath caught in her throat when she deciphered the hand-written name. *Clover.*

As she gingerly unfolded the piece of paper, she wondered how long it had been sitting there, unseen and forgotten. Weeks? Months? She struggled to read the message within as passing clouds obstructed the moon's glow. The wandering firefly, as if sensing her exasperation, flitted over, illuminating her long-lost missive.

Clover,

I'm sorry for leaving so suddenly. One day, I hope you'll understand my reasons. Please know that I will come back to you. I can only hope that you'll still have me when I do.

Yours always,
Finn

Kean tried unsuccessfully to brush thoughts of Clover aside. Even knowing it was a long shot, he had hoped for something more. She was unlike any girl he'd ever met before, so refreshingly lacking in pretension and unapologetically grounded. Being with her, he'd felt more alive in as long as he could remember, but if she didn't feel the same, there was nothing he could do about it and as much as it stung, he wasn't one to push; he'd accept her decision.

Snapping his attention back to the present, he and a handful of the Queen's men guided Helena from her carriage to the small stage where she would say a few words to commemorate the occasion. The customary crowd of onlookers gathered around their small group, eager to get a closer glimpse at the elusive monarch. Helena kept them at a slow and steady pace, making a point to shake hands and accept offerings of flowers and such from the townspeople. Each gift was then passed on to Liz, who trailed behind with a large woven bag.

Scanning the crowd, he immediately spotted Lir and surreptitiously nudged the queen while training his eyes on the sea god's direction. Queen Helena met Lir's gaze, inclining her head in a silent greeting. Although her expression remained impassive, Kean was certain she was pleased with the merrow-folk's presence there that evening, a sure indication that the merrows would fight come morning. As they inched their way to the stage amidst a throng of loyal subjects, Kean noticed Scobert duck away toward a dark alley with Anna following behind, something clasped tightly in her hand. Intuitively, his spine straightened and his skin prickled. Something was up. Instantly on high alert, a quick hand signal to the other soldiers had them forming a tighter huddle around their queen. Helena shot him an enquiring look, but by then, they received a resounding answer to all their questions.

High above, a massive horse-drawn chariot zipped through the sky, followed by a horde of Unseelie soldiers, all hooting and jeering like wild beasts. Kean immediately shielded the queen with his body while they rushed to get her back into her carriage.

"No!" snapped Helena, her eyes ablaze. "I will not cower and hide," she said as she tilted her head up to meet the oncoming attack. "Prepare to fight."

The crowd at Market Square were seemingly of the same mind, none running to hide or take shelter. Ghosts and Fae alike stood their ground, casting challenging glares at their common enemies. It was clear that the Seelie Court had had enough of the so-called Unseelie King. If there was a war to be fought, they weren't about to budge.

Suddenly amped for a long-awaited reckoning, Kean pulled his blade from its sheath and raised it overhead. "For the queen and for the realm!"

"For the queen and for the realm!" echoed the Seelie soldiers and townsfolk, brandishing weapons in the air and in some cases, raised fists their only armaments.

The chariot made a show of swooping down on the crowd and propelling upward before eventually landing on the makeshift stage. Fully expecting to see Alistair's smug face at the helm, Kean was surprised to see that it was driven by an impressive warrior with long blond hair, his torso bearing Celtic markings, a golden spear held firmly in his right hand. Clearly not an Unseelie thug, the imposing soldier looked the epitome of the heroes of lore. Bewilderment mixed feverishly with fear and bloodlust in Kean's veins, his thoughts focused on two things: the unknown identity of the warrior and the overwhelming desire to best him. When four equally impressive warriors emerged from inside the massive chariot and flanked their clear leader, Kean heard Helena take in a gasp of air.

"Do you realize who they are?" the queen asked, an uncharacteristic sense of awe and disbelief evident in her voice. Before Kean could even form a response, she continued in a reverent whisper, "Cuchulainn and his Red Branch Knights, awoken from their fabled slumber. Impossible."

Demi-gods and legendary heroes from his childhood. Could they truly be here in the flesh? Alistair seemed more than happy to offer up confirmation when he and his Unseelie soldiers soon descended on the stage.

"I caution the Seelie Court to lay down their arms," Alistair shouted, "The Great Berserker and his loyal knights stand ready to fight with me! Surrender now or perish!"

The gravity of that statement was not lost on the crowd, everyone well versed in the stories of the conquests and victories of the larger-than-life legends magically brought back to life before them. All looked to Queen Helena, who in turn searched the crowd. When the queen and the clurichaun's gazes met across the square, Helena nodded once, her expression unyielding. Scobert held the same look of steely determination, if not mired by evident resignation.

Helena stepped forward. "The Seelie Court knows no surrender. I will keep my throne, or I will die in its honor."

"Very well, *My Queen*," Alistair sneered before addressing his minions. "Attack!"

༻✥༺

Clover heard the uproar from a mile away, the hackle-raising sounds of battle. Her thoughts immediately centering on her loved ones, she soon found herself in flight, pushing herself to move faster. The closer she got, the clang of metal against metal and the deafening echo of gunshots rang through the air. Panic gripped her as she imagined the worst. What horrific scene would greet her at Market Square and were her family and friends safe?

When she was only a few yards away, she glimpsed Unseelie and Seelie soldiers fighting in mid-air, some on the ground, transforming the once quaint plaza into a battlefield. This was it—the moment she'd been dreading arrived too soon. Willing her feet to touch ground, she landed with a low thud and sprinted toward the ongoing war.

18

Amidst the melee, it was hard to tell friend from foe. Clover's eyes went to the spot where she'd last seen her family, and her heart dropped when they were nowhere in sight. As she set off to look for them, someone grabbed her arm from behind.

"Come with me," Liz screamed against the din.

Clover pulled her arm free. "I have to find my family!"

"I have them," said Liz, her look imploring.

Having had no reason in the past to do so, Clover took a chance and placed her trust in Liz, nodding in agreement.

She trailed Liz through a veritable combat zone, both shielding themselves against ongoing skirmishes. Liz expertly wove her way through the mob, leading Clover to a darkened alleyway. She stopped to catch her breath in front of an abandoned storefront, which Clover recognized instantly. It was the same shuttered flower shop where she and Finn shared a few precious hours before everything went to shreds. Liz entered, and despite a nagging sense of trepidation, she followed. What choice did she have?

Relief washed over her when she was greeted by the troubled faces of Momma Ruth, Nick, and Andie.

Momma Ruth enveloped her in a tight hug, squeezing a little

tighter than normal. "I was so worried. Where did you run off to?" she half-screamed, half-wailed. "I thought for a second that you—"

"I'm right here, Momma. I'm safe."

When her grandmother finally let her go, she had to ask, "What happened? Are you all okay?"

"Not topping my list of best Halloweens," Andie joked, "but I'm otherwise unscathed."

"It all happened so suddenly," Nick recounted. "One moment, the queen was shaking hands with the townspeople, and the next moment, a giant chariot tore through the sky and the Unseelies were swooping down from above. Alistair declared war and Queen Helena basically said over my dead body, and now here we are."

Clover turned to Liz. "You brought them here?"

"Yes," Liz said, looking as rumpled as Clover had ever seen her, with scrapes on her forearms, the hem of her dress badly torn, and a defiant gleam in her eye.

"Thank you," Clover said and meant it, then she asked the question that was really puzzling her. "Why?"

Liz cocked her chin to the side. "They're humans—not exactly at an advantage pitted against powerful supernatural creatures. I needed to get them out of there."

"Again, thank you. I owe you one," Clover said.

"Thank me if we all live to see the morning," Liz said as she peeked out from a broken window. "Alistair brings with him the full force of the Unseelie Army with reinforcements at that. Somehow, that pompous bastard was able to wake the legendary knights of Ulster and the demi-god Cuchulainn. The Seelie Army is strong, but these warriors are legendary. We're going to need all the help we can get."

"My mother," Clover offered, "and my grandfather. The merrows have pledged to fight."

"The merrow-folk were there when Alistair attacked. No doubt they're in battle right now. I just hope it's enough."

Nick approached the window. "We should try to help in any way we can. We can't just hide here."

"Nick is right," Momma Ruth said, sending Clover into a panic. It was bad enough that a full-on war was raging outside. Now her family wanted in.

Liz, thankfully, shared her sentiments. "Kudos on the valor and all, but what could you possibly do to help? Clover and I will do what we can. You can continue to take shelter in here."

"The lycanthropes," Nick said. "They'll come to the queen's aid. I know they will."

"Dad, that's crazy," Clover said.

Liz walked away from the window, thoughtful. "No, wait. That actually isn't a bad idea. There's a full moon out; the wolves will be at their strongest. Nick, do you trust them enough to go to their territories on a Hunter's Moon?"

Nick nodded. "I'll give it a shot."

"I'll come with," Momma Ruth volunteered.

Clover felt helpless. "Liz. Please tell them this is a bad idea."

Liz crossed her arms. "The Fae are at war and the Seelie Queen is threatened. We must do whatever we can. Nick has an alliance with the wolves, and Ruth is practically immortal. They're as good as any emissaries we can hope for."

"What about me?" Andie asked.

"You stay here. Without your pooka's protection, you're the most vulnerable."

"Time out!" Clover shouted in a panic. "Let's think this through."

Momma Ruth reached for her hand. "Liz is right, sweetie. This is war. Anna's out there. Mary. Scobert. Kean. Meara. We all have loved ones in danger; each of us here has something to fight for."

Try as she might to deny this inevitability, Momma Ruth was right. The time had come to honor alliances and fight for what they believed in, and although she longed for a guarantee of her family's safety, she knew she wasn't going to get it—not when they were at war.

"Okay. Let's do this," Clover conceded. "Andie, please stay in here. We'll come back for you as soon as it's safer."

"Or until Alistair kills everyone, then I'm stuck here forever," Andie grumbled.

Clover hugged her best friend. "Please understand. I can't be okay out there if I don't know *you're* okay in here."

Andie held her with equal intensity. "I know. I was just being whiny because I'm feeling so helplessly human." She let her go and wiped a tear from her eye. "Speaking of human. If you see our little elderly girlfriend out there, send her in here?"

"I will," Clover promised, suddenly filled with worry not only for Button, but for everyone whose life was in danger. With so much at stake, she knew she had to leave right then or lose her nerve. Sending a silent look to Momma Ruth and Nick, her heart swelled from the fearlessness in their expressions. Liz headed for the door, and without further ado, the four of them walked out into battle.

The first thing that caught Clover's eye, which she couldn't believe she missed before, was the massive chariot occupying at least three quarters of the makeshift stage, bright red and trimmed with gold, three sets of wheels on either side. More jarring than its size and grandeur were the five imposing men aboard it, arms crossed against their chests, very much resembling figureheads on a ship's bow. Like haughty emperors at a gladiator game, they observed the carnage before them with passive, almost bored looks on their intimidating faces.

The second thing that stole her attention was the sight of Kean and Alistair engaged in mid-air combat; Kean more than holding his own against the fearsome Major General turned Unseelie King. Searching the battlefield for the queen, she gasped when she saw Iekika aim magical currents from her fingertips at Helena's direction. As if sensing the oncoming attack, the queen spun and deflected the assault with an equally powerful one of her own. Clover tugged at Liz's sleeve and pointed.

"We have to help her," Liz declared before turning to Nick and Ruth. "Go fetch the wolves and hurry back."

Before any of them could act, all eyes went to Alistair when he dodged Kean's blade and landed on the stage, screaming at the top of his lungs. "Enough! I call on the strength of the legendary Celtic knights. I woke you from your mystical slumbers for this moment. To fight alongside the greatest faerie warrior since Cuchulainn himself. Fight with me now and end this!"

Clover mumbled a curse and fear was evident on Liz's face as she seemed to brace for the worst. For a moment, time stood still, the calm before the proverbial storm. What happened next was no less shocking as it was epic. Finn emerged from the shadows and stood side by side with Alistair.

"The Great Berserker and his Ulster Knights *will* fight alongside a faerie warrior of Cuchulainn's equal," Finn said, his voice booming and his stance undaunted. "They fight with me. And I fight for the Seelie Queen." Then he turned to Alistair, who'd paled beside him. "This ends tonight."

Rooted to the ground, Clover seemingly lost her vocal cords.

Liz exhaled audibly, a triumphant smile soon forming on her lips. "I knew it."

<hr />

Scobert watched from a distance and tugged at his beard in awe. That Finn was a better warrior than Alistair was no big surprise. That the lad was mighty enough to call the legendary Red Branch Knights his equals was something else, but to pull off a stunt so deliciously conniving and daring was the true laudable feat, and Scobert couldn't have been prouder if he'd masterminded it himself.

A deafening roar erupted from the Seelie side as battle resumed. Eyes trained on Alistair and the enchanted dagger sheathed at his waist, Scobert made his way to the stage, where a full-on clash ensued. After Finn's declaration, Unseelie soldiers rushed to their king's defense. The Red Branch Knights made easy work of picking off the advancing soldiers while Finn traded blows with Alistair.

Scobert ran as fast as he could. For the portals to reopen, both Alistair and Iekika needed to be felled by the dagger and, for his own personal reasons, he needed Alistair to die by his hands, the only fitting fate for the man who was responsible for his daughter's death.

Focused on retribution and Alistair's foreseeable demise, nothing was getting in Scobert's way—a claim quickly disproved when a distant sound stopped him in his tracks. A cry of bodily pain and ensuing wrath so visceral that it was impossible to ignore. He searched the crowd and found Helena clutching at her waist as a splotch of red blossomed on her dress and a knife's handle protruded from her belly. He followed the target of her livid gaze and saw Iekika a few yards away, a menacingly wicked smile on her face. In the next moment, Helena was rushing to her, feet afloat and arms extended like a bloodthirsty superhero. Alistair quickly forgotten, Scobert went to his queen.

⚜

After hearing jubilant cries from inside the abandoned flower shop, Andie had thought the war was over, but while she quickly debated whether it was safe to leave the safety of her hiding place, the sounds of battle returned. Not being able to contain her curiosity, she dared a peek outside and saw Alistair and Finn trying to rip each other's throats off while the warriors who looked like action figures battled with Unseelie soldiers on the rickety wooden stage that held a large, red chariot. Confused as she was as to what just happened, Andie was no doubt relieved. Finn fighting *against* Alistair was a good thing.

Never been one to do as she was told, she was having an incredibly hard time staying put while the world raged just outside her little hidey-hole. From her vantage point, trying to locate

Clover amidst the two warring sides was like trying to find a needle in a haystack. Her grandfather, on the other hand, was hard to miss. Like the god that he was, Lir dominated in every way, his otherness evident even amongst a throng of supernatural creatures. It was as if he, Cuchulainn, and the warrior knights were from a world even more mythic than the Faerie Realm, if that was even possible.

Not far from the sea god, Meara, Tony, Boann and Sinann expertly dueled with attacking Unseelie soldiers, fully demonstrating that merrows were as much a threat on land as in water. As she watched Sinann spear an Unseelie in the chest with serious ninja moves, her thoughts went to Button, hoping she was safe. She was probably holed up in a similar shop in a different alley, scared out of her mind. If they were both to cower under separate desks while the fighting ensued, wouldn't it be better if they at least took shelter together? It only made sense; strength in numbers and all. If only she could sneak out and somehow find her, everything would be fine. They'd lay low together. Having fully convinced herself of the logic of her hackneyed plan, Andie left the window and headed for the door.

༺☙༻

Finn's audacious betrayal stinging his every nerve, Alistair was determined to exact his revenge. First double-crossed by his right-hand when he sided with the imprudent immortal girl, now deceived again by his own son with his two-faced allegiance and devious maneuverings. Sorry he didn't kill him when he had the chance, he vowed that Finn would not live to see the morning.

Now engaged in a knife fight with his duplicitous son, he wished he hadn't trained him so well. There wasn't a move he was unprepared for or an attack he couldn't deflect. Fueled by anger, Alistair's moves were clumsier and less methodical than usual, and for the first time since he'd become a warrior, his confidence was sullied by something unfamiliar—self-doubt.

Finn was so on point that Alistair's brief moment of weakness yielded him two slashes to the face, one on each cheek. His own derision from the warm blood trickling down his face almost undid him. That his son was quite possibly a better warrior was too preposterous a notion to comprehend that he'd sooner die by his own sword than surrender to him.

Completely fraught with fury, Alistair reverted to magic and launched a lightning bolt of energy, which his son quickly dodged.

Finn laughed at him. "What was that? Alistair McCabe, the great warrior and purist, resorting to magic to best an opponent? I thought you were better than that."

The mockery in his voice further fueled Alistair's wrath, and Finn knew it, too. The kid was trying to get into his head and to his utter frustration, was succeeding splendidly.

"When did you know you were going to double-cross me?" he spat as they circled each other, weapons at the ready.

Finn wielded his knife lightly in his right hand—just like Alistair had taught him. He smirked. "From the start—from the moment I breached your mind and glimpsed what I'd always known but struggled to believe: That you are *nothing* like me."

"You loathsome ingrate," Alistair uttered in disbelief. "After everything I've done for you, this is how you repay me. I will take great joy in ending your sorry little life."

"Go ahead, *Father*," Finn mocked. "Give it your best shot."

With everything he had in him, Alistair attacked.

Helena all but collapsed at Iekika's feet, unadulterated fury seemingly the only thing fueling her on. With the knife still in her abdomen and blood flowing freely from her wound, she raised a feeble finger and sent an electric shock running through Iekika's body. Before the witch could retaliate, Scobert attacked from behind—a powerful punt that had her flying and sprawled on the ground in no time. A follow-up boot to the abdomen carried the point home. "Get away from her!" Scobert shouted.

Kneeling by his queen, he cradled her tenderly. "Let's get you out of here. You need to heal."

True to form, Helena shook her head vehemently. "I'll live. Do you have the dagger?"

Scobert sighed. "Yes."

Even as the blood drained from her face, fierce determination filled her eyes. "Kill her. Now."

A quick glance confirmed the witch still down a few feet away. Killing her would take a second, and yet he couldn't peel himself away from Helena's side.

"I *order* you to do it, as your queen."

Scobert's shoulders rose and fell in silent laughter. "You just had to play the queen card, didn't you?" He brushed a thumb across her cheek then laid her down on the ground with care. "I'll be right back."

Iekika struggled to get up, laughing wildly. "I must admit—I haven't had a good pummeling in a long time. It's actually quite invigorating."

"Save it, witch. This ends now," Scobert said as he pulled out the dagger and advanced.

"Come and get me, clurichaun," Iekika retorted, her ruby eyes taunting.

Just as Scobert saw red, a labored breath and a low whimper from behind stole his attention. He turned to see Helena barely moving. Torn between killing Iekika and caring for his queen, Scobert yelled for assistance. "Kean! Liz! Anybody!"

Iekika pouted. "Looks like everybody's busy getting killed, very much like your queen."

A second glance at Helena crumpled on the ground had Scobert turning his back on Iekika and running to her. Even as he was fully aware of the importance of vanquishing Iekika, nothing was more important to him than Helena. As he knelt again beside his queen, he heard the witch's footfalls grow fainter as she ran off into the distance. He couldn't have cared less.

"You fool," Helena whispered.

"Shhh. Let me heal you," Scobert said, gently stroking her hair. Then he took a steadying breath and pulled the knife from her belly.

Eliminating his wayward son was proving more difficult than Alistair had foreseen, but he was never one to throw in the towel. Both of them bloodied and bruised, it was now more a battle of grit than skill and only one would be left standing in the end.

Just as Alistair began to doubt his own shot at victory, the tides seemed to take a favorable turn when a magical lasso thrown at Finn bound his arms securely to his sides. He turned and was pleased to see Iekika tugging at the conjured restraints, effectively hampering Finn's every movement.

The tiny victory didn't seem to elicit the desired effect on their now captive opponent. Instead of fear, Finn expressed only amusement. "Resorting to magic again, are we?" He shook his head and chuckled. "Oh, how the mighty have fallen."

Alistair struck Finn with the heel of his palm. "Wipe that belligerent smirk off your face."

Iekika tugged harder at his restraints. "I say we have a little fun with him."

The witch's propensity for torture, in this instance, was a true asset. "Absolutely."

Jerking at the translucent yet surprisingly tough rope, Iekika led Finn away like one would a fettered animal. After looking around to see that no one was watching, Alistair followed the sorceress to the Enchanted Pond.

Despite the Seelie Army's clear advantage, the Unseelies were not going down without a fight. When Scobert was finally able to pull Kean from battle, he instructed him to stay by Helena's side. Now that she was somewhat comfortably healing in the carriage she'd arrived in, Scobert felt more confident in leaving her.

Kean stepped out of the carriage, looking a bit worse for wear, but battle-ready, nonetheless. "She's sleeping now. With the healing you performed and her own magic coursing inside her, she should be much better in a few hours."

Scobert clasped hands with the noble soldier. When it came to the queen's protection, there were only a handful of people he'd trust implicitly. Kean was one of them. "Thank you. I'll come back as soon as I can."

Kean glanced at the dagger by his belt. "Do what you need to do."

Scobert nodded sagely, fully recognizing the dagger's proverbial weight as it hung sheathed by his side.

Kean took in a breath. "I haven't seen Clover since this started."

"She's a lot tougher than she looks, that one," Scobert said, then sensing Kean's burgeoning worry, added, "If I see her, I'll make sure she's okay."

"I appreciate it."

With not much left to be said, Scobert nodded in farewell and headed back into the fray. Returned to the center of action, it was hard to peel his eyes away from the near poetic majesty of the Red Branch Knights in action. Like an avid spectator at a gruesome gladiator game, he was rapt. Their synchronized movements and the efficiency of the ensuing carnage was truly a once in a lifetime sight to behold. The way the knights expertly wielded their weapons while gravitating around their leader was a masterclass in the warrior arts, each of them singularly deadly, but collectively moving in tune like one lethal organism: Cuchulainn its breathing living heart. Even as he thanked the gods for having the Red Branch Knights on their side, a primitive curiosity had him wondering how he'd fare against The Great Berserker. From the looks of it, the Unseelies were quickly discovering they were no match for these mythical knights.

A long-time veteran of many a faerie war, Scobert still loathed the unnecessary loss of life, something he fully chocked-up to an army's leadership. Alistair was as much to blame for his soldier's deaths as the actual warriors who drove the blades in.

He searched the fracas for Iekika and also noticed the conspicuous absence of Finn and Alistair. As he made his way to the stage, Anna and Brielle ran up to meet him.

"Iekika and Alistair have my son," Anna announced. "You must come with me."

Potentially destroying both Iekika and Alistair in one shot had Scobert's heart pumping and his blood a-boil. "Where?"

"The Enchanted Pond."

༺༻

Finn surreptitiously tested the strength of his bonds and concluded he wasn't breaking free that easily. Still, he let Iekika yank at his restraints and lead him to seclusion, with very little resistance from his end. Satiating the witch's appetite for torture was something he was willing to endure if it provided the needed distraction. Finn had locked gazes with Anna across the square before being carted away by the evil sorceress. Soon they'd come for him, and they'd have Alistair and Iekika right where they want them—far from reinforcements and under their mercy.

He took an elbow to the back of his neck. "Hop to it, soldier," Alistair jeered.

Finn shook the pain off. "Why don't you ask your pet to unleash me so you and I can fight like real warriors?"

His comment garnering him a heavy-handed whack across the head, Finn smiled to himself triumphantly. Taunting Alistair was fast becoming a favorite pastime. When they reached the pond, Iekika stopped in front of him, loosening the slack on the lasso a tad.

"What shall we do with you?" Alistair asked no one in

particular as he circled and examined Finn like a stud animal at the county fair.

As Iekika closed in on him, Finn pretended not to notice how her witchy restraints seemed to loosen even more. Soon, he was face to face with the red-eyed imp whose scrutiny seemed even more venomous than Alistair's.

"What indeed shall we do with this one?" she breathed as she brought her face to his, their mouths almost touching.

Finn smirked and looked away, but Iekika grabbed him by the cheeks like he was an insolent child and forced him to look her in the eye.

"Don't you dare look away from me," she said. Then something happened that nearly cut Finn's knees out from under him. Very quickly and in a flash, Iekika's eyes morphed from bright crimson to deep blue, then back again. Deep blue like the ocean—deep blue like Clover's. Suspecting he'd just hallucinated, Finn blinked in disbelief.

Iekika slowly turned to Alistair. "I can think of a few choice things I'd like to do with *you*," she said, her voice like honey. Just as confusion registered on Alistair's face, Iekika released Finn and flung the lasso at Alistair, forming a loop, and pulling hard. In the split second it took to redeploy her magical restraints, a bright light flashed and what once was Iekika became Clover.

Rendered momentarily catatonic and thoroughly impressed with Clover's ruse, Finn had to consciously force himself back to the present.

"Duplicitous bitch," Alistair yelled before he shook in laughter. "Well played–very well played."

Even if he wanted nothing more than to relish a long overdue reunion with Clover, Finn reached for his knife and charged at Alistair. "Wipe that smirk off your face, *soldier*."

"Finn!" Scobert yelled as he breached the clearing and threw something at him. "Use this!"

Instinctively, he raised his right hand and caught the dagger by the hilt. Fully intent on killing Alistair, something made him do a double take. Behind Scobert and standing beside Anna was a ghost —which in itself wasn't remarkable on a night like *Samhain*. Eyes trained on the mysterious apparition, an image flitted into his head —an old photograph of a long-gone faerie warrior, one of Anna's prized possessions. A photograph of Brielle, his real mother.

"Finn!" Clover screamed as she tugged violently at the lasso, which now held an unseen captive. "He's getting away!"

The rope went slack and dropped to the ground. In a desperate last-ditch effort at salvation, Finn lunged, grasped at nothing, and roared in frustration. He couldn't believe it. In his utter astonishment at seeing his long-dead mother, he'd let his wicked father slip away.

19

Helena clutched at her side, stepped off her carriage, and wasn't surprised to be greeted by a very exasperated Kean.

"My Queen," Kean said, gritting his teeth, "you are not quite healed. I strongly urge you to return to the carriage for a few more hours, at the very least. Although your near-fatal wound is quickly mending, one wrong move could have you back where you were—basically derailing the whole healing process."

"I do understand how healing works, Mackey. I do not need a refresher course. Be that as it may, I don't intend to take a nice, long nap while my kingdom is besieged by war." She took a step and tried not to wince from the pain. "Has Scobert left with the dagger?"

"Yes, My Queen," Kean said, properly chastened.

"Good. Now tell me, how many fatalities so far?"

"About a dozen. Maybe less."

"And on the other side?"

"At least five times that number, from what I could tell."

"I would wager that number would be much higher if my best soldier were out there fighting instead of here playing nursemaid."

"Scobert asked me to—"

Helena sighed. "I know what he did, and he worries too much. I don't need you to wait on me, Kean. I need you to fight for me. Go."

"Let me at least find Liz and send her to you. You mustn't be alone. In the meantime, please stay in the carriage."

Helena rolled her eyes and wondered when everybody assumed a queen to be so fragile. "Fine. Now, leave. That's an order."

While Kean hesitated, ultimately the lad couldn't ignore an order. He ran off with a promise to send for Liz. Helena exhaled a breath she'd inadvertently been holding and clutched at her wound as she turned to board the carriage.

"I didn't think you'd be back on your feet so soon, *Majesty*," said a voice from the darkness.

Helena turned and offered up a challenge. "Show yourself, witch."

Iekika sauntered over leisurely. "It hardly seems fair, seeing how weak you are. You know, regicide is really not as challenging as I thought it would be."

"Certainly not as entertaining as burning your kind at the stake, but I suppose a worthwhile pursuit, nonetheless."

Laughing unreservedly, Iekika came closer. "Are you daring me to end your life?"

"Merely inviting you to give it your best shot," Helena replied calmly.

That was all it took to get the witch riled up. In the next moment, lightning poured forth from her fingertips, engulfing them in a miasma of sulfur and electricity. Helena deflected her magic by using her own to enclose herself in a protective bubble. In her weakened state, it was her only chance at survival.

Iekika screeched like a rabid animal. "This is how a queen fights? Hiding in a protective cage?"

"This is how a queen survives," Helena declared plainly. "Something you clearly know nothing about."

Cocking her head to one side, Iekika asked, "Is that so?"

Ickika didn't even see Liz coming. One moment she was sneering arrogantly at Helena and then she was on the ground with

Liz straddling her, delivering angry, consistent blows to her face and torso. At first, it seemed as if Iekika was too stunned to even fight back, clearly not expecting an attack from the flighty and seemingly frail faerie whom she'd spent hours torturing not so long ago. When her instincts did kick in, she fought back, not with magic but with the same brute force directed at her. Iekika grabbed at her attacker's hair, pulled, and rammed her head against hers.

A deep gash now grazing her forehead, Liz reached for the nearest rock and bashed it against the side of the witch's head, raw fury filling her every expression. Fueled by a similar hatred, Iekika lifted her hips off the ground, effectively causing Liz to lose her balance and tip to her side. The witch gained the upper hand when she got on top of Liz and thrashed her with blows to the face.

Debilitated though she was, Helena wasn't about to watch Liz get brutalized. Conjuring up all the magic she had left in her, she raised a hand to attack, but was momentarily distracted when she saw Scobert in the distance. "The dagger!" she screamed.

Despite being at the receiving end of Iekika's onslaught, Liz lifted her head, and her gaze went to Scobert. With a whispered incantation, her arm shot up and the dagger flew from Scobert's sheath to Liz's outstretched hand. She drove it in to Iekika's side with a satisfied grunt. "Payback's a bitch, witch."

The dagger's hilt glowed a bright emerald as the life went out of Iekika and she collapsed on top of Liz. Scobert ran to her and lifted the sorceress's dead body off while Finn knelt by her side. Clover, Anna, and Brielle's ghost were not far behind.

Liz clutched at Finn's hand while she lay on the dirt, bloodied, with a smile on her face. "I knew you'd come back," she croaked.

Finn ripped off a piece of his shirt and gingerly tried to wipe the blood from Liz's face. "I'm sorry this happened to you again."

Liz's peaceful expression would have seemed angelic if not for her extensive injuries. "Don't be. I'm not."

Trying desperately to keep herself upright, Helena limped over to her trusted courtier and confidante. "You did good, Liz."

When Finn glanced up at her, Helena couldn't help but laugh.

"And you," she said, still not quite certain if she was pissed off that he went away or proud that he came back. "Welcome back, soldier."

※

Andie ducked into another darkened alleyway and kept an eye out for Button as the fighting ensued in the square. Already questioning the merits of her half-baked plan to seek out and join forces with perhaps the only other person in Faerie who was as human and powerless as she was, she soldiered on regardless. She'd already made it this far; heading back to the safety of her hiding spot seemed futile at best.

"Button?" she called out softly, not wanting to draw too much attention to herself.

Walking farther in, the sudden loud crash of breaking wood had her plastered against a wall, hiding in the shadows. As she held her breath, the sounds of an apparent scuffle filled the otherwise quiet street. The clang of blade against blade and what seemed like unnecessary one-sided trash-talk could be heard.

"You're going down."

Clank. Clank. Swoosh. Clank.

"Surrender or die!"

Andie rolled her eyes. Seriously? The sword fight sounded like a bad parody of a Monty Python skit. Her curiosity characteristically getting the better of her, she peeled herself off the brick wall and ventured a peek.

An Unseelie soldier—she could tell from the ludicrous goth outfit—was battling with a Seelie soldier who, despite the disadvantage of lying against a broken wooden table on the ground, was trying his best to parry the Unseelie's attacks.

"Have it your way!" the Unseelie yelled as he continued his attack.

The identity of the trite trash-talker now revealed, Andie sighed in disgust. She searched around for something to throw at him but couldn't find anything more menacing than a rotting old peach. As she hunted for a more efficient weapon, she heard a loud grunt and a wet, scrunchy sound that made the hairs at the back of her neck stand on end. Peeking again from behind the wall, she inadvertently gasped at the sight of the Seelie soldier's vacant, lifeless, stare as a sword stuck out from his chest.

"Who goes there?" yelled the Unseelie.

Quickly, she retreated and shrunk back into the shadows, her heart beating like a deafening jackhammer.

"I hear you-ooo-ooo," the Unseelie cooed in an irritating singsong voice as he inched closer to Andie's hiding spot.

Her first instinct was to run, but her feet were lead boulders rooting her to the spot.

"Boo!" Suddenly, the Unseelie soldier was right in front of her, and she was screaming like her life depended on it.

"Shhh," he whispered as he ran a finger along the side of Andie's face, effectively silencing and disgusting her in equal measure. "Don't be frightened, pretty. I'm not going to hurt you." Then he brought his face close to hers and sniffed like a hound dog. With eyes closed and a creepy smile on his face, he declared, "It appears I've found myself a lackey."

"Get away from me," Andie hissed.

"I don't think I can do that, pretty. Not when you've so graciously landed on my lap like a beautifully wrapped present."

Panic and self-preservation now on overdrive, Andie attempted to calm herself. She cast her gaze downward, then slowly lifted her eyes to meet her would-be attacker's. "You don't look too bad yourself."

In an alarmingly failed attempt at being seductive, the Unseelie grinned like a deranged cat. "Now we're talking," he said as he leaned closer.

Andie brought both hands around the Unseelie's neck and gripped his shoulders hard.

"You don't waste time, do you? I like that in a lackey."

Clutching at the Unseelie for leverage, Andie put her weight into and delivered a hard knee to the groin. As he doubled-over screaming obscenities, she managed to slip away, but not before the Unseelie swept her right leg and brought her down. Soon, he was hovering on top of her, offering up this priceless gem, "I'll make you regret doing that, lackey."

If Andie weren't in serious fear for her life, she would have burst out laughing. What a prize, this guy. Instead, she searched her brain for an alternative plan of attack. Just as she was about to start screaming again, someone spoke from the shadows.

"Vincent," the voice said, all throaty and ominous. "Step away from the girl and I grant you a soldier's death. Refuse, and you get the death you deserve."

Not bad for a veiled warning from an invisible adversary.

"Who's there?" Vincent yelled. "Show yourself."

A few moments of utter silence Vincent's only answer, he quickly grew smug and taunted the unseen guest. "Coward," he hissed, then bent low, cupping Andie's face with his filthy, blood-caked hand.

The sound that erupted from the darkness was so frighteningly feral that it would have sent any living creature in its proximity running in the opposite direction. A hybrid between a growl and a roar, guttural and gruesome, it announced the unmistakable arrival of a blood-thirsty predator.

The next thing she knew, Vincent was hauled away by pure power and unadulterated speed. Then the street was filled with the sounds of ripping flesh and crushing bone, each grisly crunch and resounding tear the most horrific thing Andie had ever heard. Mere seconds later, the noises ceased and all she could hear was the loud, heavy panting of a large animal.

"Garrett?" she managed to squeak.

Her query was answered by a low, gruff rumbling, not exactly a roar, but not quite a purr. Her whole body turned to ice. If the creature was Garrett, she could still very possibly get morbidly hurt. If the creature was *not* Garrett, then she was most certainly someone's soon-to-be dinner.

The fearsome purring grew louder as a humungous leopard slowly approached, basically rendering Andie paralyzed where she lay. Step by frightening step, it approached until it stood towering in front of her. Then it bowed its massive head to her feet in a sort of feline act of genuflection.

"Garrett," she whispered as she reached over and cautiously stroked its huge head. "Thank you."

※

Clover was horrified at the extent of the injuries that left Liz almost unrecognizable. Before Finn carried her off to the queen's carriage to heal, she knelt beside her.

"We haven't lived to see the morning yet," she whispered, "but you just got us a little closer to the finish line. Thank you, Liz."

At first averting her gaze, eventually she reached for Clover's hand and looked her in the eye. "I have much to atone for. You don't need to thank me for anything."

Clover nodded. Something in the fervency in her grip told her that Liz was apologizing for something significant, and Clover was certain that even though she didn't know what she was sorry for, that she'd already accepted her apology.

Finn carefully lifted Liz off the ground and despite her current state, she seemed to feel no pain. She released Clover's hand and drifted to sleep.

"I'll be right back," Finn announced to their small group as he cradled Liz in his arms.

"Are you sure you can heal her and still be strong enough to fight? I've seen it take a lot out of you," Scobert said.

"I can handle it," Finn said before walking away with Liz.

Helena shifted uncomfortably and leaned on Scobert for support.

"You should be healing, too. We've got this," Scobert whispered.

Helena shook her head. "Not while Alistair still lives, and my soldiers still fight." Then, without further preamble, she turned to Brielle, who'd literally been quiet as a ghost this whole time. "I didn't think I'd ever see you again. Thank you for your service, Brielle. You were one of our finest and your death is one I still regret after all these years."

Brielle nodded. "My Queen."

The matter of acknowledging the presence of Finn's dead mother out of the way, the queen got right back down to business. "Where is the Unseelie King?"

Since she was the one who'd let him get away, Clover felt obliged to take that one. "We had him bound and captive, but he made himself unseen and was able to slip away against all our efforts. He could be long gone by now."

"He won't be far, that we can be sure of. I have never known Alistair to surrender," mused Helena. "Once he sees that I'm otherwise weak, but still alive, he won't be able to resist."

"We won't use you as bait," Scobert said. "I won't abide by it."

"Not bait," Helena clarified. "Motivation. Now, go fetch Finn and let's go back out there and end this war."

At that exact moment, Finn returned, looking stronger and more invulnerable than Clover had ever seen him.

"Ah, there he is," remarked Helena as she focused her full attention on him. "I doubted you, Finnegan, and I apologize. But you made this happen and you have my gratitude. Now, are you ready to serve your queen and end this once and for all?"

With gallantry in his stance and unmistakable confidence in his steel gray eyes, Finn was the epitome of a faerie warrior, and finally it seemed he'd begun to embrace it. "Absolutely."

Clover had never seen so many dead bodies. Relentless though they were in their dedication to Alistair and his war, the Unseelies were at a clear disadvantage against the combined forces of the Seelie Army, the merrows, and the Red Branch Knights, and were quickly being obliterated by the opposition. As Helena made her way to the heart of the battlefield, Seelie soldiers not otherwise engaged bowed their heads in reverence or took a knee, clear acknowledgements of the impending victory and their continued allegiance to the Seelie throne.

Walking amongst the soldiers, she couldn't help but notice the deferential looks directed at Finn. In the estimation of the Seelie Army, he'd gone from well-respected soldier to traitorous outcast to a warrior of mythic proportions in seemingly the blink of an eye. Though he seemed mostly oblivious to this newly acquired attention, Clover could tell he carried himself with just a little more aplomb than usual, and his piercing slate eyes, usually always warm, now contained a certain hardness to them. As she tried to imagine what he'd had to go through these past months, a sharp twinge formed in her chest. Wondering whether the Finn who'd returned was the same as the one who'd left, she realized that perhaps she wasn't the same girl he'd left behind, either. And maybe that wasn't a bad thing.

Even Brielle seemed to notice the Army's deferential reception of her son as she glided behind their group, pride evident on her face. Everything had happened so suddenly at the Enchanted Pond that mother and son were never really afforded an opportunity for a proper reunion, the necessities of war taking precedence. Not really striking Clover as the sentimental type, Brielle didn't seem to mind, which was more than she could say for herself. Selfish though it seemed in light of current circumstances, she couldn't wait to have a private conversation with Finn; he'd barely said a word to her since the debacle at the pond, but for now, all of their attentions were focused on Helena and the possibility of luring Alistair out and putting an end to this senseless war.

While some fighting still ensued, a good number of Unseelies had already laid down their weapons in surrender. The wounded lay side by side with the dead as their comrades attempted to heal those most grievously injured. The otherwise festive square, the heart of the town and the center of its life and commerce, had quickly become a hotbed of total chaos.

Helena's appearance seemed to effectively invigorate the Seelie soldiers left standing—her mere presence providing a much-needed salve for the injured and a welcome boost in morale for the entire army, but even so, Clover could tell the soldiers were weary and battle-worn. As she craned her neck in search of Kean, she whispered a silent plea for his safety. As one of Helena's top men, he would undoubtedly be in the thick of combat, leading the charge for the Seelie faction.

Just as worry for loved ones started to plague Clover anew, the sounds of a scuffle prompted her to turn around, and there he was—her nemesis in the flesh, looking more bedraggled than usual, but otherwise still annoying perfect, Alistair McCabe, with Anna in a headlock against his forearm, a gun pointed at her temple.

"Let her go," Clover hissed, not fully realizing until that moment the lengths she was willing to go to protect Anna. As an overwhelming sense of protectiveness surged through her, it dawned on her that she would do anything to defend her.

By now, their whole group was held captive by Alistair's last-ditch attempt at an upper-hand and a group of Seelie soldiers had begun to corral themselves around the Unseelie King and his hostage.

Finn advanced like a battering ram, sword out. "I swear to the gods, Alistair. If you hurt her—"

"Stay your hand, son," Anna ordered, fierce determination evident in every aspect of her bearing. Despite her compromised state, her command was firm and her stance unyielding.

"Listen to your surrogate mother, *son*," Alistair mocked. "Now, this is how this is going to play out. You will order the Seelie Army and the Red Branch Knights to stand down. Obey me or else Anna dies."

Instinctively and in obvious reverence for both Finn and Anna, the Seelie soldiers lowered their weapons.

Even with the barrel of Alistair's gun pressed firmly against her head, Anna straightened and shouted, "Disregard him, soldiers! Forward march!"

"Nobody makes a move," Finn yelled, countering her command.

Both armies at a veritable standstill, the silence that enveloped them became oppressive.

Like translucent wallpaper on a non-existent wall, Brielle's presence was mostly imperceptible, but when she glided toward Alistair, her whole essence was sharpened and heightened, and for a brief moment, she was once again a formidable warrior. "Unhand her!"

Alistair guffawed as if he'd just heard the most hilarious joke. "That is just priceless! My long-dead paramour somehow thinks she has the right to tell me what to do. Why don't you take your self-possessed sensibilities and your ghoulish corpse back to the grave where it sprung from? You didn't seem to think I had the *right* to know about my son, so I don't think you have a say in this matter, Brielle."

"Enough with your useless pontification," Anna said. "If you really intend to kill me, then shut your mouth and pull the trigger. The Seelie Army does not stand down to idle threats and self-serving pageantry. Put your money where your mouth is, *King*."

If Anna was bluffing, she had everybody fooled. Alistair responded to her taunting by squeezing just a little bit tighter on the trigger, seemingly considering the option of certain death.

"Do it," Anna dared. "Soldiers, get ready!"

"No!" Clover screamed as she instinctively lunged forward. At that same moment, a wolf the size of two grizzly bears pounced from out of nowhere, knocking both Alistair and Anna off their feet. It stood on its hind paws towering over Alistair, saliva dripping from its massive mouth as it appeared primed to attack. Even as one werewolf had Alistair in its sights, dozens more joined their ranks, nipping at Unseelie soldiers as they did.

In the chaos, Scobert shouted a command against the din. "Keep him alive!"

The werewolf turned its head in the direction of Scobert's voice, comprehending. It pushed its front paws down on the Unseelie King, pinning him to the ground.

Anna was already back on her feet by the time Finn got to her. "The dagger!" she screamed.

In the hubbub, Clover saw Alistair reach into his pocket to retrieve a small packet—surely another tool in his bag of tricks. The gleam from a discarded blade on the ground catching her eye, instinctively she grabbed it and launched it at her target, connecting with a solid *thwack*. With the blade deeply imbedded in his hand, Alistair grimaced in pain and struck the packet against the ground, enveloping them in a bright, blinding light. Shielding her eyes with both hands, the combined roars of frustration and utter chaos were her only sounds. When finally the blinding light grew dim, she opened her eyes and Alistair was gone.

Taking advantage of the distraction, Alistair escaped to one of the abandoned side streets to catch his breath. With a pained grunt, he pulled the knife from his right hand and raucously cursed the mongrel who put it there. Fully realizing the gravity of his predicament, he racked his brains for a possible out. With Iekika gone and with no foreseeable way for his Unseelie Army to best the enemy, defeat seemed inevitable. He could run and regroup, rebuild his army and strike back when the time was right. With Helena close to abdicating, the Seelie Army would clearly be more vulnerable under new leadership—but not unless their new leader was a soldier, too. If Finn was somehow named successor to Helena, morale would be high and the army strong, with a mighty warrior like Finn at the helm. Alistair chuckled to himself in near delirium. Flee now and live to battle his inglorious son another day or stay and fight—die a soldier's death. Neither option seemed tempting. Once more falling back on irrational laughter, Alistair marveled at the bizarre twists and turns that ultimately resulted in the greatest general in the Seelie Army cowering in a darkened alley, pondering an imminent end.

He would retreat. Many a war was not won on the first, second, or even third try. However detrimental it was to his pride, a decision had to be made and as a leader, he had to recognize the right time to cut one's losses. He'd regroup and retaliate. Fairly satisfied with his new plan of attack, Alistair dove deeper into the unlit alley. If his memory served him right, there was a fork down the road that led to the forest—his best chance at a stealthy escape.

Picking up his pace, he deftly maneuvered through the twisting backstreet until his foot caught on something that made him stumble. Muttering a curse, Alistair kicked the thing across the street before realizing what it was. A decapitated head—more accurately, Vincent's decapitated head. Looking down at where he stood, he realized he'd been walking on mangled body parts in varying degrees of mutilation.

Before he could utter a condemnation to whatever savage creature saw it fit to end a soldier's life in such a manner, a cold gush of air swept the area and an unseen onslaught had him tumbling forward. His uninjured hand broke his fall, hitting the pavement with brute force before sliding on the blood-soaked street. Now literally knee-deep in Vincent's remains, Alistair roared in utter rage. Having encountered his fair share of worthy adversaries, he knew right away he was facing a ghost.

His own blood seeping from one hand and Vincent's coating the other, he stood and squared off to face his invisible challenger. "Brielle, I know it's you! You think you can scare me with your ghostly assaults? Show yourself!"

His challenge was answered with a quick spectral swoosh, a hard jab, and a broken nose. Grabbing frantically and futilely at his amorphous attacker, Alistair's fury was fast approaching mythic proportions. A blow to the solar plexus had him doubling over in pain, while blood leaked from his nose.

"Coward!" he screamed. "At least have the courage to show me your face before you scurry back into whatever crypt you crawled out of."

A voice whispered from the shadows. "Not before I have the pleasure of watching you die."

Alistair's answering laugh was belly deep. "You think you can kill me? All you can do is royally piss me off. There's absolutely nothing you can do to me that I can't recover from."

Where there used to be darkness, a figure slowly materialized right in front of him. A statuesque lady with long, blonde, wavy hair and familiar indignant green eyes was staring back at him with so much wrath that it was almost too beautiful to behold.

"Mirabella," Alistair breathed.

"You're right," she scoffed, "I can't kill you, but he sure as hell can."

Before Alistair could even register her meaning, Scobert crept like a thief in the night and drove an emerald-hilted dagger through his heart.

"For my family. You sick son of a bitch."

As he drew his final breath, all he could see was Mirabella looming glorious over him, an angel of death.

20

The reverberating rumble heard across the realm confirmed Alistair's death and cemented the Seelie Court's victory, but Clover had proof enough. The moment Alistair's life ended, an invisible tether was sawed clean through, releasing her from an insidious bond that had plagued her since birth. Only when it was completely severed did she clearly detect its absence. Clover leapt in spontaneous celebration, as did most of the soldiers and townsfolk around them. Before she knew it, she was being lifted up in the air in a tight embrace.

"We did it, kid!" Nick proclaimed as he hugged her close. "The portals are open. We can go home now."

Not soon after Nick lowered her to the ground, she was besieged with hugs and kisses from Momma Ruth. "I love you so much, sweetie," she whispered.

Tears streaming down her face, she'd never been happier to see two people in her entire life. "You guys did great. That werewolf almost scared the life out of me," she joked, "but an otherwise perfect drop-in."

"Those wolves sure do know how to make an entrance, boy," Momma Ruth gushed lightheartedly before she smiled at somebody standing behind Clover.

When she turned, she was enveloped in Meara's arms. "I am so incredibly proud of you, Clover."

Hearing her mother say that was just about everything she'd ever dreamed of. She hugged Meara back with all her might. Letting her go, she noticed her cuts and bruises. "Are you okay?"

"It's nothing," Meara said, looking as exuberant as Clover had ever seen her. "Come," she said as she took her hand. "Lir will want to see you."

They were somehow able to squeeze their way through the throngs of joyous townsfolk, and soon she was reunited in celebration with her merrow family, all of them buoyant from their recent victory, their happiness contagious. Clover reveled in it. Being reunited with her family after such a horrible battle was the most precious gift anyone could ask for.

When she caught sight of Sinann, she immediately went to her. "Where's Button?"

"She's safe," Sinann confirmed, a warm smile spreading across her face. "Mary took her to Anna's when the fighting started. They should be here any minute."

Even as she sighed in relief, she couldn't help but search the crowd in an attempt to account for everyone. She still hadn't seen Kean and could only hope that Andie was still safe in the abandoned flower shop.

"I have to go," she whispered to her mom.

When Meara gave her a questioning look, she responded, "I need to see if Andie's okay."

"Of course." Meara nodded. "See to your friends."

Soldiers were reuniting with loved ones and seemingly everyone around her was locked in another's embrace as she slowly tried to make her way to the flower shop to check on Andie. With her petite frame, she felt lost in a sea of faeries, reminding her of one New Year's Eve when she and Andie braved the crowds at Times Square to watch the ball drop and she couldn't even see farther than the top of some guy's head. Trudging along, she received several congratulatory slaps on the back before walking straight into someone's chest.

"Excuse me," she blurted out.

"Hey, you."

When she looked up, she was greeted by Kean's calm blue eyes—a splash of afternoon skies against a moonlit night. Clover immediately got on her tippy toes and hugged him tightly before having a good look at him. Although the right side of his face was bloodied, he seemed otherwise unharmed.

"I was worried about you!" she shrieked in relief.

Kean grinned. "I may have wondered about you once or twice."

Clover mock-punched him. "Seriously, I really am glad you're okay."

"Ditto," Kean said with a soft smile. Then, he gestured to a quieter spot off the side. "Do you have a minute?"

Clover nodded and followed him to the front awning of a pub. She chewed on her lower lip as she waited to hear what Kean had to say.

"Finn's back," he stated plainly, "and he didn't betray the throne. He helped save it."

She simply nodded. "Yes."

Seemingly searching her eyes for the next words to say, Kean eventually took in a long breath, inched closer, and whispered, "You can say it now."

"What?" she asked, playing at innocence.

Kean smiled wistfully and took her hand. "It's okay, Clover." He lifted her hand to graze softly against his lips, his eyes piercing. "I knew from the start it might come to this," then in usual Kean fashion, added, "You weren't really my first choice, either."

Clover chuckled. Kean always had a way of defusing potentially uncomfortable situations, usually at his own expense. "Thank you. I don't know what I'd do without you."

"Hey," Kean said as he absentmindedly tucked an errant lock of hair behind her ear. "I'm not going anywhere. I'll still be in your life, right?"

Clover nodded. "You promise?"

"Somebody's got to keep Finn on his toes."

Her follow-up punch was promptly caught as Kean took both her hands in his, then he leaned forward to give her a light kiss on the forehead. "You and I; We're okay?"

"No," Clover deadpanned.

"No?" Kean asked with a playful smirk.

"We're more than okay."

"Good enough for me," Kean said, then his gaze went past Clover's head and he smiled from ear to ear.

When Clover turned, Garrett was walking toward them, partially naked except for an ill-fitting pair of ratty trousers, obviously borrowed, if not stolen. Despite looking a little rougher than normal, he was flashing them one of his trademark smiles as he walked hand in hand with Andie.

Seeing Clover, Andie immediately ran to her and squeezed her until she could hardly breathe. "I am so sorry for leaving my hidey-hole," she cried. "It was a *baaad* idea, and it almost got me killed by this stupid tough-talking sorry excuse for a faerie, but I kneed him where it hurts and then he tripped me, but a voice called out from the darkness, and Garrett ripped him into a million tiny pieces, and—"

"Slow down," Clover said as she hugged her best friend back. "It's okay. The only thing that matters is that you're fine."

Garrett clasped hands with Kean. "What happened to your face?"

"What happened to your pants?" Kean shot back.

"Touché," Garrett conceded.

"Good to have you back, man," Kean said, a genuine smile on his face.

"Good to *be* back," Garrett said, then catching Clover's eye, he lifted her up in a tight embrace. "Looks like our boy came through, eh?" he whispered, clearly referencing Finn and his epic return to the Seelie Court.

Clover felt her cheeks warm. Happy as she was to have Finn

back, she wasn't quite ready to field questions about him, seeing that they'd hardly exchanged two words since his return.

"Where is the man of the hour, anyway?" Garrett asked. "I'm not letting that bastard get off so easily; he's got a *world* of explaining to do. Heck, I almost ripped his head off."

When Clover didn't answer, Kean offered up a guess. "I reckon most of the soldiers are with the queen. I suggest we assemble by the royal carriage. Queen Helena will want a head count."

"Good idea," Clover said.

"Wait," Andie shrieked, her panic obviously bubbling back to the surface. "Button?"

"She's safe," Clover confirmed.

Andie placed a palm over her heart, exhaling audibly.

Clover realized she'd put her best friend through a lot by plucking her from her perfectly ordinary life and dropping her in the middle of a faerie war. Now that the portals were open, Andie could finally return home. *Home.* Suddenly, the word took on a different meaning and for the first time since forever, she wasn't quite sure that New York was still hers.

※

As Kean had predicted, most of the Seelie soldiers had congregated by Helena's carriage, transforming the otherwise nondescript area into a virtual throne room. In the short amount of time since the portals reopened, a makeshift throne had been erected and rugs of varying sizes had been laid on the trodden ground as faeries gathered around their queen. Oddly enough, the temporary seat remained empty as Helena sat crossed leg on the ground among her subjects, a recovering Liz at her side.

A spontaneous round of cheers and applause erupted as they joined the fast-expanding group of revelers. Clover's heart swelled when she realized they were honoring Kean. When the young soldier raised a broadsword in acknowledgement, the roar of the Seelie Army was deafening. Among the cheering crowd were the familiar faces of her merrow and human families, Anna, and even Brielle. Instinctively, her eyes sought Finn. By the wooden stage where the enormous chariot had earlier landed, Finn was huddled in quiet conversation with the imposing Red Branch Knights. Clover shook her head in awe. While certainly not the fiercest looking of the lot, Finn somehow not only commanded their attention, but their apparent respect. The behemoth warrior called Cuchulainn clapped Finn on the shoulder, bellowing at some seemingly fascinating discussion. Then Finn turned and walked toward the queen, the mythic warrior knights at his heels.

Rapturous felicitations soon quieted down to a reverential hush as Finn approached with the knights. Helena promptly rose to welcome the group.

"It is perhaps the greatest wonder of my life to see The Great Berserker and his Red Branch Knights in the flesh," Helena gushed, "and certainly the greatest honor of my lifetime to have my Seelie Army fight alongside you."

Cuchulainn bowed his head solemnly. The king-sized demi-god and the diminutive queen couldn't have been more physically different, but they shared an undeniable, if not intangible, quality: greatness.

"I assure you, Queen Helena, the honor is all ours," Cuchulainn averred, his voice crisp and resonant.

Helena inclined her head. "I would be most obliged if you and your knights might stay for a feast. We're soon headed back to court."

"I'm afraid our endless slumber beckons and our chariot awaits," the Great Berserker said with a smile. "But know this—henceforth, the Red Branch Knights stand ready to fight with Finnegan Ryan, and by extension, the Seelie Court."

The look of amazement on Helena's face was accompanied by an expression of utter curiosity. No doubt she wondered at the same question in everyone's mind—how was Finn able to wake the infamous knights and how ever did he gain their staunch allegiance? The queen expressed her gratitude and strode to see them off. Looking even more mythic aboard their gilded chariot, the knights received wild applause and cheers from the Seelie Army as they lifted off into the night sky.

A familiar voice called from behind. "Long live the Seelie Court!" When Helena turned, her face uncharacteristically lit up.

If the army and townsfolk were amped up before, seeing Scobert sent them into a frenzy. The troops even attempted to lift the returning hero upon their shoulders, failing miserably and amusing the clurichaun to no end. When someone shoved a tankard of beer into his hands, he lifted it in a toast, eliciting another round of thunderous applause. Clover hooted and clapped until her voice was hoarse and her hands were sore. Scobert downed his drink and leaned to whisper something to a nearby ghost, his eyes twinkling with laughter. Peering closer, Clover let out an inadvertent squeak.

When Clover yelled, "Mirabella!" Andie almost tripped over herself in shock. Soon they were both braving the dense crowd to get to her. Standing face to face with her fallen friend, Clover couldn't bite back the tears nor form the words.

Mirabella spoke first. "I miss you, guys."

Andie sniffed. "I want to hug you so bad right now."

Mirabella's chuckle was a soft breeze on a moonlit night. She looked around. "Where's—"

She got her answer when Button came barreling toward them, enveloping them all in a group hug, Mirabella in the middle. When she released them, tears and giggles were simultaneously pouring out of her in droves. "You don't know how happy I am to see you —*all of you*," she proclaimed to the group. Then to Mirabella, "How long do we have you for?"

"Midnight," Mirabella said, turning somber.

"Well then, Cinderella," Andie replied as she pretended to check an imaginary watch, "we've still got several precious hours to *par-tay*. I say we get to it."

"Hell yeah," Mirabella answered jovially.

Reunited with her friends, the portals re-opened and Alistair gone for good, Clover was definitely in the mood to celebrate.

At the Seelie Court, the champagne was flowing and the mood festive. Helena had opened up her residence to all, a grand feast prepared. In her throne room, only those closest to her gathered to recap and toast to the night's events. Clover sidled close to Momma Ruth to hear Scobert recount how he and Mirabella teamed up to go after Alistair. With Helena at his side and his daughter's ghost corroborating his tale with little snippets of her own, Scobert seemed happier than a clurichaun at an open bar. Even Helena, who was usually the picture of stoic composure, was as relaxed as Clover had ever seen her, giggling at Scobert's animated retelling of the fall of Alistair.

The night was fast becoming one of the most joyous occasions in Clover's young life, the spirit of camaraderie and a shared sense of victory buoying everybody's spirits. Even while she basked in the celebrations, she still longed to have a moment alone with Finn. There was, in her view, much to say. Like second nature, she scanned the crowd for her onetime love.

"I regret that perhaps my decisions have somehow led to this whole mess," Brielle confided. "I had my reasons for not wanting Alistair in your life, and yet somehow your paths still ended up intertwined."

Gawking at his birth mother was distracting Finn immensely; he barely registered what she'd just said—something about regretting something. "It's fine," he replied rather ineloquently.

Brielle lifted a hand as if to touch his cheek. "I am so proud of you."

Finn swallowed a lump that was building in his throat. "Why are you here?" he asked. "Why tonight?"

"I've been watching you, son, but ghosts can't read minds. I wasn't certain if your allegiance had truly shifted to your father."

Explaining nothing at all, it wasn't exactly the answer he was looking for. "I still don't understand."

"If you were indeed on the Unseelie's side and a raid was imminent, at the very least, I wished for Clover not to be there when you attacked, so I told her to go to Fall Valley. A while back, you'd left her a letter. I figured it was about time she read it."

Momentarily speechless, Finn struggled with a response.

Brielle continued. "I hope you'll forgive me, but I also warned Anna of the impending attack. I didn't know. It was only when you made contact using the magical compass did we learn your true intentions."

"You came back from the dead to protect Clover and Anna?"

Brielle tugged at a phantom sleeve. "Seemed as good a reason as any. I may not read minds, Finn, but it's not difficult to guess who holds your heart."

Allowing that to fully sink in, Finn rubbed self-consciously at his nape. "Thank you," he whispered, wishing he could articulate something more profound, but grateful to exchange even a single word with his long-dead mother.

"You're welcome," Brielle said before gesturing to the crowd gathered around Helena. "I have a few more hours left in this realm. Shall we join the festivities?"

Finn chortled despite himself. Of all his bizarre and epic adventures of late, spending time with his mother was on its way to topping all others. "I would love nothing more."

⁂

When Finn and Brielle's ghost joined their small group, the cautious hush that descended was quickly shattered by Scobert's gleeful felicitations. "Hip hip…hurrah!"

"Hurrah!" everyone chanted joyously in unison. "Finn! Finn! Finn!"

Finn blushed, touching a finger to his lips, imploring them to quiet down. The hibernating butterflies in Clover's belly stirred.

She hadn't really realized how much she'd missed him until that moment. When their little circle settled, Helena gestured at Finn to take a seat beside her. When he obliged, next order of business was getting Finn to tell his story. A sudden barrage of questions had Finn looking like a deer in headlights, obviously uncomfortable at being the center of everyone's attention.

"Go ahead, lad," prompted Scobert. "Fill us in. What the heck happened?"

Finn ran a hand across his head and cleared his throat. "I mean, where do I start?" he mused. "When Anna told me about Alistair, I knew I had to see him." His eyes met Anna's. "I wanted to know if he'd known all along. Turns out he was just as surprised as I was. When Alistair placed a hand on my shoulder, our minds became one. I saw so clearly into the inner workings of his mind that I almost killed him with my bare hands in disgust." Finn paused, the memory seemingly making him cringe.

Anna nodded encouragingly, urging him to continue.

Blowing out a breath, Finn resumed his tale. "When we shared minds, I found a way in. The Red Branch Knights. I knew he'd always obsessed about the notion of being the mightiest warrior in the realm, the only one worthy enough to wake the fabled knights. I played him by offering to help him wake Cuchulainn, all the while intending to have them pledge loyalty to me, and not Alistair. It gave me the perfect cover. I knew I couldn't make contact with any of you for fear that he'd read my mind, but I also knew that when the moment came, I would send out a warning at the last minute."

Helena shook her head in wonder. "Do you mind telling us how you gained the stalwart allegiance of the greatest warrior known to have lived?"

His jaw muscles contracted, and his gray eyes turned hard. "A series of tests—strength, endurance, skill, mental agility. It wasn't easy. When I gained Cuchulainn's respect, I convinced him to play the farce with Alistair. He thought it was hilarious and agreed to the charade. Later, he admitted the tests weren't actually necessary. He'd just wanted to gauge my abilities for himself. The fact that I was able to wake them was magical proof enough that I was a warrior of his equal."

Finn crossed his arms against his chest and looked down. "When the portals closed—when Mirabella died—I was with Cuchulainn. I had no idea Alistair had planned to attack on *Lughnasadh*. If I had known—"

"You were doing what you could," Mirabella spoke. "The fault was all his."

Finn's eyes watered as he turned to Mirabella, then to Scobert. "I am *so* sorry."

"Like my daughter says," Scobert said as he reached over and clasped forearms with Finn. "It wasn't your fault." His gesture was met with a look of profound gratitude from Finn. "To the Seelie Court!" Scobert once again proclaimed as he lifted a goblet above his head.

All lingering questions seemingly answered, everybody raised their glasses in an answering toast, more than happy to celebrate the war's wins, while perhaps glossing over its losses. Despite the merriment now surrounding her, Clover still had several pressing questions of her own. If Finn could even be bothered to look her way, maybe she'd get some answers.

As if he'd read her thoughts, when she glanced his way, Finn was staring directly at her, his piercing gaze thoughtful.

Clover put on a brave face and inclined her head to the side. When Finn nodded in agreement, her legs turned into hollow macaroni. Now that she finally had a chance to speak privately with him, she seemed to have forgotten how to place one foot in front of the other. When her motor skills returned, she walked away from peering eyes and ducked into the queen's receiving room—the only empty room at Court that night, it seemed.

While she waited for Finn, she took in harried breaths and mumbled practiced lines. "Welcome back, Finn. It's good to see you. You look well." Geez. She rolled her eyes. Could she sound any more like a complete dweeb?

When Finn walked in, he had both hands in his pockets, his stance tentative. "Hey."

"Hey, yourself." Off to a fantastic start.

"Look, Clover. I'm sorry for leaving so suddenly and not letting you guys in on what was happening."

Clover nodded numbly. "Yeah, I read your note."

"Oh, that."

Oh, that? This conversation was not going *at all* like Clover had planned.

Finn ogled at the tip of his boot. "After I left...I wanted to get a message to you somehow, and I figured, if you still cared, you might go to Fall Valley, so—"

"*If* I cared? What are you talking about? Why would I suddenly stop caring?"

For the first time since he'd walked in, Finn met her eyes. "You practically had me escorted out of the Otherworld."

Clover rolled her eyes. "We had a fight, but that didn't mean I didn't care! Meanwhile, you left without a word, saw fit to see Liz safely back to Court without even bothering to see me, then you literally disappeared for *months*."

And his eyes found the boot again. "I can see how that can be upsetting."

"You could have reached out. We could have found a way to communicate."

"Alistair shared a strong connection with both of us. Neither of our thoughts were safe. I did what I did to keep you alive."

Clover forced herself to take a breath and reframe her thoughts. Pointing fingers, while curiously satisfying, was not going to get them anywhere. "Listen, I'm just glad you're back, okay?"

"It's good to be back," Finn said, a small smile forming on his lips. When he looked at her, the resident butterflies in her belly whipped themselves into a frenzy, churning her legs into jelly. "You were amazing out there. I'm really happy for you—for you both," Finn said before turning to leave.

"Wait!" Clover called out. "What do you mean, *for you both*?"

When Finn turned, it was impossible to tell whether the hardness in his eyes was from anger or sadness. He took a step toward her. "I was there. The night of Helena's birthday. I remained unseen, but yeah, I was there. It had been months since I'd seen any of you, and I missed you…all of you. I figured, if I remained invisible, no harm done, right? At least I could be part of it somehow. Before escorting the Red Branch Knights to the Unseelie Court, I snuck away to see you."

Queen Helena's birthday—the night she was out with Kean. Clover stumbled back as Finn took a step closer. "What did you see?"

Finn was now standing right in front of her, the warmth from his body enveloping her. "I saw enough."

"It's over between me and Kean," Clover said, her breath hitching as she looked up into Finn's hard, gray eyes.

"Really."

"Yes."

"And why is that?"

Suddenly words seemed a paltry representation of what she was feeling. She tugged at his collar and brought her mouth to his in a burning, insatiable kiss. Finn bent his knees to match her slight frame, giving in to her, seemingly starving to be closer. With both her hands at his nape, she pulled at him urgently. His hands went to the curve of her back, bunching the fabric of her shirt around her waist.

Then, as abruptly as they crashed into each other, Finn pulled away, his smoky eyes refocusing. "I can't do this."

Clover's breath was coming out in short, ragged huffs, like she'd just ran a triathlon. "Why?"

Finn touched his forehead to hers, closing his eyes. "Because I am in love with you, and if there's someone else…"

Clover cupped his beautiful face in her hands. "It's always ever been you."

Finn kissed the back of her hand. "We've made a total mess of things this year, but we have all the time in the world to figure things out. What do you say we start over and take it one step at a time?"

"I'd like that."

Finn cleared his throat. "Would you like to go out on a date with me?"

"Only if I get to make out with you afterwards," Clover teased.

"I'm all yours," Finn whispered as he leaned in for a soft kiss.

※

In the months following *Samhain*, Clover had settled into a certain calm even as the realm was awash with preparations. For the first time in a long while, she felt safe again, like it was okay to make plans and look forward to the future. Even though the future promised changes and challenges still, she felt steady enough to weather them.

To her, New Year's Eve always signified endings and beginnings and tonight, that couldn't ring truer. At the evening's feast, Helena was to name her successor, and after they rang in the new year, it would be time to say her goodbyes—to Helena and Scobert as they embarked on a new adventure, to Andie as she returned to New York, and to her dad, who after being given a new lease on life, was more than ready to give it a second shot. Though she would have loved nothing more than to see her parents back together, in the end, it was never meant to be. Asking Meara to leave her home was akin to imploring her to abandon her true self and wanting Nick to stay was perhaps as cruel as pushing him away.

She'd decided to stay in Faerie a while longer. Still learning every day and mastering her powers, she wasn't eager to return to New York just yet. Momma Ruth was staying in the realm with her. When she'd asked her why, she'd simply answered that now that she had eternity to look forward to, she couldn't imagine it not beginning and ending with her.

Garrett had left the day after *Samhain,* promising to return on

New Year's Eve to pay respects to the queen and her successor, but Clover would wager he'd be gone again before the last bit of confetti fell. Creatures like him were too wild and too singular to be caged into any one place or time.

Finn snuck up from behind and planted a kiss on the hollow of her neck. "What are you doing here, all quiet and pensive?"

Mesmerized by the miniature harps floating over the lagoon in Helena's throne room, Clover hadn't even heard him approach. She leaned against him and craned her neck to meet his eye. He was looking exceptionally dapper in a black tux, festive twinkly lights casting shadows on his pale, blond hair. Clover was wearing a shimmering silver gown that Cordelia had picked out, totally making her feel like she was at the prom. A supernatural prom featuring an abdication for an opening act and a coronation as the main event.

Clover hummed a tune and sang softly, "Should auld acquaintance be forgot and never brought to mind…"

"Ah. Feeling sentimental, I see," Finn said as he wrapped his arms around her waist.

She turned to face him. "I just hate goodbyes is all."

He planted a kiss on her forehead. "It doesn't have to be goodbye. You belong in this realm and the one above. Nobody's asking you to choose—you can have both and see your family and friends anytime you feel like it."

"But what about you? You belong here."

"I belong with you," he said softly. "Everything else is just logistics."

Clover rested her cheek upon Finn's chest and reminded herself of how truly lucky she'd been. The past few months had been surreal, to say the least, dangerous at best, but still by far the most meaningful and extraordinary time of her life, and she owed a lot of that to the leprechaun standing in front of her.

"You really are my lucky charm. Do you know that?" she whispered.

Finn chuckled. "I think you've been pretty good at making your own luck."

She looked up at him. "I have, haven't I?" A melodious dinner bell rang, signaling the start of the feast. "Who do you think she'll name as successor?"

"It's anybody's guess, really," Finn said, then offering his hand to her, "shall we?"

As she intertwined her fingers with his, a weight lifted. With the promise of Finn by her side, suddenly she was more focused on beginnings than goodbyes.

***

After donning her fine, regal robes one final time, Helena observed the girl looking back at her from the mirror. What a glorious life she'd lived, she marveled, but now it was time to finally turn the page, a long overdue tomorrow for the girl-queen who'd served her people well.

Liz walked over and placed a silver tiara on head. "There. Now, you're absolutely perfect."

Helena's smile quivered when she realized how much she'd miss her trusted aide. After a seeming eternity of years by her side, she'd sooner lament Liz's absence than her own shadow. Looking at their reflections, her heart swelled. "We had a good run of it, don't you think?"

Casting her gaze to the floor, Liz sighed. "My Queen—"

"Helena. Call me Helena."

She took in a shaky breath. "Helena, there's something I need to get off my chest." Barely even able to finish her sentence, Liz's eyes filled with tears.

Helena turned to face her, taking her shaking hand in hers. "I know."

Liz wiped at her cheek, her eyes wide. "What do you mean?"

"When have you ever known me to let things go?" Helena smiled. "When Iekika escaped and Boris was left dead in my dungeons, did you really think I wouldn't have gotten to the bottom of that?"

Covering her face with her hands, Liz let out a soft wail. "I am utterly reproachable. How ever did you stand to be around me knowing what I've done?"

Helena gingerly peeled Liz's fingers off her face and looked her in the eye. "I'm hardly in a position to cast judgement. I cannot even count the duplicitous and Machiavellian things I've done in my lifetime."

Liz sniffed. "You're only saying that to make me feel better."

Helena shook her head. "I knew who you were on the inside, Liz, so I stepped aside and watched you grow into your true nature."

Suddenly, she was enveloped in the fiercest of hugs. "Thank you for believing in me."

"Thank you for giving me a reason to."

※

Gathered at the feast, Clover looked around at the happy faces surrounding her. Garrett and Andie, despite agreeing to stay friends, couldn't deny their shared chemistry as the pooka nuzzled close and whispered something likely inappropriate in Andie's ear, causing her best friend to giggle uncontrollably. Meara and Nick sharing a quiet moment, their heads bent low. Momma Ruth having the time of her life coaxing Mary to dance the merengue. Button smearing icing on Sinann's cheek and clearly thinking it was the most hilarious thing ever. Kean surrounded by a loyal throng of Seelie soldiers, looking like he'd finally found his rightful place in the army. Anna sharing a laugh with Scobert; the clurichaun's gaze shifting to the stage as soon as Helena walked in, pure love and admiration in his eyes.

She belonged to the humans and faeries in that room, and she couldn't have been happier for the realization. Even Liz, who she'd once despised, she now considered a true ally and her heart swelled to see her by Helena's side again, her usual flawlessness and confidence returned. When Helena cleared her throat to speak, everyone quieted and turned their attention to the stage.

"Tonight heralds the end of an era and welcomes the beginning of a new day. I assure you my decision to leave was not taken lightly, nor was the selection of a successor. In the many years I've been your queen, I've had the chance to personally get to know a lot of you. The virtues I laud in a potential monarch are at times the same qualities I've considered flaws in the past. Heart. Humility. Humanity. A good leader must possess all these traits and more. Courage. Bravado. Hardness. Softness. Honor."

Helena paused as her gaze fell on the guests there gathered.

"After careful consideration, I nominate a faerie who I feel encapsulates what it is to be a member of the Seelie Court, of what it means to be Fae." Helena took in a breath, standing a little taller. "Anna Ryan, please rise."

Audible gasps were heard across the room as Finn stiffened beside Clover, his mouth agape. Anna, pale as a sheet, followed her queen's bidding and rose from her seat.

"Anna," said Helena. "Do you rise to accept this great honor if the Seelie Court should grant it?"

Even as tears threatened to fill her eyes, Anna stood tall and resplendent. "I do."

Helena smiled. "Very well. Does the Seelie Court accept my nomination of a new Seelie Queen?"

Not even a moment after Helena asked her question, everyone leapt from their seats in thunderous applause. "Aye!" Finn yelled against the deafening cries of assent.

As the clock ticked close to midnight, in a year wrought with numerous wins and losses, the Seelie Court had unanimously elected their new queen.

Later that evening at the Enchanted Pond, a handful of them congregated to see friends and family off, giving the portal entrance the proper feel of an airport boarding gate.

Clover had hugged Nick and Andie for what felt like a million times that night, but it hardly felt like enough. Meara and Garrett were to escort them through the portal and see them back to Earth safely. Anna, Mary, Button, Sinann, and Kean were all there to bid their newfound friends goodbye. Even Helena and Scobert had made the trek through the woods to say their final farewells and Momma Ruth, still intent on prolonging the party, even snagged a couple of bottles of champagne for the send-off.

Momma Ruth popped the cork and retrieved flutes from a nearby picnic basket, filling and passing the glasses around until everybody had one. She raised hers in a toast, "To what we've lost and what we've gained, to things long gone and still remain. To new adventures and to new beginnings!" Then she finished with, "Long live the queens!"

They all raised and clinked their glasses. "Hear, hear!"

Clover downed her champagne and found her way to Andie and Garrett.

"Hey, Garrett. You better make sure Andie gets home safely."

"Oh, please," replied the pooka with a smirk. "She's perfectly capable of taking care of herself. If she's lucky, *maybe* I'll see her home and tuck her in."

Andie landed a hard punch on Garrett's shoulder, a look of mock loathing on her face.

"Ouch," Garrett faked. "Will you tell her to stop hurting me? Jaysus, this one's got a temper."

Clover giggled at their banter, then turned to her best friend. "I'll see you soon?"

"Absolutely. This isn't goodbye, okay? Besides, portal travel is fun. I may apply for frequent flier miles."

Finn clasped hands with his friend. "I probably shouldn't expect to see you anytime soon."

Garrett's grin was the embodiment of mischief. "You never

know, man. Seems like every time you get yourself into trouble, I turn up to save your sorry ass."

"I'll try *not* to keep out of trouble then," Finn joked.

Garrett offered his arm to Andie. "Mademoiselle, shall we?"

Andie nodded and blew Clover a kiss before jumping into the pond with Garrett.

Just as tears began to form anew, Nick and Meara approached.

"Hey, kid," Nick said. "I suppose we better get going, too."

Clover hugged her dad for the umpteenth time, squeezing until her arms hurt. "I love you, Dad."

Nick kissed the top of her head. "Me, too, sweetie. More than you know." Starting to choke up, he released her and turned to Meara. "Ready to board?"

Meara laughed and offered her hand to her once-husband. Before they jumped into the pond, Momma Ruth wrapped Nick in a bear hug. "I love you, son. Go out there and be happy."

"I will," Nick promised before jumping in the portal with Meara.

Clover blew out a breath she'd been holding for a while, relieved to have survived the goodbyes without falling to pieces.

Their small group dwindling even further, Scobert raised his walking stick above his head. "I reckon now's as good a time as any."

"You're leaving tonight, too?" Clover asked. "Can't it wait?"

"Nah," Scobert said. "You guys have it covered here. Helena and I have a whole lot of travelling to do."

Helena rested her head contentedly against Scobert's arm. Now that she wasn't queen anymore, she looked like a really happy teenage girl.

Mary kissed the happy couple on their cheeks. "Don't go forgetting the Seelie Court, you hear? I expect you two to visit as often as you can."

Scobert rolled his eyes. "I haven't even left yet; you're already telling me to come back."

Helena took Mary's hands in hers. "I will make sure we make time to visit."

"Thank you," Mary said, then to Scobert, "see, was that so hard?"

Anna approached Helena. "I still don't know what to say. I will forever strive to deserve this honor."

"You'll soon get used to it," Helena confided. "And should you ever feel the need to get away, just let us know and we'll bring the *shillelagh* right over."

Anna laughed and accepted the offer, promising again to do her best to follow in Helena's legendary footsteps.

While Clover was happy for Helena and Scobert, she was still sad to see them go. "Good luck to you both. Thank you so much for all you've done to help me."

Helena smiled graciously. "You've done much for us in turn. Don't forget I still owe you a favor."

Back when she'd saved the queen from King Boris's attack while inadvertently unleashing her own dormant powers, Helena had vowed to be in her eternal debt.

"Perhaps the magical *shillelagh* could make its rounds?" Clover offered.

Helena laughed unreservedly then. "Perhaps."

After they'd all said their goodbyes and there wasn't a dry eye in the bunch, Scobert and Helena disappeared in a puff of smoke.

Clover tilted her face to the night sky, feeling the evening breeze on her cheeks. This was where it had all begun. Who would have known that jumping into the portal that summer day would have led to such a magical world of adventure, romance, and possibilities?

Finn planted a soft kiss on her neck. "Deep in thought, again?"

She looked up into his deep, silver eyes. "I'm just happy to be here." With worlds to discover and an eternity unfolding before her, Clover couldn't imagine being anywhere else.

He kissed her forehead and pulled her closer. "I'm happy you're here, too. Are you ready to start heading back?"

Clover nodded.

When Finn took her hand and started walking, she stopped in her tracks. "Wait."

"What is it?" Finn asked

A mischievous smile formed on her lips. "Why walk, when we can fly?"

Don't miss your next favorite book!

Join the Fire & Ice mailing list
www.fireandiceya.com/mail.html

ACKNOWLEDGMENTS

My heartfelt thanks to Nancy Schumacher and the whole team at Fire and Ice Young Adult Books.

My utmost appreciation goes out to my family, for cheering me on, holding my hand, and supporting me every step of the way. To my sister, Deanne-Deanne, my writing guardian angel; I couldn't have done any of this without her constant encouragement and positivity. She was Clover's first and biggest fan and I will forever be grateful (Team Finn!).

Thank you to my readers, Alethea Semian and Heidi Denman, for tirelessly proofreading my drafts and providing insightful input along the way.

Boundless thanks to my husband, Bobby, who believed in me even before I did. Achieving my dreams is made easy with him by my side.

Finally, my profound gratitude goes out to the readers who read and enjoyed *Clover*. If not for them, *Fae's Ascent* would never have come to be.

THANK YOU FOR READING

Did you enjoy this book?

We invite you to leave a review at the website of your choice, such as Goodreads, Amazon, Barnes & Noble, etc.

DID YOU KNOW THAT LEAVING A REVIEW...

- Helps other readers find books they may enjoy.
- Gives you a chance to let your voice be heard.
- Gives authors recognition for their hard work.
- Doesn't have to be long. A sentence or two about why you liked the book will do.

ABOUT THE AUTHOR

Nicole Kilpatrick is the author of the young adult fantasy novels, *Clover* and *Fae's Ascent*. Aside from books, she's passionate about all things food and travel related. Visiting her home country of the Philippines tops her list of favorite things; a close second is binge-reading while consuming copious amounts of chips, cheeses, and cured meats. When not writing, she can be found lounging in a cabin by a river, curled up on a couch reading a book, or concocting recipes in her cozy kitchen. She lives in Brooklyn with her husband.

nicolekilpatrick.com

- facebook.com/NicoleKilpatrickAuthor
- twitter.com/npkilpatrick
- instagram.com/npkilpatrick
- goodreads.com/nicolekilpatrick

ALSO BY NICOLE KILPATRICK
WITH FIRE & ICE YOUNG ADULT BOOKS

Clover

Printed in Great Britain
by Amazon